BOOK ONE

THE FRIENDSHIP LETTERS

Letters *of* Trust

BOOK ONE

THE FRIENDSHIP LETTERS

Letters *of* Trust

WANDA & BRUNSTETTER

BARBOUR
PUBLISHING

ISBN 978-1-63609-334-5
Adobe Digital Edition (.epub) 978-1-63609-335-2

For more information about Wanda E. Brunstetter, please access the author's website at the following internet address: www.wandabrunstetter.com

Cover Model Photography: Richard Brunstetter III

Published by Barbour Publishing, Inc., 1810 Barbour Drive, Uhrichsville, OH 44683, www.barbourbooks.com

Our mission is to inspire the world with the life-changing message of the Bible.

 Member of the
Evangelical Christian
Publishers Association

Dedication

To each of my dear Amish friends who keep in touch with
me often, even though we live miles apart.
I appreciate each of you, and the wisdom and prayers you
have offered when needed.

———— ≈ ————

God is our refuge and strength,
a very present help in trouble.

PSALM 46:1

Prologue

Grabill, Indiana

"I can't believe that Vic and I will be moving to Pennsylvania in the morning." Eleanor Lapp choked back tears as she stood in the Schwartz family's yard and gave her friend Doretta a hug. "You and I have been good friends for such a long time, and I'm going to miss our special times together."

Doretta teared up. "Oh, my dear friend, I shall miss you too, but a new adventure awaits you and Vic in what I've heard is the beautiful state of Pennsylvania." She paused to wipe the moisture on her cheeks. "Our friendship will remain strong, because we'll keep in touch through lots of letters and some phone calls. I'll write to you often, I promise."

"I will send you letters as well, but it won't be the same as getting together for long chats and doing fun things together, the way we have since we were *kinner*." Eleanor glanced toward the barn, where her husband of one week had gone to say goodbye to Doretta's brother, Glen.

Days prior, Vic and Eleanor had packed up all their belongings with some help from her family. With the exception of their wedding gifts and Eleanor's personal things, the newly married couple didn't have a lot of items to bring along on their move. But maybe that was a good thing, since it would make moving easier and a little less stressful. Soon after Eleanor accepted his marriage proposal, Vic had purchased a home for them in

Paradise, Pennsylvania, and he'd recently bought a few pieces of furniture, so that when he and Eleanor arrived they wouldn't have to sleep or sit on the floor. He had taken care of that when he'd gone home for a few weeks before his and Eleanor's wedding. Eleanor looked forward to helping her husband pick out the rest of their furnishings, which they planned to do within the first few days of their arrival.

Doretta gave Eleanor's back a few gentle pats. "Your place is with Vic now, and you knew before you married him that his plan was always to return to the area where he grew up."

Eleanor gave a slow nod. "I'm excited to go and start my new life, but it's going to take a little time to adjust to being apart from my family and friends. Don't worry about me," she quickly added. "I'm sure I'll be fine once we get there and have settled into our new home. I love Vic very much, and I won't let anything about this move come between us."

Chapter 1

Colorful red, gold, and pale green autumn leaves crackled beneath Eleanor's feet as she made her way down the driveway to the mailbox in front of her and Vic's new home. Although it had two stories and four bedrooms, the house was smaller than many other Amish homes in their area, where couples with large families lived. Someday when children came, Vic would no doubt want to add an extension out the side or back of their house that would include more rooms.

How quickly the time had gone since Eleanor and her husband stood in the presence of their families and friends and responded to Bishop John's questions. Eleanor still got choked up when she thought about the sincerity behind their wedding vows. She loved her husband with all her heart and wanted to be the kind of wife he needed. Eleanor looked forward to the years ahead, and hopefully to raising a family here together. It wouldn't matter whether they had one child or ten. The bishop had reminded Eleanor and Vic during the wedding service that as long as they put God first in their marriage, their family unit would be strong. He also stated that whatever happened in the years ahead—the good or the bad—with the Lord's help, they would be able to face it together.

Redirecting her thoughts, Eleanor stopped in front of the mailbox and opened the flap. While pulling the mail out, a gust of late September wind came up, causing the top envelope to blow off the stack of letters, magazines, and other correspondence. Keeping a firm grip on the rest of the mail, Eleanor bent down and picked up the envelope that had fallen. She smiled, noticing that the return address was Doretta's.

Oh good. I can hardly wait to see what my dear friend has to say. I miss her and my family so much, but I won't let Vic know that I've been feeling kind of homesick. He might believe that I want to return home, and I would never want to disappoint Vic or plead with him to move back to Indiana.

At times Eleanor wished she and Vic had remained in Indiana instead of moving here, but she never allowed herself to dwell on it. Her responsibility as Vic's wife was to him now, and that meant living in the state, town, and home he had chosen.

Eleanor hurried back to the house, shivering as the wind continued to blow. Although she wasn't pleased to see the colder weather setting in, at least it was no longer hot and muggy, the way it had been this summer. Even though there was something about each season that she liked, there were unpleasant aspects as well. She particularly didn't care for frigid temperatures, but there were some winter outdoor recreations that she enjoyed. Eleanor looked forward to the pond at the back of their property freezing well enough that they could ice-skate on it. It would also be fun to build a snowman or make snow angels, the way she had done with her three older brothers when they were all children. Sometimes their winter frolicking had ended up in snowball fights. Of course, Eleanor, being the youngest, had taken the brunt of things when Gabe, Sam, and Larry ganged up on her. It had evened things out a bit when Doretta came over and joined in the fun, but if Doretta's brother Glen came along, he'd always sided with Eleanor's brothers. Four against two was hardly fair, but Eleanor and her friend had done their best to hold their own against those rowdy boys.

Eleanor's musings ended when she entered the house and placed the mail on the narrow table inside the entryway. She removed her sweater and hung it on a wall peg, then picked up Doretta's letter and took it to the kitchen table. Eagerly, she tore the envelope open and read the letter silently.

———————≈———————

Dear Eleanor,

Thank you for the lovely card you sent me a few weeks ago. The butterfly stamp you used to make it made me wish it was summertime again. Just think—in two months it will be Thanksgiving, and we'll be thinking about pumpkins and turkeys. Do you have any rubber stamps for either of those?

It would be nice to come visit you sometime and see your new place, but with my teaching position, it's hard to get away. I do miss getting together with you and sharing our thoughts on different matters.

I was wondering if you will be looking for a job to provide some extra income, or have you decided to stay at home at this time and concentrate on being a homemaker?

I hope things are going well for you there, and that you've established a friendship with one or both of Vic's sisters, or perhaps someone in your church district.

I'm keeping busy with my teacher's position, and my relationship with William Lengacher has gotten stronger. I'm sure it's just a matter of time before he asks me to marry him, and when he does, I'm prepared to say yes. William is so kind and polite. He gets along well with my dad, and they have a shared interest in hunting. Mom likes him too, and so do all of my siblings. Even though William has a good job at the Farm Building Supply, he's thinking about partnering with his twin brother in a new business venture.

———————≈———————

Eleanor stopped reading and set her friend's letter aside, after noting that the rest of it appeared to be mostly about the weather they'd been having in the Grabill area, along with some local news, which she could read about later. She focused instead on a brief note from her mother, and that lead to Eleanor thinking about how her parents had disapproved of Vic soon after they'd met him. When he'd first showed up in Grabill, to attend a friend's wedding, Eleanor had been attracted to him. He was good-looking and outgoing and took an interest in her right away. Vic had made her blush when he'd said the minute he'd laid eyes on her, he had told himself, *She's the girl for me. I am going to marry her someday.*

Vic had returned to Pennsylvania a few days after his friend's wedding, but he'd written letters and made phone calls to Eleanor and gone back to Grabill several times so they could get better acquainted. As their relationship progressed, Vic had taken a job working for one of the Amish men in Grabill who owned a carpentry shop. It had been wonderful having him living so close, and during that time her love for Vic had grown deeper. Soon after he'd proposed to Eleanor and she'd said yes, Vic had made it clear that once they were married, he wanted them to live in Pennsylvania. She had agreed with that, because the thing Eleanor wanted most was to be with Vic.

During Vic's time in Grabill, he had done a few things her parents hadn't approved of. Mom had stated that Vic seemed to want things his own way, and Dad had commented that Eleanor's boyfriend had been seen smoking cigarettes and drinking beer with some of the other young fellows his age. Eleanor had told her parents that they had nothing to worry about. Vic would set his days of doing worldly things behind him when he quit *rumspringe* and joined the church. And he had done just that.

Eleanor let her musings go and finished reading her mom's letter, as well as the rest of Doretta's letter, and then she went through the remainder of the mail. Once her morning chores were complete, she would take the time to respond to her friend with either a letter or one of the pretty cards she'd made, using one her favorite rubber stamps—a cardinal sitting on the branch of a tree, which she had stamped with red ink. Cardinals were one of her friend's favorite birds. Of course, Doretta was a bird-watcher when she wasn't teaching school, so she liked many feathered species, especially the more colorful ones.

Eleanor smiled, remembering the day she and her friend had graduated from the eighth grade and gone for a leisurely walk to look at birds. They'd had a wonderful time, laughing, talking, and taking turns pointing out birds that appeared to be unusual or sang pretty tunes. Eleanor looked forward to buying a few feeders so she could be entertained this winter while watching the birds that would find their way into her and Vic's yard in search of food.

Eleanor thought more about her special friend, and she teared up a little bit as she reflected on some of the wonderful times they had spent together. She wondered if it might be possible for Doretta to come to Pennsylvania for a visit sometime next summer. It would be wonderful to see her again and have time to do some catching up. She had to admit, planning for that day would be a way of making this transition easier, and it would be ever so nice to see a familiar face from home for a little while. Of course, next summer was several months away, but when the time drew closer, Eleanor would talk to her husband and see if he was okay with the idea. Maybe it wasn't good to plan this far ahead, but if Vic agreed, Eleanor would invite Doretta to come, which would give her something to look forward to. Her and Vic's home had enough room for guests, so that wouldn't be a problem.

Eleanor had been working on decorating the rooms in the house, and she liked the colors she'd chosen for each one. Pale blue for the bathroom, a light shade of yellow for the kitchen, and an off-white for their living room, dining room, and all four of their bedrooms. Eleanor seemed to be gifted with a green thumb of sorts and had put in plenty of flowering plants in the sunny places around the yard. She looked forward to planting their vegetable garden early next spring, once the temperatures warmed. Until then, Eleanor was content to keep busy with cooking, cleaning, and doing whatever inside chores needed to be done. But the thought crept into her mind, based on what Doretta had mentioned in her letter, that she could consider working, at least part-time, for extra money. In fact, being away from the house for a while might help her feel less lonely.

Perhaps I should bring that idea up to Vic, she told herself. *It might be nice to get out and work again. Even if I didn't make a lot of money, it would be fun if I could find a job where I could socialize with others.*

Eleanor had finished washing her lunch dishes and was about to get out her card-making supplies when a knock sounded on the back door. Since it was the entrance that neighbors, friends, and family normally used, Eleanor figured it must be someone she knew. The mailman, whenever he had a package, always came to the front door. The same held true for someone trying to sell something, or people from their church district whom Eleanor didn't know very well. Since Eleanor was the newcomer to this area, there were many folks, even from their church district, whom she was not well acquainted with yet.

After wiping her damp hands on a dish towel, Eleanor left the kitchen and opened the back door. She was greeted by her ever-cheerful mother-in-law, Susie. It seemed like every time Eleanor saw the brown-eyed brunette, she wore a smile. At age forty-eight, the large-boned but by no means overweight woman always seemed to have a cheerful attitude. Susie was the mother of five children, ranging in ages from twenty-seven to eight years old. Vic was the oldest, followed by Clara, age twenty-two; Kate, who was eighteen; fifteen-year-old Stephen; and Eddie, who would turn eight later this week. Susie was an excellent quilter and often sold her quilted items to some of the local quilt shops in Lancaster County. She had given Vic and Eleanor a lovely wedding-ring-patterned quilt as a wedding present, which they used on their bed. Vic's father, Ethan, was a kindly man type who enjoyed telling jokes and humorous stories. He owned a small shop on his property in Strasburg, where he made doghouses, birdhouses, picnic tables, and a variety of lawn furniture. Vic had told Eleanor once that he had begun working for his dad when he graduated from the eighth grade, but after a few years he'd quit and sought employment at a few other places that dealt in handmade wooden items. Vic had also stated that he wouldn't be happy doing any kind of job unless it involved wood and working with his hands. His new position at a local company that was based in Lancaster specialized in custom-built homes, additions, decks, garages, and remodeling of barns. Vic had stated several times that working at the new business was by far his favorite place of employment. He'd also explained that he liked building larger items and didn't think he could ever go back to working for his dad. Eleanor had no problem with that; she just wanted her husband to be happy.

"Good afternoon, Susie. Please, come inside." Eleanor opened the door wider, and after Vic's mother stepped in, Eleanor took her mother-in-law's outer garments from her, hung them up, and then invited Susie to join her in the kitchen.

"Something smells real good in here." Susie tilted her head back and sniffed the air. "Have you been doing some baking?"

"Just a bit this morning. I made Vic's favorite, chocolate chip pie." Eleanor motioned toward the pantry and then gestured for her mother-in-law to take a seat at the table. "Would you like a cup of *kaffi*, or some *tee*, perhaps?"

"If I weren't in a hurry to get to the quilt shop in Bird-in-Hand, I would take you up on the offer for either coffee or tea. After I leave the quilt shop, I'll get a bite of lunch before heading back to Strasburg."

"I've already eaten my noon meal, but I'd be happy to fix you something," Eleanor offered.

"*Danki* for the invitation, but I've made plans to meet my friend Lavina Beiler at the Bird-in-Hand Family Restaurant." Susie fiddled with the long white ties on her heart-shaped *kapp*—the type of head covering Eleanor felt she must wear now that she lived among the Lancaster County Amish. It was quite a bit smaller and shaped differently than the cone-style, pleated-at-the-back coverings worn by Amish women in Indiana. Eleanor had determined before her wedding that if she was going to live in Lancaster County, she would dress in the same style of clothing as other Amish women whose homes and families were here. She certainly did not want to stand out among these Plain people as looking, or even acting, different than them.

Susie's hands moved from her covering ties to the front of her black apron, which concealed most of her dress. "The reason I came by was to invite you and Victor to Eddie's birthday supper that we'll be hosting at our home this Friday evening. I mentioned it to Victor a week or so ago, but he may have forgotten to tell you."

Eleanor pursed her lips to keep them from forming into a broad smile. It seemed so strange to hear Vic's mother refer to him as "Victor." However, that was his given name, and if his mother preferred to call him that, instead of Vic, it was certainly her choice.

Susie's cheeks turned crimson as she gave a slow shake of her head. "That son of mine can be so forgetful at times. From the time he was a young child, he got preoccupied easily and would forget important things, even with my constant reminding. Did he, by any chance, mention the birthday gathering to you?"

"No, he did not, but I will tell him that you came by and make sure he knows we are invited." Eleanor pulled a paper napkin from the wicker basket in the center of the table and wiped a damp spot where she had set her water glass during lunch. She didn't know how she had missed it when she'd cleared her lunch dishes from the table. Hopefully Susie hadn't noticed. Eleanor didn't want her mother-in-law to think she was a slovenly housekeeper and hadn't cleaned the table.

"It's no surprise to me that he forgot, which is why I came here to tell you about the plans." Susie leaned slightly forward and gave Eleanor a genuinely warm smile. "I'm so glad my son chose a sweet woman like you who can make sure he stays on the straight and narrow—if you get what I'm saying. Victor is a hard worker and quite talented when it comes to working with wood, but he can be a bit scatterbrained sometimes and needs someone to help him remember certain things."

"I hope he won't see my reminding him as pestering. I doubt that any man would appreciate a *gebeller* wife."

"It's not nagging, dear. It's loving." Susie winked. "Seriously, though, if Victor didn't have someone to remind him, he probably wouldn't remember his own birthday, let alone his youngest brother's."

Eleanor sat quietly for several seconds before responding. "I'll do my best, Susie, but only if I can see that it doesn't irritate my husband." She shook her head slowly. "I would never want to say or do anything that might drive a wedge between us."

Susie rose from her chair and came around to give Eleanor a hug. "I don't believe you have to worry about that. My son loves you very much, and I can't imagine him letting anything disrupt your marriage—especially not something like a few gentle reminders when needed."

Chapter 2

"We worked hard today, Vic. Should we stop someplace for a beer before I drop you off at your place?"

Vic looked over at his English coworker, Tom Brooks, and shook his head. "No thanks. Not interested."

Tom gave his truck's steering wheel a thump. "Oh, that's right. You're one of those religious fanatics who goes to church every Sunday and doesn't smoke, drink, or cheat on his wife."

Vic's coworker's tone sounded like mocking, which caused Vic's throat to constrict. *Do we Amish come off as acting as though we are righteous to outsiders? I'm no saint, and I've got my own share of problems, even as a Christian. But maybe some other people don't realize that. I just wish that folks weren't so quick to judge.*

Vic's face tightened as he inhaled a long breath through his nose. After he released it, he responded. "First off, I believe in God and go to church, but I am not a religious fanatic. Second, I quit smoking and drinking after I joined the church, and for your information, I would never be unfaithful to my wife." Vic hoped his tone wasn't too harsh, but he felt the need to get his point across.

"Okay, no problem. I didn't mean to get you riled up. Just figured after a long day at work you might need to chill out before going home, where you'll no doubt have chores to do." Tom pushed a hunk of his sandy-blond hair away from his eyes.

"Yes, I usually have jobs that need to be done, but I don't mind, nor do I need to 'chill out,' as you put it." Vic tried not to let his irritation show, but Tom could probably hear it in his voice. "Are you married?" he asked.

"Not anymore. My wife, Cheryl, was too demanding, and all we ever did was argue. So we finally decided to call it quits and go our separate ways." Tom grimaced. "I'm glad we don't have any kids, 'cause that would've made things even stickier when she left. She'd have probably wanted full custody, and I'd have been stuck paying child support."

As he watched the scenery pass by, Vic weighed the information Tom had shared. *I can't help wondering how much of their marital problems started with Tom. I'm finding him to be a bit annoying right now, and we've only been together a few minutes.*

"Are you divorced or just separated?" Vic asked.

A muscle on the side of Tom's jaw quivered. "We've been divorced for a year."

"That's too bad. Sorry to hear it."

"Yeah, well. . .you win some, you lose some. My folks got a divorce when I was twelve. The way those two fought over every little thing, I'm surprised they didn't split up sooner." Tom made a grunting sound that reminded Vic of a bear. "I'll have to admit, it was hard on me and my brother—especially after Dad got married again and then we were stuck with a stepmother who neither of us liked and still don't. Fortunately, my mom found a decent man and married him a few years later." He turned his head in Vic's direction before looking back at the road. "As I said, Cheryl and I have no children, so that's a good thing—especially if, down the road, either of us should decide to get married again to someone else."

Vic wasn't sure how having no children could be a good thing, since he looked forward to the day when he and Eleanor would become parents. He supposed his coworker must have meant that he wouldn't have wanted to put his kids through what he and his brother dealt with when their parents got divorced.

The rig was quiet, with the exception of the engine's dull droning, but it wasn't long before Tom turned on the radio. Vic wondered if it was because of the awkward topic that had been shared. *I can't fathom how people can be in love and then down the line give up on their marriage. Why don't couples try harder to work on the problems that come up day to day?*

Vic thought about what Bishop John had said in the message he'd preached during his and Eleanor's wedding service. He had stressed several times that divorce was not an option and that any marital problems the couple might have should be worked out through communication, prayer, and if necessary, counseling.

Vic smiled inwardly. So far, he and Eleanor hadn't had even one disagreement, let alone any major problems. He felt sure that if something unpleasant did come up, they would be able to work things out between them. The love he felt for his wife was strong, and Eleanor had made it clear that she felt the same way about him.

———— ≈ ————

Paradise

Eleanor hummed as she stirred the kettle of chicken-noodle soup simmering nicely on the gas stove. The delightful aroma wafted up to her nose, and she sniffed deeply. She hoped Vic wouldn't mind having soup and sandwiches for supper this evening. Eleanor's original plan was to fix stuffed cabbage rolls, but she'd lost track of time today while making cards and decided to heat up the soup she'd made for lunch instead. Although cabbage rolls always made a tasty meal, they were time consuming to make, not to mention the mashed potatoes she liked to serve with them. Hopefully Vic wouldn't mind soup, crackers, and a ham-and-cheese sandwich for supper tonight.

Eleanor turned and glanced at the battery-operated clock on the other side of the kitchen. It was almost five thirty. Vic should be home soon.

She turned the stove to its lowest setting and went down the hall to the bathroom to check her appearance in the mirror. Eleanor wasn't vain, but she did want to make sure she looked presentable, with her head covering on straight, and check that ink wasn't left on her fingers from stamping or any blotches of food on her clothes from cooking.

Once Eleanor felt satisfied that she looked okay, she started back toward the kitchen. Halfway there, she heard Vic's mixed-breed dog, Checkers, barking from his pen in the yard. She had put the dog there a while ago when she'd caught him digging a hole in one of her flower beds. *Oh good. If Checkers is carrying on in such a way, it must mean that Vic is home.*

Eleanor hurried to the front entrance, and as she opened the door, she saw Tom's truck pull into the yard. After Vic got out and closed the door on the passenger's side, he headed across the yard and let Checkers out of his pen. It wasn't long before the dog started yapping and running in circles around her husband. When Vic bent down and gave Checkers' head a pat, he was rewarded with a few doggie tongue slurps on his chin.

Eleanor resisted the urge to roll her eyes. She didn't have a fondness for the shaggy-looking dog, but Vic certainly did. Checkers had been his dog when he was a teenager still living at home with his parents. When Vic lived in Grabill for a time, Checkers had remained in Pennsylvania with Vic's folks. As soon as Eleanor and Vic had moved into their home here in Paradise, however, Vic had brought Checkers to live with them. Eleanor was glad that her husband hadn't pushed to bring the dog into the house, because if he had, she might have put her foot down. Ever since Eleanor had been bitten by a neighbor's dog when she was a young girl, she'd developed a mistrust for most dogs—especially the larger ones that had a threatening bark. Vic had assured Eleanor many times that Checkers wouldn't hurt her, but she kept her distance anyhow. Even though the dog had shown no sign of aggression toward her, Eleanor didn't relish the thought of allowing the dog inside the house, where it would have the opportunity of having an accident, shedding hair, or leaving dirty paw prints on her clean floors.

Eleanor waited near the door until Vic headed for the house; then she stepped out onto the porch to greet him. "Did you have a good day?" she asked after he'd given her a hug.

"*Jah,* I did—at least till the ride home with Tom."

"What happened?"

"I'll tell you when we get inside."

"Okay." Eleanor entered the house and felt relieved when her husband hurriedly shut the door. Sometimes when he wasn't quick enough, Checkers got in, and then Vic had a hard time getting the dog back out.

"Should we go to the kitchen to visit while I get supper on the table, or would you rather wait and talk while we're eating?" she asked.

"Whatever you like. I'm okay with either suggestion."

"All right then, let's talk while I get supper on the table. There's chicken-noodle soup heating on the stove, and I thought I'd make ham-and-cheese sandwiches to go with it, if you're okay with that."

Vic pulled Eleanor into his arms and gave her a tender kiss. "I'm fine with whatever you fix."

Eleanor smiled. She felt blessed to be married to such a thoughtful, easy-to-please husband.

"Is there anything I can do to help?" Vic asked after he'd washed his hands at the sink.

"Not really. I'm sure you must be tired after working all day."

"Yeah, kind of, and thirsty too."

Eleanor poured Vic a glass of apple cider and gestured for him to take a seat at the table. "So what happened on the way home from work that involved Tom?"

Vic lowered himself into a chair and took a drink before responding. "He wanted me to stop with him for a beer, and when I said no, Tom kinda gave me a hard time about it." Vic grimaced. "I think he was trying to see if I'd get riled."

"Did you?"

"Nope. I kept my cool and just stated the facts, although I was a bit irritated with him." Vic took another drink. "How'd your day go?"

"It was good. I got a letter from Doretta, which got me to thinking how nice it would be if she could come for a visit sometime next summer." She glanced over at him. "Would that be okay with you?"

He nodded. "If you two can work it out, I'd have no problem with it. It is a ways off, though, so we'll need to talk about it again when the time gets closer."

"Agreed." Eleanor felt a sense of giddiness about the prospect of spending time with her friend. She took a loaf of bread out of the pantry and placed it on the table. "Oh, and your mamm stopped by today. She wanted to invite us to supper at their place this Friday evening to celebrate Eddie's birthday."

Vic gave a wide grin. "Oh, that's right. My little *bruder* will be turning eight on October first. Did you tell her we'd be there?"

"Jah, and I'm looking forward to going. I bet it'll be a *schpass* evening." Eleanor made no mention of her husband's forgetfulness.

"With Eddie involved, it's bound to be fun." Vic scratched his head. "He's such a special kid. I'd like to give him something that he'll really like."

"You know him better than I do, so I'm sure you'll come up with the right gift."

"I hope so. Sure wouldn't want to disappoint the little guy."

"I bet he will like anything you choose to give him. From what I've heard, your youngest brother thinks the world of you."

Vic gave a brief shrug. "I don't know why he would. There's nineteen years between us. By the time Eddie was born, I was almost old enough to be his *daed*."

"Well, there you go. Your mamm told me once that you've always taken an interest in Eddie and treat him like a son."

"Guess you're right." Vic reached down and untied his work boots, then pulled them off of his feet. "Ah . . .that feels better. Boy, these new *schtiwwel* are sure taking some time to break in."

Her brows wrinkled. "Are they hurting your feet?"

"Some, but not to where I've gotten a blister from them." He pointed at his old pair setting by the back door. "My older boots seemed easier to wear, even when they were first out of the box the day I bought them." He slid his new ones over toward the wall. "But these are a different brand than the last pair I purchased."

"Hopefully they'll break in soon, or else you'll need to start looking for another pair."

Eleanor took jars of pickles, along with mayonnaise and mustard from the refrigerator and placed them on the table beside the bread. Then she got out two packages of ham lunch meat and some sliced cheddar cheese. "Do you mind if I change the subject? There's something else I'd like to talk to you about."

"Go ahead. Why don't you take a seat and tell me what's on your mind?" Vic gestured to the chair across from him.

She did as he asked, but unsure of how to bring up the topic she wanted to talk about, Eleanor couldn't find the words to begin.

"Is something wrong? Have I done anything to upset you?"

Eleanor shook her head vigorously. "I've been wondering if you would mind if I looked for a job."

Vic's dark eyebrows shot up. "You have plenty to do right here at home."

"I—I know, but I get lonely during the day, and if I had a job I'd be around people."

"If you're lonely, why not take a walk over to the neighbors' and get better acquainted? Or you could hitch up your horse and buggy and go over to Strasburg to visit my mom."

Eleanor swallowed hard. She wasn't doing a good job of getting her point across. "I've done waitressing before, and there are plenty of restaurants in our area, so I'm sure one of them might hire me. I'd really enjoy working, Vic, and it would give us some extra money."

Vic pinched the bridge of his nose. "My boss pays good wages, so we are getting along fine with what I make."

"I understand, but—"

He shook his head. "I'm not for the idea, Eleanor, and if we're not in agreement on this, then it will mean you'll either have to abide by my wishes or go ahead and get a job without my permission."

She flinched at the sharp tone of his voice, and tears sprang to her eyes. "I'm sorry, I just thought. . ."

Vic got up from the table, and when he came around to stand by her chair, he placed a hand on her shoulder and gave it a tender squeeze. "I'm sorry. I didn't mean to upset you. Please don't cry."

Eleanor sniffed and swiped a hand across her hot cheek. They'd only been married a few months, and now she and Vic had experienced their first major disagreement. She didn't care for the way it made her feel.

"Listen, my love," Vic said, stroking the side of her cheek with his thumb. "We both like kids, and we agreed before we got married that we want to have a big family. So think about this: What if you got a job and then you became pregnant? You'd have to quit and disappoint your boss."

"True."

"And haven't we been hoping that it won't be long before we'll be able to announce to our families that we're expecting a baby?"

"Well, yes, but that hasn't happened yet."

"But when it does, don't you want to be ready?"

She gave a slow nod.

"All right then, let's make an agreement."

"What kind of agreement?"

"If, after we've been married a year, you are not in a family way, I'll consider the idea of you finding a job outside of our home."

Although Eleanor wasn't thrilled about waiting that long, she gave an affirmative nod. Her husband was right about one thing—if and when she did get pregnant, she would definitely want, and need, to be at home with their baby.

Chapter 3

Strasburg, Pennsylvania

"Come on, Domino. You need to get moving, or we're gonna be late for my brother's birthday party." The firm set of Vic's jaw let Eleanor know he was irritated with his pokey horse this evening. It was unusual for the black-and-white gelding to amble along at a snail's pace. Normally, it was all Vic could do to hold Domino back.

"Maybe there's something wrong with your horse," Eleanor commented, looking over at her handsome husband. "He might be sick or could have thrown a shoe."

"I checked each of Domino's hoofs yesterday morning while cleaning them." Vic's brows furrowed. "He's been eating well and hasn't shown any sign of being sick. Guess I'd better pull over and check his hooves. Sure don't want to make him run if he has lost a shoe. He could have some missing pieces of the hoof wall, and any cracks or nails embedded in the hoof will need to come out."

Eleanor sighed. "That's one of the downsides to using a horse for transportation."

Vic waited until they came to a wider spot in the road and guided his horse and carriage over as far as possible. Handing the reins to Eleanor, he said, "Hold him steady while I check his hooves."

Eleanor did as her husband asked and sat quietly while he got out of the buggy and went to examine Domino's hooves.

A short time later, Vic got back into the buggy and took the reins. "You were right—he lost his right front shoe. I'll take it easy with him, and when we get there, I'll see if Dad's neighbor Abe, who's a farrier, is free to come over and replace the shoe." He took the reins from Eleanor. "If Abe's not available until tomorrow, I'll leave Domino in my daed's barn and borrow his horse, Buster, for our trip home."

"Are you sure he won't mind?"

Vic shook his head. "Since Dad's shop is right there on his property, he usually sticks close to home, unless he has to make a run into town for something or meets up with his best friend, Lloyd Zook, for coffee someplace. If that should happen, he can use my mamm's horse, Polly. Mom sticks around home most of the time anyway, unless she has some of her quilted items to deliver, and then she often will hire a driver."

Eleanor wasn't keen on using a horse they weren't familiar with. Even though the horse belonged to Vic's dad, there were no guarantees that it would behave itself. The whole idea bothered Eleanor as she thought about how sometimes animals acted funny with a stranger in charge of them. What if Buster decided to act up on them? *I'm sure if I press Vic concerning my uneasy feelings about using that horse, he'll dismiss it. But I'll try, even though he will do what he wants.*

"Why don't we borrow your mamm's horse instead of your daed's?" Eleanor questioned.

"No way. Polly's about as slow as sticky molasses being poured from a jar. Dad's horse has some get-up-and-go, and he'll get us home a lot quicker than Pokey Polly."

Eleanor drew in a couple of short, quick breaths. She would much rather travel home at a leisurely pace then race down the road with a rambunctious horse.

As if he could read her thoughts, Vic let go of the reins with one hand and reached over to touch Eleanor's arm. "Now, don't you worry. If we end up taking Buster, I'll have no trouble keeping him under control. He just needs a firm hand and a little reminder of who's boss."

————— ≈ —————

When they arrived at the Lapps' farmhouse, Vic led his horse into the barn while Eleanor got their gift for Eddie out of the buggy and headed for the house. She wished Vic had chosen to ask for his mother's horse to borrow for their return trip home, rather than his dad's. *But then,* she reasoned, *Vic must feel that he can handle Buster or he wouldn't have mentioned that he might ask if he could borrow the horse.*

Letting her thoughts go with the wayward wind that had picked up, Eleanor stepped onto the front porch and rapped on the door.

A few seconds later, Vic's eighteen-year-old sister, Kate, answered her knock. "It's nice to see you." She gave Eleanor a hug, and when she looked past, Kate blinked her brown eyes in rapid succession. "Where's Vic? I don't see him or his *gaul.*"

"Domino threw a shoe on the way here, so Vic took him to your daed's barn, where he'll end up spending the night if we can't get a farrier to come out this evening."

"That makes sense. I'm sure Dad will let Vic borrow one of our horses for your trip home after Eddie's party."

A mix of mouthwatering flavors drifted out the door. One was the faint, sweet smell of chocolate cake, and the other Eleanor recognized as savory chicken baking in the oven. She couldn't wait to eat, since she'd only snacked for lunch. "Speaking of your little brother. . ." She held up the gift bag in her right hand. "Where would you like me to put this?"

"I'll take it to the living room, which is where we'll all gather after we've eaten supper." Kate gestured to several brass hooks on the wall, above a long wooden bench. "You can hang your purse and sweater there if you like, and then join me, Clara, and Mom in the kitchen."

"Where's the rest of your family?" Eleanor asked.

"Dad's in the shower, and Stephen went to the barn with Eddie to look at the batch of *busslin* that were born early this morning. They got a look at them after breakfast, but then Mom went out and reminded Eddie that he needed to get his lunch pail and head for school, and Stephen should go straight to Dad's shop."

Eleanor smiled, remembering the joy she had always felt when she'd seen new life that had been born while growing up on her parents' farm in Indiana. She was tempted to run out to the barn right now and take a look at those kittens but didn't want to be rude. Vic's mom and sisters might need her help in the kitchen. Holding back a wistful sigh, she hung up her sweater and purse.

––––––––≈––––––––

Vic had just gotten Domino situated in one of the empty stalls when he heard the sound of laughter coming from the other side of the barn. Certain that it must be his two brothers, he left the stall and hurried to see what they thought was so funny. He found both fifteen-year-old Stephen and eight-year-old Eddie holding a black-and-white kitten against their faces.

When Vic knelt on the concrete floor beside them, Eddie showed him the kitten he held. "I'm gonna keep this *bussli*, and call it *Gebottsdaag*, 'cause it was born on my birthday."

Vic struggled to keep from rolling his eyes. "The Pennsylvania Dutch word for birthday is a pretty long name for a kitten, don't you think? And it looks too little to be away from its mother." Vic's gaze went from Eddie to Stephen, and then he pointed at the tiny, meowing kittens. "You both should put those busslin back in the box. You can play with them when they get a bit older and stronger."

Vic was tempted to lecture Stephen, because at his age, he ought to know better. But Vic chose not to say anything more on the topic as he watched his brothers return the little critters to the box where four other kittens burrowed against the mama cat's belly.

"Well now, birthday boy," Vic said, "should the three of us head on up to the house and see if Mom's got supper ready? The sooner we eat, the sooner you can open your presents."

Eddie bobbed his dark brown head. "And we'll eat some cake and ice cream too, right?"

"Absolutely. I'm sure Mom baked a chocolate cake for you, and she might even have bought your two favorite flavors of ice cream."

Eddie's pale blue eyes seemed to light right up. "*Schocklaad* and *aebeer*?"

Vic nodded.

"Don't you get sick of chocolate and strawberry all the time?" Stephen bumped Eddie's arm with his elbow. "You know, you could be satisfied with vanilla for a change."

"No way!" Eddie gave a firm shake of his head. "Vanilla's boring."

"No it ain't. You can put strawberries, chocolate syrup, nuts, or whatever you want on top."

"I know what I want, and—"

Feeling the need to put an end to this discussion, Vic stepped between the boys and put one hand on each of their shoulders. "I'm getting *hungerich*, so let's go to the house now, okay?"

"Jah, sure, 'cause I'm hungry too." Stephen made a dash for the barn door, and Eddie was right behind him.

Vic chuckled as he brought up the rear. Seeing the interaction between his two young brothers made him think about his childhood days when he and his sister Clara, who was five years younger than him, used to squabble about the pettiest things. When things got out of hand, Mom would have to separate them for a while, which usually meant that they were given some chore to do on opposites sides of the house, or else Mom would send one of them outdoors and keep the other child in the house with her. Vic didn't care for that at all back then, but as an adult, he could now understand why their mother did what she did and said what she meant. It was good parenting—plain and simple.

I wonder how it'll be when Eleanor and I have children. Vic thought as he stepped outside and closed the barn door. *What goes around comes around, Mom's always said. So I won't be one bit surprised if two of our kinner end up pestering each other.*

———— ≋ ————

Eleanor sat quietly at the supper table, listening to Vic engage in conversation with his parents and siblings. Although she didn't know all of them very well yet, Eleanor could tell they were a tight-knit family who enjoyed each other's company and liked to crack jokes and tell humorous stories of things that had happened in their area recently. It was nice to hear their laughter, but Eleanor thought she would enjoy listening to some topics that didn't necessarily involve humor. It wasn't that she liked hearing bad news or listening to unpleasant stories, but life was not a piece of cake with a dollop of ice cream on top. It was full of ups and downs, and hearing of other people's problems gave an opportunity to pray for those situations.

Eleanor had always been a strong believer in prayer. Many places in the Bible instructed people to pray and even told them what to say, such as in Matthew 6:9–13: "After this manner therefore pray ye: Our Father which art in heaven, Hallowed be thy name. Thy kingdom come. Thy will be done in earth, as it is in heaven. Give us this day our daily bread. And forgive us our debts, as we forgive our debtors. And lead us not into temptation, but deliver us from evil: For thine is the kingdom, and the power, and the glory, for ever. Amen."

"Would you like some more chicken?"

Clara's question caused Eleanor's thoughts to change direction. "No thank you," she said to Vic's younger sister. "I've already eaten more than my share." She took the offered platter and passed it on to Vic.

"I'll have another drumstick, but that's enough for me. I need to save some room for a hefty piece of my little brother's birthday cake." Vic looked at Eddie, who sat across the table from them, and grinned.

The boy smiled back at him and smacked his lips. "I can't wait for that."

"Can you hold off until you've opened your gifts?" his mother asked.

Eddie responded with a quick nod. "I hope I got the pony I've been asking for."

"You're too young for a pony." Stephen bumped his brother's arm. "I didn't get mine till I was twelve."

Ethan, the boy's dad, spoke up. "Don't worry, son, Eddie won't be getting a pony until he's old enough to take care of it and can be trusted to stay out of the road with his pony and cart."

Eddie shook his head vigorously. "I'd never go in the road, 'cause that wouldn't be safe."

"You're right," his mother interjected, "and that goes for you too, Stephen."

"I've seen other kids with their pony carts riding along the shoulder of the road," Stephen responded.

"That may be true, but it's dangerous, and it's my job as your daed to protect you." The boys' father pointed at their plates. "Now please finish your supper so we can move to the living room and Eddie can open his birthday presents."

"Okay, Dad," the brothers said in unison.

Vic leaned close to Eleanor and whispered, "See what we have to look forward to when we have kinner someday?"

She nodded and put her index finger to her lips, shushing him. This was not a conversation they should be having with family present.

———— ≈ ————

"Wasn't that a nice evening we had with my family?" Vic asked as they traveled home around nine o'clock with his father's horse pulling their buggy.

"Jah," Eleanor agreed. "Supper was good, the cake was delicious, the strawberry and chocolate ice cream were real tasty, and Eddie seemed happy with all the gifts he got."

"I think he liked ours best, though, don't you?"

She shrugged. "Maybe. His eyes did seem to light up when he saw the box of Legos you had chosen for him."

"He's a creative kid. I bet he'll build a lot of neat things with that big set of pieces."

They rode in silence for a while. Then Vic commented, "You seemed kinda quiet during supper."

"I was listening. Your family had a lot to say, and I could hardly keep up with all the humorous stories your daed shared."

"He does tell some whoppers."

"You mean they weren't true?"

"They really happened all right, but he likes to exaggerate a bit." Vic laughed. "Ever since I can remember, my daed's been quite the storyteller."

Eleanor thought about her own father. He'd always been the more serious type and didn't crack jokes very often. On the rare occasions that he did, it had always taken her by surprise. Even without all that humor, he was a good man who cared about Eleanor's mother, as well as Eleanor and her brothers.

A vehicle whizzed by, going in the opposite direction, and the driver blew his horn a couple of times. Buster clearly didn't like it, for he whinnied and took off in a fast-paced gallop.

Vic pulled back on the reins, but Buster kept running at what felt like lightning speed.

Eleanor's heart pounded. She hoped and prayed that her husband could get the horse under control. Otherwise, they might end up in an accident.

Chapter 4

Vic gritted his teeth and pulled back on the reins with all his strength, but Buster kept running at an even faster pace. He wished now that he'd asked to borrow Mom's docile mare instead of Dad's frisky horse. Even though Polly may have spooked when the car roared past, Vic was sure that he could have easily gotten her under control. Well, it was too late for regrets. He had to get Buster under control or deal with the potential consequences of the buggy toppling over.

After what seemed like hours but was only a few minutes, Vic managed to get Buster slowed down to a decent trot. "Whew, that's a relief." He felt a trickle of sweat run from his forehead to his cheek, but he didn't risk letting go of the reins with one hand to swipe at the moisture. Vic felt the adrenaline fading from his limbs; this unexpected event was all the excitement he needed for one day.

He glanced over at Eleanor, surprised that she hadn't said anything, but then he realized why. His wife's hands were clamped against her mouth—no doubt to keep from screaming.

"It's okay, Eleanor. This horse is under control now, and we're almost home." Vic spoke calmly, in spite of his quivering muscles and dry mouth. He would never admit it to his wife, but this episode with Buster had left him feeling drained and more than a bit frustrated.

Eleanor released her hands and placed them in her lap. "That was too close for my comfort," she said in a near whisper. "I hope we never go anywhere with your daed's gaul again. This situation could have ended badly with our buggy ruined and us getting hurt." Eleanor leaned closer to him. "Maybe you should have your father come by our place tomorrow and take his horse home."

"There's no need for you to worry," Vic was quick to say. "I plan on taking Buster back when I go to get my horse once he's been shod. I'll keep the horse and buggy close to the shoulder of the road and pray that nothing happens to spook him again."

———— ≋ ————

Paradise

Eleanor entered their home and turned on a few battery-operated lamps, letting much-needed light spill into the living and dining rooms. She'd never cared for a dark house, especially if she was by herself. But she wasn't alone. Vic was in the barn putting Buster away, and he'd be in soon.

Eleanor took off her sweater, hung it on one of the wooden pegs, and headed straight for the kitchen. As soon as she entered that room and had lit the overhead gas lamp, she got out the teakettle, lit the gas stove, and placed the kettle on the burner. She hoped a cup of warm chamomile tea might calm her nerves before going to bed. The ride home with Buster had made Eleanor feel like she might have a panic attack. She had covered her mouth to keep from screaming, knowing it may have upset Vic and could've riled the horse even more.

The house was quiet except for the ticking of the battery-operated clock. Eleanor stood by the kitchen sink, looking out the window, although it was too dark to see much of anything. She knew Vic would be in the barn for a little bit, getting Buster settled in for the night. There was time before the water heated, so Eleanor checked the African violets on the windowsill to see if they needed watering.

By the time she'd given them all a drink, the teakettle had begun to sing, just as Vic entered the kitchen. "I'm going to fix myself a cup of chamomile tea to calm my nerves," Eleanor stated. "Would you like some too?"

"No thanks. It would take something a lot stronger than a cup of tea to settle me down." Vic's features tightened. "That stubborn horse of Dad's kept moving all over the stall while I was trying to rub him down. If Buster was mine, I'd have gotten rid of him by now. He's too jumpy for me, and I certainly wouldn't want you to try and handle a horse like him."

"I wouldn't want to either." Eleanor poured hot water into her cup, added a tea bag, and took a seat at the table. "What were you referring to when you said it would take something stronger than chamomile tea to settle you down?"

"A bottle of beer might have helped." Vic lowered himself into a chair and shrugged. "But that's not going to happen because we have no beer in the house." He looked over at Eleanor. "And don't worry. I'm not going out to get any beer either. The last one I drank was several months before I joined the church, and I have no intention of drinking any now."

She figured after the incident with Buster her husband might close his eyes and take a nap in the chair. Eleanor was put off, hearing Vic bring up the topic of alcohol. Feeling a sense of relief that he no longer drank or smoked, Eleanor pressed a palm to her chest. She'd known some young Amish men in her community who'd drunk and smoked to excess during their *rumschpringe*, or time of running around, before joining the church. Even some of the wilder girls had indulged in those practices. Not her, though. Eleanor had seen what drinking too much could do when a couple of those young men who owned cars had gotten arrested for driving while under the influence of alcohol. It was a wonder no one had been in a serious accident. She felt comforted knowing that her husband no longer drank beer.

———≋———

Vic's dog ran along beside him as he headed for his phone shed Saturday morning. Last night after putting his own horse in Dad's barn, Vic had gone to his parents' phone shed and left a message for Abe, the farrier, asking when he could meet him to replace the shoe Domino had lost. He'd also left his phone number and asked Abe to give him a call as soon as he could. Since this was Saturday, Vic's day off, he hoped Abe could take care of Domino today.

Vic opened the door to the phone shed and stepped inside. Checkers darted in after him and nudged Vic's leg.

Vic grunted. "I know what you want. You want to play fetch, don't you, boy?"

Normally, when Vic came out of the house in the morning and let his dog out of the pen, he would toss a stick or throw one of Checkers' well-used balls for his eager pet to fetch. This morning, however, he'd been in a hurry to get to the phone shed, so he'd neglected his routine of playing with the dog. Vic figured if he didn't do something to get Checkers out of the phone shed, he'd be stuck with the mutt bugging him the whole time he was listening to messages. Vic wished Eddie was here right now, with his dog, Freckles. Those two could keep Checkers entertained for hours.

"Okay, okay. . . . Let's go get you something to fetch." Vic stepped out of the small wooden building and picked up a stick. He flung it hard, and as soon as Checkers chased after it, Vic returned to the shed and quickly shut the door.

After taking a seat on the wooden stool, he checked the answering machine for messages. The first one that came up was from Eleanor's father, asking Eleanor to call him at noon today. Al stated that he would be in their phone shed at that time, waiting for Eleanor's call.

Vic's forehead wrinkled. *I wonder what that's about. Sure hope everything's all right with my wife's family.*

He jotted down his father-in-law's message and listened to the next one. It was from the farrier, stating that he could meet Vic in his dad's barn today at two o'clock to take care of giving Domino a new horseshoe and check all the others as well. Vic was glad he didn't have to be there until later this afternoon. He wanted to be here when Eleanor made the phone call to her dad. If she should receive bad news of some kind, he wanted to be available to offer his wife the support she would need.

Holding the piece of paper he'd written the messages on, Vic stepped out of the phone shed and nearly tripped on his dog.

"For goodness' sakes, Checkers, couldn't you have at least given me some warning that you were there?" Usually when the dog went after a stick or ball, he would drop it near Vic and let out a few barks. At the moment, however, the black-and-white ball of fur sat near the phone shed with the chunk of wood in his mouth.

"Are you done playing, or did you want me to throw it again?" Vic asked.

Checkers dropped the wood and gave two loud barks.

Vic's gaze flicked upward. "Okay, buddy, whatever you say." He leaned over, took the stick from the dog's mouth, and gave it a pitch. When the dog took off running, Vic made a beeline for the house.

"Are you sure my daed didn't say why he wanted me to call?" Eleanor asked Vic as the noon hour approached.

He shook his head. "I would have told you if he'd said anything more."

"Then why were you insistent on coming here with me?" Eleanor stepped into the phone shed behind her husband.

"I figured if it was bad news, I ought to be with you."

She moved closer and gave him a hug. "Thank you. I appreciate your support."

They stood quietly for several moments, with Vic gently rubbing Eleanor's back. Finally, at his suggestion, she took a seat, and he stood behind her with both hands resting on her shoulders.

In an effort to calm her nerves, Eleanor drew in a few quick breaths. She was tempted to pick up the phone and call her parents' number right now, but Dad might not be in his phone shed yet, and then all Eleanor could do was leave a message.

She looked at the small battery-operated clock sitting beside the phone and watched as both hands moved until they pointed to twelve. It was time to make the call.

Eleanor dialed the number and was relieved when she heard her father's voice.

"I'm glad you got my message and were able to call." His voice deepened. "I wanted to let you know that your mamm is in the hospital."

Eleanor clutched her sweater, pulling it tightly closed. "What's wrong with her, Dad? Is she sick or was she involved in an accident?"

"It wasn't an accident. Your mamm has been in extreme pain for several days and managed to hide that fact from me until around midnight last night." He paused a few seconds before continuing. "The pain in her stomach got so bad that she couldn't sleep, so she woke me, saying she thought we ought to call a driver to take us to the hospital so she could find out what was wrong and see if they could help with her pain."

"Did they know what the problem was?" Eleanor questioned. "Did they run any tests?"

"Jah, they did a blood test and an ultrasound, and ran a few other tests. It didn't take long for them to determine that the pain and nausea your mamm had experienced was due to a very sick gallbladder."

"What are they going to do about it? Is there some medicine she can take?"

"There was a lot of inflammation and infection, so they did an emergency surgery and removed her gallbladder this morning."

"Oh dear. I wish I'd known sooner. I would have been praying for her."

"I knew you'd be sleeping when I made the first call, which is why I asked you to call me at noon."

"You must have come home from the hospital then."

"That's right. Your mamm won't be released until Sunday or Monday, but that's only if she's doing well enough to come home. I have a few things to do here, and then I'll be going back to the hospital. Your brothers will probably go there later today."

"I need to be there too, Dad. Mom's going to need my help when she comes home from the hospital."

"Would you mind? I'm sure she would appreciate having you there to help out and see to her needs."

Eleanor turned her head to look at Vic. When he made no objection, she spoke into the phone again. "I'll see if I can get one of our drivers to take me up. If we can leave within the next few hours we should be there by midnight tonight."

"Are you sure about this? I can call on your sisters-in-law or some of the women from our church district for help."

"No, Dad. My place is with Mom right now."

"Okay, Daughter. I'll wait up for you tonight and keep the battery lamp lit near the window. If something comes up and you can't make the trip, please leave me a message. I'll be going out to the phone shed when I get back from the hospital this evening."

"No problem. If I can't get a ride tonight, I'll get one for tomorrow and be sure to let you know." Eleanor swiped a hand across her damp forehead. "Tell Mom I'm praying for her and that I'll be there to see her soon."

"I will. Take care and tell your husband I said hello."

"Vic's standing right here, Dad. He's heard everything that's been said, because the phone is in speaker mode."

"Oh. Greetings, Vic."

Vic leaned closer to the phone receiver. "Hello, Al. I'm sorry to hear about Lydia. I hope she gets better soon."

"Thank you. I hope so too." There was a brief pause, and Eleanor's dad posed another question. "Is there any chance you might be able to come to Indiana too?"

"I wish I could," Vic responded, "but my boss has several big jobs scheduled for the next few weeks, so he's gonna need every available man."

"That's understandable. Sorry you can't make it, but hopefully we'll see you both for Thanksgiving or Christmas."

"Maybe so. We'll have to wait and see how it goes."

Eleanor said a few more words to her father and told him goodbye. When she hung up the phone, she turned to face Vic again. "Would you mind calling a driver for me while I go pack?"

His brows furrowed. "Do you really have to go take care of your mother? Wouldn't one of your brothers' wives be willing to help out?"

"I'm sure they would be, but all three of them have young children to care for. Besides," she quickly added, "I want to be there to take care of my *mudder*. When I lived at home, she took care of me whenever I was sick or needed her, and now it's my turn to return the favor."

He nodded. "I guess you're right. I'll make a few calls if necessary while you're up at the house putting things in a suitcase." Vic bent his head and gave her a strong kiss. "I'm sure gonna miss you, though."

Eleanor stood and wrapped her arms around his waist. "I'll miss you too, my love, but if things go well for Mom, I'll be back before you know it."

Chapter 5

Grabill

Eleanor's mother had already removed her head covering and asked for a scarf to wear instead. Eleanor agreed that it would be more comfortable to rest in the soft material than the stiff kapp she'd removed. She went to her bedroom dresser and brought out a brown one for her mother. Eleanor watched Mom tie on the scarf and nestle herself into the soft cushions the couch offered.

"Are you sure I can't fix you something to eat?" Eleanor leaned close to her mother.

"No food right now, but I am thirsty and would appreciate something cold to drink."

"Sure, no problem. Would you like some apple cider?"

"Maybe later. Right now I'd be fine with just a glass of *wasser*."

"Water it is then. I'll be right back." Eleanor hurried off to the kitchen. When she returned to the living room a few minutes later and approached Mom, she saw that her eyes were closed. Believing she must be asleep, Eleanor set the water on the small table near the couch and took a seat in the rocking chair. Her mother had come home from the hospital shortly before noon today and had been resting on the couch for well over an hour.

Eleanor figured Mom should have been hungry by now, and it worried her that she didn't want to eat.

Dad had mentioned that before they left the hospital, the doctor said it might take a while for Mom to get her appetite back. He'd also stated that she would need to change her diet, at least until her digestive system got used to being without a gallbladder. The best foods for Mom to consume at this point in her healing were broth, decaffeinated herbal tea, juice, bananas, applesauce, and other soft, nonfatty foods. It was also important for her to get plenty of rest, which meant taking the prescribed medicine for her post-surgery pain.

Eleanor was glad she could be here to look after her mother and take over all her household chores. If she hadn't come here to help out, Mom might very well have tried to do too much.

From the sound of her deep breathing, it appeared that Mom had indeed fallen asleep, so Eleanor sat quietly, not wanting to disturb her by making any more noise from the wooden rocker. But the longer she sat there and waited, the more anxious Eleanor became. *I should get started prepping the food for us to eat.* She looked over at Mom once more. *I'll try to be as quiet as I can.*

Eleanor rose from the creaky, rocking chair and hesitated for a moment. Her mother never stirred, so Eleanor headed for the kitchen to heat some chicken broth. She would offer it to her mother when she woke up. As soon as Dad came in from the barn, she would fix him whatever he wanted for lunch.

Maybe I'll make toasted cheese sandwiches. Eleanor had always liked those, and her dad did too. Truth was, Eleanor was more like him than she was her mother—at least as far as their likes and dislikes of foods. In other ways, she wasn't like either of them. Mom tended to be a worrywart, and Dad was usually quite easygoing.

Eleanor took a jar of chicken broth from the pantry and paused to glance around Mom's newly painted kitchen. The walls had been an eggshell white when Eleanor lived here, but they'd since been changed to a light beige color.

Eleanor missed living in Grabill near her friends and family, but being here now with plans to stay at least a week, she longed to be with Vic.

I wonder what he's doing right now, she thought. *Does he miss me as much as I miss him?*

———≈———

Bird-in-Hand, Pennsylvania, Monday afternoon

"I'm gonna swing in here and get me a beer before we head for home," Tom said, glancing at Vic before pulling his truck into the parking lot of a minimart on Old Philadelphia Pike Road. "Should I get one for you too?"

Vic's top teeth came down on his bottom ones with an audible click. "How many times do I have to tell you that I'm not a drinking man?" *At least not anymore.*

Tom shrugged his broad shoulders. "Figured with the wife gone and all, you may have changed your mind about that."

"The reason I choose not to drink has nothing to do with Eleanor, so please leave her out of this conversation. For that matter, let's not talk about it at all." Vic gestured to the minimart. "If you need a beer that bad, go on ahead. I'll just wait for you right here."

Tom's elbow connected with Vic's arm. "Calm down. There's no reason to get riled about it."

Vic's fingers curled into the palms of his hands. "I'm not riled, just irritated because you won't let up on the topic and keep trying to get me to drink with you. I've told you enough times, and I'm getting tired of repeating myself."

Tom sneered at him. "You're sure the self-righteous one, you know that?"

"I'm not self-righteous—just using common sense." Vic slid a finger down the side of his nose. "You have the right to drink a beer if you want to, and I have the right not to, so let's leave it at that."

"Okay, buddy, whatever you say." Tom opened his door and hopped out of the truck. "Be back soon," he said before slamming the door.

"That fellow doesn't have a lick of good sense, much less any manners," Vic muttered. He closed his eyes, and when he pressed the back of his head against the headrest, a vision of his sweet wife took over Vic's thoughts. He was eager to get home and check for messages. Hopefully there would be one from Eleanor, suggesting a time for him to call so they could talk. She'd been away only two days, but it would be a lot better to hear her voice in real time rather than merely listen to a recording, unable to give an immediate response. Conversations via messages were so impersonal, and a person couldn't say much before their message would get cut off if the voice mailbox became full.

I hope Eleanor's mother heals well from her surgery and my wife can come home to me soon.

Vic's eyes snapped open and he sat up straight when Tom got back into the truck. His coworker gave him a smug-looking smile as he set a brown paper sack on the seat between them. "I got myself a six-pack, and I'm gonna open a can right now."

Vic watched as Tom pulled the tab from one of the cans and took a big swig. "Ah, that sure hits the spot." He moved his hand so the can was right under Vic's nose. "Doesn't that smell good?"

"Not to me." Vic turned his head away. "Can we get going now? I need to get home. I have chores to do. I imagine you do too."

"Nope. Since Cheryl moved out, there's no to-do list waiting for me anymore."

Vic pulled his fingers through the long hairs growing from his chin as he reflected on that. Although Eleanor had never made a list of chores for him to do, there were times when she'd asked him to do certain things. It had never bothered him, though, because she had always asked nicely. Besides, Vic wanted to please his wife, and he'd never viewed doing things to help out as a bother. After all, they were married, and he felt that certain chores were his responsibility.

Tom finished off his beer and started the truck. Soon he pulled out onto the road in the direction of home. Vic was glad Tom had only downed one can of beer, or he would have said something. It wouldn't be good to drink alcohol while driving, and if they were involved in an accident or Tom got pulled over for speeding, it would not go down well.

———————≈———————

Paradise

By the time Tom pulled into Vic's yard, Vic felt like he could scream. From the time they'd left the minimart he'd been forced to listen to his coworker's foul mouth as he shouted at other drivers and complained about all the idiots on the road. On top of that, Tom had his radio blaring so loud it vibrated the cab of the truck. Vic felt as if his head might burst open. He wished someone else from work lived close to him so he didn't have to rely on Tom for a ride to and from their boss' shop. If it wasn't so far, he would ride his scooter to and from work every day, but the shop in Lancaster wasn't close enough for him to do that.

"Thanks for the ride." Vic got out of the truck. "See you tomorrow morning." He barely heard Tom's reply over the blare of his radio. It would feel good to get away from the loud music and be home where he could relax from his long day at work.

Vic glanced at the barn and thought about how things had gone when he'd returned his father's horse to him the other day. It was sure nice having Domino reshod and back in his own stall again. Vic appreciated his dad's generosity in loaning Buster, but he still couldn't get over that rambunctious horse's nature. *How in the world can my daed put up with such an unpredictable animal?* he wondered. *If Buster was mine, I'd get rid of him for a less headstrong horse.*

Vic stopped at the dog run to let Checkers out, and then he sprinted for the house. Barking frantically, the dog ran alongside him. Vic bent down and gave Checkers' head a few pats; then he picked up a stick and gave it a fling. Instead of going after it, like he normally would, the dog brushed against Vic's leg and followed him into the house.

Vic chuckled. "You missed me today, didn't you, boy?"

Checkers wagged his tail and let out a yip.

"I missed you too, buddy." *But not as much as I miss my wife,* Vic thought. He took a glass down from the cupboard, filled it with water from the faucet at the sink, and took a big drink. Next, he put some water in the dog's dish and watched as his faithful companion drank eagerly.

Vic pursed his lips. *Guess my dog got real thirsty today, or else I didn't put enough water in the dish inside the dog run this morning. I'll make sure to give him plenty of water tomorrow before Tom comes by to pick me up for work.*

After Vic finished the refreshing liquid in his glass, he refilled the dog's dish, went out the front door, and headed for the phone shed. Checkers trailed after him again. At the rate things were going, Vic figured the dog might try to get in bed with him tonight. "Well, that's not going to happen," he mumbled. "No matter how much I like my *hund,* his place is not on the bed. But I may let him sleep on the floor in my room. It would be nice to have the company, even if it is only that of a dog."

When Vic opened the door of the phone shed, Checkers darted in ahead of him and plopped down near the wooden stool.

"Okay, buddy, you can stay here with me, but you'd better keep quiet while I'm listening to messages." Vic took a seat and punched the MESSAGE button. There was only one, and he was pleased to hear Eleanor's voice.

"Hi, Vic, it's me. I'm sure you're at work, but I wanted you to know that Mom came home from the hospital today. As you can imagine, she's not feeling the best, but with some rest and time to recover from her surgery, I'm sure she'll be fine. I'll call again tomorrow and give you an update, but the way it stands now, I'm pretty sure I'll be here at least a week." Eleanor's message ended with "I love you."

"I love you too." Vic's words were spoken in a near whisper, but Checkers must have heard, for his ears perked up and he gave two loud barks.

Vic grinned. No doubt the dog thought the words he'd spoken had been meant for him.

He picked up the phone and dialed Eleanor's parents' number. When he heard their recording, he left a message, letting Eleanor know that he'd listened to her message and looked forward to hearing from her again. He ended by saying he loved her and was eager for Eleanor to come home. Before Vic hung up, he remembered to add, "Tell your mamm that I'm glad she's out of the hospital, and I hope she gets better soon."

Vic heaved a sigh. *The sooner she gets better, the sooner my wife will be coming home to me.*

———— ≈ ————

Grabill

Eleanor had just placed sandwiches on the table when Mom entered the kitchen and headed for the pantry.

"What do you need? I can get it for you."

"There's no reason for you to baby me," Mom said, wrinkling her forehead. "I can certainly do something as simple as getting out a box of crackers to go with the broth you heated for me."

Eleanor cringed. She hadn't meant to upset her mother. She'd come here to help out, and now it seemed her mother didn't want her help.

"Sorry." Eleanor looked down at her toasted cheese sandwich, which now held no appeal.

"No, I'm the one who should apologize." Mom placed her hand on Eleanor's arm. "I appreciate you coming here, but I'm not an invalid, and I need the freedom to do some things myself."

"I understand. I'm just concerned that you'll try to do too much."

Mom shook her head. "I'll follow the doctor's orders. I promise."

"You'd better do as he said." Dad's deep voice resonated when he entered the kitchen.

Her mother turned to look at him. "Oh, I didn't realize you had come in from outside, Al."

"Yep. I entered through the front door, because I'd gone out front to get the mail and check for messages in the phone shed." He leaned down and gave Mom a peck on the cheek. "How are you feeling, Lydia?"

"I am sore from the surgery, of course, but it's not unbearable."

"I'm glad to hear it, but you need to be careful and not do too much."

"I know my limits."

"That's good, but if you forget, we're here to remind you." He looked at Eleanor and winked. "Right, Daughter?"

She nodded slowly. Truth was, she didn't look forward to reminding her mother of anything for fear of getting another reprimand. Eleanor had always been sensitive to harsh words. Growing up, she'd often cried whenever her mother or father corrected her behavior.

"Two of the messages on our recorder were for you." Dad handed Eleanor a slip of paper.

She smiled when she read them. One was from Vic, and the other came from Doretta, saying she'd heard Eleanor was here and that she'd come by soon. Eleanor looked forward to her good friend's visit and hoped it would be soon, for they had lots of catching up to do.

Chapter 6

Eleanor had put the last of the clean breakfast dishes in the cupboard when she heard a horse and buggy come into the yard. Peering out the kitchen window, she watched as the woman driver guided the horse and open buggy to the hitching rail near the barn. Eleanor did not recognize the horse pulling their rig, which threw her off for a moment. From the back, she couldn't tell who the two women were in the buggy, but when one got down and went to secure the horse, she recognized her dear friend immediately. Excited to see Doretta, Eleanor hurried out the back door and into the yard. She'd just reached the buggy when Doretta's mother, Amanda, stepped down.

"It's so nice to see you, Eleanor." The small-boned, slender woman stepped forward and gave Eleanor a hug. "We came by to check on your mamm and say hello to you."

Doretta had finished securing the horse and turned to face Eleanor with her arms outstretched. "I'm happy to see you as well."

"Same here. I didn't know who had pulled into the yard at first." Eleanor hugged her friend.

"You didn't?" Doretta tilted her head, and then she waved her question away. "Oh, that's because we have a new horse." She gave Eleanor another hug. "How have you been, and how's your *mudder* doing?"

Eleanor bit back a chuckle. Leave it to Doretta to ask two questions at the same time.

"I'm fine, and my mother is doing as well as can be expected. This is only her second day home from the hospital, and her incision is still pretty sore. She doesn't have much of an appetite yet, either."

"That's predictable," Amanda stated. "And certain foods may not agree with her. That's how it was when my sister, Sylvia, had her gallbladder removed last year." Amanda gave a slow shake of her head. "Poor thing. She still can't eat certain foods without suffering the consequences."

Eleanor hoped that would not be her mother's case. "Let's go inside." She gestured to her parents' sprawling, two-story house. "I'm sure my mamm will be pleased to see you both."

Amanda reached into the back of the black open buggy and withdrew a small cardboard box. "I brought your mamm starts from two of my prettiest pink African violets."

Eleanor smiled. "I'm sure she will appreciate them."

A gust of wind came up, and Doretta shivered. "Wow! It's sure turned chilly today."

"Let's go inside before the wind gets any stronger. We can visit better in there and enjoy sitting in a warm house with a cup of tea or some hot apple cider." Eleanor started walking toward the house, and her friend matched her stride, with Doretta's mother just a few steps behind.

———≈———

"Tell me all about your new home in Pennsylvania," Doretta said after they'd visited with their mothers in the living room for a while and then excused themselves to go to the kitchen to talk privately. "Is Paradise a lot different than here?"

"Jah. There are a lot of hills in Pennsylvania, and we certainly have more traffic to deal with in Lancaster County than you do here in Grabill."

Doretta pushed a wisp of her reddish-brown hair back in place under her white, cone-shaped head covering. "I've never been to Pennsylvania, but I've heard it's a beautiful state." She smiled. "I'm looking forward to visiting you there, hopefully sometime next year."

Eleanor reached across the span between them at the table and clasped her friend's hand. "Summertime, like we talked about before, would work well, since you won't be teaching school then."

Doretta nodded. "I hope we can make it happen."

"Same here." Eleanor thought about that time in the future. *I wonder by then if I'll be expecting Vic's and my first child.* She took a sip from her mug filled with hot apple cider. *If so, it might seem a little strange, since Doretta and I would no longer be in the same stage of life. Of course, with me being married now, and her not yet engaged, our lives are already a bit different. I'm sure my being with child would not affect my close relationship with Doretta in any way, however.*

"How are things going between you and your husband?" Doretta's question broke into Eleanor's thoughts. "Have you had your first disagreement yet?"

"Vic and I are two different people, so we don't see eye to eye on everything, but nothing big has come between us, and I hope it never does."

Doretta smiled. "You're easygoing, so I'm sure if any problems should arise, you'll be able to work them out with your husband."

"I hope so." Eleanor fiddled with the ties on her heart-shaped head covering. "I'm surprised you haven't commented on my prayer kapp. It's quite different than the one I used to wear when I lived here."

Doretta reached up and touched the front of her own stiff white covering. "There is quite a contrast between the two. Mine hides the back of my hair and bun, but I can see your bun through the back of your kapp."

"It is sheer in comparison, but it's also lighter weight, which is kind of nice."

Doretta picked up her mug and took a drink of cider. "I see the skirt of your dress does not have pleats like the ones we women wear here in Grabill."

"That's true. After moving to Lancaster County, I felt like I should dress the way other Amish women there do."

"I understand. Have you made some new friends from your church district or community?" Doretta asked, taking their conversation in a different direction.

Eleanor shook her head. "Not really—just a few acquaintances. Most of the women my age are married with children, so I don't have much in common with them. Maybe after Vic and I have our first child, I'll fit in more and can relate to the women who are mothers."

Doretta opened her mouth as if to say something, but Eleanor spoke first. "How are things going with you and William? Has he asked you to marry him yet?"

Her friend's cheeks colored. "I think he was about to when he brought me home from the singing last Sunday night, but Isaac showed up and interrupted our conversation." Doretta's forehead wrinkled. "My dear brother wouldn't stop talking to William, so I finally said good night and went in the house."

"That's a shame. I bet you weren't too happy with Isaac for sticking around and monopolizing the conversation."

"No, I wasn't, but it was partly William's fault because he kept talking to him."

"Maybe he was only being polite and didn't want to hurt your brother's feelings."

"I suppose. I just hope William gets up the nerve to try again when we're not likely to have any interruptions."

Eleanor hoped Doretta would have more opportunities to spend time with William and that a permanent relationship would eventually develop between them. *Maybe by the time she comes to Pennsylvania to visit me, she and William will be engaged.*

"I've been praying for you ever since I heard about your gallbladder attack and the surgery that followed." Amanda's tone revealed her obvious concern. "Are you in a lot of pain?" she asked when Lydia winced as she repositioned herself on the couch while trying to find a comfortable position.

"I appreciate your prayers." Lydia adjusted the light blanket that covered her from the waist down. "And to answer your question: my pain isn't too bad. I just have to sit or lie a certain way so that I don't put pressure on my incision." She placed a thin pillow behind her back.

"I'm sure it will take a while for you to heal." Amanda leaned forward in her chair. "Is there anything we can do to help out while Doretta and I are here?"

"Not really. Eleanor's been taking good care of things." Lydia sighed. "I'll certainly miss her when she returns to Pennsylvania. It was difficult for me to accept the idea of her moving to another state and adapting the Amish ways in Lancaster County."

In fact, it was difficult for me to accept the man Eleanor chose to marry. Lydia was careful not to voice that thought. If her daughter had come back to the living room and overheard her saying such a thing, it would not go over well. Besides, Lydia had never said anything negative about her son-in-law to anyone in their church district and wasn't about to now. The last thing she needed was for any gossip to get started, which in the long run would make Lydia look bad for saying unpleasant things about her daughter's husband. Although Vic had done nothing specific to cause Lydia to distrust him since he and Eleanor had gotten married, she had voiced her concern to Eleanor when she and Vic had begun dating. Eleanor had shrugged it off, saying that Vic was a really nice guy, and to her knowledge, he hadn't done anything that other young men his age hadn't done. Lydia and her husband had heard through the grapevine that Vic had done a few things they disapproved of before joining the church. Even though, as far as she knew, he hadn't smoked cigarettes or drunk alcohol since he and Eleanor had gotten married, Lydia couldn't get past the nagging feeling that Vic still had a wild side and couldn't be trusted. She hoped her son-in-law would be a good husband and not break her daughter's tender heart someday.

Lydia shook her concerns aside when Amanda posed another question. "Are the Amish in the area where Eleanor and Vic live much different than we are here?"

"Not in the respect of how they worship, but the women's dresses, aprons, and head coverings are different from ours. Also, their carriages are gray and closed, which look much different than our black open buggies."

"Some in our area are getting closed buggies now."

"You're right. I've seen some, but most, like the carriages my family use, are still open."

"The closed ones would be much nicer for cold winter weather."

Lydia bobbed her head. "I certainly can't argue with that."

Amanda glanced toward the kitchen door. "Should we join our daughters in the kitchen for hot tea and some of that banana bread I brought along?"

Although Lydia felt no hunger, she nodded. "I need to get up and move around anyway. The doctor said I should do some walking, and even a few steps to the kitchen is better for me than sitting or lying on the couch all day."

Paradise

Vic entered the house via the back door and pulled off his work boots. It was lonesome without his wife there to talk to. He looked around the empty kitchen where she'd normally be busy putting something together for them to eat. Vic wished he could call Eleanor just to hear her sweet voice, but he'd have to leave a message and schedule a day and time for them to talk, like he'd done a few days ago.

After placing his boots in the utility room, he went to the bathroom and washed up. Looking at himself in the mirror, it wasn't hard to see the lines of strain on his face. Between missing his dear wife, working harder than normal, and putting up with Tom's irritating ways, Vic had a hard time finding anything to smile or laugh about.

It was difficult to be enthused about fixing something for supper, but he'd worked hard all day on the new house his boss had contracted to build, and Vic was as hungry as a bear. He had never liked cooking that much and wondered if he should go out to a restaurant for supper or drop by to see his folks. Most likely when Mom heard that Eleanor was gone, she would invite him to stay for supper.

Although it was difficult to say the words out loud or even think them, Vic did not relish the idea of his mother knowing that he was on his own, without a wife to cook his meals this week. Mom was, and always had been,

"]

the kind of mother who worried about her children and often tried to do too much for them. While she would surely understand Eleanor's need to go home to care for her mother, she would no doubt fret about whether Vic was getting enough to eat and also comment about how important it was for him to eat the proper foods.

Vic left the bathroom and started down the hallway toward the kitchen. He was almost there when he heard his dog's familiar bark, followed by a scratching sound on the back door.

"Okay, little buddy, I'm coming." Vic opened the back door, and when Checkers raced in, he ran straight for the kitchen. Vic had a rough time saying no to his pet's puppy-looking eyes staring up at him, as though asking for permission to stay.

Vic squeezed out a small laugh. "Are you hungry, or do you just want to be in here with me while I fix supper?"

The dog's response was a few wags of his tail.

Vic was not in the mood to turn on the stove, so he got out a loaf of bread in preparation for making a tuna sandwich.

"I sure had a busy day, Checkers. You probably would've enjoyed wandering around the construction site with me while I worked in various places." He looked down at his furry buddy and back at the bread. "I don't see why you can't have one slice of this. Here you go, boy." He tossed the bread, and Checkers caught it in his mouth.

Vic stepped over to the refrigerator and returned with mayonnaise and pickles. He then grabbed the can opener from one of the drawers and proceeded to work on the tin container.

The dog's nose twitched when Vic opened the can of tuna.

"You in the mood for some fish?" Vic put some dry dog food in Checkers' dish and poured the oil from the tuna on top. "Maybe a little fish oil will make your coat shine. It has omega-3 in it, which is also good for the brain. That way you can remember where you've buried all your bones."

Checkers dived right into the tuna delight.

"You like that, don't you boy?"

The dog kept eating, and Vic went back to the refrigerator for some lettuce. This was not going to be a great meal, and it would certainly be nowhere near as good as anything Eleanor had fixed since they'd gotten married, but at least it would fill the hole in his empty stomach.

———— ≋ ————

Vic woke up the following morning feeling as though his head was surrounded by a dense fog. He'd gone to bed later than usual last night and had fallen into a deep sleep. To make matters worse, he had forgotten to set his alarm. *Sure hope my ride doesn't show up before I'm ready to head out the door. Tom won't be happy if I make us both late for work.*

Vic was on the verge of rolling onto his right side when he felt a slurpy tongue brush his cheek. His nose wrinkled at the smelly odor of dog fur, not to mention the wet spot Checkers had left on his face. "What are you doing on my bed?" He pushed the mutt aside and then pointed to the floor. "Get down, Checkers! What was I thinking, letting you stay in the house last night and allowing you to sleep on the floor in here?"

The dog jumped down and slunk out of the room with his tail between his legs.

From the looks of the dog hair on the sheets, Vic figured his faithful companion might have slept in his bed the whole night.

"Not good," he mumbled as his feet touched the floor. "Now I'll have sheets to wash when I get home from work this evening, not to mention putting a new set of sheets on the bed." Vic made a mental note to be sure to put Checkers in his dog pen tonight. The last thing he needed was for Eleanor to return home and find out that his smelly hund had been sleeping in the house, not to mention their bed.

Chapter 7

Grabill

Eleanor glanced at the calendar hanging on the kitchen wall. It was hard to believe that she'd been here two whole weeks and would be going back to Pennsylvania today. Eleanor had thought when she'd first come here that it would be for only a week, but it had taken a while for Mom's pain and fatigue to subside, so she had decided to stay an extra week to help out.

"Would you like another cup of tea?" Eleanor asked her mother, who sat at the table paying some bills while Eleanor dried the breakfast dishes.

"No thanks. One cup was enough for me." She placed her pen aside and sealed an envelope.

"Are you sure you can manage on your own without me now? I could stay another week if you need me to."

"I appreciate all that you've done, but you have been here long enough. It's time for you to return home, because I'm sure your husband needs you more than I do right now. Maybe even more than he's willing to admit," Mom added. "Besides, you've already scheduled a driver, and she'll be here soon to pick you up."

Eleanor nodded. She had to admit that it would be good to get home and be with Vic again. She'd missed him something awful and knew from Vic's messages, plus the few times they'd spoken on the phone, that he missed her too. If her driver arrived on time, she would be leaving within the next ten minutes, and by suppertime she should be home and in her husband's strong arms. Oh, how she looked forward to that.

"Your mamm is right," Dad interjected. "Your place is with Vic now, and you've done plenty around here since your arrival. Besides, your mother is doing better, and anything she cannot do I'll take care of when I come in for the evening after a day's work."

"Don't worry, Daughter, I promise not to overdo. Believe me, I know what my limits are, so I'll only do what I'm able."

"Good to hear." Eleanor felt some relief hearing her parents' words, but she also knew how determined Mom could be when she wanted to do something. Eleanor could only hope that Mom would keep true to her word. If not, she'd end up coming back here again, which Vic would probably not be happy about.

Eleanor wished she'd had more time to spend with her brothers and their families, but at least they had made time for a few visits and to check on Mom. She smiled, thinking how cute it had been when Gabe's eleven-month-old girl, who'd been named after her grandma Lydia, had taken her first step during one of the visits. With each step Lydia Ann had taken, everyone had clapped and cheered her on. Seeing how sweet the little girl was caused Eleanor to yearn for a child of her own. Hopefully that dream would come true for her and Vic soon. Although she was only twenty-five and still had plenty of childbearing years left, she wanted to start having children while she was young and had enough energy to keep up with them.

A horn honked outside, breaking into Eleanor's musings. She looked out the kitchen window and saw her driver's vehicle pull into the yard. It was time for a tearful goodbye with her parents, followed by a long nine-to-ten-hour drive.

———————≋———————

Lancaster

Vic laid his hammer down and paused to swipe the sweat from his forehead. He, along with four other men, had been working hard to finish a house his boss had been contracted to build. They needed to get it done before winter set in with snow and heavy rains. He looked forward to getting off work this afternoon and was more than ready for his wife's return. Eleanor had been at her folks' house a week longer than she'd expected, and Vic had been happy last night when he'd gone to the phone shed and found a message from her saying she'd be home by suppertime this evening.

Maybe I'll take her out to a restaurant to eat so she doesn't have to cook, Vic told himself. *After a long day of traveling, she'll be tired and shouldn't have to worry about fixing supper.*

"What are you standing around for?" Tom bumped Vic's arm. "The boss will be here soon to check on things, and we need to get this done."

"Yeah, I know. Just taking a short break is all." Vic picked up his hammer again. "I'm just as eager to finish this job as you are."

Tom's forehead wrinkled. "Never said I was eager. I've got plans for this evening, and I don't want the boss saying we've gotta work overtime."

"Me neither." Vic nodded. "My wife's on her way back from Indiana and should arrive home about the time I get there."

Tom gestured to the cabinets they'd been installing. "It may not be the usual time if you don't get busy."

Vic's coworker swung his hammer, and Vic followed suit. This day couldn't end soon enough to suit him, and he hoped Tom wouldn't feel the need to stop for beer or anything else on the way back to Paradise.

———≈———

At four o'clock, Vic's boss, Ned Duncan, showed up to check on their progress. Since the cabinets weren't finished, he instructed Vic and Tom to keep working until they were done, while Allen and Bill installed two smaller cabinets in the utility room above the place where the washer and dryer would go. "I'd like you all to stay until these projects are done," he said, "because tomorrow we need to move on to another job that's been waiting."

Vic groaned inwardly. He'd wanted to be home by the time Eleanor arrived, but unless she was late getting in, it looked doubtful that he'd be at the house before she was.

Vic waited until the boss left, and then he asked to borrow Tom's cell phone so he could call home and leave a message for Eleanor. Hopefully she would walk out to the phone shed to check for messages when she saw that he wasn't there at the usual time.

Paradise

"Thank you for the ride." Eleanor handed her driver, Reba, the money she owed before stepping out of the vehicle and retrieving her luggage from the back. The sun had almost set for the day, and a beautiful pinkish-orange color glowed in the west.

Eleanor felt a feeling of lightness in her chest as she made her way up to the house. She heard Checkers barking from his dog run and figured Vic was either not home from work yet or had put the dog there while doing his chores, because sometimes Checkers got in Vic's way, begging and wanting him to play.

She stepped onto the porch, put her key in the door, and entered the quiet house. None of the gas lamps or battery-operated lights were on, and her shoulders drooped with disappointment. Vic was obviously not at home. *I wonder how late he'll be this evening.*

Eleanor took her suitcase to their bedroom and placed it on the end of the bed. Then she went back outside and headed for the phone shed to leave a message for her folks, letting them know that she'd arrived safely. Eleanor would let Checkers out of his run after she'd made the phone call, because if she did it now, he'd sit barking outside the shed and her voice might not be heard above the noise.

Upon entering the phone shed, Eleanor saw the light on the answering machine blinking. *Vic may have called, so maybe I should check for messages before calling my folks.*

The dog's frantic barking had increased, so Eleanor leaned close to the answering machine to listen to the first message. Sure enough, it was Vic, saying that he would be later than usual getting home.

Eleanor's disappointment increased. She had so looked forward to greeting her husband with a warm hug and a kiss. *Life is full of disappointments,* she told herself, *but this is a minor one compared to what some people must face.*

With determination not to let this displeasure get to her, she picked up the phone and made the call to her folks. After leaving a quick message, Eleanor left the phone shed and hurried across the yard to let the barking dog out. As soon as the gate to the dog run opened, Checkers ran out and jumped up on Eleanor's dress. She pushed the dog away and stepped back. "I know you're happy to be out of your pen, but you need to stay down." Eleanor bent down and grabbed a stick, then gave it a fling. Checkers took off like a flash.

Her legs moved quickly as she hurried to the house. It was time to go to the kitchen and see what was available for supper. Eleanor had a feeling that during the two weeks she'd been gone, Vic had eaten most of his evening meals at his parents' house. Either that or he'd gotten by with heating soup from a can or making cold sandwiches, because he wasn't much of a cook.

Eleanor opened the refrigerator and soon realized that there wasn't much to choose from. All the packages of chicken and beef were in the freezer and would take too long to thaw. There were a few packages of sliced ham in the refrigerator, so she took them out, along with a brick of cheddar cheese. Eleanor found six medium-sized potatoes in the pantry, which she peeled and cut into slices. In a casserole dish, she layered the potato slices with pieces of lunch meat, cheese, and butter. After sprinkling the ingredients with salt and pepper, Eleanor poured milk over the top. Once the oven was heated to the proper temperature, she slid in the scalloped potatoes and set the timer. At least they would have a main dish to eat, and it should be filling.

Eleanor found a few carrots in the refrigerator, which she peeled and cut. She also opened a jar of pickles and a can of black olives. It wouldn't be the best meal she'd ever cooked, but it wouldn't be the worst either.

While the potatoes cooked, Eleanor returned to the bedroom and opened her suitcase. Even though her husband was absent, it felt good to be here in her own home. Eleanor reached over by the nightstand and clicked on the battery-operated light. Her suitcase held a couple of things from her mother. It was just like Mom to be generous, and one of the items was some nice dark green material, enough for Eleanor to make a new dress. Her mom had also added some natural home remedies. Eleanor appreciated the gifts. It wouldn't take long to empty out the suitcase and put everything away, so she got busy on it right away.

Eleanor had hung the last dress in the closet when she heard Checkers carrying on outside. Thinking Vic might be home, Eleanor's heart pounded with anticipation as she hurried to the living room and opened the front door. Instead of Vic, however, their nearest neighbor, Anna Stoltzfus, stood on the porch, holding a good-sized plastic container.

"Welcome home, Eleanor." The middle-aged Amish woman offered a friendly smile. "I spoke to your husband last evening, and he mentioned that you would be coming home today." She handed the container to Eleanor. "I baked two applesauce cakes this morning and thought you might like one of them."

Eleanor matched Anna's smile. "Danki, that was very thoughtful of you." She stepped to one side. "Won't you come in?"

"Maybe some other time. I really need to get back home and start *nachtesse* for my family right now." Anna tilted her head back and sniffed. "Based on the wonderful odor I'm smelling, I bet you have something in the oven for supper too."

Eleanor nodded. "Vic isn't home from work yet, and there wasn't much in the refrigerator to work with, but I was able to put together what I needed for scalloped potatoes." She gestured to the plastic container in her hand. "Thanks to you, we'll be blessed with a tasty dessert now too."

"If I'd known exactly what time you'd arrive home, I would have planned better and invited you and your husband to our house to join us for the evening meal." Anna's plump cheeks turned a light shade of pink. "I only realized you were here when I saw your driver's vehicle pull into your yard, and then you got out and walked up to the house with your suitcase."

"It's okay," Eleanor assured the kindly woman. "We'll do fine with what we have."

"All right, then, I'd best be on my way. Have a nice evening, Eleanor."

"Danki. I hope you and your family will have the same."

After Anna left, Eleanor returned to the kitchen. When she checked on the scalloped potatoes and determined that they were almost done, she glanced at the clock. It was almost six thirty, and still no sign of Vic.

———— ≈ ————

It was seven o'clock by the time Tom pulled his truck up near the end of Vic's driveway, and Vic was more than a bit irritated. In addition to working an hour and a half overtime, Tom had made two stops on the way here—one for gas, the other for beer. Thankfully, he hadn't downed any of the alcoholic beverages before driving. Vic figured Eleanor must be home, because Checkers was out of his dog run and waiting for him on the front porch. As soon as Vic stepped down from the truck, Checkers raced into the yard and headed straight for him. Vic bent down to pet the dog about the same time as Tom spun his tires and drove out of the yard, sending several pieces of gravel flying.

Vic's jaw clenched as Checkers started barking and chasing after the vehicle. He cupped his hands around his mouth and hollered, "Come back here, right now! You know you're not supposed to chase cars."

Checkers stopped running and returned to Vic with his tail between his legs.

"I'm going in the house now, boy," Vic said. "I want to say hello to my *fraa*."

When Vic entered his home and smelled food, he had no doubt that his wife was not only here, but she'd obviously cooked a meal. So much for his plan to take her out for supper. He followed the tempting aroma and found Eleanor setting the kitchen table. The sight of his lovely wife took

Vic's breath away. He set his lunch box down and smiled as she called out his name and stepped into his embrace.

"It's good to be home; I've missed you so much," she murmured against his chest.

"I've missed you too." He lowered his head and their lips met in a sweet, warm kiss. When they broke apart, he gazed deeply into her eyes. "It's been real lonely here without you. I hope we never have to be separated again."

Eleanor's eyes sparkled with tears. "Till death do we part."

Chapter 8

Lancaster

"I don't think you need another one of those before we get back on the road, Tom." Vic's jaw clenched as his coworker downed a third can of beer. "You know I'm not comfortable with you driving after consuming alcohol, and if you get pulled over for some kind of infraction, and the officer discovers that you've been drinking. . ."

"I know how many cans of this stuff I can handle." Tom glanced at Vic with a sneer. "Don't take this the wrong way, but you remind me of my wife when she used to carry on about me having a few cold ones."

He gave Vic a dismissive wave. "You worry too much, and I'm sick of you getting in my face about this." Tom lifted the can to his lips and took another swig. "There's nothing wrong with a few beers now and then, especially after a stressful day at work like we had today—the boss expecting us to do more than we could handle."

Vic couldn't get over his coworker's defensive attitude. And the more he drank, the more aggressive Tom became. Vic shook his head in disapproval. *It's too bad you've gotta have a crutch like this to wind down your day.*

Vic had to admit that today had not gone well all the way around. He looked at the dried blood on his hand from a minor cut he'd received this morning. A few hours later, he'd caught his pant leg on a nail, which caused a tear he'd have to ask his dear wife to mend. There was no doubt about it—this had been a hectic and nerve-wracking Monday. Despite the issues he'd faced today, Vic didn't need a beer in order to deal with it. He didn't think his coworker needed one either. What the misguided fellow really needed was a few months' counseling to help him deal with his troubled marriage.

I'm sure I'd be willing to see a counselor if my marriage was on the rocks, Vic told himself. *I would do anything to keep my wife from leaving me if we were having marital problems. I bet Eleanor would be willing to go for counseling too.*

Vic glanced at Tom again and noticed that he drove with one hand on the wheel and the other holding the beer, close to his lap. As far as Vic was concerned, that was not good driving. On top of that, Tom had the radio turned up so loud that Vic could hardly hear himself think. At a moment like this, Vic wished he had his own car and would be allowed to drive it and still be considered Amish. *I really need to find some other way to and from work. Riding with Tom is hard on my nerves. If only there was another employee who lived close to me, I would have asked that guy to take me home instead of Tom today.*

The tension in Vic's shoulders made riding in the passenger seat less than relaxing, especially after their long day at work. Riding in Tom's truck on the slick, snow- and ice-covered pavement didn't help either. The roads had been that way yesterday too, while traveling by horse and buggy to and from church. Vic always took it easy on these roads, especially during bad weather, and thankfully his senses weren't tainted by alcohol, meaning he could react quicker if a problem presented itself.

As the truck sped down the road, going faster than Vic liked, it fishtailed a couple of times, due to the snow and ice. Tom's one-handed steering combined with his drinking made things even worse. Vic couldn't wait to get home and be with Eleanor for the rest of the evening, but at the rate they were going, it would be a miracle if they made it home in one piece.

Eleanor stood in front of the living room window, staring at the mounds of snow in their yard. They'd had a snowstorm two weeks ago, on Christmas Day, and even though it hadn't snowed again, the cold temperatures had kept the ground covered with white. It was lovely to look at it, but the frigid air took some of the joy out of being outside. At least the fireplace gave her warmth as the burning wood crackled and snapped.

Eleanor swirled her mug, which was half full of coffee with a dab of cream. It added soothing comfort on this chilly day as she took slow sips. The children in their area seemed to enjoy the snow. Eleanor took pleasure in watching them, bundled up, as they frolicked in the snow on their way home from school.

She placed one hand against her flat stomach and closed her eyes. *Lord, will Vic and I ever become parents?* She hoped there was nothing wrong with either of them that would prevent her from becoming pregnant. It was a pleasing thought to picture a new baby in their home. The excitement of an infant would bring joy to her, as well as Vic, and what a difference having a child would make in their home.

Things for now were quiet and a tad boring. Eleanor still thought about going out into the community, looking for work. If only she could convince her husband of that idea. Since she'd tried before and hadn't gotten anywhere, she figured there was no point in bringing up the topic again. Vic's answer would most likely be that his income was enough, so there was no reason for her to consider getting a job.

Eleanor saw a familiar vehicle pull up to their mailbox out by the road. Normally the mail was delivered by noon, but she figured with the road conditions being what they were, it had probably taken the mailman longer to make all the stops on his route today.

Although the thought of bundling up and tromping through the snow to retrieve the mail held no appeal, the hope of receiving any correspondence from home was a driving force.

Moving away from the window, Eleanor finished her beverage, took the mug to the kitchen, and went to the hall closet to get her outer garments.

When Eleanor stepped outside, she paused on the porch and watched as the wind picked up and snow drifted across the road. *Is it wrong to wish for spring already?*

Pulling the scarf around her neck a little tighter, she stepped off the porch and made her way carefully down the slippery driveway. Checkers bounded along beside her, yipping and snapping at snowflakes. She couldn't help laughing at the dog's antics. Although Eleanor still didn't have a real fondness for the mutt, she was able to tolerate Checkers more than she had before.

I wish I had half as much energy as Vic's playful dog. Just think of everything I could get done in a day.

They reached the mailbox, and while Checkers poked his nose into a pile of snow, she opened the box and withdrew the mail. It was too blustery to look through the contents, so she told Checkers to come and headed toward the house, eager to get in out of the cold.

Eleanor hastened her steps because the bite of winter had penetrated her outer garments. The wind blew the winter chill everywhere, it seemed, and she shielded her face with the sleeve of her jacket. All she could think about was getting back inside the welcoming warmth of her home. Meanwhile, Checkers ran around in circles, barking and snapping at the snow. Eleanor was tempted to let him play for a while as she retreated to the house, but if he darted out in the road and got hit by a passing vehicle, Vic would really be upset. The truth was, she would also be sad if the dog got hurt or, worse yet, killed.

The wind picked up, and Eleanor held tightly to the mail, wondering if she should take the dog back to his pen or let him come in the house for a while. She waited on the porch until Checkers settled down and then called him again. As if he knew what she had in mind, Checkers leaped onto the porch and sat near the door, looking up at her expectantly.

"Okay, you can come in, but you'd better be good. And there will be no running all over the house." She opened the door and stepped inside,

Checkers right at her heels. After she took care of her jacket, boots, and gloves, Checkers went with her into the kitchen.

Having put the mail on the table, Eleanor gave Checkers a bowl of water and poured herself another cup of coffee. When Checkers gave a grunt and flopped down on the throw rug in front of the sink, Eleanor smiled. It felt good to be back inside the cozy house, and she was glad there wasn't anything else that had to be done outside for now. At least their horses were in the barn, out of the wind, and here lay Vic's dog, all cozy and warm, despite the fact that Eleanor had said on numerous occasions that she didn't want the mutt to come in the house.

Eleanor sat at the table, took a cautious sip of coffee, and sorted out the mail. She was pleased to discover a letter from Doretta and eagerly opened it to read:

―――――≈―――――

Dear friend Eleanor,

I hope this letter finds you doing well and enjoying the quiet, peaceful days of winter.

My mamm and I have been busy making some new dresses, and of course, teaching school occupies much of my time. The students did well with their parts during the Christmas program last month, and the schoolhouse was filled to capacity with parents and other family members. A good time was had by all.

Lots of ice-skating has been going on in the area, and I've seen many children pulling each other on sleds. Do you remember how much fun you, Irma, and I used to have when we were young girls and it snowed? I miss those days sometimes, and occasionally I even wish I was a little girl again.

It's too bad Irma's family moved to Montana soon after we all graduated from the eighth grade. I never did understand why her stepfather wanted to move there, but I suppose he had his reasons. Irma never liked it there, but from a recent letter she wrote to me, it would seem that she's been much happier for the past few years—ever since she married LaVern Miller and they moved to Ohio.

I'd better close now and help Mama with supper. Write back soon and let me know how things are going with you.

Love & blessings,

Doretta

⎯⎯⎯⎯ ≈ ⎯⎯⎯⎯

Eleanor sat for a minute, reflecting on the things her friend had said. She'd lost touch with Irma a while ago, but it was nice that Doretta still heard from their old friend. Eleanor would respond to Doretta's letter soon and ask for Irma's address. It would be nice to send their childhood friend a note, or maybe one of the homemade cards Eleanor liked to make. In the meantime, there was more mail to go through, and she needed to make out a grocery list for tomorrow's shopping trip. Following that, Eleanor would begin supper preparations.

It took a few minutes to sort through the bills. When Eleanor finished, she picked up *The Connection* magazine. She'd no more than turned to the first page when the screech of tires, followed by a deafening crash, brought Eleanor to her feet.

She rushed out of the kitchen and hurried to the living room window, which faced the road in front of their house. Eleanor gasped when she saw that the front of Tom's pickup truck had collided with a tree near the edge of their property. Her heart pounded as she raced out into the cold without stopping to grab a jacket.

Dear Lord, Eleanor prayed as her shaky legs propelled her forward, *please let Vic and Tom be okay.*

Chapter 9

Ignoring the slippery snow and patches of ice beneath her feet, and with heart pounding against her chest, Eleanor hurried down the driveway. She approached the vehicle, and both Vic and Tom got out.

"What in the world were you thinking?" Vic shook his finger in his coworker's face. "When we neared our driveway, I told you to slow down. If you hadn't been drinking—"

"I can handle my liquor just fine," Tom said with a sneer. "The slippery road was the problem, not my beer."

Drinking? A chill ran down Eleanor's spine, and she knew it wasn't from the cold. It was not safe for her husband to be riding with a man who drank alcohol while driving.

"Are—are you okay? Were either of you hurt?"

Vic and Tom both shook their heads.

"Just shook up a bit," Tom said.

"One of your headlights is busted, and it looks like some damage was done to your fender." Vic looked at Tom. "You just missed our mailbox before you hit the tree."

Vic's grim expression let Eleanor know that he was quite upset about this unexpected mishap. She couldn't blame him, given how anxious she felt. If the accident had occurred because of the slippery road, it would have been understandable. But Tom had no business drinking alcohol while driving his truck. Maybe he drank too much at home. She wondered if that might have been a factor in his wife leaving him.

"Don't worry about your mailbox. If I'd wrecked it, I would have given you some money to buy a new one." Tom waved his hand. "Right now, I need to get my truck away from that tree and head for home." He studied his vehicle. "I won't worry about the fender yet, because it doesn't look too bad, but I'd better get a new headlamp before this day is out. Sure wouldn't want to get pulled over for driving with only one light."

"You're right. That wouldn't be good," Vic muttered. "And you'd be in big trouble if the officer who pulled you over took a whiff of your breath. He'd haul you straight to jail for driving under the influence."

His words resonated in Eleanor's ears as she stood beside him. *Maybe a night in jail would be what Tom needs to help change his behavior.*

Tom shrugged. "I've gotta go. See you tomorrow morning, Vic." He got into his truck, backed it up, and headed on down the road.

"I'm sure that hitting the tree sobered him up a little, but he'll probably have another beer before the night is over." Vic shook his head. "He needs to get his life in order."

Eleanor drew in a deep breath in an effort to calm herself. The thought of her husband riding in Tom's vehicle again caused her to shudder. Next time, it might be more serious than running into a tree and breaking a headlight. Another accident due to bad weather or Tom's drinking could leave Vic or his coworker seriously injured.

Vic slipped his arm around Eleanor's waist and pulled her close to his side. "Don't look so worried. If Tom stops for a beer after work tomorrow, I'll find another way home, even if I have to walk."

"You can't do that. It's too far and too cold. I think you should see if one of our drivers can take you to and from work from now on."

"That'd be okay in an emergency, but it'd be too expensive to hire someone to drive me to and from work every day—especially with the higher rates most drivers are charging these days—thanks to the price of gasoline going up." Holding on to Eleanor's hand, Vic began walking toward the house. "Don't worry, dear wife; things will work out."

Eleanor waited until they entered the house and had taken seats in the living room to ask a question that had come to mind. "I'd still like to see about getting a job, Vic. We could use the money I earn toward the expense of hiring a driver for you."

Vic's facial muscles visibly tightened as he shook his head. "You have enough to do here at home, and I won't have my fraa working at some job so I'll have enough money to pay a driver." He looked deeply into her eyes. "Besides, if you were working in town, then you'd need a driver to take you there and back home. Basically, the only thing you'd be working for is the money to pay both of our drivers."

Eleanor blinked rapidly. She hadn't thought about that. "Maybe I could find a job close to home so I could walk to and from work."

"Walk to work and back home in the cold, snowy weather?" Vic's brows lowered. "And what about spring when it rains, or summer's heat and humidity?" He shook his head. "That's not reasonable, Eleanor, and I think we should end this conversation."

I used to walk to school in the same kind of weather, and it wasn't that long ago. She lowered her gaze so he wouldn't see the tears that had gathered in her eyes. "I'm going to get supper started now." Eleanor hurried off to the kitchen. *Why does my husband have to be so stubborn? Shouldn't I have the right to get a job if I want one?*

She went to the sink and poured a glass of cool water because her throat felt parched after their conversation. There was a housekeeping job available just down the road from them. The elderly couple had been asking around the neighborhood and even put an ad in the paper. Eleanor felt compelled to go speak to them.

She finished her drink and set it aside. *Maybe it wouldn't hurt to stop in and inquire about the housekeeping job. You never know; since their place is so close to our home, Vic might change his mind.*

———— ≋ ————

"I see you got your headlight fixed," Vic said after he'd climbed into Tom's truck the next morning and shut the door. At least in the mornings his coworker didn't have a beer in his hand.

"Yep. Took care of it after I left your place yesterday." Tom pulled out of Vic's driveway and headed down the road. "And the fender doesn't look too bad, so I won't worry about getting it fixed right away." He gave the steering wheel a thump. "I don't want to put in a claim with my insurance company, 'cause I might get canceled."

Vic cleared his throat in preparation of the question he was about to ask. "Are you going to stop drinking while you're driving home after work?"

Tom jerked his head and glared at Vic. "You ain't my mother, you know."

"I'm not trying to be. Just don't want to put my life in jeopardy. If you're not going to stop drinking while driving, I'll need to find another way to and from work."

Tom grunted as he turned back to face the road ahead. "As if you have so many other options. Did you forget that none of the other fellows who work for our boss live close to you?"

"I'm well aware."

"Then what are you gonna do—travel by horse and buggy? There's no place to keep a horse at the boss's shop while you're out on jobs all day, so I don't see how that idea could work."

Vic clamped his teeth together with an audible click.

"Well, you're not saying anything, so guess I got you on that one, huh?"

"If you insist on drinking and driving I'll have no other choice but to hire one of my own drivers."

"Oh yeah? And what's that gonna cost?"

Vic was about to respond, but Tom cut him off. "Have you forgotten that I have not charged one red cent to haul you back and forth to work with me?"

"I'm aware, and I appreciate it, but if you'll recall, I have offered to pay for the gas on several occasions, and you've always declined."

"That's true. I was trying to do you a favor."

Vic crossed his arms. "The biggest favor you could do me is to stop drinking alcohol when you're behind the wheel of your vehicle. If you must drink, can't you wait till you get home?"

A few minutes passed before Tom gave a nod. "Yeah, okay. Guess that'd be the best thing all the way around."

Vic drew in a quick breath and let it out slowly. "Thank you."

After Eleanor did the breakfast dishes and cleaned up the kitchen, she sat down at the kitchen table and wrote a letter to Doretta. She thought awhile about the things she planned to say but felt certain that her friend could be trusted not to repeat any of it. Vic wouldn't appreciate it if he knew she had discussed their private life with Doretta or anyone else, for that matter.

Eleanor started the letter by telling her friend about the weather they'd been having. From there, she moved on to describe what had happened when Tom's truck hit the tree near their yard.

Eleanor paused long enough to pick up her mug of warm apple cider and take a drink. When she took up her pen again, she mentioned in the letter that she'd like to get a job to help with the expense of hiring a driver to take her husband to and from work each day.

"But he doesn't want me to work outside the home!" Eleanor added with an exclamation point. *"Our place is as neat as a pin, and there's not that much to do around here. I wish he wasn't so stubborn."*

She went on to say that it concerned her that Vic was riding to and from work with a coworker who drank beer while he drove. Although there was nothing Doretta could do about the problem, it felt good to write down her frustrations and ask for prayer.

When she'd finished writing, Eleanor folded the letter and placed it inside the prepared envelope. She put on her jacket and scarf and went outside to mail it.

Checkers followed on her heels and barked until Eleanor picked up a stick and threw it. After the letter had been delivered to the mailbox, she headed back to the house. The chill of winter made her wish for an early spring, and she was eager to see the first flowers poke through the soil. Eleanor had planted daffodils in one bed and red tulips in another. It would be a friendly reminder of being back at home, where her mother's well-tended flower beds bloomed every spring.

Eleanor missed Doretta, but it would be a while before she'd be able to go back to Grabill for a visit. If she could keep busy here, there wouldn't be as much time to dwell on feeling homesick.

Eleanor pondered the idea of talking with Vic's mother about the situation with Tom and mentioning that she wanted to get a job. Perhaps Susie could convince her son that it would be a good thing if Eleanor earned some money so he could hire a sensible driver.

By the time she reached the back door and took hold of the knob, Eleanor had changed her mind. If she told Vic's mother and the woman brought up the topic to Vic, he would know Eleanor had talked with her about it behind his back, and that would not go over well at all.

She had recently made the acquaintance of a young, newly married woman named Mary Petersheim, but Eleanor didn't think she ought to start dumping heavy topics onto her new friend right away. Besides, she did not know Mary well enough to be sure she could be trusted not to repeat anything Eleanor said. And she certainly couldn't tell her own mother about the situation. Every time Mom learned that Vic had done something off-key, she'd go on and on about it. Eleanor had already been through enough stress with her mother's attitude toward Vic. She wanted her husband to be accepted fairly. There was no point in giving Mom something else to dislike about him.

I guess for now, the best thing I can do is quit asking Vic about getting a job. I just need to pray for God's will to be done.

Chapter 10

Over the next few months, things moved along fairly well. Vic was pleased that Tom kept true to his word and didn't drink while driving them home from work. After Vic had assured Eleanor that Tom wasn't drinking while driving anymore, she dropped the topic of getting a job, and Vic felt relieved. There was no need for her to earn extra money, since he didn't have to pay a driver to haul him to and from work every day. Besides, Eleanor had plenty to do at home, and he figured that if his wife got caught up with her work and became bored, she could always visit one of their neighbors or get together with some of the women from their church district.

Today was Saturday, and he was on his way to pick up his little brother for a day of fishing. Vic had invited their father and brother Stephen to go along, but as expected, Dad had said he and Stephen would be busy in his shop.

Dad's business of making doghouses, birdhouses, picnic tables, lawn furniture, and several other items related to the outdoors was on the same property as his and Mom's home, which made going to work easy for him. Before moving to Indiana, Vic had worked for his father, and even though he'd been offered his old job back when he returned to Pennsylvania after marrying Eleanor, Vic had turned the position down. In addition to earning more money at his current job, he had never cared for the way his dad had critiqued his work in the past. Vic had always felt that nothing he did was quite good enough in his father's eyes.

What a shame, Vic thought. *Eddie and Stephen need to spend more time doing recreational things with our daed, just like I needed it when I was a boy. The only time we really spent together was when I was working in Dad's shop, and now Stephen's stuck with that job.*

"A father should never be too busy to do fun things with his kinner," Vic muttered as he guided his horse down the road toward Strasburg. "When Eleanor and I are blessed with children, I'll come up with lots of fun things for us to do as a family."

Strasburg

When Vic arrived at his parents' place, he found Eddie sitting on the front porch, holding his fishing pole. As soon as Vic pulled his horse up to the hitching rail, Eddie picked up the small cooler that had been sitting beside him and hurried out to Vic's buggy. "Sure am glad we're going *fische*," the boy said after he'd put his pole and cooler into the back of Vic's open buggy and taken a seat next to Vic.

"Jah, me too." Vic kept a firm grip on the reins as he backed his horse away from the rail. "Too bad Stephen couldn't join us, but Dad mentioned that he and Stephen would be working in the shop today."

Eddie nodded, his dark hair waving in the breeze. "Too bad they'll both have to miss out on all the fun."

I'm surprised Dad didn't come up with something for Eddie to do in the shop too. Vic didn't voice his thoughts to his youngest brother. It wouldn't be right to say anything negative about their dad—especially to a youngster, who would be apt to repeat it. Besides, working in the shop might be the only quality time Stephen, or even Eddie when he got older, would ever get with Dad. That was pretty much how it was for Vic growing up. Truth was, Dad probably thought he was doing the right thing by training his boys to be good workers. Maybe he saw their hours of working together in the shop as quality time spent with his sons.

Vic pushed his thoughts aside and concentrated on driving the horse as he left the driveway and entered the road. He sure looked forward to the time he would spend with Eddie today, and he wanted to be sure they'd make it safely to the pond where some of the best fish in the area could be caught.

Paradise

As Vic had rushed out the door to get his brother, he'd asked Eleanor if she would have time to brush their horses before letting them out in the field. He'd also stated that the new salt lick needed to be set out by the corral. Eleanor didn't have anywhere to go today, so taking care of the things he'd mentioned had not been an issue, and she'd already checked both of those items off her list.

Upon entering the kitchen, Eleanor decided to bake some peanut butter cookies from the batch of dough she had made up yesterday. She removed it from the refrigerator, turned the oven on, and soon had a dozen cookies baking and filling the room with a tantalizing aroma. She set the timer, and while the cookies baked, Eleanor went to the utility room to start a load of sheets in the wringer-washer. When the kitchen timer went off for her second pan of cookies, she ran back and took them out. After pausing long enough to get a drink of water, Eleanor put a third tray of cookies in the oven and went outside to hang the clean sheets on the line to dry. So far, it had been a productive morning, and multitasking was an easy and quick way for Eleanor to get more done.

Once the baking and laundry were done, she crumpled up her to-do list and tossed it in the garbage. *Now that those things are done, what else should I do?* she asked herself. Eleanor tapped her chin as she studied the bare kitchen walls. *Maybe I could decorate it with a stencil. I'd like to add a saying or an uplifting scripture—something Vic and I could reflect upon whenever we're in the kitchen.* A few ideas came to mind. Since Eleanor liked to stamp and create pretty cards with sayings, the blank wall seemed to call out, *Decorate me.* She even thought about doing something along the same lines in their living room. Although they had been living in this house for a while, Eleanor thought some spaces still needed a few things to make the place look and feel a bit homier.

She went back outside to check on the drying sheets and discovered that they were still a little damp. The plot where the garden sat had been tilled, planted, and kept weeded. So far there were peas, onions, lettuce, and strawberries, all doing well. Eleanor looked forward to seeing what the other plants they'd chosen to put in their garden would produce. Tomatoes were one of her favorites, and she planned to use some of them to make different sauces for canning.

Remembering the cookies she still hadn't sampled, Eleanor went back to the house. When she stepped inside, the fragrance of freshly baked cookies lingering in the kitchen was a pleasant welcome. *I wouldn't mind sharing some of these. Vic and I can only eat so much anyway.* It wasn't quite lunchtime, and she didn't feel all that hungry yet. *It's probably because I sampled some cookie dough earlier,* she mused. Checkers had even eaten one of the broken cookies, but Eleanor had since put him outside in his dog run so he wouldn't beg for more people food.

Eleanor donned a lightweight sweater, picked up a plastic container she had filled with a dozen cookies, and went out the front door. It was a lovely spring day, and she looked forward to taking a treat to her elderly English neighbors, Homer and Dottie Bennett, who lived down the road. They were the couple she had hoped to work for, but they'd found a good housekeeper a few months ago. Besides, Vic had still not put his stamp of approval on Eleanor working outside their home, so it was probably just as well that the job had been filled. When she'd brought up the topic of her working recently, he had reminded her that since Tom wasn't drinking beer while driving anymore, he didn't have to hire a driver to take him to and from work. That meant less expense, so there was no need for Eleanor to get a job. Besides, he'd stated, she would probably be in a family way soon, which would mean she'd need to stay home anyway.

Eleanor paused from her introspections and turned to look at Checkers, barking from his dog run. "Sorry, but you can't go with me to the neighbors'. I'll let you out when I get back home."

Checkers kept jumping and barking at the fence, but Eleanor hurried on, doing her best to ignore him. Once she was out of sight, the dog would no doubt settle down.

The Bennetts lived less than half a mile away, and Eleanor enjoyed her trek as she walked slowly on the shoulder of the road. It was lovely to see all the trees along the way bursting with a bevy of colors—some white—some pink—and some with no flowers, only green leaves. She took her time, listening to the birds twittering while they flitted from tree to tree, which only added to her enjoyment on this relaxing springtime walk.

Although no cars went by, a few horse-pulled carriages passed her on the road, and to each one, Eleanor gave a cheery wave. Pennsylvania, and particularly the area in and around Paradise, was finally beginning to feel like her home. Of course, Eleanor still missed her friends and family in Indiana, but keeping in touch through letters and phone calls helped a lot. The other day, she'd received a letter from her childhood friend Irma, a few weeks after Eleanor had sent her a card using the address Doretta had provided. She had also gotten another letter from Doretta. Eleanor was surprised that Doretta's boyfriend still had not proposed marriage. If he had, surely her friend would have mentioned it.

Maybe William is taking his time, to make sure Doretta is the right woman for him. Eleanor pursed her lips. *Although I can't imagine that he wouldn't see what a wonderful wife she would make.*

Her thoughts ceased when the Bennetts' home came into view. It was time to do the neighborly thing and bring a little cheer into the elderly couple's day.

Strasburg

"Are you sleepy or just tired of fishing?" Vic moved closer to where Eddie lay on the grassy bank, with eyes closed and hands propped beneath his head. He leaned down and gave the boy a nudge.

Eddie's eyes opened, and he pulled himself up to a sitting position. "I ain't sleeping—just thinking is all."

"About all those sneaky fish neither of us has caught today?" Vic pointed to their fishing poles lying near the pond.

"Nope. I was thinking about how much I'd like to learn how to swim." Eddie's vivid blue eyes focused on Vic. "Would you teach me, Vic?" He pointed to the pond.

"You mean, right now? Here at this *deich*?"

"Jah, I like this pond."

Vic shook his head. "No way, little bruder. The water's too cold for that. We'll have to wait for the warm summer weather to do any swimming."

Eddie's chin jutted out. "That's a ways off. Sure wish we could do it now."

"Well, we can't. We'd probably both turn blue from the cold. Besides, we didn't bring our swimming trunks along."

Eddie offered Vic a crooked grin. "Guess we could go skinny-dipping if the wasser wasn't so cold."

Vic's deep laugh ended on a snort. "You know what, Eddie?"

The boy shook his head.

"You remind me of myself when I was your age."

"We do have the same dark hair and blue eyes."

"True, but I was thinking more about our personalities being alike."

Eddie squinted and rubbed the bridge of his freckled nose. "What do you mean?"

"I was referring to the fact that we're both adventuresome and like to try new things. We also enjoy being outdoors." Vic gestured to the trees and clouds reflected on the pond's surface, and then he pointed to a turtle sticking its head out of the water. "I enjoyed hanging around this pond when I was a boy, and now I'm fortunate enough to have a pond on the back of the property, not far from Eleanor's and my home."

"Is that the one where you're gonna teach me how to swim?"

Vic nodded. "It's not as big as this one, and it's not a good fishing hole, but it's plenty big enough for a person to learn how to swim."

"*Geb mir dei?*"

"Jah, Eddie, I give you my word." Vic gestured to the cooler Eddie had brought along. The boy had said earlier that it had been filled with sandwiches and cookies made by their mother. Vic had brought a thermos filled with hot coffee for him, along with several bottles of water for them both to drink. "You ready to eat some lunch?"

"That's fine by me." Eddie opened the cooler and handed Vic a sandwich wrapped in waxed paper. "It's got peanut butter and grape jelly on the pieces of bread. That's what I asked Mamm to make." He looked up at Vic with all the innocence of a child. "Hope it's okay."

Vic ruffled his brother's thick crop of hair. "That's fine and dandy with me. I've always liked peanut butter and jelly sandwiches."

They both took seats on the old blanket Vic had brought along. Eddie opened his mouth and was about to take a bite of his sandwich when Vic stopped him and said, "Don't you think we oughta pray first?"

His brother's cheeks colored. "Oh jah, that's right. Guess I'm so hungerich, I forgot about praying." He bowed his head, and Vic did the same. When their prayers ended, they opened their eyes at the same time.

Vic chuckled.

"What's so schpassich?" Eddie tipped his head.

"It struck me as funny that we're so much alike, we even opened our eyes after praying at the same time."

Eddie gave a wide grin. "Bet I'm gonna grow up to be tall, just like you. Maybe I'll even build houses too."

Vic gave a nod. "I wouldn't be one bit surprised."

They ate in silence for a while, and after they finished their lunch, Eddie grabbed his pole again and leaped to his feet. "Think I'll see if I can catch at least one fish before you take me home. Maybe Mamm will cook it for supper tonight."

"Good idea." Vic leaned back on his elbows and watched his little brother throw his line into the water. *He's such a cute kid. Sure can't wait till I'm a father and have a son of my own. Of course,* Vic reminded himself, *the good Lord might give me and Eleanor daughters instead of sons.* He tugged his left earlobe. *But I'd be just fine with that, 'cause there are lots of girls who like to fish.*

Chapter 11

Paradise

Eleanor flipped the calendar on the kitchen wall to the next page. It was hard to believe it was already June, although the warm weather they'd been having was proof of that. She had been rubber-stamping some cards earlier today. Eleanor enjoyed making each of her creations personal, using favorite colors, scenery, animals, and other things liked by the person she would be giving them to.

She had collected quite a few stamps and had them organized in a container she kept in one of their spare bedrooms downstairs. In another box, she'd stored several different types of card stock, an assortment of colored ink pads, and a mixture of embellishments, along with the tools to make detailed decorations on each of her cards. Whenever Eleanor went into her craft room and got started on making a card, she spent a fair amount of time with her creative juices flowing. Sometimes the minutes could get away from her, and she'd be surprised by how quickly an hour or two could go by. At least she had a battery-operated clock on the wall, but sometimes Eleanor would ignore the time because of the fun of making something pretty and creative.

Standing in the kitchen and staring face-to-face with the calendar, she saw the dates she or Vic had circled. Eleanor made sure that they both put each of their family members' and close friends' birthdays and anniversaries, as well as other special events, on the calendar. She didn't want to miss anyone's special day. By looking at the dates, Eleanor knew who to make up cards for and when to send them off so the recipients would get them in plenty of time.

Doretta's birthday is coming up soon. Eleanor put her finger on June 22. Oh, how she wished she could be there to help Doretta celebrate her twenty-fifth birthday.

She tapped her chin. *I wonder if Vic would mind if I went to Grabill to surprise my friend. Maybe I could stay a few days, which would give me time to see a few other friends and, of course, my family.*

Excitement welled in Eleanor's soul as she thought more about the possibility. She could hardly wait until Vic got home to talk to him about it. In the meantime, some weeds poking up in the garden were waiting to be pulled.

———— ≈ ————

Eleanor had been working in her garden about an hour when she heard the familiar sound of a horse and buggy coming down the road, although it wasn't close enough to see. She glanced back at the row she'd just finished, pleased that it looked so nice. Her goal when she had first started this garden was to make sure that the plants she'd bought from the garden center were added into a plot of rich soil. Vic had let Eleanor know that he liked raspberries fresh or even frozen, so they'd purchased several berry bushes from one of their church members. They'd decided on just the right place to plant them and had made a long row of raspberries that bordered the far side of their garden. All the plants were doing well, and Eleanor could easily imagine later in the season picking the ripe, red berries and enjoying their succulent flavor. But it would be a while yet, so she'd have to be patient.

As the *clip-clop* of a horse's hooves drew closer, she turned to look and was surprised to see Vic's mother pulling into the driveway in her open buggy.

Susie rarely came by unannounced, so Eleanor figured her mother-in-law must have been in the area and decided to stop in for a visit.

It's a good thing I'm home, Eleanor thought, rising from her kneeling position. After removing her gardening gloves and brushing dirt from her skirt, she headed across the yard toward Susie, who was guiding her horse, Polly, up to the hitching rail.

Eleanor stepped forward and secured the horse. "It's nice to see you this morning. If you came to see Vic, he left for work a little over an hour ago."

Susie shook her head and climbed down from the buggy. "I figured he wouldn't be here. I had some quilted pot holders to deliver to someone in Gordonville, and since we haven't seen you or Vic for a few weeks, I decided to come by and see how you've both been doing."

"We're fine," Eleanor replied. "Sorry for not checking in with you by phone. Vic has been working overtime some days, and I'm keeping busy with the garden, card making, and doing some of his chores when he gets home late."

"I would send Stephen over to help you with chores, but he stays real busy with his daed in the shop." Susie's forehead wrinkled as she lowered her brows. "I am fully aware that my husband is good at his trade and needs to earn a living, but sometimes I think he works harder and longer than he should." Susie heaved a sigh. "Ethan says he's going to take a week off soon and take me on a trip for our thirtieth wedding anniversary."

Eleanor smiled. "Thirty years is a milestone. You both certainly deserve a trip to celebrate. Where do you plan to go?"

Susie shrugged. "I'm not certain, but he did mention Niagara Falls. I've never been there, but I hear it's beautiful, so of course I said I would like to go."

Eleanor nodded. "I don't blame you. I've heard good things about those magnificent falls."

Susie pushed a wayward strand of light brown hair back under her prayer covering where it had escaped near the back of her head. "I'm just not sure we could be gone a whole week."

"Because of Ethan's job?"

"That likely won't be a problem, since he's already said he would take the time off. My concern is for Eddie. Kate and Clara won't be around during the day because of their jobs, and it wouldn't be good for an eight-year-old to be on his own during the day."

"What about Stephen? Wouldn't he be around to keep an eye on his little brother?"

Susie shook her head. "Ethan has already said that he plans to line out some work for Stephen in the shop to do while we're gone. Otherwise, it would put him behind on orders."

"What day does your anniversary fall on?" Eleanor questioned. "Maybe Eddie could stay here with us."

"The twenty-second of June." She paused and a smile formed on her lips. "Eddie isn't hard to manage. His disposition is good, and he likes to help out. So I'm sure you would appreciate the extra pair of hands around your place." Her smile lingered. "I would be sure to help with his packing, making certain that he had everything he needed to wear, and of course his toiletries too."

Eleanor broke eye contact with Susie, as she debated about whether or not she should agree to have Eddie stay with her and Vic during his parents' absence. It would mean giving up her tentative plans to be with Doretta on her birthday. She'd need to talk to Vic first, but most likely he wouldn't have a problem with Eddie staying with them for a week. Her husband had a soft spot for the boy and would no doubt enjoy having him around. Vic would be gone at work during the weekdays, however, so the responsibility of keeping an eye on Eddie would fall upon Eleanor. It would mean not being able to get as much of her own work done as she did when she was here by herself.

"Would you like to sit at the picnic table with me and have a glass of cold lemonade?" Eleanor asked. "I'm about ready to take a break anyway, and we can discuss the possibility of Eddie staying here while you're gone."

Susie clasped Eleanor's arm. "Really? You wouldn't mind having an energetic boy around for seven whole days?"

Eleanor shook her head. "It'll help prepare me for the day when Vic and I have some kinner of our own. I'll need to check with Vic first, but I'm fairly sure that he'd be fine with the idea of having his brother here."

"That would be *wunderbaar*." Susie gave Eleanor a hug. "I can't tell you how much this means to me."

Unless Vic said no to the idea of Eddie staying with them, which seemed doubtful, Eleanor would not be going to Grabill for Doretta's birthday. It felt good to know that Vic's mother wouldn't have to worry about her youngest child while she and Ethan were gone, but Eleanor was disappointed that she wouldn't be there to help Doretta celebrate her birthday.

I'm glad I haven't said anything to Doretta's mother about the possibility of my going to Grabill, Eleanor thought as she led the way to the picnic table across the yard. *Maybe after Ethan and Susie return from their anniversary trip, I can go to Indiana for a few days to spend some time with my dear friend, or better yet, my friend can come here, like we talked about before. With school out for the summer, Doretta won't be teaching, so she should have plenty of time to spend with me, and I can show her around Lancaster County.*

Eleanor smiled inwardly. *I bet she would enjoy seeing some of the covered bridges in our area. We could also take a tour of some of the quilt shops where Susie sells her quilted items. We have lots of things to see around here, including a trip to the all-you-can-eat buffet at Shady Maple Smorgasbord in East Earl.*

———————— ≋ ————————

That evening when Vic arrived home after another long day on the job, he saw the hammock in their yard and felt tempted to lie down in it for a while. *But that would not be a good thing,* he told himself. *As tired as I feel right now, I'd probably fall asleep, and then none of my chores would get done.*

After pausing to greet Checkers and throwing the dog a stick, Vic stepped onto the porch and turned to watch his exuberant pet chase after the slender piece of wood. He grinned and shook his head. *Goofy mutt.*

When Vic entered the house, he was greeting by a tantalizing aroma coming from the kitchen, and he knew right away that supper was cooking. "Is that fried chicken I smell?" he asked when he entered the kitchen where Eleanor stood at the counter near the sink, mashing potatoes.

She whirled around, offering him a dimpled smile. "It sure is, and you're just in time. Supper will be on the table in a few minutes."

"Do I have time to wash my hands and kiss my fraa?"

"Of course."

He stepped close to Eleanor and leaned down to give her lips a firm kiss. "It's great to be home."

"It's good to have you here. Did you have a good day?"

"It was a busy one, that's for sure." He fanned his face with both hands. "And a hot one too. That new house we've been building hasn't been wired yet, so there was no air-conditioning inside to keep us cool."

She gave his arm a little poke. "Seriously, Vic? We don't have electricity or air-conditioning in this house, and I've never heard you complain about the heat."

"That's because I'm not sawing wood or pounding nails all day when I'm at home. Besides, we usually have a nice little breeze blowing through our open windows to cool the house off."

"Yes, that's true. I'm also thankful for all the trees in our yard that provide much-needed shade when we need it the most." Eleanor reached for the container of salt and sprinkled some on the fluffy potatoes. Then she added some pepper, butter, and milk. "The *grummbeere* are done now, so we can eat as soon as you've washed up."

Vic didn't have to be asked twice. While he hurriedly washed his hands, Eleanor put the chicken on a platter and placed it on the table. Then she spooned the mashed potatoes into a hefty bowl and set it next to the chicken. "I was going to cook a vegetable to go with the meat and potatoes," she said after Vic took his seat at the head of the table. "Instead, I changed my mind and put a tossed green salad together." She took it from the refrigerator and set it on the table. "What kind of salad dressing would you like?"

"It doesn't matter. I'll take whatever you've got."

Eleanor came back to the table with a bottle of ranch dressing. After that, she poured water into their glasses and took her seat. Following Vic's lead, Eleanor bowed her head.

When Vic finished praying, he waited for Eleanor to open her eyes, and he picked up the platter of golden-brown chicken. After passing it to Eleanor, Vic took a few bites from the drumstick he'd taken. "I was right. This *hinkel* is the best—so tender and moist." He winked at her. "Sure am glad I married such a good cook. Danki for fixing this lip-smacking meal."

"You're welcome."

As Vic and Eleanor ate, they chatted about the weather for a bit.

"Your mamm dropped by here this morning," Eleanor said after a short time had passed.

"Did she come for any special reason?" he asked. "Or did she simply wish to pay a call on her favorite daughter-in-law?"

Eleanor rolled her eyes. "I'm her only daughter-in-law, silly."

"Of course, I knew that." Vic spooned some more potatoes onto his plate. "What'd Mom have to say?"

"She mentioned that her and your daed's thirtieth anniversary would be coming up in a few weeks."

"Oh, that's right. I almost forgot about that. When I took Eddie home after our fishing trip, Dad did say something about wanting to take Mom somewhere special for their anniversary."

"Your mom said he'd mentioned going to Niagara Falls." Eleanor paused and took a drink of water. "She also brought up the topic of needing to find a place for Eddie to stay while they're gone. Since Stephen will be working in your daed's shop on the weekdays and your sisters will be at their jobs, it wouldn't be good for Eddie to be on his own all day." Eleanor set her glass down and looked directly at Vic. "I told her we could probably keep Eddie while they're gone. Would you be all right with that, Vic?"

He offered her a wide smile. "Of course. It'll be fun to have my little brother here for a whole week. But are you certain you don't mind taking on the responsibility of making sure he behaves himself while I'm at work?"

"It won't be a problem, and I'd be glad to do it. You can enjoy spending time with Eddie in the evenings and on the weekend while your parents are gone."

Vic chuckled. "I'll bet Eddie will be after me to teach him how to swim while he's here. I did make my little bruder a promise that I would teach him when the warm summer weather came." Vic grabbed a piece of carrot from the salad bowl and took a bite. "I just hope I have the time to make good on my word."

Chapter 12

"I'm bored; I miss my hund." Eddie slumped in his chair at the kitchen table. "There ain't nothing for me to do that's fun, and I wish Vic was here so he could take me to the pond like he promised."

"I'm sure he will teach you to swim, either some evening or this Saturday when he's home all day. And how can you be bored when you're eating lunch?" Eleanor pointed to his peanut butter and jelly sandwich.

The boy's chin jutted out. "Didn't mean right now. I was talking about being here by myself all day."

Eleanor drank some of her iced tea and set the glass down. "You're not here by yourself, Eddie. I'm with you, and you have Vic's dog, Checkers, to play with."

"All that hund wants to do is chase after a *dumm* old *schtecke*." Eddie frowned. "I'm glad my hund don't pester me like that all the time. The only thing Freckles likes to do is chase any squirrels that come into our yard."

"You're right, Checkers does enjoy chasing a stick, but there are other things you can do with him."

"Like what?"

"Why don't you try teaching him some new tricks? He can sit and speak, but I'm sure you could teach him to do more tricks."

Eddie took a bite of his sandwich, followed by a drink of milk. "Maybe I could teach the hund to roll over or put his paw in my hand when I say, 'Shake.'"

"Those are both good tricks. Why don't you begin working with him after you've finished your lunch?"

The boy shrugged his slim shoulder. "I'll see."

"Wouldn't it be fun to surprise your brother when he gets home this evening by showing him what you taught Checkers to do?"

"I guess so."

Eddie didn't sound too enthused, but Eleanor figured once he started working with the dog, he might see things in a different light—especially if he succeeded in teaching Checkers to do a few new tricks.

As she ate her sandwich with Eddie, Eleanor had some time to think. It was obvious that her husband had a hard time squeezing in time to keep the promise he'd made to his little brother. She hoped Vic would follow through so Eddie wouldn't be disappointed. It would be a shame if, when Vic's brother left after his folks got home, he told them that he hadn't had a good time this week and never wanted to stay with Vic and Eleanor again. She could only imagine how frustrated Eddie must feel because of seeing Vic only in the evenings and not getting to do much in the way of fun with him.

Eleanor took another bite of her peanut butter and jelly sandwich. *This isn't turning out so well with Vic not making more of an effort with Eddie. I hope he can spare some time with his little brother this evening.*

She glanced at the boy as he continued to eat. *Between his father having no time to teach Eddie to swim, and now Vic promising every evening and not following through, Eddie must feel more discouraged each day. I can't help feeling sorry for him.*

Eleanor picked up her glass to have more iced tea. It was a pretty day, and the open window brought the sweet trill of birdsongs inside. The feeders were full, and the birds seemed happy as they flew from one feeder to another.

Eleanor's thoughts took her in another direction. She'd made a chocolate chip pie to serve this evening after their supper. Maybe something sweet and tasty would put Eddie in a better mood toward the end of the day. She figured her husband would be thrilled with a thick slice of chocolaty pie too, since it was one of his favorites. He'd no doubt want a cup of coffee to go with it, and so would Eleanor. That would be a pleasant way to end the day, relaxing and enjoying a yummy dessert.

Turning her attention back to Eddie, as she watched him finish his glass of milk, Eleanor had to admit that having Vic's little brother here for the past five days had been more of a challenge than she'd expected. Eleanor had tried to keep the boy occupied by asking him to help her with a few simple chores. She'd also gotten out a simple puzzle for him to work on. Nothing had held his attention very long, and it soon became difficult to listen to him complain all the time about Vic's absence and failure to keep his promise to teach Eddie how to swim. Last night during supper, the boy had brought the topic up again. He'd reminded Vic that he would only be here a few more days before his folks got back from their trip and came to get him. "Then it'll be too late," Eddie had stated, speaking the words with emphasis. "I'll probably never learn how to swim."

Eleanor felt sorry for her husband's youngest brother. Eddie looked up to Vic and expected him to keep his promise. But she also understood why Vic hadn't taken Eddie to the pond for a swimming lesson yet. He'd gotten home late every evening so far and explained to Eddie that he was too tired to trek back to the pond near the back of their property, much less find the energy to get in the water and give a swimming lesson. Before Eddie went to bed last night, he'd once more brought up the topic of learning to swim. Vic had reminded his brother that on Saturday he wouldn't have to leave home and go to work, so he'd give Eddie his first swimming lesson then. The boy had given Vic a hug and headed to bed with a hopeful-looking smile.

Parenting involves sacrifice, and it's filled with many challenges, Eleanor thought as she watched Eddie gobble down the rest of his sandwich. *Even so, I look forward to being a mother someday, and I'm sure I'll feel differently when it's my own flesh-and-blood child I am dealing with every day.*

When Vic arrived home from work that evening, he'd no more than stepped out of Tom's truck and said goodbye when he was greeted by Eddie and Checkers, waiting at the end of the driveway, both vying for his attention.

He threw a stick for the dog and then put one hand on top of his little brother's head. "Did you have a good day?"

Eddie shrugged. "It was okay, but I wish you could've been with me."

"I wish that too, but you knew I had to work, right?"

"Jah, that's what our daed always says too." Eddie's chin lowered, almost to his chest.

"Someday, when you're older and out of school, you'll get a job and will most likely work five days a week, same as me."

Eddie looked up at Vic and wrinkled his nose. "If I hafta get a job and go to work every day, I don't wanna grow up."

Vic chuckled and started walking toward the house. "You'll change your mind about that when you start needing money."

Eddie gave Vic's free hand a tug. "It's still hot out, Vic. Can we go swimming now, 'stead of waiting till Saturday?"

Vic shook his head. "Sorry, buddy, but I have some chores to do in the barn. After that, I'm sure Eleanor will have supper ready. I will take you out back to the pond sometime tomorrow, though."

"You promise?"

"Jah. Now let's go inside so I can say hello to my fraa."

The following morning, at the crack of dawn, Vic was awakened when someone pounded on his and Eleanor's bedroom door. He rolled over in bed and groaned. *If that's my little brother, it better be something important.*

Of course it's Eddie, Vic told himself as he clambered out of bed and stepped into his trousers. *Who else would it be?* He looked over at his wife, now sitting up in bed.

"What's going on?" she asked, followed by a yawn.

"I don't know, but I'm about to find out." Vic plodded across the room and pulled open the door. There stood Eddie in his bare feet, wearing a pair of swim trunks.

Vic grimaced. "What are you doing up so early, and why are you wearing your swimsuit?"

"We're going to the pond so you can teach me to swim. Remember, Vic? You said we'd do it today."

"Course I remember, but I didn't say it would be this early. Why, the sun's not even up all the way yet. You should go back to bed."

Eddie's shoulders drooped. "I ain't tired. Besides, I'm *hungerich.*" He gave his belly a thump.

"Why don't you go find something in the kitchen to tide you over till Eleanor gets up and fixes breakfast? I'm sure there's a banana or an apple you can eat."

"Okay."

When Eddie headed down the hall, Vic turned to face Eleanor, who was now sitting on the side of the bed. "Don't get up. My determined little *bruder* can wait awhile to have his breakfast."

"It's all right," she said. "I'm awake now anyway, so I may as well get up and fix the morning meal. If I were to lie down again and close my eyes, I'd probably sleep longer than I should and then wake up with a *koppweh.*"

"I hear what you're saying. I'm used to getting up early for work during the week, and whenever I sleep in on a Saturday, I usually end up with a headache." Vic grabbed one of his work shirts and put it on. "While you're getting breakfast made, I'll go out to the barn and take care of the horses. Oh, and don't worry about Checkers. I'll feed him too."

"*Danki,*" Eleanor said, followed by another yawn.

Vic came around to Eleanor's side of the bed and gave her hug. "Thanks for keeping Eddie occupied all week while I was at work. I'm sure there were lots of other things you would have rather done."

"It was fine, Vic. I'll admit that finding enough things to keep him occupied was a bit of a challenge, but it was kind of fun." She smiled. "I especially enjoyed watching Eddie teach Checkers how to do a few new tricks."

"Jah, it was humorous last evening to see the dog flop on the floor and roll over with both feet in the air." Vic chuckled. "I'm not sure how Eddie got him to do that trick. I've tried before, but with no luck whatsoever."

"I guess maybe you didn't offer Checkers enough treats."

"Maybe so. Either that or the hund likes my little brother better than he does me."

"I doubt it, but Eddie did spend a lot more time with the dog this week than you're able to do each day."

"True. Between eight hours of work, and sometimes more on the weekdays, plus the commute to and from the job, I'm not home as much as I'd like to be." Vic sat on the bench near the bottom of their bed and put his socks and boots on. "Even when I'm here, I always have lots of chores to do."

She nodded. "I try to do as much as I can when you're gone, but there are some things I'm not able to do by myself."

"It's all right, Eleanor. I don't expect you to do any more than you're doing already." Vic kissed her forehead. "I probably don't say it enough, but I love and appreciate you so much."

She smiled up at him and stroked his short beard. "I love and appreciate you too."

———————≋———————

After a hearty bacon-and-eggs breakfast, Vic pushed back his chair and headed for the back door.

"Are we going swimming now?" Eddie jumped up from his seat and started across the room.

"Not yet. I have a few more chores to do, and then I need to go out to the phone shed to see if there are any messages." He put his hand on Eddie's shoulder. "Maybe there's one from our mamm and daed, letting us know what time they'll be home on Monday."

Eddie's eyes brightened. "Won't they be surprised when I tell them that I learned how to swim? You're still planning to teach me, right, Vic?"

"Jah, sure. Just have a few things I need to get done first. You can come out to the phone shed with me if you like."

Eddie shook his head. "Naw, that's okay. Think I'll see if I can teach Checkers one more trick."

Vic gave a brief nod and hurried out the door. On the way to the phone shed, he noticed a hole in Checkers' dog run, and he made a mental note to get that fixed before the day was out. If he didn't repair it today, then tomorrow while they were at church, Checkers might figure a way to squeeze out.

"Sure seems like there's always something that needs to be done around here," Vic muttered as he approached the phone shed. "There just aren't enough hours in the day."

<hr />

It was well past noon before Vic finished making all the repairs to the dog run. He'd not only replaced the one section he had first seen, but after inspecting the rest of the run, he'd found several more spots that needed fixing. Apparently his determined dog had managed to create several holes that could have offered an escape route if they'd become large enough for Checkers to squeeze through. Vic had heard Eleanor ring the dinner bell some time ago, but determined to get the job done, he'd kept working, figuring that lunch could wait.

Finally, when the last hole had been repaired to Vic's satisfaction, he put his tools away and went up to the house. Upon entering the kitchen, he found Eleanor sitting at the table by herself. "I rang the dinner bell several times, but you didn't come, so I hope you don't mind, but I decided to go ahead and eat without you," she said.

"Don't mind at all, and I'm sorry I didn't respond to the bell. I was determined to finish fixing the dog run." He glanced around the room. "Where's Eddie?"

Eleanor shrugged. "I figured he was with you."

"Nope. I haven't seen him since I started working on the dog run. He came out to see what I was doing once and brought up the topic of learning to swim. I told him I couldn't do it until I got done with my project."

"What'd he say?"

Vic pulled his fingers down the side of his face. "I'm not sure. He mumbled something, but I couldn't make out the words." Vic turned back toward the door. "I'd better go out and see if I can find him. He's probably in the barn playing with the *katze*, or maybe he took Checkers there to work on some more tricks to surprise us with."

"Okay, let me know if you can't find him, and I'll help you look."

"Will do." Vic hurried out the door.

Vic's first stop was the barn, and when he didn't find his brother there, he went out and stood in the middle of the yard. Cupping his hands around his mouth, Vic hollered, "Eddie! Where are you, my little brother?"

There was no response, but when Checkers, barking frantically, ran into the yard from the back side of the house, Vic's pulse quickened. *Could the dog be trying to tell me something?*

"What's wrong, boy? What are you barking about?"

Checkers bumped Vic's leg with his nose and took off like a flash toward the back of the property. Vic followed close on Checkers' heels as the dog continued to bark and run, leading him in the direction of the pond.

The muscles in Vic's legs tightened as he continued to chase after the dog. *Surely Eddie would not have gone to the pond without me—especially since he doesn't know how to swim.*

As Vic approached the pond, his heart pounded, while his breath caught in his throat. His little brother floated facedown and unmoving in the water.

Chapter 13

With a fervent prayer, Vic leaped into the water. He grabbed hold of Eddie and pulled him out. *This can't be happening. Please, Lord. Don't let my brother die.*

Vic placed Eddie faceup on the ground and put his ear next to the boy's mouth and nose. He desperately hoped he would feel air on his cheek, but there was none. Feeling helpless and frustrated, Vic looked to see if Eddie's chest was moving. It was not.

Although Vic had been trained in CPR, his thoughts were so scattered right now, he had to take a few deep breaths and force himself to concentrate. He needed to remember everything he'd learned about administering CPR to a drowning victim. One thing Vic knew for sure—drowning could have only one of three possible outcomes: death, survival with brain damage, and survival without brain damage. The third option was what Vic hoped and prayed would be the outcome for his little brother.

He checked Eddie's pulse, and finding none, Vic started CPR with rescue breathing. With Eddie lying on his back, Vic first tilted the boy's head back and lifted his chin. Then he pinched Eddie's nose closed and put his own mouth over the boy's mouth, forming a tight seal. Vic blew into his brother's mouth for one second then repeated the breath another time. Next, he began chest compressions. Since Eddie was a child, he placed the heel of his one hand in the center of the chest at the nipple line. Then he pressed down about two inches, making sure not to press on the ribs or the end of Eddie's breastbone. Vic did thirty chest compressions, letting Eddie's chest rise completely between pushes. He paused to see if his brother had started breathing. After two minutes of CPR, with no response, Vic knew he had to get help, and quickly.

Vic heard his dog barking again and looked up to see Eleanor approach. Apparently Checkers had gone after her, as he'd previously done for Vic.

"I found my bruder facedown in the water, and he hasn't responded to CPR. I'll continue to work on Eddie, but I need you to run out to the phone shed and call 911," Vic shouted. "Hurry! Quick! There's no time to lose!"

Slapping a hand across her mouth as if to silence a scream, Eleanor turned and ran back in the direction of their home.

Vic would continue the cycle of thirty chest compressions and two breaths until help arrived. All the while, he prayed, *Dear God, please don't take my little brother. If Eddie dies, I will never forgive myself.*

Strasburg

Eleanor held her husband's cold, sweaty hand as they sat with his sisters and teenage brother in their parents' living room, waiting for their mother and father to get home. Vic had been so upset when he'd received the news that Eddie had died, he hadn't been able to call his parents at their hotel in New York and tell them what had happened. As much as it hurt her to do so, Eleanor had taken care of that dreadful task. The same thing held true in notifying Vic's siblings, who had all been at their jobs when the drowning happened. The full responsibility had fallen on Eleanor's shoulders. Poor Vic could barely utter a coherent word.

She shuddered when she thought about Susie and Ethan's response to the earth-shattering news. Susie had let out a shrill scream, and Ethan had released a guttural cry that sounded like it had come from a wounded animal.

Eleanor had called her own parents too and left a message, telling them what had happened and asking them to pray for Vic and his family. Vic blamed himself for his brother's death—he'd said so several times while the paramedics had worked on Eddie. He kept repeating that he should have taken his brother to the pond for a swimming lesson when he'd asked. Vic had broken his promise to his brother, and he couldn't do anything to right the wrong.

Eleanor could blame herself too. She had told her mother-in-law that she could take care of Eddie while she and Ethan were gone. Closing her eyes for a moment, she remembered the comment she'd made right after that to Vic's mom. *"It'll prepare me for the day when Vic and I have some kinner of our own."*

What was I thinking? she chided herself. *Why did I say that to her? If I'd been on my toes earlier today, I would have kept a closer eye on Eddie. I should never have assumed that he was with Vic the whole time he'd been working on the dog run.*

Eleanor opened her eyes and swiped at the tears on her cheeks. This was new territory for her. She hadn't experienced losing a close family member before. The pain of loss weighed heavily on her, but she needed to stay strong for Vic and his family as they dealt with this horrible, unexpected tragedy. Eleanor swallowed against the lump in her throat. *My poor husband—he truly believes that he's the cause of his brother's death.*

Eleanor had never seen Vic so despondent. She wished there was something she could do to ease his emotional pain and the deep-seated grief he felt.

Vic's sisters were seated close to each other on the other sofa in the room, with their hands folded and eyes closed. No doubt they were both praying. Stephen sat on the floor in one corner of the room with his knees pulled up to his chest. Eleanor could only imagine what was going through his mind. Did Stephen, and perhaps Clara and Kate, blame Vic for Eddie's drowning? And what about Ethan and Susie? Would they hold their oldest son responsible for his brother's death? So many unanswered questions and so much grief. It was unimaginable that their morning could have begun on a positive note and ended up in anguished pain by afternoon.

Evening light poured into the room, but no one wanted to eat a thing. Their world had stopped, and they'd been left hanging over a cliff filled with the darkness of grief.

Unable to bear the deafening silence in the room, Eleanor left her seat and went to the kitchen. Her bare feet silently crossed the hardwood floor, while her sniffles continued. Eleanor went to the window, and with her arms folded, she stared out. Life was unchanged in Ethan and Susie's yard. The birds sang, and the next-door neighbor mowed his grass. *If only we could go back and change the outcome of today.* A few tears escaped Eleanor's eyes and dripped onto her dress. *The next several days, weeks, and perhaps even months will be difficult, and we all need to trust God. Only He can see Vic and his family through this immense trial.*

Eleanor returned to the living room with cups, glasses, a jug of cold water, and a pot of chamomile tea for anyone who wanted it.

"Please, come have something to drink," she said, placing the tray she held onto the coffee table in front of the couch where the sisters sat.

No one moved from their seat or gave any response. Eleanor wondered if she should pour them each a beverage, but she didn't want to appear pushy or try to force something on them that they didn't want. She turned from the table and went back to her seat. Eleanor's heart clenched when she saw Clara and Kate weeping as they embraced each other. Eleanor looked at Vic, with his head lowered, and Stephen, who appeared to be staring off into space.

Help me, Lord, Eleanor prayed. *I need to know what to say or do to help ease this family's pain.*

———— ≈ ————

It was ten o'clock that night when Ethan and Susie came into the house via the front door. Clara and Kate were the first to leave their seats and give their parents a tearful embrace. When Vic and Stephen held back, Eleanor stepped forward and offered her condolences, along with a hug.

Finally, Stephen got up and practically fell into his mother's arms, releasing heart-wrenching sobs, mingled with those of his parents.

Eleanor looked at Vic, wondering and waiting to see what he would do. He continued to remain on the couch, head down and shoulders shaking. It was all Eleanor could do to keep from clasping her husband's hands and guiding him across the room to where his parents stood with his siblings. Vic was clearly in a state of deep depression and shock, but it was important that he let his feelings out and express the way he felt to his parents.

She stood off to one side, waiting to see what would happen while praying for each one of the bereaved.

Finally, Vic got up and went over to stand in front of his parents. In a voice barely above a whisper, he said, "It's my fault Eddie drowned, because I didn't teach him to swim when he asked, and I didn't keep an eye on him like I should." He paused, cradling his head in his hands. "I wouldn't blame either of you if you didn't speak to me for the rest of your lives."

Eleanor's heart nearly broke. She waited to hear his parents' response, and she wasn't surprised when Susie pulled Vic into her arms and said with a tremor in her voice, "Our hearts are broken over the loss of our boy, but oh, Victor, your daed and I do not hold you responsible for what occurred."

Then Ethan hugged Vic. "Your mamm is right. When Eleanor called and gave us the tragic news, she said you had done everything in your power to bring Eddie back to life."

"Only God could do that," Vic mumbled. "But no. He just sat up there in heaven on His regal throne and watched it all happen. If He could bring His Son back to life after Jesus' death on the cross, why couldn't God have brought Eddie back to us?"

"There are no answers for that, Son." Ethan put his hand on Vic's shoulder. "God's ways are not our ways. As much as it hurts to know that Eddie is gone, it must have been his time to go."

Vic stood up straight and pulled his shoulders back with a huff. "How could it be time for a fun-loving eight-year-old kid like Eddie to die?" His voice rose with each word he spoke. "If that's the kind of God we serve, then I want no part of Him!" Vic jerked the front door open and rushed outside.

"He needs time to grieve and forgive himself for what he's convinced is his fault." Eleanor hoped the words she'd spoken were true. She couldn't imagine how it would be for Vic, her, or any of his family in the days and years ahead if he turned his back on God and never came to grips with his brother's untimely death.

Vic paced the length of his parents' porch a few times and then stepped into the yard and took off for the barn. It didn't matter what his parents said about not blaming him for Eddie's death. He blamed himself, and eventually when their numbness wore off, they probably would blame him too. *Who knows,* Vic thought, *my daed may not have verbalized it, but he might also feel guilty, because he never spent enough time with Eddie or taught the boy to swim. If that's the case, maybe when Dad comes to grips with his own sense of guilt, he might understand the way I feel right now.*

Vic kicked at a clump of weeds. *Life isn't fair, and neither is God.* Vic had heard their bishop say on more than one occasion that the heavenly Father was a just God. *Would a just God take a young child from his parents?* Vic felt a tightening in his throat, and he blinked several times to keep tears from coursing down his cheeks. *I've gotta get out of here. I can't remain at my parents' house any longer and be reminded of my shame.*

He entered the barn and took Domino out of the stall he'd put him in earlier when he and Eleanor had come here to wait for their parents. *I need to go home, whether Eleanor's ready to go or not. But I can't go back in the house and face my family again. I wish I could send her a message.*

Vic led his horse out to the buggy and was in the process of hooking him up when Domino let out a loud whinny. A few minutes later, Eleanor came out of the house.

"What are you doing?" she asked, joining him at the buggy.

"I'm getting my horse and carriage ready to go home."

"Without me? Were you going to leave and not say anything?" He heard the hurt in his wife's tone of voice.

"No, I. . .uh. . .planned to come get you, but I didn't think I could deal with seeing my family again tonight—especially Mom and Dad."

"I understand you're upset, and so are they, but don't you think you owe them the courtesy of at least saying goodbye?"

He shook his head. "I can't. Would you please go into the house and tell them we're leaving?"

Vic noticed her expression change from soft to hard.

"I hate that pond of ours! I wish it wasn't there." Tears streamed down her cheeks. "It's going to be hard going back to our place since that was where your brother died."

"Don't you think I know that? I've been sitting in my parents' house, wishing that we didn't have that pond either. I'm gonna have it filled in so we never have to look at it again." Vic's eyes welled with tears, and his voice shook with all of the emotion he felt deep within his chest. "I truly need to leave here, Eleanor—right now."

"I think it would be best for us to stay."

"I can't! I have to get out of here. It's harder for me to be here than to go back to our place."

Eleanor didn't respond at first, but then she touched Vic's arm and said, "Okay, for your sake, I'll let them know we need to go home." She turned and hurried back to the house.

Vic sagged against the buggy, feeling a sense of relief. Suddenly, a strong desire came over him. He wished that he had something strong to drink in his hands right now to numb the pain.

Chapter 14

Paradise

The last three days had been agonizing, with funeral arrangements being made and then Eddie's viewing. It had been all Vic could do to look at his brother's cold, lifeless body, lying in an Amish-made coffin inside his parents' home. Family members, friends, and others in their community had come to pay their respects. Vic felt as if the weight of the universe rested on his shoulders. He couldn't eat, barely slept, and wasn't able to work. Fortunately, his boss had given him a week off for bereavement, but it wouldn't be long enough. Regardless, he would have to return to work when the week was up, or they would have no money coming in. At a time like this, Vic actually wished his wife did have a job that would help pay the bills.

He wandered around the house, wearing nothing but a pair of old trousers. The weather had turned stifling hot and muggy, and he could not stand the feel of a shirt clinging to his body like flypaper. Truth was, he hadn't been able to stand much of anything the past few days. Nothing took his mind off the image of his little brother's body facedown in the pond. *If I'd just gotten there a little sooner, maybe I could have saved Eddie. If I'd known he was planning to sneak off to the water by himself, I would have stopped him.*

Vic's head jerked at the sound of Eleanor's voice calling him to get dressed for his brother's funeral. His neck bent forward as his stomach clenched. He had no idea how he would make it through this day.

"Vic, are you coming?" Eleanor stepped into the living room. "If we don't leave soon, we're going to be late."

Vic swiped a hand across his sweaty forehead and flinched. Short of death or coming down with some serious illness, he couldn't get out of going to his brother's funeral service this morning. Then there'd be the graveside committal and a light meal at his parents' home. He grimaced. *If only I had something to help squelch the pain.*

"Vic, did you hear what I said?" Eleanor stepped up to him and touched his arm.

"Jah, I heard." He hesitated a moment then walked out of the room and down the hall toward their bedroom, feeling as though he was moving in slow motion. A part of Vic wanted to pray and ask God to help him get through the day, but then he was reminded that God hadn't cared enough to answer his prayer to save Eddie, so why should he bother to pray for anything now?

———≈———

Eleanor couldn't miss her red-rimmed eyes as she looked in the bathroom mirror to set her white head covering in place. She'd not only shed tears because of Eddie's passing, but she also hadn't gotten enough sleep these past few days. Every night, she had lain awake for several hours, worrying about and praying for her husband, as well as the rest of his family. Eleanor couldn't imagine what it must be like for Susie and Ethan to have lost one of their children. It wasn't normal—not the natural order of things—for a young child to die before his parents. Even to lose a baby while it was still in the womb would be difficult. She remembered how sad her mother had been when she'd had a miscarriage six years after Eleanor was born. Although Eleanor had been too young to understand it all, she'd seen Mom's tears and heard her sobs.

Eleanor was thankful that her parents would be at the funeral today. Although they'd only met Vic's family on the day of her and Vic's wedding, they'd told Eleanor when she'd notified them of Eddie's passing that they wanted to attend the funeral to offer their support to her and Vic, as well as to his parents and siblings. Her folks had arrived late last night and insisted on staying at a hotel near Strasburg. Eleanor had invited them to stay with her and Vic, but Mom said they didn't want to impose. Eleanor appreciated this courtesy on her parents' part, as it would have been difficult to have anyone at the house last night with the way Vic had been dealing with Eddie's death. When she'd last spoken to her mother at the hotel, she'd filled her in about how bad Vic felt over the loss of his young brother. Mom had commented that she could ask Dad to speak with Vic, if she thought it would be helpful. But Eleanor simply thanked her mother and explained that the topic was too painful for Vic to discuss with anyone at this time. She hoped that no one would say the wrong thing to Vic at the funeral today.

The whole situation was hard on Eleanor, not knowing what to expect. Vic had been different since the accident, and she wanted her old husband back. But what could she do? She wasn't sure how to deal with the way he'd closed himself off from the people who cared deeply for him. Eleanor prayed for help in caring for her husband. How long would this trial go on until things turned around and became bearable? Only God knew the answer to that question, and she would have to trust Him through this ordeal.

Eleanor's thoughts came to a halt when she spotted Vic in the hallway outside the open door of the bathroom. He was fully dressed, in the same black Amish men's attire he wore on Sundays. Eleanor's dress was also black, as would be the color of the clothing the other mourners wore on this solemn occasion.

"Is the horse and carriage ready?" she inquired.

With lips pressed together, Vic nodded, making no eye contact with her.

At a loss for words, Eleanor clasped her husband's arm and walked him to the front door, much like one would lead a child. Although this day would be heart-wrenching for all, she hoped that in the weeks ahead, Vic would come to grips with his brother's death and stop blaming himself for something that could not be undone.

———— ≈ ————

Strasburg

Susie wasn't sure how she or their family members had made it through Eddie's two-and-a-half-hour funeral service, held at their home, but here they were, standing at the Amish cemetery, watching as her little boy's six-sided coffin was lowered with ropes into the predug grave. The raw, painful emotions welling up in her soul screamed for release. Somehow, by the grace of God, Susie had held herself in check during the funeral service. But the finality of viewing the pallbearers shovel dirt into the hole to cover the pine casket was nearly her undoing. *Why, Lord? Why did You allow our son to drown?* She kept replaying the nagging questions, even though no answers would come. Susie had always been a cheerful, positive person, but she wasn't sure she would ever be able to smile or laugh again.

Susie was fully aware that her husband was also grieving, and so were their four remaining children. She heard muffled sobs from Clara and Kate, while Victor and Stephen, along with the other four pallbearers, continued to fill in the grave.

My poor sons, Susie thought, as she continued to observe their sorrowful faces. *Although I am certain that Victor and Stephen are hurt in different ways, they are both grieving heavily over the loss of their brother.*

Susie glanced back at her husband. The lines of fatigue and devastation showed clearly on his bearded face. *Does Ethan think, like I do, that we should have spent more quality time doing fun things with Eddie when we had the chance? Now it's too late, and there's no way to undo the past. What's done is done, and we have to find the strength and courage to move on.* Susie closed her eyes in prayer. *Lord, please help me and each member of our family to accept Eddie's death as Your will. Help us in the days ahead not to cast blame upon anyone for the accident—especially not on our son Victor. He already blames himself and is hurting too much.*

———— ≈ ————

Vic's muscles tensed and sweat rolled down his back in rivulets as he stood with the others to silently pray the Lord's Prayer. He couldn't do it, however. All Vic could manage was a six-word prayer: *Why did You take my brother?* No answer to his question came, of course. God was silent and probably pointing a finger at Vic, just as he was doing himself. There was nothing anyone could say or do to change the fact that, for the rest of his days, he would have to live with the guilt he felt over his brother's death.

When the brief committal ended, Vic hurried off to his horse and buggy to wait for Eleanor. He saw his wife across the way, talking with her parents, but there was no way he could join them right now. All Vic really wanted to do was to be alone with his negative thoughts and pent-up emotions. He had an obligation to go back to his parents' home for the meal some of the women in their church district had prepared, but the idea of trying to eat nearly made him gag. Even worse was the thought of having to talk to well-meaning people offering their condolences and trying to say the right things. *There are no right things to be said at this time,* Vic told himself as he swallowed past the lump in his burning throat. *I certainly have nothing right to say to anybody, and I have no wish to hear what anyone might say to me.*

———— ≈ ————

When it was time to eat, Eleanor went looking for Vic. He'd wandered off toward the barn shortly after they'd arrived at his parents' house after leaving the cemetery. It was rude not to talk to anyone, but she couldn't really blame him. He'd told her on the trip from Paradise to Strasburg this morning that he dreaded having to make conversation with anyone today. Vic had stated firmly that he wanted to be left alone.

He needs to eat a little something and spend some time with his family and close friends at least, Eleanor thought as she made her way across the yard toward the barn, where she figured he might still be.

When she entered the oversized building where the funeral service had been held in order to accommodate all the people, it appeared to be empty. The usual smell of horse flesh and nose-tickling straw had been cleaned and swept away in preparation for the benches that had been placed here for the service.

Although the barn was devoid of the usual thump of horses' hooves in their stalls and the skittering noise of cats scampering across the floor, the sound of gut-wrenching sobs could be heard coming from somewhere near the back of the barn.

Eleanor felt sure it was Vic, releasing the emotions he'd kept bottled up all morning. While it was good for him to get those feelings out, it broke her heart to hear his pain. She felt a deep need to go to him and offer comfort.

Following the sound of his increasing cries, she made her way past the empty horse stalls. When she approached the last one, she found her distraught husband curled up in a fetal position in one corner of the cubicle, shivering and weeping like a small child who had lost his favorite toy and could not be consoled. Only it wasn't a toy Vic had lost—it was his little brother whom he'd loved so much.

Eleanor knelt beside her husband, cradling him with her arms. "Let it out, Vic, let it all out. You have the right to grieve."

He continued to sob, rocking back and forth in Eleanor's arms, and she cried with him.

Once their tears subsided, she stroked his damp cheeks with the palm of her hand. "I'm here for you, Vic—now and for as long as you need me."

"I need you more than ever," he murmured. "Can you promise that you will always love me?"

With a gentle touch, she stroked his forehead. "Of course, my love. I'm your wife, and I will always love you." She took hold of his hand. "Can you go in the house with me now and have a little something to eat? I'm sure there are several people inside who are waiting to speak with you."

He sat up straight, pulled a hankie from the pocket of his trousers, and blew his nose. "I need to go home."

"Vic, we can't go yet. It wouldn't be right to leave your family so soon after—"

"It might not be right, but I can't face any of them this afternoon." A muscle clenched along his jawline. "I mean it, Eleanor. I can't go in and act as if nothing is wrong."

"No one is asking you to act a certain way. You just need to—"

He held up one hand. "I'm going home now. The question is: Are you coming with me?"

Eleanor had to make a decision, and quickly, for Vic was already on his feet. If she said no to his request, he would undoubtedly go home without her, and that would be more embarrassing than the two of them leaving together. Besides, it would mean she'd have to find another way home later on.

After a moment's hesitation, she nodded. "I will go inside and let your family and my folks know that we are leaving. If they ask why, I'll tell them that you're not feeling well." *Which you're obviously not,* she mentally added.

"Fine. I'll be waiting out by our horse and buggy." He gripped her arm. "Please hurry, Eleanor. If I stay here much longer, I might say or do something to embarrass you."

"I'll join you shortly. I promise." She followed Vic as he hurried from the barn. Before they went their separate ways, she paused and said, "I think it would be a good idea if you sat on the passenger's side of the buggy, and I'll take the reins for the ride home."

Eleanor felt relieved when Vic nodded. It would not be good for him to drive the horse in his emotionally charged condition. Eleanor could only hope and pray that Vic's family would be understanding, and that in the coming weeks, things would get better for Vic and everyone who had been hurt so deeply by Eddie's passing.

Chapter 15

Paradise

"I'm not sure this is a good idea," Lydia Wagler's husband, Al, whispered to her as their driver's van approached the road that Eleanor and Vic lived on.

Lydia blinked rapidly as she looked at him. "Of course it's a good idea. It wouldn't be right if we left Pennsylvania without saying goodbye to our daughter and son-in-law. I am sure they would be hurt if we did not stop and see them."

"Eleanor might be hurt, but I'm not sure about Vic." Al frowned. "He barely said two words to us yesterday after his brother's funeral, and I doubt that he would care one way or the other if he said goodbye to us or not."

She reached across the seat and placed her hand on his, giving it a few gentle pats. "I'm sure that's not true, and even if it is, we still have to do what's right."

Al gave a brief nod. "You're right."

She leaned forward and tapped their driver, Ike, on the shoulder. "This is our daughter and son-in-law's place. I see their address on the mailbox over there on your side of the road."

"Okay." Ike made a left-hand turn and drove his vehicle up the driveway, stopping close to the house.

The home was small compared to many other Amish houses in the area, but the barn adjacent to it was twice the size. Lydia figured her son-in-law would probably add on to the house if needed, once children came along and their family grew. Either that or they would find a bigger place and move.

"We should have called to let them know we were coming," Al said when Lydia opened the door on her side of the van.

She turned and squinted her eyes at him. "Unless one of them was in the phone shed when we called, we'd have had to leave a message. And," she added, "they may not have gone out to check for messages before we got here, so our stopping by would have still been a surprise."

"Good point." Al told their driver they shouldn't be too long and asked him to wait for them.

"Sure, no problem," Ike responded. "If you decide to stay awhile, let me know, and I'll drive into town and find someplace to eat."

"Sounds good. I'll come back here shortly and let you know if we plan to stay longer than half an hour or so." Al gave a wave and followed Lydia up to the house.

Lydia reached out to knock on the door, but it opened before her knuckles even connected to the wood, and Eleanor stepped out onto the porch. "Mom. Dad." Looking a bit perplexed, she glanced out toward the van. "Are you heading for home?"

"Yes, we are," Lydia replied, "but we wanted to stop here first to say goodbye and see how you and Vic are doing today."

"Vic's still sleeping, and I was about to start breakfast. If you haven't eaten yet, you're welcome to join us."

"Danki for asking," Al said, "but we ate breakfast at the hotel where we stayed last night."

"You look *mied*." Lydia reached out with both hands and touched her daughter's pale cheeks.

"Jah, I am tired. The last few days have been exhausting. We haven't had much sleep since. . ." Her voice trailed off, and tears sprang to her eyes. "It's been really hard for Vic and everyone in his family—especially his mom and dad."

Lydia bobbed her head. "I can only imagine how devastated Susie and Ethan must feel."

"Like I said when we talked on the phone, Vic blames himself for his brother's death." Eleanor swiped a hand across her tearstained cheeks. "I don't know what to do or say that might make him feel better."

"It'll take time," Al said. "When a tragic accident occurs that takes someone's life, it's not unusual for a person who was close to the deceased to take the blame."

"Your daed's right," Lydia interjected. "Eventually your husband will work through his grief and realize it was not his fault that his bruder got in the water without waiting for Vic to teach him how to swim." She moved closer to her daughter and enveloped her in a tender hug. "It must be hard being here, though, so close to where the accident happened."

When Eleanor pulled back from the hug, she wiped at more tears. "Jah, Vic and I have both had a difficult time dealing with the idea that the pond is still back there. We wish it wasn't on our property, and we'll probably avoid going there from now on, which is why Vic wants to hire someone who has the proper equipment to come and fill in that small body of water. If it's taken out, there will be no ice-skating or bonfires at the pond to look forward to this winter, though." Eleanor sniffed. "I had thought that maybe someday, when the pain wasn't so raw, we'd be able to go there again and enjoy spending time at the water, but if Vic has his way, there will be no more pond out behind our home."

"I can understand why he would want to take out the body of water where his little brother perished," Al put in. "But it could be quite costly to have it done, and would removing the pond really solve anything? The memory of his brother's drowning will most likely stay with Vic for as long as he lives." He moved closer to Eleanor and placed his arm around her waist, pulling her close to his side. "The important thing is for Vic, and you too, Daughter, to allow God to heal your emotional wounds, and realize that it will take some time."

Eleanor sniffed. "I—I know, Dad, and I've been asking for God's comfort and help."

Lydia's eyes watered, and she wiped away the tears. It hurt to see their grown child in such heart-wrenching pain. Oh, how she wished she had the power to make things better for Eleanor and Vic, but like her husband had said, God would be the one to heal her daughter's and son-in-law's emotional wounds.

Moving away from Eleanor, Al cleared his throat and nudged Lydia's arm. "We shouldn't make our driver wait much longer. Besides, Vic is resting, and we don't want to disturb him."

Eleanor gestured to the partially open door. "Would you like to at least come in for a quick cup of kaffi or something else to drink? I'm sure it won't wake Vic if we go in the kitchen."

Al shook his head. "As much as I'd like to, I think we should head out. We've kept our driver sitting out there in his van long enough, but if we did stay longer, I'd have to go there and let him know."

Lydia shook her head. "No, you're right, Husband. We should be on our way. It's a long trip back to Indiana." She gestured to Eleanor. "You are clearly exhausted and should probably rest."

"You're right, Mom. I do feel the need to lie down for a while. I appreciate you both coming all the way to Pennsylvania for Eddie's funeral. I'm sure it meant a lot to all of his family, and it certainly did to me." She gave them both a hug. "I'll be praying for you to have a safe trip home, and when you get there, would you please call and leave us a message?"

"Of course." Lydia gave her daughter's back a few gentle pats. "And we'll certainly be praying for you, Vic, and all of his family."

"Danki. We need all the prayers we can get right now."

Eleanor waved before the van pulled out, and after it was out of sight, she stepped off the porch. *May as well go get the mail, because there's probably some since we didn't check the box yesterday.*

She looked toward the barn and shook her head. *I suppose I'll be checking on the horses and the barn cats again since Vic won't pry himself from the bedroom. Seems like all he wants to do is stay put in bed.*

Eleanor had fed Checkers early that morning and fixed their breakfast, now being kept warm in the oven, but she wasn't sure her husband would want to eat anything when he finally got up. The past few days, Vic hadn't said more than a few words to her. That made it even more difficult to offer him the comfort he needed. Vic's attitude had become more and more negative, and when he did say anything to Eleanor, he tended to snap at her for no good reason. She wondered whether Vic would be able to go back to work next week. If he couldn't communicate with her or anyone in his family, how would he be with his boss and coworkers? Her steps slowed while she asked herself, *How far could Vic sink into himself, and how long can I handle all of this alone?*

Eleanor had only made it halfway to the mailbox when Checkers came alongside her, pawing at her skirt and begging for attention. For a moment, looking at the dog made her smile. It was a normal action for Checkers to want to play, and right now Eleanor craved some sense of normalcy. The last time she'd seen the dog, he'd been sleeping on the floor beside Vic's side of the bed. Eleanor was sure that Checkers sensed the pain Vic felt, for nearly every minute since the accident during the time they were at home the dog had been at Vic's side. Eleanor figured it might be good therapy for Vic to have his pet close by, which was why she'd decided not to make a fuss about Checkers being in the house.

"Did you come here because you knew that I needed your company?" Eleanor bent down and stroked the dog's ears.

Checkers looked up at her and let out a *Woof!* Then he darted off and came back with a stick in his mouth. Eleanor gave it a good toss, and while the dog chased after it, she hurried to the mailbox, where she discovered a few bills, some advertisements, and two envelopes. The return addresses showed that one had come from Doretta's parents and the other one was from Doretta. She figured they were probably sympathy cards.

Eleanor carried the mail back to the house and seated herself on the porch swing. The first envelope she opened was a sympathy card from Doretta's parents, Elmer and Amanda Schwartz. They had written a note stating how sorry they were to hear about the passing of Vic's young brother. On the bottom of the card beneath their signature, they had written the words of Matthew 5:4: "Blessed are they that mourn: for they shall be comforted." Eleanor hoped that when she showed the card and verse to Vic, it would offer him some comfort.

She opened the second envelope and found a card from Doretta, along with a letter:

———— ≈ ————

> Dear Vic and Eleanor,
>
> My heart goes out to both of you and the entire Lapp family during this difficult time. I cannot begin to comprehend the grief you must feel, but I'm sure that our heavenly Father understands. Please know that I am, and will continue, to pray for you in the days ahead.
>
> May you feel God's presence as you grieve and allow your hearts to heal. I hope this passage of scripture from 1 Thessalonians 4:13–14 might help: "I would not have you to be ignorant, brethren, concerning them which are asleep, that ye sorrow not, even as others which have no hope. For if we believe that Jesus died and rose again, even so them also which sleep in Jesus will God bring with him."
>
> Love & blessings,
> Doretta

———— ≋ ————

Eleanor squeezed her eyes shut in an effort to keep tears from falling. *Oh, dear friend Doretta, I do hope that my husband will heed your words and allow God to heal his broken heart.* She released a heavy sigh. With Vic inconsolable, it seemed that she wouldn't be able to have Doretta come and stay with them for a while this summer. Right now, and for the foreseeable future, Eleanor's focus needed to be solely on her husband.

———— ≋ ————

Vic rolled over onto his right side and groaned. His head felt like someone had pounded on it with a hammer. The last time he'd had a headache this bad was when he had suffered a hangover from drinking too much. Of course that had been a few years ago, before he and Eleanor had become serious about each other. Once he'd decided to settle down and join the church, Vic had given up all the wild and crazy things he'd done during his time of running around. He was a twenty-seven-year-old man now, with a wife to support. He had set his desire to party and drink aside, replacing it with hard work and the determination to make a good life for him and Eleanor. Things were different now, with Eddie gone and himself to blame. Vic felt empty inside—like he had no purpose in life. He didn't want to eat, sleep, or do any work. He just wanted to find a way to numb the pain bottled up inside of him, screaming for relief.

He shielded his puffy eyes from the ray of sun streaming into the room through the partially open window shade. He looked at the empty spot on Eleanor's side of the bed and wondered if she had lifted the shade a bit when she got up, hoping the light coming through would wake him.

"Well, it worked," Vic muttered, pulling the covers over his head. *But I have no reason to get up, so I may as well lie right here for the rest of the day.*

He closed his eyes and tried to sleep, but when the sheet and blanket were lifted from his face, he turned onto his back and opened his eyes. Eleanor stood beside the bed, looking down at him and holding two envelopes in her hands. "These are sympathy cards. They came in today's mail. Would you like to know who they are from?"

"Not really. I'm sure there are lots of people who feel sorry for me right now."

"Not just you, Vic, but your whole family." Eleanor took a seat near the edge of the bed. "The first card is from Elmer and Amanda Schwartz. They included a verse of scripture at the bottom. Would you like me to read it to you?"

"No." He started to pull the covers up again, but she reached for his hand and clasped it firmly.

"You're not solving anything by closing yourself off like this. Doretta's parents care about you, and I think you should listen to the verse they included."

"Okay, whatever."

"These words are from Matthew 5:4. It says, 'Blessed are they that mourn: for they shall be comforted.' "

Vic sat straight up in bed. "That's baloney! People who mourn are not blessed. I mean, where is the blessing in grieving for someone who has died?" His face scrunched up until his cheeks ached, which forced him to relax his facial muscles a bit. "An innocent child like Eddie did not deserve to die, and I have every reason to mourn."

"Of course you do, Vic." Eleanor spoke softly, and she looked at him with a tender expression. "But God will offer comfort if you allow Him to."

He shook his head vigorously. "I don't need God's comfort or anyone else's, for that matter. I need to be left alone."

"You can't pull inward or stay in bed all day, feeling sorry for yourself. I'd like you to get up, wash your face, put your clothes on, and come to the kitchen. Breakfast is ready to be put on the table, and you need to eat."

Eleanor's forceful tone irked Vic to no end. Who did she think she was, telling him what to do? "You are not my mother!" he shouted. "And I'm not a child who needs to be told when he should get out of bed or eat a meal. I'll leave this room when I'm good and ready, is that clear?"

Eleanor flinched as though she'd been slapped. "I–I'm sorry. I didn't mean to sound like your mother. I'm your wife, and I'm very concerned about you."

"Well, you needn't be. Just worry about yourself for a change."

"I will lay the other card we received on the table, in case you wish to read it later on." Eleanor's chin trembled and her eyes filled with tears, but before he could offer a response, she turned and rushed out of the room.

Vic had been too harsh with her, but he couldn't keep the words from pouring out like water when a dam had broken, creating a destructive flood.

He rolled over onto his stomach and gave his pillow a few good punches. *I am not only a lousy brother, but I'm also a horrible husband. I wish I had drowned in that pond. Eddie did not deserve his fate.*

Chapter 16

"You don't look so good. Are you sure you're ready to come back to work?" Tom asked when Vic got into his truck the following Monday morning.

Vic's jaw tightened. "There's no need to worry. I'm fine."

"Okay, whatever you say." Tom shrugged his shoulders and pulled out onto the road.

Vic leaned back in his seat and closed his eyes. Truth was, he didn't feel like he had enough strength to lift a hammer, much less put in a full day's work. But he couldn't sit around home forever, groveling in his grief. He had to earn a living so the bills could be paid and he could provide for his and Eleanor's needs.

Vic thought about how he'd stayed home from church yesterday, using the excuse that he had a pounding headache along with an upset stomach. Eleanor seemed understanding, and even though he'd told her to go to church without him, she had stayed home, saying she was worried about him and wanted to be there in case he needed anything.

She's a good person, Vic thought. *I chose well when I asked her to be my wife.*

———— ≈ ————

Eleanor sat at the picnic table to write a letter to Doretta. She had planned to do it at the table in the kitchen, but it was more peaceful here in the yard, where birds chirped and a light breeze caused the leaves on the trees to flutter.

Eleanor tapped her pen against the notepaper. *Where do I begin? How much should I say to Doretta?* She felt certain that whatever she said, her friend would not repeat it to anyone—especially if Eleanor asked her not to say anything. She held the notepaper firmly with one hand and began to write.

Dear Doretta,

Today we received your parents' sympathy card, as well as the one from you. Losing Eddie has been difficult for everyone in the Lapp family, and we truly do appreciate your prayers.

Vic is taking his brother's death especially hard, and I'm worried about him. He blames himself for Eddie's death—not only because he hadn't been watching him close enough, but mostly because he'd promised the boy that he would teach him to swim and kept putting it off. Vic figures his little brother got tired of waiting and went to the pond to see if he could learn to swim by himself. Now my poor husband is riddled with guilt.

Truthfully, I also feel somewhat to blame. I'd told Eddie's mother that I would take good care of him while they were gone, and I didn't live up to my promise. I should have been keeping a better eye on Eddie that day. I realize, however, that no matter how sorry or how much to blame any of us feels, it won't bring Eddie back. I feel confident that the boy is in heaven with Jesus now, and that offers me comfort.

Please write again soon. I always look forward to hearing from you.

Love,
Eleanor

PS: I would appreciate it if you didn't share with anyone what I've told you in this letter.

Eleanor folded the paper and slipped it into the matching envelope. She was currently out of stamps and would take it to the post office later this morning so it could go out with today's mail. Since she would be leaving soon and had plenty of time today, Eleanor planned to go see her in-laws to find out how they were doing. She would also take them some baked goods that she had made on Saturday.

Strasburg

Eleanor shook the reins to get her horse, Buttons, moving a bit faster. The mare had done well on the first part of the trip, but for the last half hour she'd been poking along.

"Come on, girl, let's get moving," Eleanor prompted. "We'll be at our destination soon, and then you can rest."

The Lapps' place came into view, and Eleanor guided Buttons up their driveway and over to the hitching rail. She stepped out of the carriage, secured the horse, and then reached inside for the plastic container full of cookies. If Susie and Ethan weren't at home or in his shop, she would leave the cookies on the porch and head for home. But if they were there and seemed to be up for a visit, Eleanor would put Buttons in the barn until it was time for her to leave.

As Eleanor approached the house, she spotted Vic's mother hanging sheets on the line. The wind had come up, and seeing that Susie seemed to be struggling to keep the sheets from tangling, Eleanor set the container she'd brought on the picnic table and hurried to offer her assistance.

"Here, let me help you with those," she said, taking hold of one corner and pinning it to the line while Susie did the other.

"Danki. This is a pleasant surprise." Susie smiled, although it didn't quite reach her tired eyes. In addition to her obvious fatigue, the poor woman's shoulders drooped as if they bore a heavy burden. No doubt Vic's mother felt weighed down with grief.

"I came to see how you are doing, and I brought some ginger-spiced cookies." Eleanor gestured to the container on the wooden table.

"Danki. Those are Ethan's favorites." Susie pulled another sheet from the wicker laundry basket near her feet, and Eleanor assisted her again. When they were finished, she put her hand against the small of her mother-in-law's back. "How are you and Ethan doing?"

"We're getting by. Ethan's working in his shop with Stephen this morning, and I'm sure it helps both of them not to dwell on our loss if they keep busy." Susie placed the palm of her hand against her chest. "I've been trying to keep busy too, but it's awfully hard to turn off the thoughts that keep swirling through my head. So many times during the daylight hours, I find myself wanting to seek Eddie out to see if he wants something to eat or. . ." She paused and inhaled deeply, then blew her breath out slowly. "It doesn't seem possible that he's really gone." Her voice broke on the last word.

Eleanor wrapped her arms around her mother-in-law and held Susie as she emitted heart-wrenching sobs. Finally, Susie pulled away and wiped her tears with the corner of her apron. "I'm sorry for blubbering like that. I just begin to think that I have myself under control, and then another rush of tears comes. I wonder if I'll ever be able to talk about Eddie without breaking down."

"You have a right to feel that way, and I'm sure in time it will get better." Eleanor hoped her words, spoken with feeling, might help to make Susie feel a little better. If nothing else, she wanted Vic's mother to know that the emotions she felt were a natural part of the grieving process.

"How is Victor doing?" Susie asked once she'd gotten herself under control. "Is he still blaming himself for Eddie's death?"

Eleanor wasn't sure how to answer that question because Vic had become so sullen and unwilling to talk since his brother's funeral that she could only guess what he really felt. He barely looked at Eleanor these days, but even without him saying so, she was certain that he still blamed himself. "Your son is still grieving, I know that much," Eleanor said. "He went back to work today, so I'm hoping that having something constructive to do will help take his mind off his pain."

"I hope so too," Susie said. "But it doesn't really answer my question. Does he still blame himself for Eddie's drowning?"

Eleanor swallowed past the thickness in her throat. "He hasn't spoken those words for a few days, but Vic's actions speak louder than his words. I'm quite sure he's still blaming himself."

Susie shook her head. "I'm real sorry to hear that. I'd hoped that once Victor had a few days to think things through he'd come to the conclusion that he was not to blame for his brother's death. Eddie made his own choice that day to go to the pond by himself. He chose to get in the water even though he knew he couldn't swim."

"You're right, Susie, and I've been praying that Vic will soon come to that realization himself."

"I pray for that too." Susie picked up the empty basket. "Can you come in the house for a while to visit? I would really enjoy it if you'd stay for lunch. Ethan and Stephen will be coming into the house around noon to eat, and I'm sure they would like to see you."

"That sounds nice. I'll put Buttons in the barn and give her some water, if that's all right."

"Of course. It wouldn't be good for her to stay at the rail too long in this hot sun."

"I'll take the *kichlin* into the house first and then come back to take care of the horse."

"I can take them, if you like. The plastic container can go in my laundry basket."

"All right. I'll see you in the house soon." Eleanor watched as Susie got the container of cookies and headed for the house. Her shoulders didn't droop so much as she stepped onto the porch. Eleanor was glad she'd decided to come here today. Even if she could only bring a little happiness into her mother-in-law's day, it was worth the drive and having to deal with her slowpoke horse to see Susie perk up a bit when she'd invited Eleanor to stay for lunch. Besides grieving the loss of her youngest child, Susie had most likely been feeling quite lonely. *I can relate to the lonely part. Since Vic has pulled away from me, I can't help feeling lonesome myself these days. I need to make an effort to come by here regularly,* Eleanor told herself as she moved across the yard to her waiting horse. *I may not be able to do much for Vic right now, other than pray for him, but Susie seems to need and want my company, and I could use some companionship too.*

Bird-in-Hand

"It was a long day, wasn't it?" Tom asked after he and Vic had left the jobsite and climbed into his truck.

Vic nodded and brought a shaky hand to his forehead. He had thought a full day of working might keep him from thinking about Eddie's death and help ease the burden of his guilt. But it hadn't. In fact, Vic had struggled to keep his mind on the job and knew the work he had done was probably not his best. If only he could blot out the image of his little brother lying facedown in that pond. Vic and the rescue squad had done everything in their power to bring Eddie back, but it was too late.

"I think what you need is a drink."

Tom's comment halted Vic's thoughts, and he opened his eyes. "I'm not thirsty. I drank plenty of water today."

Tom gave the steering wheel a smack with the palm of his left hand. "I was thinking you needed something a little stronger than water. How about a beer or two? We could stop by one of the taverns on the way home."

Vic shook his head. "Not a chance. And if you'll recall, you promised not to drink any alcoholic beverages while driving."

Tom glanced over at Vic, then back to the road. "Who says I was talking about me? I suggested that you might need a beer."

"Oh, and like you'd just sit there and watch me drink it and not have one too?"

Tom shrugged his shoulders. "Could be."

"Yeah, right." Vic pointed straight ahead. "Just keep driving, please."

"Okay, whatever, but if you change your mind—today, tomorrow, or any other day when you feel you can't cope, let me know. I've got plenty of beer at my home too, so if you get a hankering for one some evening, come on by."

"I doubt that'll ever happen." Vic would never have admitted to his coworker or anyone else for that matter, but the thought of drowning his sorrows with a few beers was more than a little tempting.

But with my luck, he thought, *as soon as I stepped in the door, Eleanor would get a whiff of my breath and she'd know I'd been drinking. I can only imagine what she'd have to say about that.*

———— ≈ ————

Paradise

When Eleanor heard a vehicle pull into the yard, she looked out the window and saw her husband. Eager to find out how Vic had done on his first day back at work, she hurried outside to greet him. As expected, Checkers followed her out the door. Vic's dog spent more time in the house than outside these days, and Eleanor had discovered that she found a sense of comfort and companionship with the dog around.

Before Eleanor had a chance to say hello to Vic, Checkers ran up to him, barking and wagging his tail. Vic barely acknowledged his pet or Eleanor as he shuffled toward the house, looking down at the ground.

"It's good to see you. How was your day?" Eleanor asked as she walked by his side.

"It went okay."

"I made some meadow tea this afternoon. Would you like some iced?"

"I guess."

Checkers, not about to give up, ran circles around Vic, yapping all the way. Vic continued to ignore the poor dog as he walked toward the house.

When Vic sank into one of the porch chairs, Checkers leaped onto his lap and started licking his face.

"Get down! I don't want your sloppy tongue kisses." He pushed the dog away.

Eleanor cringed. Was her husband really so tired that he couldn't spare a few minutes for his dog? She had been on the verge of going inside for the tea, but feeling sorry for Checkers, she went in search of a stick instead. She found one not far from the house and called for the dog, who bounded off the porch and raced up to her. With tail wagging and body posed to run, he waited for her command.

"Go get it!" Eleanor shouted after she'd thrown the stick.

Checkers took off after it, and Eleanor returned to the porch. "I'll get your iced tea now." She placed her hand on Vic's shoulder and gave it a gentle squeeze. He offered no response, and she couldn't help feeling a bit hurt. Was he really that tired, or could it be depression Vic felt? Either way, she'd hoped her husband would want to talk with her.

Eleanor waited for a moment, then opened the door and went inside. She returned a short time later, carrying a tray with two glasses of iced tea and a plate of cookies. Setting the tray on the small table next to Vic's chair, Eleanor took a seat on the other side of the table. "I went over to see your folks this morning," she said, handing Vic one of the glasses.

No comment—not even a shrug.

Eleanor decided to try again. "I took them a container of the ginger cookies I made, but of course I saved some for us too." She picked up the plate and held it out to him. "Would you like a few?"

Vic shook his head before drinking half of his tea.

She clenched her fingers into the palms of her hand. *Isn't he ever going to say anything? Vic is tired—I get that—and he's still grieving, but why won't he talk to me? I just want to carry on a normal conversation with my husband. Is that asking too much?*

"Your mother invited me to stay for lunch while I was there." Eleanor looked over at Vic, but he just sat there, staring straight ahead.

Finally, when Eleanor thought she could stand it no longer, Vic looked over at her and said, "I'm going out to the barn for a while."

"Oh, okay. I'll call you when supper's ready."

"Don't bother. I'm not hungry."

"But you have to eat something."

He turned and glared at her, his eyes filled with anger and hatred. "Don't tell me what to do! I don't *have* to do anything, and I'll eat when I'm good and ready!" Vic set his glass down, took the stairs two at a time, and ran all the way to the barn.

Eleanor closed her eyes and lowered her head. *Dear Lord, will my husband ever be himself again? Please show me what I can do to help him.* With tear-filled eyes, she stared off into the distance. He'd never looked at her like that before, and it frightened her. How had their loving marriage gone so wrong?

Chapter 17

Philadelphia Pike Road

It had been a month since Eddie's death, and now here they were in July—one of the hottest months of summer. Vic came home from work every evening feeling like he'd spent the entire day in a steamy sauna. Not that he was an expert on saunas. He'd only been inside one once, before he'd joined the church. He remembered that being in there had felt pretty good for the first several minutes, but the longer Vic and his buddies had stayed, the worse he'd felt. He couldn't tolerate too much heat and had ended up getting out before the rest of them did.

In addition to being hot and sweaty right now, Vic still had no ambition and had to force himself to get his work done while on the job. By the time he got home, he had no energy for doing his chores and felt thankful that Eleanor had done most of them while he was gone during the day.

Today, like all the others since his brother's death, Vic fought the urge to drown his sorrows. In fact, the feeling was so overwhelming, he broke the promise he'd made to himself and let Tom talk him into stopping for a few beers after work. Vic had convinced himself that a couple of drinks wouldn't hurt. The cool liquid would taste good, and it might numb his increasing emotional pain. He'd thought about Eleanor, knowing she would be upset about his decision to drink, but Vic's desperate need took over. All he wanted was that numbing feeling he'd experienced from the past. The relaxed state the alcohol had seemed to create made him feel good for a while, at least until it had worn off.

"It's about time you took me up on my offer," Tom said, pulling his truck into the parking lot of one the minimarts on their route home. "We can drive to my house to drink our beers, and that way you won't have to worry about anyone seeing you with a drink in your hands."

"What makes you think I'd be worried about that?" Vic pulled his sunglasses down and looked at Tom with raised brows.

"Well, for starters, you're Amish, and you've always told me that you thought drinking was wrong."

"I never said it in those exact words."

"May as well have. You sure let it be known that you don't drink."

"I used to," Vic admitted, "but it was before I joined the church."

"What's different now? Is it because you're still fretting about the loss of your kid brother?"

Tom's unexpected words hit Vic like a punch in the gut. "I've been feeling uptight lately and need something to help me relax." He glanced toward the store. "Would you mind going in to buy a carton of beer? I'll reimburse you for it."

Tom flapped his hand like he was swatting at some pesky fly. "Don't worry about it, Vic. These cans of beer will be my treat." He gave Vic's back a few solid pats. "Take my word for it, friend. By the time this evening's over, you'll be relaxed and won't even be thinking about your problems."

Paradise

"Have a seat and make yourself comfortable," Tom said when they entered his sparsely furnished house. The living room had a fairly decent-looking recliner, but the only other place to sit was a well-worn leather couch. It was hot and stuffy in the room, until Tom clicked a button on the wall and the cool air from his air-conditioning unit came on.

"You want a glass or would you rather drink your beer from the can?" Tom asked after Vic had taken a seat on the couch.

"Don't bother with a glass. A can is fine for me." He glanced at the clock on the far wall. "I can't stay long. I don't want Eleanor to worry."

"A little worry on the wife's part might be good for your marriage. She'll appreciate you more when you get home." Tom opened the carton of beer he'd brought in and tossed one to Vic. "Here you go—enjoy!"

At that moment, with the can of beer in his hands, Vic realized that there was still an opportunity for him to change his mind. If he started drinking, could he control himself this time? His past had already been bumpy due to the last time he drank some alcohol, but Vic rationalized his doubts away. *I've missed having a beer and the way its flavor hits my taste buds.* He held the frigid-cold can and stared at its icy label. *It shouldn't be a problem for me this time. I'm older now, and I think I can drink responsibly.*

Vic didn't believe being late for supper would do anything good for his marriage, but right now all he could think about was downing the beer he held in his hands and hoping it would help soothe his jangled nerves. If Eleanor got upset because he was late getting home this evening, he'd think of something to calm her down.

Vic opened the beer and took his first drink. "Oh boy. . .that felt good going down, and I like the fruity, funky taste."

"Not bad, huh?"

Vic bobbed his head. He'd barely finished with his beer when Tom tossed him another can.

"If the first one was good, then two will be better." Tom chuckled and opened another one for himself.

"Okay, but after I finish this, I should get going."

"What's your hurry? You just got here, and I doubt you've had a chance to relax yet. Just kick back and enjoy the moment." Tom lifted his can. "And the beer."

———— ≈ ————

Eleanor glanced at the clock on the kitchen wall. The chicken dish she'd made was in the oven, staying warm, and the tossed green salad in the refrigerator would go with it. She also planned to serve green beans, and some chow-chow, a condiment that Vic really liked. Today was their first anniversary, and she'd made his favorite pie for dessert. Eleanor had hoped Vic might give her a gift or even a card this morning, but he'd left the house without saying a word about their anniversary. She'd made a special card for Vic and had decided to wait until this evening to give it to him. She figured with the stress he'd been under, he must have forgotten the date of their anniversary. Would he be upset if she asked? Would Vic feel bad when she gave him the card if he had none for her?

She glanced at the clock again. *I wish Vic would get here. I wonder what's taking him so long. Could he be working longer hours than normal this evening?*

Eleanor took a seat at the table and tried to relax. It was hard not to worry about her husband—especially since he wouldn't communicate with her the way he used to before Eddie's death. Vic also lacked ambition and didn't eat or sleep as much as he should. He'd lost some weight, and the bags and dark circles under his eyes were clear evidence of his exhaustion.

Eleanor got up and went over to the desk where she kept notepaper as well as a file folder for keeping incoming bills and receipts separate from those that had been paid. It helped to stay organized, especially when it was time to pay bills and do tax preparation at the end of the year.

Eleanor figured that while she waited for Vic, she might as well write a few letters. She owed one to her mother and also Doretta. She'd received another letter from her friend a week ago and hadn't responded to it yet. Doretta had said she would continue to pray for Vic and all of the Lapp family as they dealt with the loss of Eddie. She'd stated that she had been praying for Eleanor too, that she would be patient with Vic and know what to say or do to help with his emotions and healing process.

Eleanor picked up two sheets of paper and a pen and went back to the table. Writing letters was an easy way to get her thoughts down on paper, and it did help some to ease the stress and tension she often felt these days.

———≈———

"Hey, buddy, you'd better ease up. I think you've had enough of those, and I'd better take you home," Tom said when Vic reached for a fifth can of beer.

"Ah, come on. . .I'm feeling so relaxed, and one more will make me feel even better." Vic's tongue felt thick, and he couldn't keep from slurring his words. He stood up, rocked back and forth, and stumbled across the room, where more beer cans sat by Tom's chair.

Tom leaped to his feet and grabbed Vic's arm. "I said no more! You can barely even stand on your own two feet."

"I–I'm fine. Haven't felt this good in a long while." Vic looked at Tom and blinked multiple times. "That's sure funny. . . . Think I'm seeing two of you. Have you got a twin brother?"

"No, pal—you're drunk, and I'm taking you home right now." Tom got a good grip on Vic and led him out the door.

Vic didn't want to leave yet, but he was too unstable, and his head felt so fuzzy he couldn't think straight. Well, at least he'd be going home in a jolly mood for a change. That ought to make Eleanor happy.

———≈———

Eleanor had finished writing letters to her mother and Doretta and was about to turn the oven to its lowest setting when she heard a noisy vehicle pull into the yard. No doubt it was Tom's truck bringing her tired husband home from a long workday.

Eleanor left the kitchen and hurried to open the front door. She was surprised to see that instead of dropping Vic off at the end of the driveway like he normally did, Tom had pulled his truck up close to the house. What surprised her even more was when Tom stepped down from his truck, went around to the passenger's door, and helped Vic out.

Her throat constricted. "What's wrong with my husband?" She rushed forward. "Is he sick, or did he get hurt on the job?"

Tom shook his head and walked Vic slowly up the porch steps. "He had a little too much to drink, and he's feeling pretty tipsy right now."

Eleanor's fingers touched her parted lips. "Are. . .are you saying that he's drunk?"

"Yep. I'll help him inside, and then you can take over from there."

Coldness hit Eleanor to the core of her being. How could this be? To her knowledge, Vic hadn't partaken of any alcoholic beverages since he had joined the church. And even before then, she'd never seen him drunk and unable to walk on his own.

She ground her teeth together. *So much for spending a nice anniversary together this evening. This day is now ruined.*

Eleanor followed the men inside and closed the door. She had put Checkers in his dog run a few hours ago, so at least she didn't have to deal with the dog carrying on when he saw his owner. She did, however, need to figure out how to deal with Vic. No one in her family drank alcohol, other than the little bit of wine they partook of during church communion, so she'd never had to deal with a situation like this before.

After Tom helped Vic onto the couch, he turned to Eleanor and said, "You can try to sober your hubby up now or just let him sleep it off, which would be my suggestion. He'll probably be sick as a dog, but sober, by morning." He started for the door, then turned back to face her. "Sorry about this. When we stopped by my house and I offered Vic a few beers, I thought he'd stop at two, but he drank two more and then wanted a fifth before I insisted on taking him home."

Eleanor followed Tom out the door. "What I don't understand is why you offered my husband any beer at all."

"He's been stressed out since his brother drowned. I thought it might help Vic to relax and unwind for a bit, so I invited him to my house for a few beers." He reached out his hand and touched her arm. "Don't look so serious. I'm sure he'll be fine when the buzz wears off."

Before Eleanor could offer a retort, Tom got into his truck and drove away.

Eleanor's heartbeat raced as she closed the front door. It shook her to the core to see her husband like this. Although she knew Vic had been dealing with depression due to his brother's death, she'd never imagined that he would start drinking. She hoped it was only a one-time event, and that when Vic sobered up, he would have learned his lesson and never touch another alcoholic beverage.

———— ≈ ————

Groaning and shielding his eyes against the light permeating the room, Vic rolled onto his side and nearly fell off the couch. "What time is it, and what am I doing in here?" he mumbled as a sharp pain shot through his head. His lips felt dry as sandpaper, and the bad taste in his mouth reminded him that he'd obviously not brushed his teeth last night. He tried to sort out what had happened from the time he'd finished his last beer at Tom's place yesterday until now.

"You'd better change your clothes and wash up or you'll be late for work," Eleanor announced when she entered the room a few seconds later.

Vic pulled himself to a sitting position and rubbed his forehead. "It's morning?"

"Jah."

"And I slept here on the couch all night?"

She gave a brief nod. "You fell asleep there after Tom brought you home, and you were too drunk for me to put you to bed."

Before Vic could respond, Checkers darted into the room, jumped into his lap, and began licking his face. Vic pushed the dog away and looked at Eleanor again. "Would you put him outside? I can't deal with this right now. Fact is, I'm not sure I can go to work today at all. My head's pounding so hard I can barely think straight."

"I don't think you should go to work either." Eleanor moved toward the front door. "I'll let the dog out and then go to the phone shed and call your boss."

"Don't tell Ned I'm suffering from a hangover." He spoke with an urgent tone.

Eleanor looked straight at him. "So you want me to lie to him?"

"No. Just say I–I'm not feeling well today, 'cause that's the truth—I feel terrible."

"And who's to blame for that?" Her lips flattened as she crossed her arms.

"Only me. I'm the one who messed up, and I am truly sorry, Eleanor. I should not have put you through that."

"What about yourself? Did getting drunk do anything good for you, Vic?"

"Last night it did, because after drinking a couple of beers I felt relaxed, and then I had a couple more and the painful grief I've been carrying for the last month was gone."

"How about now? Is it still gone?"

He shook his head. "It's back, and now there's the additional shame I feel for being so stupid and getting drunk. Will you forgive me, Eleanor? I promise it will never happen again."

"Jah, Vic, I forgive you, but more importantly, you need to forgive yourself—not just for getting drunk, but for not teaching your brother how to swim and believing that you are to blame for his death. You need to allow God to help you work past that and not turn to alcohol as a crutch." She spoke in a soothing tone but with obvious conviction.

Vic nodded very carefully while continuing to rub his throbbing head. "You're right, and from this moment on, I will do my best."

She reached for a card that had been lying on the coffee table and handed it to him. "Here. Happy belated anniversary."

His eyes widened. "Oh boy! I really blew it. Our first anniversary was yesterday, right?"

"Yes."

"I'm really sorry, Eleanor. I'll make it up to you, I promise."

Chapter 18

Throughout the rest of the summer and into September, Vic managed to keep his promise to Eleanor and stayed away from drinking any alcoholic beverages. To combat the continued feelings of self-hatred and blame for Eddie's death, Vic kept as busy as he could, sometimes driving himself into a state of exhaustion. Instead of coming home after work and collapsing on the couch, he found extra projects to do around their place.

This tactic also kept Vic's wife off his case, with all the concern she kept saying she had for him. Vic didn't enjoy being mothered by Eleanor, which she often seemed to do. Telling him what he should or shouldn't do, as if he were a child, had gotten his dander up on more than one occasion. A little too much mothering, and he'd lose his patience real quick. He couldn't understand after telling her repeatedly not to treat him like a child why she would turn around and do it again. Vic loved his wife and hoped that one of these days she'd figure out what he needed. But for now it was the same old thing around the house: Eleanor would nag him about what he was or wasn't doing.

Since today was Saturday and he didn't have to report for work, Vic planned to build Checkers a bigger, better doghouse that he could go into more easily when he was inside his pen. He could have asked his dad to build the doghouse, since that was one of the many things Dad made in his shop. But building it himself would give Vic another excuse to keep busy. He would get started on the doghouse right after breakfast.

Eleanor placed a platter of scrambled eggs mixed with cubed ham on the table and took the seat across from Vic. After they'd prayed silently, she passed the platter to Vic and smiled. "It looks like it's going to be nice today, and thankfully, a lot cooler now that fall is here and we're in the beginning of October."

"What?" Vic's head came up, and he set the platter down. "What day is it?"

"October first. I turned the page over from September to October after I came into the kitchen this morning." Eleanor gestured to the calendar on the far wall.

Vic leaped out of his chair and rushed over to take a look. Sure enough, it was the first day of October. "It's Eddie's birthday. He would have. . . And should have turned nine today." Vic winced at the realization and thought about the Legos he'd given his brother last year. He had no idea what his mother had done with Eddie's toys and wondered if she'd thrown them out or given them to some other family's kid.

"Birthdays, Christmas, and other special occasions are a time when we think about our loved ones who have passed on."

Although Vic figured his wife's words were meant to be comforting, they hit him with the force of a freight train. He didn't need a birthday or some other special day to remind him that Eddie was gone, because the pain was always with him. Even more so today, however. Vic could still see the look of joy on his little brother's face when the family had gotten together to celebrate Eddie's eighth birthday. *If I'd had any idea it was going to be his last*, Vic berated himself, *I would have done things differently.*

"The eggs are getting cold," Eleanor said as Vic continued to stand there, staring at the calendar.

He turned to look at her and shook his head. "I've lost my appetite."

"You really should eat something. You've gotten so thin since—"

He pointed a finger in her direction. "Don't start nagging again. I'll eat when I want, and I don't need to be mothered. If I did, I'd still be living at home, listening to my mamm telling me what I should and shouldn't do." Vic grabbed his jacket off the wall peg near the back door and put it on.

"Where are you going?"

"Out to the barn. I still have some chores out there that need to get done."

"Can't they wait until after you've eaten?"

Vic's irritation mounted. "Weren't you listening to what I said before—I have no appetite." Vic grabbed his hat, slapped it on his head, and rushed out the door without giving Eleanor a chance to respond. He wanted to be alone, and if he was being honest with himself, he desperately needed something that would quiet his pent-up emotions.

Eleanor looked at Checkers, asleep on the throw rug in front of the sink. She was surprised that he hadn't gotten up and followed Vic out the door. *I wish I'd never said anything about it being October first,* Eleanor fretted. *I wouldn't have mentioned it if I'd remembered that today would have been Eddie's birthday.* She looked at her husband's empty plate and took a deep breath to calm herself. She'd thought Vic was doing a little better, but seeing him so upset, she couldn't help but worry. *I hope he won't turn to alcohol again. Drinking is not the answer to Vic's problems.* She released a heavy sigh. What her husband needed most was to talk about his feelings with someone who had been through something similar and had dealt with their emotions constructively. She wondered if any of their church leaders could help Vic deal with his problem.

It was getting old, having him snap at her so often, when all she was trying to do was show some concern for his well-being. *I wouldn't mind talking about my feelings to someone about this,* she thought. *It might help my nerves to settle down if I could pour out my pent-up emotions. Sometimes when Vic snaps at me, I just want to let out my anger, but I'm sure that would only make things worse.*

Eleanor took a sip of tea. *Should I go ahead and speak to the bishop or one of the ministers about Vic?* She tipped her head, weighing her choices. *If I did talk to one of them, they would probably approach Vic, and then he'd suspect that I had turned to the church leader for help, which I am certain he would not appreciate.*

Eleanor set her empty cup down. *I'd better pray about this before I say anything to anyone. I don't want to do something that would upset Vic even more, which in turn could affect our marriage in a negative way.*

———— ≈ ————

Vic entered his horse's stall and picked up the brush. "At least you won't get on my case about anything, will you, boy?" He patted the horse while it munched on some hay. "You've got it made, that's for sure. No worries, just eating, sleeping, and a little exercise to keep you fit." As he groomed Domino, Vic began devising a plan. If he could just drink one or two beers, he would feel more relaxed. It had worked before, when he was at Tom's place. Only Vic had learned his lesson and would stop at two. The problem was he didn't have any beer here, and if he went to one of the local stores to get some, he might be seen by someone he knew while he was purchasing the beer. He grimaced. *That would not be a good thing.*

Vic stopped brushing Domino and planted his feet in a wide stance. *I know just what to do. I'll hitch my horse to the buggy, drive over to Tom's place, and see if he has a few beers I can buy. Maybe I could even drink them while I'm there, because if I bring the beer home and drink here in the barn, I'd be taking the chance that Eleanor might walk in, not to mention that I'd have to make sure the empty cans were well hidden beneath other garbage in the can. Then again, I could hide it in the barn. There are places Eleanor never goes.*

Vic gave Domino a few pats. "How about it, big fellow? You ready to go for a ride?"

The horse's response was a little whinny, and then Domino turned his head and nuzzled Vic's hand.

Vic's forehead wrinkled. *If Eleanor sees me pull out of the yard, with no explanation, she'll be worried and upset. Guess I'd better go tell her that I'm leaving and come up with some kind of a believable excuse.*

———— ≈ ————

Eleanor had cleared the dishes from the table and was about to put the leftover scrambled eggs in the refrigerator when the back door opened and Vic entered the house. She assumed he had changed his mind about eating.

"Did you get your chores done in the barn?" she asked.

He nodded.

"There are plenty of eggs left. Would you like me to put them in a skillet and reheat them for you?"

"No, that's okay. I hitched my gaul, and I'm going into town, so I'll be gone for a while."

"Oh?" Eleanor poked her tongue against the inside of her cheek. "I didn't realize you'd be going anywhere today. You never said anything about it before." She picked up the egg container and put it away in the refrigerator. Eleanor waited for his response and wondered if he was still upset with her from the things she'd said earlier.

Vic reached up and rubbed the back of his neck. "I. . .um. . .didn't know I'd need to go until now."

"Would you like me to go with you? I can soak the dishes and be ready to leave shortly."

Vic shook his head. "No, don't bother. I can get done with my errands a lot quicker if I'm by myself."

Eleanor's voice dropped as she whispered a quiet, "Oh, I see." She couldn't help feeling disappointed. What had happened to the man she'd married, who used to enjoy spending time with her? Had his brother's death changed him so much that he didn't want to be with her anymore?

"Don't look so down in the mouth. I'll be back before you know it. Besides, I'm sure you have plenty of things here to do that'll keep you busy while I'm gone."

Eleanor didn't bother to refute what he'd said. She just told him goodbye and went to the sink to wash the dishes. A few seconds later, she heard the back door shut and knew that Vic had gone.

Hot tears pricked the back of her eyes. *Will anything ever be right in this house again?*

—————≈—————

As Vic neared Tom's place, he thought after he'd had some beer and left Tom's house, he should go into town to purchase something. That way he would return home with whatever he purchased and Eleanor wouldn't suspect that he had lied to her. Vic had set a tarp in the back of his open buggy to cover up the beer if he was able to buy some from Tom. When he went to town, the alcohol would be out of sight from anyone who might look in the back of his open rig. It wouldn't be good if another Amish person walked by Vic's buggy and saw beer inside. No doubt the news would get out and around pretty fast in their community.

He gave the reins a jiggle. *I'll just swing by the hardware store after I'm done at Tom's and take a look at some paint for Checkers' new doghouse. That way my wife won't give my errand any thought.*

When Vic guided his horse and buggy onto his coworker's driveway, he was relieved to see Tom's truck parked in front of the garage, which meant he must be home. *I sure hope he has some beer I can buy.*

Since there was no hitching rail in this English man's yard, Vic got out of his buggy and tied Domino to a fence post. Then, after taking the porch stairs two at a time, he knocked on the front door. Several seconds passed, and then Tom, wearing jeans and a T-shirt, pulled the door open.

"Well, this is a surprise." Tom pointed to the fence post. "I see you found a place to secure your horse."

Vic nodded. "I hope you don't mind."

"As long as he doesn't pull the fence down, it's perfectly fine." Tom stepped onto the porch in his bare feet. "So what brings you to my house this morning?"

Feeling a bit unsure of himself all of a sudden, Vic stuck both hands in his jacket pockets while shuffling his feet a few times. "I—uh—was wondering if you might have some beer I could buy."

Tom's eyes widened. "You're kidding, right?"

Vic shook his head.

"Have you forgotten how things turned out the last time you were here?"

"No, I remember."

"Then what are you looking for today—a repeat performance?"

"Course not. I just want some beer, which I'll pay you for, of course."

"Why are you asking me? Why don't you go to the store and get your own beer, which I'm guessing you think you must need."

Without commenting on how badly he needed the beer, Vic replied, "I can't take the chance of anyone I know seeing me at a store with beer in my hands."

"So you're man enough to drink it but afraid to let anyone know?"

Vic shrugged his shoulders. "I guess so, if that's how you want to put it."

Tom leaned against the doorjamb. "Why now? What's brought you to the point that you think you need alcohol again?"

Vic explained about it being his brother's birthday and said he needed the beer to help him relax and hopefully forget.

"It'll do that, all right," Tom said. "But remember, it's only a temporary fix. When the buzz wears off, reality always sets in."

"I know." Vic pulled out his wallet. "Do you have some I can buy or not?"

"Yeah. I bought a whole case after I dropped you off at your home yesterday. I can sell you half, if you want that much."

"I do." Vic bobbed his head, feeling a mixture of guilt and relief.

"I assume you'll be taking it back to your home?"

"Yeah, but I don't want my wife to see it, so I won't take it in the house." Vic pulled his fingers through the ends of his ever-growing beard. "I can hide my beer in the barn."

"How do you know your wife won't find it there? I'm sure there must be occasions when she goes into the barn."

"Yeah, of course." Vic held on to the brim of his hat as a gust of wind came up. "There are plenty of places to hide things there, so I'm not worried."

"Okay, whatever you say." Tom stepped into his house and told Vic to follow him.

Vic's throat tightened and he swallowed hard. *Sure hope I'm not making a mistake, keeping the beer in the barn. But I'm fairly certain I can find a safe place to hide the stuff there, and Eleanor will be none the wiser. The only thing I'll have to worry about is making sure she doesn't smell the booze on my breath. And I can't allow myself to get drunk again, because then she would know for sure what I've been up to.*

Chapter 19

Strasburg

Susie grabbed a hunk of weeds growing close to the carrots in her garden plot. As she gave it a good yank, a puff of dirt nearly hit her face when the unwanted plant pulled free. With her two able-bodied daughters helping her today, Susie hoped to get every single weed gone within the next few hours, leaving a clean-looking garden plot. So far, they'd gotten a good amount of green beans from the garden this year, and with Kate and Clara's help, most of the beans had either been canned or frozen. The three of them had also canned beets and pickles, so the pantry looked well stocked with an abundance of veggies and also some fruits and berries. Susie had appreciated her garden, especially this year, as caring for it and putting up all the produce had helped to occupy her mind after losing her youngest child.

She paused and looked at the nicely manicured plot of ground as Clara and Kate continued weeding. The only produce left in Susie's garden were carrots, winter squash, onions, and potatoes. There was also some swiss chard, which they needed to pick before the end of October, or else it could likely freeze in the colder weather.

Susie's youngest daughter plucked several weeds by the potato patch and threw them into the garden cart. "Do you realize what day this is, Mom?"

She brushed some dirt from her gardening gloves and blinked her blue eyes rapidly as she looked over at Susie.

"Jah, Kate. It's the first of October. Last year at this time we were getting things ready in the house for your little bruder's birthday supper."

"That's right," Clara interjected. "What a wunderbaar time we had celebrating Eddie's gebottsdaag." She leaned close to her sister and snatched up a few weeds that Kate had missed. The girls looked so similar that, if it weren't for the four years' difference in their ages, they could almost pass as twins.

Susie blew out her breath in a rush of emotions. She had been fully aware of what day it was and didn't need the reminder, but she would not avoid talking about it with her girls. If there was one thing Susie had realized during the four months since her son's death, it was that holding things in wasn't good. She had learned early on that talking about her loss helped her deal with the pain.

She still missed Eddie and always would. After all, how could a parent not miss their dear child? There wasn't a day that had gone by since her son drowned that Susie hadn't thought about him. It had been difficult not to sink into depression after he died, but reading God's Word, praying, and sharing her feelings with friends and family had gotten her through the most difficult months. Today would be one of the hardest days for Susie, as she tried not to dwell on the fact that Eddie would not be here to celebrate his ninth birthday. There would be no party or cake and ice cream. This would be like any other day this week, except for the memories of her youngest boy.

Susie couldn't help but think about what it would have been like if Eddie hadn't drowned. Would he have learned how to swim by now? What would he have wanted for his ninth birthday? Would he have been out here helping them weed the garden today? Susie could almost picture her son, right here, mingling with them, and tossing an occasional dirt clod at one or both of his sisters. Or maybe the little rascal would be out in the barn, hanging around the cats or playing with his dog. But all was gone—all except her memories of him, which she would carry deep within her heart forever.

Susie felt the weight of another clump of weeds in her grip give way as she gave a tug. Tossing it in the garden cart, she felt a sudden wave of peace come over her as she looked up at the cloudless sky. Her boy had gone to heaven when he died, and for that she was ever so thankful. *Dear Lord,* she prayed, *if it's possible, please give Eddie a big hug and tell him that his mama said, "Happy birthday."*

Susie opened her eyes and looked out past the barn, to the building where her husband's shop was located. *I wonder how Ethan and Stephen are doing. Do either of them remember that today would have been Eddie's ninth birthday?*

———— ≈ ————

"Hey, Dad." Stephen bumped Ethan's arm as they worked side by side in his shop. "You know what today is?"

"As a matter of fact, I do. Today is the first day of October."

Stephen's brown eyes darkened as he gave a slow nod. "If Eddie was still alive, today would have been his ninth birthday."

Ethan scrubbed a hand over his face and down his full beard. It had been a sad day when his boy drowned, and since that time, he'd dealt with many regrets. He regretted not having spent more time with his boy. *I should have set my work aside and taught Eddie how to swim,* he thought. *If he had learned, I'm sure he wouldn't have drowned in Vic's pond—maybe wouldn't have even gone there at all.*

Ethan stared straight ahead, pondering how hard Vic had taken Eddie's death. He too blamed himself for not taking the time to teach Eddie how to swim. Vic had also stated several times that he felt guilty for not watching his brother that day. *If only the past could be undone. But all the shoulda, woulda, couldas cannot bring back my son.*

Ethan wondered how his wife was doing today. No doubt Susie knew what day it was. He figured she'd be feeling down, same as Kate and Clara. Although Eddie pestered them some, both girls loved their little brother dearly. It seemed so strange without their youngest son around. Ethan visualized Eddie's face and all those freckles he had. Things were definitely different now, without Eddie asking multiple questions about whatever popped into his curious head. His boy had enjoyed nature too and would often ask if they could go fishing. It was one more thing Ethan hadn't done enough of with Eddie or any of his children.

He shifted his stance. *If only I had taken more time out to spend with my boy.* That was a regret he'd have to live with from now on. Some people's lives could be long, and some were cut short, like Eddie's. *We really don't know how much time we have on this planet,* he thought. *But I'd best get back to my work, because now isn't the time to waste on pondering life's many mysteries and things I can do nothing about.*

He reached for a piece of sandpaper and began working on the rungs of a chair. It felt good to feel the rough surface slowly becoming smooth beneath his fingers. He'd cut a lot of wood and done a lot of sanding today and had sawdust coating the hair on his arms to prove it.

Now that the weather was cooling, Ethan figured he wasn't likely to get many orders for outdoor furniture, so he'd recently begun making some indoor chairs and tables. He'd made some last year too but planned to make even more this winter, if for no other reason than to keep his hands and mind busy.

"Remember the kitten Eddie wanted to name Gebottsdaag?" Stephen's question pulled Ethan's thoughts aside.

"Jah."

"Can you imagine wanting to call a bussli 'Birthday'?" Stephen snickered while rolling his eyes.

Ethan stopped sanding and gave a little chuckle. "That would have been pretty silly, all right. I'm glad he gave up that silly notion and called the kitten 'Fluffy' instead."

Stephen dipped his brush into the can of stain near his feet. "I sure do miss my little bruder."

"I miss him too, but he's in a much better place now."

"You mean *himmel*?"

"That's right. I believe God took Eddie's soul straight to heaven when he died."

Stephen gave the chair he'd been staining a few swipes with his brush. "How do you know? Eddie never got the chance to grow up and join the church, like I'm planning to do next year when I turn sixteen."

"That's good, Son. You're at the age of accountability, but your little brother was not."

"You mean 'cause he hadn't taken classes, gotten baptized, and joined the church?"

"Jah."

"But Dad, I'm sure Eddie knew what was right and wrong. He sinned just like every other person who's been born."

"That is true, but I know for a fact that Eddie went to heaven, because one night before he went to bed, he tearfully admitted to your mamm and me that he'd done something wrong that day. Then he asked me to pray the sinner's prayer with him." Ethan gave a decisive nod. "Eddie prayed, asking Jesus to forgive his sins and to come live in his heart. That boy's in heaven, as sure as you and I are sitting here in this shop."

Stephen sat for several seconds, as though pondering Ethan's words. Then a smile formed on his oval-shaped face. "I'm glad, and it helps to know that someday, when I get to heaven, I'll see my little bruder again."

Ethan nodded one more time. "Those of us who have accepted Christ as our Savior will be reunited with Eddie, my parents and grandparents, as well as many other people we know who have passed away."

Paradise

When Vic pulled his horse and buggy into the yard, he was glad that Eleanor wasn't outside. If she had been, she might have followed him into the barn when he went to put Domino away. That would have been bad, especially if she'd tried to kiss him and gotten a whiff of his beer breath. Although he'd struggled with the desire to do it when he'd gone to Tom's place, Vic had downed one can of beer before he'd left there. It had taken the edge off a little bit, but he needed another one now to truly calm down. The realization that today was his little brother's birthday had been like a punch in Vic's gut. He would do almost anything if there was a way he could bring Eddie back to his family.

Vic heard Checkers barking from his pen, but he chose to ignore him for now. There was something more important that needed to be done before he let the dog out. He stepped down from the buggy and reached inside for the cardboard box that held his haul. Vic glanced around one more time to be sure he wasn't seen, and then, satisfied that he was alone, he hurried to the barn and set the box inside Domino's stall. Pausing to wipe a trickle of sweat from under the warmth of his hat band, Vic went back outside to unhitch his horse. His mind was on only one thing at the moment, and he barely took notice of the sparrows chirping as they flew from tree to tree in the yard.

After leading Domino into the barn, Vic put the gelding in his stall, made sure he had fresh water, and gave the horse's warm flank a brief pat. "I'll be back soon to brush you down." While Domino slurped his water, Vic picked up the box that was filled with cans of beer and hoisted it onto his shoulder. Using his left hand to hold the box steady, he stepped onto the wooden ladder, holding on with his right hand, and hauled his purchase up to the loft. In no hurry to go back down, Vic opened one can and leaned against a bale of straw to drink it. *Ah, that tastes good. I feel better already.* When Vic finished the beer, he was tempted to have another but didn't want to take the risk of feeling tipsy. The last thing Vic needed was to end up drunk again. That would not go over well with his wife. And since tomorrow was a church day, Vic couldn't risk waking up with a hangover that would no doubt include a pounding headache. No, he had to play it safe today.

An aggravating fly buzzed around Vic's head, and he waved it away. Domino's whinny was a reminder that Vic still needed to brush the horse. He put the empty can of beer in the box with the full ones, pushed it to the back of the loft, and covered it with straw. It was unlikely that Eleanor would climb up here for any reason or start snooping around, so Vic felt safe about leaving the box here. If he found a better hiding place, he could always move it, but for now he felt confident that the box was safe.

Vic climbed down the ladder, and when his feet touched the creaky floorboards, he reached into his pocket and pulled out a pack of mint-flavored gum. If Eleanor came anywhere near him, he needed to make sure that his breath did not smell like beer.

———— ≈ ————

"I'm glad you're back," Eleanor said, trying to sound cheerful when Vic entered the house with Checkers at his side. "You were gone quite a while, and I was beginning to worry."

He shrugged. "Errands can take time, especially when traffic is bad."

"That makes sense." Eleanor left the kitchen sink, where she'd been washing several canning jars, and walked over to him. "Would you like a cup of kaffi?"

Vic's eyes narrowed and his cheeks flushed a bright pink hue. "Why would I need any coffee?"

"I didn't say you needed it. Just thought you might enjoy drinking a cup with me."

Vic shook his head. "The only thing I need right now is a nap." He brushed past her and quickly started down the hall.

"Wait a minute, please." She followed. "I thought it would be nice if we could sit down and talk for a while."

"Not now. I'm tired, and I need to lie down." Vic kept his back to her and continued to move toward their bedroom at the end of the hall.

Eleanor wasn't sure what to do. Vic rarely hugged or kissed her anymore, and she craved his attention and touch. Had the thrill of being married to her worn off for him, or did it have more to do with the despair he felt over Eddie's death?

Eleanor quickened her steps, hoping to catch up with Vic before he entered their room. "I hope you have a good rest," she said, reaching out to touch his shoulder.

He just shuffled into the room and closed the door.

Eleanor's eyes watered as she gave a frustrated shake of her head. Was there nothing she could say or do to bring her husband out of the pit of depression he'd been in for the last four months? She turned and headed back to the kitchen. *Maybe I will have a talk with our church bishop sometime next week, but I won't make any mention of that sorrowful evening Vic came home drunk.* She swallowed hard. *I fear, though, that if something isn't done soon to help my husband deal with his deep-seated grief, he might resort to drinking again.* Eleanor's lips compressed. *If that should happen, I don't know what I will do.*

Chapter 20

Sunday morning, as Vic sat on a backless wooden bench, listening to their bishop, Michael Zook, preach, it was all he could do not to bolt. Although Vic had not said the words out loud, he dreaded going to church every other Sunday. Sometimes on their off-Sundays, Eleanor would suggest that they visit another church district, but Vic always made up some excuse not to go. It was too difficult to sit for three hours, listening to songs and sermons he wasn't sure he believed anymore. He couldn't help feeling that the Lord had let him down. Vic struggled with this issue day in and day out. If only there was a way to fix what had happened, but the truth was, he couldn't do a single thing about the past. It was gone and lost forever.

The bishop's sermon today was on the topic of faith and how Christians should not allow their faith to waver during difficult times.

That's easy enough for him to say, Vic thought. *He's not responsible for the death of his brother.*

"Without faith it is impossible to please him: for he that cometh to God must believe that he is, and that he is a rewarder of them that diligently seek him," the bishop quoted from Hebrews 11:6.

Vic still believed in God and had acknowledged Christ as his Savior the day he'd gotten baptized and joined the church. But he'd never fully committed his life to Jesus and rarely took the time for Bible reading and devotions at home. This had been especially true since Eddie's passing. Although Vic felt responsible for his little brother's death, he was angry at God for allowing it to happen.

His jaw clenched and he dug his fingers into the palms of his hands. *Why, Lord? Why did You take my little brother? Why couldn't it have been me?* Vic swallowed hard. How many times had he asked those questions? Of course, no answer had ever come.

A young child sitting on his father's lap on the bench in front of Vic began to fuss. Vic watched as the Amish man gently patted the baby's back. It seemed to do the trick, for the little one quieted right down.

I hope Eleanor and I never have any children, Vic thought, *because I'm not dependable and would not be a good father.*

After church was over and the noon meal had been served, Vic went out to check on Domino. His horse had acted kind of spooky on the ride to church, and Vic wanted to be sure the animal hadn't broken free or become tangled. When he got to the line of horses, Vic was relieved to see that Domino was okay and appeared to be quite docile. Vic concluded that the horse should be fine until Eleanor was ready to go, which he hoped would be soon, because he didn't feel like socializing with anyone today.

Vic walked over to where his buggy was parked, thinking he might get in and take a nap, but before he could put one foot into the buggy, his dad showed up.

"Hey, Son, you're not leaving already, are you?" Dad questioned.

Vic shook his head. "Not yet. I'm feeling kind of tired today and thought I'd rest for a while, until my *fraa* is ready to go."

"Busy week at work, huh?"

"Jah. Always busy, and some days more than others."

"I understand." Dad gestured to Vic's carriage. "Why don't we both get in? We can rest our weary bones and visit awhile."

Vic was not in the mood to talk, but he could hardly tell his dad no. He and Mom weren't a part of this church district, since they lived in Strasburg. However, Vic was sure they'd come all this way today so they could see him and Eleanor, and he would not turn his dad aside.

"Okay." Vic climbed into the driver's side, and Dad went around to the left and took his seat on the passenger's side. He didn't mind a little idle chat with his father, but it appeared from the expression on Dad's face that it was going to be more of a serious talk. *I hope he doesn't mention anything about Eddie. I'm not up for that today. In fact, I'd like to avoid talking about my little brother with anyone, because all it does is increase the agony I feel over his untimely death.*

"Other than being tired from work, how are you doing in other ways?" Dad placed his hand on Vic's arm as he looked over at him.

Vic shifted on his seat. "I'm getting by. How about you?"

"Yesterday, with it being Eddie's birthday, was kind of tough."

Vic just swallowed around the thickness that had formed in his throat. He really did not want to talk about this.

"Was Saturday kind of hard for you too?" Dad persisted.

He's not going to let the topic drop. Releasing his father's hand from his arm, Vic stared straight ahead. "Yeah, it bothered me a lot." He felt his facial muscles quiver and wished he could control the action. "Eddie should not have died. He was cheated out of his whole life."

"But he's in heaven now. I'm certain of it. Don't you find that comforting?"

Vic shrugged. "Guess I would if I was there with him."

Dad clasped Vic's arm again. "It wasn't your time to go."

"Maybe it should have been." Vic couldn't keep the bitterness out of his tone.

"Please don't talk that way, Son. I'm sure you don't mean it."

"Jah, I do. And can we please change the subject? I don't want to talk about this anymore."

Dad opened his mouth like he was about to say something more when Eleanor stepped up to the buggy. "I saw you come out here and figured you must be ready to go, Vic, but now I have a feeling I'm interrupting something."

Vic shook his head. "We weren't saying anything important, and I am more than ready to go."

She glanced over at Vic's father. "I'm truly sorry for the interruption."

"It's fine," he said. "There are some other people here today who I'd like talk to, so I'll do that right now." He gave a nod and sprinted across the grass to where a group of men stood talking near the barn.

Vic's brows lowered as he turned to Eleanor and said, "Go ahead and get in the buggy. I'll be back soon with my horse, and then we can be on our way home."

Eleanor sat rigidly on her seat as they headed in the direction of home. She wished she knew what Vic and his dad had been talking about but thought it would be best not to ask. If Vic wanted her to know, he would tell her.

Well, maybe not, she told herself. *Vic hasn't shared much of anything with me lately. I really wish he would open up and talk to me about his feelings—or anything else, for that matter.*

Eleanor reached over and placed her hand on his knee. "What did you think of the bishop's sermon today?"

"It was okay, I guess."

"I think we all needed the reminder that without faith it's impossible to please God."

Vic kept his gaze on the road ahead.

Eleanor folded her hands in her lap. "I sat next to your mamm during our noon meal today. She didn't say too much, other than that yesterday had been difficult for her. I'm sure it was hard for everyone in your family."

Once again, Vic did not comment.

What is wrong with him? Why won't he talk to me? Eleanor released a heavy sigh. What was the point in trying to communicate with her husband when all he did was sit there not saying a word? She decided to remain quiet for the rest of the way home, but tomorrow, after Vic left for work, Eleanor would definitely make a trip to see the bishop and his wife.

———— ≋ ————

An hour after Vic left for work the next day, Eleanor had hitched her horse to the buggy and was on her way to Michael and Letty Zook's home. She hoped they would be there and have some free time to talk to her about Vic. Eleanor had also written another letter to Doretta this morning, asking for continued prayer. She still had not mentioned anything about Vic's drinking episode, but since he hadn't gotten drunk again and to her knowledge had not indulged in drinking any more alcohol, she'd chosen not to mention it to Doretta. But if Vic had kept drinking, she probably would have felt the need to tell her friend about it, because she trusted Doretta not to say anything to anyone about the things Eleanor wrote in her letters.

Eleanor's thoughts took a new direction when she approached the Zooks' home and guided Buttons up the driveway. Michael was getting up in years and no longer worked at the shoe-and-boot store he owned, so she hoped he might be home.

After securing her horse to the rail, Eleanor climbed down and reached inside the buggy to get the container of cookies she'd brought along.

Letty and Michael lived in the newer addition that Eleanor had been told was added onto their original home a few years ago, for the grandparents to live in. Their son, David, and his wife, Salome, now lived in the big house with their four children. David had taken over the shoe-and-boot store, but on occasion Michael would go there to help out. Their business sat out in front of their home, and coming in today, Eleanor had seen several buggies parked outside, which meant that the shop had customers.

Eleanor wondered how things would be when she and Vic were Letty and Michael's age. Would they have any children to take care of them?

As she made her way up the path to the *daadihaus*, Eleanor stepped around several hens clucking and scratching at the ground.

Maybe I should raise some chickens, she thought. *It would give us fresh eggs, and maybe I could even sell some to the neighbors or other people in our area who might enjoy getting eggs that aren't store bought. I'll talk to Vic about it soon.*

Eleanor stepped onto the porch and knocked on the door. It didn't take long until it opened and Letty greeted her with a welcoming smile. "It's nice to see you, Eleanor. I didn't get the chance to speak to you yesterday after church, so I'm glad you came by." A few strands of gray hair peeked out from under the sides of the elderly woman's kapp, and she pushed them back into place before giving Eleanor a hug. "Please, come inside and take a seat."

"These kichlin are for you." Eleanor handed the container of cookies to Letty.

"Danki, how thoughtful of you." Letty smiled. "Would you care for a cup of tea or some coffee? We could have some of your cookies to go with it."

"Maybe later." Eleanor removed her plain dark-colored jacket and hung it on a wall peg near the front door. "Is Bishop Michael here? I was hoping to speak with him about something important."

"Certainly. He's in one of our guest rooms, which he uses for his study. I'll put the cookies in the kitchen and go get him."

After Letty left the room, Eleanor took a seat in one of the living room chairs. She picked at a hangnail on one of her fingers, feeling a bit nervous all of a sudden. Eleanor hoped that coming here had not been a mistake. What if the bishop or his wife mentioned her visit to any of their family members or someone in their church district? If Vic found out she'd told Michael and Letty about the problems they were facing, he'd be quite upset.

Well, I'm here now, she told herself. *So I may as well state what I came for. I will just kindly ask that the Zooks don't repeat anything I've said or mention to anyone that I came here seeking their advice.*

A few minutes passed before Michael and Letty entered the room. He shook Eleanor's hand and said, "My fraa said you wish to speak with me about something."

Eleanor nodded. "That's true, but only if I'm not interrupting anything and you can spare a few minutes to talk."

"I have plenty of time." He took a seat in a chair across from her.

"If you'd like to speak privately to my husband, I'll wait in the kitchen until you're done." Letty looked at Eleanor, tipping her head to one side a bit.

"No, it's fine if you stay. Maybe the both of you can help me figure out what to do."

"About what?" Michael asked after Letty took a seat on the couch.

"My husband, Vic." Eleanor moistened her lips with the tip of her tongue. "As you may realize, Vic's been quite depressed since the death of his little brother, and he blames himself for the accident." Eleanor swallowed hard, struggling for the right words to continue.

"I am aware of his sadness, and that of the rest of his family too," the bishop said. "But why would Vic blame himself because Eddie drowned?"

Eleanor explained about Vic's promise to teach his brother to swim, and also how neither she nor Vic had watched Eddie close enough that dreadful Saturday in June. "We had no idea, of course, that Vic's brother would wander off to the pond and get in the water without either of us being there with him."

"Children can be very spontaneous sometimes," Letty put in. "Quite often they don't think about whether what they want to do is safe or not."

"That's right," Michael agreed. "Neither you nor your husband can be held accountable for Eddie running off without telling you where he was going." He paused and rested his hands on his right knee. "If the boy did not know how to swim, he was wrong for going into the water without an adult there to supervise."

"While that may be true, it doesn't change the fact that Vic is still grieving and it's affecting everything he says and does."

"Would you like me to talk with him?" Michael questioned.

"I–I'm not sure. You see, I don't want Vic to know that I've spoken to you about this matter. I'm sure he would not like it."

"We will definitely pray for your husband," Letty interjected.

"And perhaps if I ask Vic how he is doing the next time I see him, he will open up and tell me what's on his mind." Michael sat very still for several seconds. "If he does, I won't hold back from sharing my thoughts and some verses from the Bible with him." He glanced at Letty. "And as my wife said, we will be praying for Vic, you, and the whole Lapp family."

"I appreciate that." Eleanor managed to smile as she wiped tears from her eyes. She felt a bit better after sharing her concerns with their bishop and his wife.

"Umm. . .one more thing before I go," she said. "Would you please not mention to anyone that I was here or repeat what I have said to you today? Vic would not appreciate it if he knew I had come seeking your help."

"Don't worry," Michael was quick to say. "Letty and I will not mention this conversation to anyone at all."

Eleanor sagged against the back of her chair, feeling such relief. She felt confident that she'd done the right thing by coming here today. *Now, if Vic will just open up and share his feelings with Bishop Zook the next time they talk, maybe his emotional pain will lessen and our marriage will improve.*

———≋———

Vic arrived home from work early that evening, feeling tired and out of sorts. He let Checkers out of his pen, said a quick hello to Eleanor, and headed straight for the barn. Without bothering to do any chores, Vic quickly climbed the ladder to the loft, pulled out the cardboard box he'd hidden, and took out two beers. *I'll need to get more of this stuff before I run out,* he told himself after he'd consumed the lukewarm liquid in the first can. *After a couple of beers I feel like I can cope. I just need to make sure I don't drink too many and end up getting drunk again. And I don't dare let Eleanor get a whiff of my breath.* Vic figured the smart thing to do was to keep a safe distance from his wife. It was the best way to be sure she wouldn't catch on to the fact that he'd been drinking.

He drank the second can of beer and reclined in the straw with his eyes closed. *I wonder if what my dad said yesterday is true, about Eddie being in heaven. Is he better off there than here? Has he forgiven me for not teaching him how to swim?*

So many confusing thoughts swirled through Vic's head. If only he had some answers.

Chapter 21

Grabill

"When I went to the mailbox this morning, I found a letter for you from Eleanor," Doretta's mother said soon after Doretta arrived home from teaching school.

Doretta smiled. "Oh good. I haven't heard from my dear friend in a while, and I've been wondering how she is doing."

Mom went to the desk where she kept the mail and handed Doretta the envelope. "It's always nice to receive mail from a good friend or family member."

"Jah." Doretta turned the envelope over and grinned when she noticed that Eleanor had used one of her rubber stamps to put a rose on the back flap. Stamping was a fun hobby, and Eleanor was good at making beautiful cards and decorating notepaper. "I think I'll take this to my room to read after I change out of my teaching dress. Then I'll come back downstairs and help you start supper."

"No hurry," Mom replied. "In case you weren't listening, your daed said this morning that he might be working later than usual this evening, so supper might not be at the same time as we normally would have it."

"I didn't hear him mention that. Guess I must have been thinking about something else while we ate breakfast."

There was a glimmer in Mom's eyes as she gave Doretta's shoulder a pat. "I have a pretty good idea who you were thinking about too."

Doretta's cheeks warmed. "Guess there's no point in denying it. I was thinking about William."

"Has he asked you to marry him yet? You've certainly been going steady long enough."

Doretta's gaze lowered as she shook her head. "I'm beginning to think he may never ask."

"If he doesn't, are you prepared to move on if some other nice fellow comes along and takes an interest in you?"

Doretta's head came up, and the heat in her cheeks deepened. "I'm in love with William, and I can't imagine spending the rest of my life with anyone else." She didn't understand why her mother felt it necessary to discuss this topic. Was it out of concern or something else?

"How does he feel about you?" Mom questioned. "Has William declared his love too?"

"Jah, he has."

"Maybe you should bring up the topic of marriage."

Doretta gasped, shaking her head vigorously. "Oh no, I could never do such a thing. It would be too bold and embarrassing. It might even scare William away." She hoped her mother would drop the questions about William and move on to a different topic.

"Should I ask your father to have a talk with your boyfriend—find out what his intentions are toward you?"

Doretta's arm muscles quivered as she made flighty hand movements. "Please don't do that. It would be humiliating, and William might think that I put Dad up to it."

Mom slipped her arm around Doretta's waist. "Now don't look so worried. I wouldn't ask your daed to speak to William unless you wanted him to."

"Well, I don't. If William wants to marry me, then he will ask in his own good time." She held up Eleanor's letter. "That's enough talk about me and my boyfriend now. It's time for me to go read my friend's letter."

Clutching the envelope in one hand, Doretta hurried up the stairs and into her room. At least her mother had promised not to ask Dad to speak to William about a proposal of marriage.

Doretta tore open the letter and read it silently. When she finished, she set it aside and bowed her head. *Dear Lord, please give my friend Eleanor a sense of peace today. Guide and direct her in knowing how to help Vic through his struggles, and show her how to be the kind of wife her husband needs. Don't allow their marriage to suffer because of Vic's guilt and grief. Instead, please strengthen their relationship and let Vic and Eleanor both feel Your presence every day.*

When Doretta opened her eyes, a new realization hit her. The frustration and concern she felt because William had not asked her to marry him was nothing compared to what Eleanor and Vic had been dealing with. Her vision blurred, and she blinked to keep tears from spilling over. *I need to be patient and realize that if it's God's will for me to marry William, he will propose at the right time. If not, then maybe it's not meant for us to spend the rest of our lives together as husband and wife.*

———— ≈ ————

Lancaster

Vic put his tool belt and lunch box on the floor in the back seat of Tom's truck and closed the door. "Sure am glad to have this workday over," he said after climbing into the front of the vehicle.

Tom nodded with a groan. "Yeah, it was a tough one all right, and I'm glad to be heading home. It was kind of hard to keep a good attitude today when the owners of the new house we're building kept asking to make changes."

"You're right, and there were a lot of them." Vic stretched both arms over his head. "You know what I could use right now?"

"A vacation?"

"I'd like to stop somewhere so we can have a few beers." Vic lowered his arms and exhaled the deep breath he'd taken in. "Guess a vacation wouldn't hurt either."

Tom's eyes widened, and he blinked a few times, as if trying to process what Vic had said. "Are you serious?"

Vic gave a decisive nod. "I need something to help me relax, and after the way things went today, I'm sure you do too."

"Correct me if I'm wrong, but I thought you were opposed to me drinking while driving."

"I—I was, and I still am, but if you don't have more than two drinks, you'll probably be okay to drive. You didn't have a problem the last time you did it, remember?"

"Yeah, and I've done it plenty of times when you haven't been with me." Tom glanced over at Vic briefly. "Where do you want to stop for the beers?"

Vic shrugged. "Beats me. I figured you'd probably know some of the good taverns and pubs in Lancaster."

"I admit, I've been to a few. Molly's Pub on East Chestnut Street is good, and so is the Lancaster Brewing Company on North Plum Street. Either of them would probably be fine, but I know a bit more about the Brewing Company, since I've been there more often."

"What do you know about it?"

"I read on the internet that they have an obsessive commitment to quality ingredients with skill and experience to brew great ales and lagers."

"Okay, that sounds impressive." Vic smacked his lips in anticipation. "Let's go there and see if they live up to their commitment and skill."

"I'm on it." Tom turned his right blinker on at the next corner.

***

Paradise

Two hours later, when Tom stopped his truck at the entrance of Vic's driveway, Vic turned to him and said, "Thanks for stopping off for the beers, and for the lift home again. They had some pretty good beer, and I wouldn't mind going there again sometime."

"Sure, no problem. Oh, and if you'll let me know when you need some more beer to have here, I'll pick some up for you."

"Sure, but I'll have to be careful bringing it in so my wife doesn't see it." Tom's brows nearly squished together. "She doesn't know you've been drinking?"

Vic shook his head. "Not since the night I came home drunk. The next morning I promised Eleanor that I wouldn't drink again, so I've been keeping the beer you got for me in the barn, up in the hayloft."

"Friend, if you're not careful, you might end up like me."

"In what way?"

"Wifeless."

"That'll never happen," Vic stated firmly. "Eleanor loves me, and getting a divorce is not an acceptable option among the Amish. Although," he added with a frown, "there have been a few Amish I know of who left the church and decided to divorce their spouse."

"Do you think your wife would ever leave the church and put a permanent end to your marriage?"

"No way, and I don't plan on leaving or getting a divorce either." Vic stepped down from the truck and took his tool belt and lunch box from the back. "I'll see you tomorrow morning."

"Sure thing." As soon as Vic shut the truck door, Tom took off down the road. Vic began to walk toward the mailbox, thinking how nice it had been at the pub. At least he hadn't noticed any familiar faces coming in or going out. He wasn't sure, however, with him being Amish, if it may have left a lasting negative impression on the bartender who worked there. It wasn't a normal sight to see a Plain person out in public drinking beers. *Maybe I'm overthinking this,* Vic told himself.

Vic checked the mailbox but found nothing. He assumed Eleanor must have gotten the mail already. Pausing before heading up the driveway, he reached into his pocket for a package of gum but found none.

"This is not good," he mumbled. *I must have forgotten to put some mint-flavored gum in my pocket this morning before leaving for work. I'll need to make sure not to get close to Eleanor, or she'll be able to smell my breath and know that I've been drinking._*

———— ≈ ————

Paradise

Eleanor felt relieved when she heard the rumble of Tom's truck outside. Vic was later than usual this evening, and she always worried when he didn't get home on time. Accidents could happen at any time, but even more so during the after-work traffic, when people were in a hurry to get home.

Eleanor watched from the front room window as her husband exited the vehicle. He'd headed right to the mailbox. Normally, she was the one who would go for their mail each day, and it seemed a little odd for him to do it.

As usual, their supper was in the oven, keeping warm. Tonight Eleanor had made a tangy meatloaf and baked potatoes, so she was eager to say hello to Vic and put their meal on the table.

Eleanor went to the front door and opened it to greet her husband. Checkers was by her side, tail wagging and poised to greet his favorite human.

When Vic came up the steps carrying his tool belt and lunch box, Eleanor stepped out onto the porch. "I'm glad you're home." She opened her arms for a hug, but he breezed right past with his head turned away from her. She followed him into the house, and Checkers, who had come back in also, began nipping at Vic's boot laces.

"Knock it off!" Vic shooed the dog away and then set his stuff on the floor.

"Vic, I was hoping for a hug and a kiss." Eleanor moved toward him again and was disappointed when he took a few steps back. "What's wrong, Vic? Why are you pulling away from me? Aren't you glad to be home?"

"Sure, I just. . ." He dropped his gaze to the floor.

"You just what?" Eleanor slipped her arms around his waist and went up on tiptoes to kiss his cheek. It was then that she detected a sickening aroma—she remembered it well from the night Tom had brought her husband home, too drunk to stand on his own. She sniffed deeply and frowned. "Have you been drinking, Vic?"

"No, I...uh... You see, Tom had a beer after work, and he spilled some. I think a little of it may have gotten on my clothes."

Her jaw clenched. "The odor I smell is coming from your breath, not your clothes."

Vic averted his gaze, and Eleanor noticed that a film of perspiration had quickly formed on his forehead. "I'd appreciate it if you were truthful with me, Vic."

He stood with his arms folded, staring at the floor. "Okay, I admit it—Tom and I stopped at a place in Lancaster for a couple of beers." He looked up at her with a somber expression. "Don't look so worried. It's no big deal. I am not drunk, and I don't see anything wrong with having a few beers now and then to help steady my nerves."

Before she could form a response, Vic rushed on. "Tom and I had a rough day at work, and we both needed to relax, but I'm not going to make a habit of it, so you have nothing to worry about." He bent down and scratched his dog behind the ears. "Right now, I'm going to go take a shower and change into clean clothes. When I come out, will supper be ready?"

"It's ready and waiting to be served. And Vic, I am not happy with the way you're making light of this. You said you were not going to drink alcohol again."

Scrambling for the right words, he turned to face her. "I'm sorry, Eleanor. I hope you will forgive me."

"I'll forgive you, but I hope you will not do it again."

"I won't. So can supper wait till I get my shower?" Vic asked, in need of a topic change.

"Jah, we'll eat when you're done." Eleanor gestured to the stove. "It's keeping warm in the oven and has been for a couple of hours."

"Great. I'll be back soon and we can eat."

Vic disappeared down the hall, and Eleanor retreated to the kitchen. She saw Checkers lying by the table and felt the need to reach down and pet him. While doing this, the dog looked up at her with his soft brown eyes. It felt as though Vic's dog could almost feel her pain. Eleanor spoke in a whisper: "I don't want to feel sad, but it's hard not to with everything that's been happening around here." Her throat hurt so badly from holding back tears that she could hardly swallow.

Eleanor moved away from the dog and went to the refrigerator to get out the iced tea. After pouring some into her husband's glass, she filled her glass too. Eleanor took a long drink, and the coolness soothed the discomfort in her throat. She had begun to wonder if her husband was even capable of keeping his promises. If he continued to drink, would he deny it again, or would Vic be honest with her?

Chapter 22

Three weeks had gone by, and even though Eleanor had not smelled beer on Vic's breath during that time, she had a feeling he was not being honest with her when he said that he'd had no beer to drink since that last time. Sometimes he appeared to be calm, relaxed, and more talkative than usual. At other times, however, Vic appeared sulky and seemed jittery and unresponsive if Eleanor tried to make conversation. She didn't want to keep asking if he'd been drinking, but she couldn't help worrying about him, as well as their strained marriage. What if Vic never snapped out of his depression? How could they have a happy life together?

Eleanor picked up the canning jars she'd placed on the kitchen counter and put them in a cardboard box. She had finished all her canning for the season, and several empty jars were left over, so it was time to put those away.

After hanging the handle of a battery-operated lantern over her wrist to guide the way, Eleanor hoisted the box and went carefully down the creaky wooden stairs. When she reached the bottom and her bare feet touched the cold, hard cement floor, Eleanor wished she'd had the good sense to put on a pair of shoes or bedroom slippers before coming down to the basement. Around the house, Eleanor often went barefoot and had since she was a child. She enjoyed the freedom of not wearing shoes, although she guessed it wasn't very practical at times.

Eleanor made her way over to an old wooden table and placed the lantern and box on it. Between the light spilling into the room through the basement windows, plus the glow of the lantern, she could see fairly well.

The shelves in the cellar had been lined with jars full of a variety of produce from her bountiful garden. Although it seemed like a lot of food, the jars would quickly empty over the winter months, especially if they had visitors for any meals. No doubt they would have some company during the upcoming holidays. At least Eleanor hoped so, because it would be nice to share some meals with other people who would be full of good conversation, not sullen like Vic.

Thinking about the holidays caused Eleanor to frown as she picked up the first two jars and placed them upside down on one of the empty shelves. *What if my folks want to come here for Thanksgiving or Christmas? It would not be good for them to see how Vic has been acting, and I'm sure they would catch on to the fact that things aren't going well in our marriage.* She pursed her lips. *Maybe having people over to our home isn't a good idea right now, no matter who they are. I'm actually glad Doretta didn't come for a visit after Eddie died. She can be kind of assertive at times and may have said something to Vic about his attitude toward me.*

Vic's affections toward Eleanor weren't what they used to be before the accident that took his brother's life. He still kept his distance, which hurt her feelings. Eleanor often found herself tearing up whenever he ignored her or treated her unkindly. It was frustrating to do kind things for him, like making his favorite foods, keeping the house neat and clean, giving him space to relax, and pitching in to help whenever he needed her to, only to have him unappreciative of her efforts. It was hard to keep praying about the situation and seeing no results. *I wish someone who had been through a similar situation could tell me what to do. I suppose the best thing for me to do at this point is not to give up praying and never lose hope.*

Eleanor grabbed two more jars and set them in place. *If we went to Grabill for Thanksgiving or Christmas, it's doubtful we could hide the way things are between us.*

She stared across the room at her wringer washing machine, which was not in use at the moment, and continued to ponder the situation. *I wish we could go somewhere for the holidays that's far from here and where nobody knows us. Then we wouldn't have to deal with any of this for a while, and maybe that would help. Taking a vacation can often help a person relax, and Vic and I both could surely use a little relaxation.* Eleanor released a deep sigh. *I guess that's not likely to happen. Knowing Vic, he will say he's too busy to go anywhere. But if we stay here for the holidays and have any company, most likely he won't be very sociable. Staying home by ourselves would be even worse, because Vic would probably avoid me as much as possible by hiding out in our room or going to the barn. He'll let Thanksgiving and Christmas go by without any celebration on his part at all.*

She glanced at the box of jars again. *I'd better stop feeling sorry for myself and finish this job. When I go back upstairs, I'll put on some shoes and a jacket, then get out to the barn and check on the gray-and-white cat whose kittens should be born almost any day.*

After Eleanor put on her warm outer garments, she left the house and headed for the barn. On the way, she paused to look at the half-built chicken coop Vic had started two weeks ago and never finished. After she'd asked him if he would mind if she raised some chickens, he'd said, "If that's what you want to do, I have no objections." Vic had even said he would build the coop, but of course he hadn't followed through with that, so they hadn't bought any chickens.

"It's nothing new," Eleanor muttered as Checkers raced alongside her. "Vic rarely follows through with anything anymore. There's probably no point in bringing up the idea of raising chickens again." With the weather turning colder, Eleanor was aware that it would be more of a challenge to keep baby chicks alive. If, by some chance, Vic finished the coop and she got some chickens at this late date, they would have to be fully grown.

Maybe I'll wait till spring to bring the topic up again, she thought. *Hopefully by then Vic will feel better and might be more willing to finish the chicken house project.*

Eleanor put the dog in his pen and moved on toward the barn. When she entered the building through the tall double doors, she heard the horses' huffing breaths and the swish of their tails coming from the stalls. "I'll be there shortly, Buttons," she called. "I know you and Domino want to be let out of your stalls so you can roam free in the pasture."

Before tending the horses, Eleanor decided to take a quick peek inside the cat's box she had fixed up last evening. It would only take a few minutes to see if the kittens had been born.

Eleanor hurried across the room and was surprised when she looked into the box and saw no sign of the gray-and-white cat. From the looks of the undisturbed bedding she'd placed inside the box, it didn't appear that the cat had slept in there at all. After Eleanor had made up the birthing box for the mother-to-be, the cat had seemed kind of restless. Eleanor was sure it wouldn't be long till the kittens were born, and she looked forward to the pleasure of seeing them.

I wonder where that cat went. Sure hope she didn't leave the barn and find someplace outside to have her babies. It's too cold out there for that.

Eleanor moved toward the horses' stalls but halted when she reached the ladder leading to the hayloft and heard a distinctive meow coming from above. She looked up. *I bet the cat didn't like the box and went up there to make her own birthing bed.*

Curious to know if she was right, Eleanor climbed the ladder. At the top, she stood quietly and listened. *Meow. Meow.* There it was again. Crunching through the prickly straw, Eleanor followed the sound until she came to the place where the mama cat and four adorable kittens lay. "Oh, they're so cute.

You did good, little mama." Eleanor resisted the urge to pick up one of the wee felines because she didn't want to upset their mother. There would be plenty of time to hold and pet the kittens when they were a few days older. She was glad the cat had found a safe place to give birth to her babies.

Eleanor was about to go back down the ladder when a section of what looked like a cardboard box, sticking partway out of the hay, caught her eye. Wondering what might be inside, she went to investigate.

Sure enough, it was a cardboard box, and when Eleanor pulled the flaps aside, she gasped. The box was filled with beer cans. Many were empty, but some had not been opened.

Heat rushed through her body. *No wonder Vic has been coming out to the barn so often. He's been up here drinking, and this is his hiding spot.* With a sinking feeling in the pit of her stomach, Eleanor slowly shook her head. She'd had an inkling that Vic had been lying to her, and now she knew for sure. Eleanor picked up one of the cans. *I wonder what he's going to say about this when he gets home this evening and I show him what I found.*

———— ≈ ————

Vic stepped onto the porch that evening and was greeted by Checkers with a few loud barks and several wags of his tail. "Hey, buddy, just give me a sec, okay? I just got home and I'd like to wash up." Vic opened the front door. "Just stay outside and have a good romp. I'll be back to throw your stick soon."

After Checkers ran into the yard, Vic shut the door and headed for the kitchen, wondering why there were no delicious smells floating from that room this evening. When Vic entered, he saw Eleanor facing him with her hands behind her back. "I see you finally made it home." Her lips flattened. "Did you and Tom stop somewhere for a few beers, or were you waiting till you got home to drink your hidden stash?"

"Wh–what do you mean?" Vic's voice cracked, and he lowered his gaze, unable to look her in the eye.

"Please, look at me, Vic. This is what I mean."

He forced himself to lift his head and flinched when he saw the can of beer Eleanor held, as she brought her hands out from behind her back. "Where'd you get that?" He could barely get the words out.

"I found it in your secret hiding place in the barn."

Vic grimaced and bit down on his bottom lip until he tasted blood. "What do you have to say about this?"

"What were you doing being all *schnuppich* up there in the hayloft?"

Eleanor's eyebrows shot up. "You want to talk about who's being snoopy? You hid the truth and have been drinking again, even though you said you would stop." She planted her free hand against her hips. "And for your information, I wasn't being all snoopy. I heard a meow and went up to see if the gray-and-white cat had found a place to have her babies." Eleanor set the can of beer on the table. "I not only found the *katz* and her *busslin*, but I discovered a box full of beer cans—some full like this one and some empty."

Vic cleared his throat a few times. "Okay, I believe that you weren't being snoopy, but let me explain—"

"You're obviously addicted to this stuff and apparently need it more than you do me." She gestured to the can of beer.

Vic felt an uncomfortable tightness in his chest as his thoughts filled with self-loathing. In addition to living with being the cause of his brother's death, he'd been hiding the truth about his drinking from Eleanor, and now he felt guiltier than before. He couldn't deny it—she'd seen the proof—and now Vic had to find a way to make it up to her. So far the stupid things he had chosen to do had only made things worse.

If the tension continued mounting between him and Eleanor, soon there would be no more trust. Vic wasn't listening to any good advice from his folks or even his wife. It was easier for him to go off alone and brood in the barn. He didn't make any quality time for the Lord in his life or for his wife and members of his family. They seemed to only get the crumbs from Vic these days. But he had no problem taking care of his need to drink alcohol to help calm his nerves. It was all about number one—himself—and he felt like a selfish brat.

"Eleanor, I am truly sorry."

She placed both hands over her face and sobbed. "Am I not enough for you, Vic? Is that the problem?"

Vic couldn't believe what he had just heard. *Look what my lies and selfish ways have done to the woman I love.*

He pulled Eleanor gently into his arms and patted her back, not even caring that his breath most likely smelled like beer, even with the gum he'd chewed on the ride home in Tom's truck. She'd found him out anyway, so he no longer had anything to hide. "You are everything I need, Eleanor." He blinked against the hot tears pushing the back of his eyes. "Please don't ever leave me. I couldn't make it without you."

She sniffed deeply and remained in his embrace. "I am not going to leave you, Vic, but things have to change. You can't go on trying to drown the pain of losing Eddie by getting drunk or even drinking until you're relaxed enough to squelch the pain."

"I know. It's just that being here, where I see my family all the time, is a constant reminder that my little brother is gone. If we could get out of here for a while, maybe I'd feel better and wouldn't need to drink."

She moved closer again and looked up at him with a hopeful expression. "Would it be possible for us to make a trip someplace where it's warm, like Florida? Maybe we could go there for a couple of weeks and be gone for Thanksgiving. I was thinking about that idea this morning and wishing it could just be the two of us, without spending the holiday with either of our families."

"That does sound nice." He clasped her cold hands and gave them a gentle squeeze. "I have some vacation days coming, so I'll talk to my boss about it tomorrow. If he says I can take a few weeks off, we can make our plans, start packing, and see if my folks will keep Checkers for us while we're gone."

She pressed a palm against her chest as a faint smile formed on her inviting lips. They were lips Vic wanted desperately to kiss, but he couldn't do it right now—not with beer on his breath. So instead, he wrapped his arms around Eleanor and held her close. He hoped that his boss would be okay with him being gone for a couple of weeks. He also hoped that his craving for alcohol would not go with him on their vacation. He somehow needed to break free from his apparent need for the intoxicating stuff.

Chapter 23

Sarasota, Florida

Eleanor sniffed deeply of the sea air and smiled while listening to and watching the crash of waves as they swept ashore. She had not been to the beach since she was a teenager and had come with a group of her friends. Doretta had been among them, as well as two other young women. They'd stayed in the village of Pinecraft, at a home owned by Doretta's paternal grandparents. The elderly couple had bought the place to rent out when they weren't there on vacation themselves. Staying in Pinecraft, where so many other Amish folks were, had been fine back then. But Eleanor was glad she and Vic had been able to rent a small cottage within walking distance of Lido Beach. They'd tried to get something right on the beach, but those places were either too expensive or had already been rented. Well, it didn't matter. Eleanor was glad to be here, away from the stresses of home and where the weather was nice and warm. It didn't even bother her that they would be alone to celebrate Thanksgiving in a few days. In fact, she looked forward to it being just the two of them.

She glanced over at her husband, busy putting up the colorful red-and-blue beach umbrella they'd found at the cottage for guests to use. They'd only been here one day, but already Vic seemed more relaxed.

Last night, after Eleanor had finished writing a postcard to her parents, as well as one to Doretta, she and Vic had eaten a delicious meal at a little café in St. Armands Circle. Following that, they'd taken a walk out to the beach. It had almost seemed magical as they'd sat on a blanket, holding hands, while viewing a most glorious sunset that had turned the sky a vivid gold. Vic had whispered sweet words of love against her ear and made promises she hoped he would be able to keep. Eleanor also hoped that when they returned to Pennsylvania in two weeks the memories they'd make here would go with them, and Vic would feel no need to drink away his pain.

"Okay, we're all set. The umbrella is up and our beach chairs are in place. We can get some vitamin D from the sunshine now." Vic's deep voice drove Eleanor's thoughts aside.

"Not too much, though." Eleanor reached into the wicker basket she'd brought along and pulled out a tube of sunscreen. She smiled as he flopped into one of the chairs and gestured for her to take the other one.

"Ah, this is the life." Vic grinned over at her as he lathered some sunscreen on his arms, face, and lower legs. "I could get used to lounging around like this. Couldn't you?"

She nodded and seated herself. After pushing up her dress sleeves and pulling her skirt a little above her knees, she put plenty of sunscreen on too. She wiped off her hands on a towel she had in the bag and retied the lightweight scarf that covered her hair. She didn't want to mess with her stiff prayer kapp while on the beach. It was nice to enjoy the relaxing rays of the sun and have quality time with Vic. Even though a good many people were at Lido Beach today, it was still a nice place to unwind and relax.

As Eleanor lay back in her chair, she could smell food in the air. Since there was a snack bar not far from where they sat, she assumed that the pleasant odors were coming from there. Eleanor wondered if she'd find very many shells on this beach. It would be nice to bring home some pretty ones. She could display them on a shelf and have them to remember this trip to Florida. Once children came, the trips they'd be taking would probably be fewer and closer to home. Eleanor imagined them going camping to some popular places that the Amish often visited. When she was growing up, her family went on camping trips a few times each year. Her parents often chose a beautiful place where the family could soak up the views and enjoy seeing wildlife.

She paused her thinking and swatted at a pesky bug, then let out a long sigh. *Those were some good days, but I'm glad Vic and I are here now, creating new memories to share.* Eleanor turned her face more toward the sun, eager to get nice, sun-kissed coloring to replace her pale skin tone.

They remained like that for a while, until Vic said they should walk out to the water and get their feet wet.

Eleanor didn't have to be asked twice. "That's a great idea." She got off her chair and grabbed a plastic bag from the picnic basket with a small cooler inside.

"What's the bag for?" Vic asked.

"Shells. I'm sure we'll find some on the shoreline, where the water's coming in, and maybe on the dryer part of the sand as well."

"Okay." He glanced around. "You think our stuff will be okay here while we're gone?"

"I'm sure it'll be fine." Eleanor gestured to all the other giant umbrellas, beach chairs, and colorful towels that had been laid out on the sand. "No one else seems to be worried about their belongings when they go running off to get in the water."

"Guess you're right, so let's go see what treasures we can find." Vic took hold of Eleanor's hand and gave her fingers a tender squeeze.

Joyful tears sprang to her eyes. It was a delight to see her husband looking so happy and sounding so positive. This was the man she'd fallen in love with and had agreed to marry. Was it possible that Vic would remain this cheerful and calm when they returned to Pennsylvania? Eleanor hoped and prayed for that. Maybe this getaway was all her husband needed to release the tension he'd felt for so many months.

As they walked toward the surf, the soft, white sand sifted between Eleanor's bare toes. It felt good to be without shoes in such a warm, tropical place. Others on the beach must have thought so too, for many of them were barefoot.

Eleanor shielded her eyes from the glare of the sun when a plane flew overhead with an advertising banner. Her gaze flitted to two young children tossing a striped beach ball to each other in the shallow, frothy water. It looked like fun as the young kids smiled, continuing to play. The shrill sounds of their happy voices couldn't be missed. A breeze blew in off the gulf, but it wasn't cold at all. The sun was intense, and she wondered how long they should remain under its warm rays. At least they had their beach umbrella set up, and Eleanor could easily set her chair under the shade it provided.

As they walked farther, Vic spoke in Pennsylvania Dutch. "You look pretty, Eleanor."

"Danki." She smiled back at him.

A gust of wind tugged at the skirt of her dress, but she held it in place as they hurried along. A trickle of sweat ran down her forehead and nose, but Eleanor didn't mind one bit. This was all a part of being on the beach, and she loved every minute of it.

Vic rolled his pant legs up past his knees and waded into the water. It felt surprisingly warm. Not cold like their pond at home. He squeezed his eyes shut as an image of Eddie lying facedown in the water flashed into his mind. *Don't think about it,* Vic told himself. *I'm in sunny Sarasota with my beautiful wife, and I need to keep my concentration on what we're doing now.*

He opened his eyes, paused, and drew in a few deep, calming breaths. The truth was, being here on the beach had caused Vic to feel more relaxed than he had in a long while. This was much better than the temporary stress release he'd gotten from drinking a few beers. The euphoric feeling made him wish that he and Eleanor could stay right here and never go home. *But it's just wishful thinking,* he reminded himself. *The man we hired to bring us to Florida will be driving us back to Pennsylvania in two weeks, so I am determined to make every minute count while Eleanor and I are on vacation. I want this to be a special trip that we'll always remember. And hopefully, by the time we get home, I'll have no desire to drink beer or any other alcoholic beverage.*

Vic turned his head to the left and spotted Eleanor on her knees in the sand. One by one, she dropped pretty shells into her plastic bag. He smiled. *I wish we would have come here sooner.*

He knelt next to her, not caring in the least that he now had sand stuck to his knees. "Looks like you've gotten quite a collection of shells already."

She turned her head toward him and smiled. "Jah, and this is so much fun. I think I can use some of the little ones I've found to decorate greeting cards that I'll be stamping after we go home."

Vic found a shell in the sand. "How about this one?"

"That's nice. It looks like a corkscrew." She held the bag closer to him.

He put his shell in and found another one right away. "This same corkscrew shell is bigger than the previous one I found. Let's keep it too." Vic placed the pretty shell inside the bag. "I have to admit, it is fun looking for different kinds of *seeschdal* on the beach. There seems to be an endless supply of them."

Eleanor flashed him another heart-melting smile. He wished he could take his lovely wife in his arms right now and kiss her soundly, but that would have to wait until they were away from the crowd of people and had returned to their rented cottage.

As a young English couple walked by holding hands, Vic nuzzled Eleanor's neck with the tip of his nose. He did wonder if the couple walking past or anyone else who might be nearby could be watching them. It wasn't the norm for a married Amish couple to show affection in public. But in this quick moment, Vic didn't care what anyone else might think or what was normal or not. Today he felt like he and Eleanor were on a date and didn't have a single care in the world.

When Eleanor had done enough shelling and Vic said he was hungry, they returned to their beach chairs. The umbrella was still in place, despite the wind, and so was their picnic basket. Vic pulled the chairs under the umbrella for shade. Eleanor was glad they had put the basket under the umbrella before going down to the water, because it had become quite hot over the last few hours. Even with the cooler inside the basket, the heat of the day might have melted some of the ice she'd put in before leaving their rental this morning.

"I'm glad we remembered to put sunscreen on." Eleanor opened the picnic basket and reached into the small cooler bag inside. "Otherwise, we'd probably both be red as lobsters," she added after handing Vic a bottle of cold water, along with a ham and cheese sandwich.

He pointed to his bare legs. "I think the sunscreen got washed off while I was in the water."

Eleanor grimaced when she saw how pink her husband's legs had gotten. "I guess the sunscreen I bought wasn't the waterproof kind. I'll give you some aloe vera gel to put on your legs after we get back to the cottage. In the meantime, you might want to pull your pant legs down so you don't get any more direct sunlight on them."

"You're right about that." Vic placed the water bottle and sandwich in his lap and bent over to do as Eleanor had suggested. "My arms are often exposed to the sun when I'm working outside, at home or on the job, but I don't usually go around with my pant legs pulled up." He chuckled. "Now wouldn't that look schpassich?"

"Jah, it would look rather funny." Eleanor smiled. It was good to see her husband in such a pleasant mood. Even with sunburned legs he'd managed to keep a positive attitude. "Guess we'd better pray before we eat our lunch," she said.

Vic nodded, bowed his head, and closed his eyes. Eleanor did the same. Her prayer was one of praise—thanking God not only for the food they were about to eat but for allowing them to have this special time together. She ended her prayer by asking God to continue healing her husband's emotional wounds so that he wouldn't be tempted to start drinking again once they got back to their home in Paradise.

Eleanor took her sandwich from the cellophane wrap. While savoring the taste of ham, cheese, and mayonnaise, she watched the seagulls screeching and swooping overhead. Every gull on the beach seemed to know when someone had dropped a piece of food, for they converged within seconds of it landing in the sand. A young girl sitting with her parents under their umbrella nearby began to cry when a hungry bird swooped too close, nearly snatching a cracker from her hand. The girl's father shooed the seagull away, and his daughter's crying stopped as suddenly as it had begun.

"Oh yuck!" Vic's nose wrinkled.

"What's wrong?"

"I just crunched down on some gritty sand that must have blown into my sandwich."

She couldn't help but laugh. "Guess that's what happens when a person chooses to eat a meal while sitting on the beach."

"Yeah, you're right. Just didn't think it would happen to me."

She rolled her eyes and giggled. "Drink some water. I'm sure it will push the gritty sand right down."

"You won't think it's so funny if you end up with some sand in your sandwich." Vic reached over with a feather he'd just found and tickled Eleanor under her chin. "There, now you have something to laugh about."

She pushed Vic's hand away and gave his arm a gentle poke. "You don't play fair."

"You're right—not when it comes to teasing my beautiful fraa." He pulled the feather across the back of her neck. "There. How's that make you feel?"

She feigned a frown. "You gave me goose bumps, even though we are sitting here in what feels like at least eighty-some-degree weather."

"Good. Then this should help you cool off." Vic tickled Eleanor behind the ear and slid the tip of the feather slowly up and down her arm.

She reached over and tousled his thick brown hair. "If you keep teasing me like that, you might end up sleeping on the couch tonight."

Vic quickly pulled the feather aside. "No, please. I surrender, and I promise to be good. At least for now, anyways," he added with a wink.

All Eleanor could do was shake her head and smile. What a blessing it was to see this playful side of Vic again. Although it was too soon to tell for sure, at this moment, Eleanor felt more hopeful than ever that things would be better for them during, and even after, their vacation was over. Vic had already changed so much since they'd left home. Surely he would not sink back into depression.

Chapter 24

Strasburg

"It's too bad Eleanor and Vic couldn't be with us for this Thanksgiving meal," Ethan said after he'd taken a second helping of turkey and passed the platter to Stephen. "I miss them." He gestured to the array of food spread out on the table. "And they don't know what they're missing by not being here today."

"I miss them also, but those two are exactly where they need to be." Susie picked up the napkin by her plate and blotted her lips. "If the weather is good in Sarasota, they'll probably return home with some nice tans and maybe a few shells from the beach."

"You're most likely right. I hope the kids have a real good time on their getaway." He smiled at Susie, gave her an approving nod, and looked at the crowded table laden with food still left to eat. "You really outdid yourself on this meal. Everything smells and tastes *appeditlich.*"

"I'm glad you think the food is delicious, but I can't take all of the credit for it." Susie motioned to her daughters, seated on her side of the table. "Kate and Clara helped me cook the meal, and I couldn't have done it without them."

"Danki, Mom." The sisters' cheeks reddened as they spoke in unison.

"And if you think that this meal is good, just wait till we bring the pies out for dessert," Clara said. "We have pumpkin, apple, and chocolate chip pie—Vic's favorite."

"I am eager to try a small slice of each kind, and my thanks goes out to all three of you for spending long hours in the kitchen to make such a nice meal that we won't likely forget." Ethan nudged Stephen's arm. "What do you have to say to your mamm and *schweschder*?"

"Danki, Mom, Clara and Kate." Stephen spoke around a mouthful of sweet potatoes.

Susie was tempted to scold her son for talking with his mouth full but decided to let it go. She wanted this day to be as pleasant as possible. Susie's gaze came to rest on the empty chair where Eddie used to sit. She blinked rapidly and swallowed hard, hoping tears wouldn't follow. Susie still missed her son terribly and felt sure that the rest of the family did too. But special occasions still came and went regardless of a death in the family. They had to get through each holiday without giving in to despair.

Susie hoped that Victor and Eleanor were having a nice Thanksgiving and that their time in the Florida sunshine was doing them both some good. Hopefully when they returned home, Victor would be feeling better emotionally and could finally say that he'd come to realize he wasn't to blame for his little brother's death. *Eddie should not have gone to the pond by himself that day,* she told herself. *Even so, as our bishop stated after he'd been told the sad news, "It may have been Eddie's time to die."* That was a hard pill to swallow, but the truth was everyone at some point would face death. Susie just hadn't expected her youngest child would be called away so soon.

Sarasota

"Well, it isn't a big turkey, but this game hen you fixed for our Thanksgiving meal is sure tasty."

Eleanor smiled from across the small table where they sat on the sunny lanai at the back of the cottage. "I'm glad you like it. With it being just the two of us, I didn't see the point in fixing a large turkey, because we'd probably never eat all the leftovers."

"That's true, especially when we've been going out for some of our meals." Vic reached for his glass of iced tea and took a drink. "Sure is different being here, just the two of us, instead of spending the holiday with a house full of relatives."

Eleanor nodded, and then she helped herself to more mashed potatoes. "I kind of like having you all to myself. Of course," she quickly added, "I enjoy spending time with our families too."

Vic didn't respond to Eleanor's statement. He kept his gaze on his plate of food. Eleanor figured he might be thinking about Eddie and felt sad, so she decided to change the subject.

While thinking of something to say, she hoped that this trip would bring out Vic's old self completely, and that he wouldn't grow quiet again once they returned home. For Vic's sake, Eleanor would try to stay positive during this vacation, because there were moments like now when she wondered what negative thoughts may have crossed her husband's mind. Some flashes from the past invaded her own thoughts. Those days of feeling miserable with him sulking around their house and barely speaking to her had been unbearable.

With a shake of her head, Eleanor dismissed her own negative thoughts. She would continue to lift Vic up in prayer and always try to aim for a positive topic. "Is there anything special you'd like to do with the rest of our day?" she asked.

He shrugged his broad, suntanned shoulders. "Whatever you want to do is fine by me. I've enjoyed everything we've done so far, especially our bike rides and walks to the beach."

"Same here," she agreed. "We still have a week left before it's time to go home, so I think we should make every day count."

Vic's eyes brightened. "I agree, and for our last day here, I've planned something really special for us to do."

"Oh, what's that?"

He put one finger against his mouth. "My lips are sealed. You'll know when it happens."

She spooned some cooked carrots onto her plate and flashed him a smile. "Since you put it that way, I guess I'll have no other choice."

He bobbed his head. "And believe me, it'll be the worth the wait."

Grabill

"This is sure a mighty fine meal, Mom. Everything I've put on my plate tastes great."

Lydia looked at her son Larry and lifted the meat platter. "I'm glad you're enjoying it. Would you like some more *welschhaahne?*"

"Don't mind if I do. Turkey's one of my favorite meats—especially when it's this tender and moist." He grinned at his brother Sam before passing it on down to him.

"What is that now—your third helping?" Sam's brows lowered.

Larry gave a noncommittal shrug and forked himself two hefty pieces of white meat. Following that, he spooned some mashed potatoes onto his plate and covered it and the meat with plenty of gravy. Then he cut up the piece of turkey, picked up his fork, and popped it into his mouth.

Larry's wife, Nancy, rolled her eyes. "You won't sleep tonight if you eat too much and end up with indigestion."

"I'll be fine. Besides, I've had a good many Thanksgiving meals from Mom's table and have never had any stomach problems or heartburn," he mumbled before sinking his fork into the mound of potatoes.

"Don't forget to save some room for your mamm's pumpkin pie." Al reached over and patted Lydia's arm. "I remember when the two of us started going steady." He looked at their family members, who all stared at him intently, seemingly glued to his every word. "I went to her folks' house to visit your mamm almost every Friday evening, and she always served me some kind of a delicious dessert." He patted his stomach and chuckled. "It's a wonder I'm not fat like one of those squealing pigs out there in our barn."

Everyone laughed, and the conversation changed back to how good the food tasted. Gabe's wife, Priscilla, commented about the creamy mashed potatoes and mentioned that she'd been glad when Lydia had passed her secret recipe on to her soon after she and Gabe got married.

Lydia smiled as she looked at each family member. "I'm glad you're all enjoying the meal, and I'm sure you'll also enjoy the desserts my gracious daughters-in-law have brought along to share."

Lydia's mother, Esther, spoke up. "I wish Eleanor and her husband could be with us today. It's been a while since any of us have seen them, and I'd like to know how they are getting along these days."

"We miss them too, Grandma," Sam said. "But I think maybe going to Florida was what they both needed."

"Sam is right," Al agreed. "In the last letter we got from Eleanor, she stated that Vic was still grieving pretty hard over his younger brother's death. I believe that getting away for a while will be good for both him and Eleanor."

"That's right," Lydia agreed. "Reading between the lines of our daughter's letter, I had the feeling that she has been greatly affected by her husband's moods—although Eleanor didn't come right out and say so." She looked at her mother while musing a moment. *If there's more going on than just Vic's sad feelings, I do hope my daughter will feel free to confide in me. I know my son-in-law is having a very difficult time getting through his grief. I'm also aware that Vic seemed quite unstable when Al and I were there for his brother's funeral.*

Lydia noticed her mother's soft expression change to one of concern. Mama was a caring person and didn't mince her words when conveying things she felt important to the family.

"We need to keep them both in our prayers," Lydia's mother said. "Perhaps when they get back from Florida, things will be different for both of them."

———≈———

Sarasota

When Eleanor woke up the next morning, she was surprised to discover that Vic's side of the bed was empty. *He's up early,* she thought. *I wonder if he's in the bathroom and plans to come back to bed.* She yawned. *I'm still tired from staying up too late last night, and I could easily go back to sleep.*

Eleanor glanced at the alarm clock setting beside the bed. It was seven thirty. The sun shone around the edges of the window dressings, which kept a majority of light out of the room. This cottage was quite accommodating for their needs. Eleanor almost disliked the idea of leaving when it was time to travel back to Pennsylvania. In a lot of ways, it had been like an oasis for her, with a happier husband, nicer weather, and plenty of quality time for just the two of them, with no one they knew coming by unannounced.

Eleanor waited a few minutes, but when Vic didn't come back, she got up and slipped on her lightweight robe. *Maybe he's up for the day, which wouldn't be a surprise. Ever since the first morning we woke up here, my husband has been getting up early.*

As soon as Eleanor opened the door to their room, the pleasant hickory scent of bacon greeted her. She hurried into the kitchen and smiled when she saw Vic wearing a pair of shorts, standing in front of the stove with a spatula in one hand.

"This is a surprise," she said, stepping up to him. "I wasn't expecting you to cook breakfast."

He leaned close and kissed her forehead with several soft kisses. "You always cook for me, so I wanted to surprise you this morning." Vic flipped the bacon over in the pan. "I still have eggs to fry, but I did slice a grapefruit earlier, and it's in the refrigerator. So if you're hungerich, you could start with your half."

"I am hungry, but I can wait till you're done, and then we can eat together." Eleanor glanced at the kitchen table and noticed that it hadn't been set yet. "While you're finishing up the bacon and eggs, I'll set the table."

"Oh, that's already been done. I put paper plates, silverware, napkins, glasses, and cups on the table out on the screened-in lanai." Vic spoke in a bubbly tone. "It's another gorgeous day, so I thought it would be nice if we began it outdoors."

"I like that idea." She gave his bare back a gentle kiss. "I'll go change into something more appropriate. I don't think it would be proper for any of our neighbors to see me sitting outside in my nightgown and robe."

Vic nodded and turned the bacon one more time. "Good point. Seeing you in your bedroom clothes is for my eyes only."

"You're right about that." She gave the other side of his back a kiss and hurried from the room.

———— ≈ ————

It didn't take Eleanor long to choose something from the closet to wear. She popped into the bathroom to freshen up and ran the brush through her long hair, forming it into a ponytail, which she tied and left that way. Then Eleanor slipped on her flip-flops and lifted the window shade. The bathroom filled with sunshine, and she glanced out the window, admiring a peach-colored hibiscus shrub full of its tropical-looking blooms.

When Eleanor returned to the kitchen, wearing a plain pale blue dress, the inviting aroma of coffee greeted her, along with the pleasant odor of bacon that still lingered. Vic had everything set out on two trays—one with bacon and eggs, along with two grapefruit halves. The other tray held a bottle of orange juice and the stainless steel coffeepot.

"If you'll hold the door open for me, I'll carry the first tray out," he said. "After I set it on the table, I'll be back for the second tray."

"I can bring that one out." Eleanor opened the back door and held it for him.

"No, that's okay. Just keep holding the door, and I'll get the second tray after I've set this one down." Vic offered Eleanor a wide smile. "Today is your day off, so you won't be cooking or doing any kind of work. Unless you call pedaling your bike work, that is," he added with a wink.

"Where are we going with our bikes?" she asked once all the food had been set out and they were both seated at the table on the lanai.

"I thought it would be fun to take a ride across the bridge that goes from Bird Key into the downtown area of Sarasota. Then when we've worked up an appetite, we can eat lunch on the outside deck at Marina Jack restaurant. We'll have a great view of the bay, and I hear they have some pretty good food. But we can talk about it more after we finish our prayers," Vic added.

"Okay."

Vic closed his eyes, and Eleanor did the same. *Heavenly Father,* she prayed, *thank You for this meal my husband graciously fixed for us this morning. I thank and praise You for the beautiful day You have given us and for the opportunity Vic and I have had to spend quality time together. It's a joy for me to see him so calm, and attentive, and with such a peaceful expression on his face. Please let Vic's positive attitude continue when we return home at the end of next week.*

Chapter 25

A week later

Reaching into the bedroom closet, Eleanor withdrew a new pair of bright coral flip-flops. The color was almost neon, and it made her feel happy wearing the summery look. She had picked out a bluish-green dress with short sleeves to wear today—anything to feel cooler and more comfortable during their long bike ride into town.

Eleanor filled a small tote with a couple of water bottles to quench their thirst and put a little snack bag of trail mix inside, in case either of them needed a pick-me-up on this outing.

Vic locked up the cottage and waited near the garage door for Eleanor to close up the tote. She soon joined him and watched as Vic checked the rear tire on his bike. It looked like it might be a little low, but Vic declared that it should be fine for their ride.

Eleanor placed the tote into the basket of her bike, where it would be safe. "I can't believe that this is our last day in Sarasota," she said, wheeling her bike out of the small garage attached to the cottage. "It's going to be hard to leave the warm sunshine and go back north to the colder weather." Even though the day had started out cloudy with some sprinkling of rain, she felt the heat rising and the humidity starting to climb. It would be another bright and cheerful day to enjoy with her husband. Eleanor had brought along a small notepad on their trip to jot down any highlights she wanted to remember. She was sure that today there would be something else to add to the growing list of memorable items they'd experienced.

Eleanor looked up toward the sky, watching the clouds breaking up and moving more inland. She didn't think there would be any need to bring an umbrella on their outing today.

Vic pushed his bike out behind hers. "I can't say I'm looking forward to much of anything about going home."

Eleanor could tell from the way his shoulders drooped that seeing their vacation almost at its end was a disappointment for her husband. The thought of leaving saddened her too, but they couldn't stay here indefinitely. Vic's family was in Pennsylvania, not to mention his job and the house they were buying. Moving to Florida would mean starting over, with a new home, new job, new friends, and no family living here. If only they could afford to come back again. The cottage had been just right for them to stay in, with all that it had to offer. The location was nice, and it had a homey feeling about it. If she and Vic could afford to buy a cottage by the beach like this one, they would be able to come anytime they needed a vacation and relax from the pressures of life.

She squelched a sigh. *I wish we could afford to have a second home, but that's only a fantasy for us since we don't have enough money.*

Eleanor looked over at Vic and offered what she hoped was a reassuring smile. "When we leave this lovely cottage tomorrow morning, we'll take all the wonderful memories we made here with us."

"Guess you're right." Vic pushed his shoulders back and stood solidly, holding on to the handlebars of his bike. "That's enough talk about going home. We have someplace important to go, and they'll leave without us if we're late."

Eleanor tilted her head to one side. "Who will leave without us, and where are we going?"

Vic gave her nose a light pinch and jiggled his brows. "It's a surprise, and it is for me to know and you to find out."

Eleanor couldn't imagine why he was being so secretive, but she was eager to discover what the surprise was all about.

———— ≈ ————

"Are we eating lunch here again?" Eleanor questioned as she followed Vic into the parking lot of the Marina Jack restaurant.

"Nope, not this time." Vic found a place for them to chain up their bikes. "When we were here the last time, I made reservations for us to go on the *Marina Jack II* boat cruise, where we will take a tour of the bay while eating lunch. I picked up a brochure about it and learned that the cruise vessel is ninety-six feet and it's docked behind the Marina Jack restaurant."

Her eyes widened. "Seriously?"

"Jah."

"I—I don't understand. When would you have had the chance to make reservations for the cruise without me knowing about it?"

"After we finished eating lunch that day, while you were in the restroom, I hurried over to the gift shop, where they take care of reservations." He flashed her one of his biggest grins. "I wanted it to be a surprise."

"Oh, Vic, everything you've done on this trip has been a surprise." She got off her bike and clasped his hand. "Danki for making this the best vacation I've ever had."

He gave her fingers a tender squeeze. "It's been my best one too."

Once their bicycles were safely locked up, they headed for the gift shop, where Vic said they'd need to go to check in and pick up their tickets.

Eleanor's pulse quickened. She could hardly wait for this afternoon's adventure to begin. Although they had seen Sarasota Bay, as well as the Gulf of Mexico from the shoreline, she and Vic had not seen either body of water while on a boat. And how nice it would be to eat lunch while they cruised the waters of this beautiful bay. She was also eager to find out what food would be served.

After picking up their tickets, they were instructed to wait on the deck out back until it was time to board the boat. Eleanor took a seat beside Vic on one of several wooden benches. Most of the other people waiting had also found seats, but a few stood around in clusters excitedly talking and laughing. Numerous boats of different sizes were moored in the marina, most empty. The *Marina Jack II* loomed over them by the deck, obviously the largest boat in the marina. There were two decks, with covered seating on both. They'd been told that the boat also had restrooms. Eleanor couldn't wait to board and see how this cruising vessel looked inside.

The sun sparkled on the surface of the water, which appeared to be quite calm on this warm, windless day. If not for her eagerness to board the boat, Eleanor thought she could probably just sit here all day on the bench, watching boats come and go and observing the many pelicans and seagulls hanging around the waters surrounding the marina.

"I wonder what they will serve us for lunch." Eleanor leaned close to Vic's ear and spoke quietly.

Vic pointed to the ramp leading down to the boat. "They are starting to load the people now, so I think we're about to find out the answer to your question."

⸺⸺⸺≋⸺⸺⸺

Once they were on the boat, Vic guided Eleanor into the dining area on the lower level and found the table marked with their name. Every table had been draped with a white cloth, and a place setting of silverware with red cloth napkins had been placed in front of each seat.

"Pretty fancy, huh?" He looked at Eleanor and wasn't surprised to hear her deep intake of breath.

"It's a lovely setting. I've never been on a luxurious boat like this before." She motioned to the large windows. "It looks like every seat on this level offers a view of the water."

"It does," a middle-aged English woman commented as she and the man who accompanied her headed to a nearby table. "And on a hot day like this, it's so nice that the boat has air-conditioning."

Eleanor looked at Vic with a bemused smile. "Were you tempted to mention that we Amish don't have air-conditioning in our homes?" she whispered as the couple walked away.

He shook his head. "Naw, she'd probably wonder how we survive without it, and then I'd have to explain."

They seated themselves, and soon a server came and asked if they would like a glass of iced tea.

"Yes, please. We both would," Eleanor said before Vic could respond.

Vic smiled and reached for Eleanor's hand. "You know me so well."

"Of course I do. All wives should know what their husbands want."

The waitress returned a short time later and set tall glasses filled with iced tea and a fresh lemon wedge in front of them.

"Thank you," Vic and Eleanor said.

Seeing the look of awe on his wife's pretty face confirmed to Vic that this boat ride and everything else they'd done on this trip had been worth every penny he'd spent. Not only had the last two weeks been fun, but Vic and Eleanor had gotten back the closeness they'd once had. Vic felt stronger emotionally, and he was sure that his and Eleanor's marital relationship would continue to grow even stronger in the days and years ahead.

———— ≋ ————

Eleanor listened with interest as the boat's captain shared his knowledge of the sea and pointed out various things to look at on the intercoastal water journey. The boat had left the dock at noon and would return at one thirty, which meant Eleanor and Vic had one and a half hours to absorb everything about this wonderful cruise.

Soon their waitress came again and said it was time for them to get their food from the buffet table. Eleanor and Vic followed a family of four who'd been seated at a nearby table. Eleanor and Vic picked up plates and dished up their salads. From there they loaded their plates with chicken marsala, the chef's daily fish catch, a mix of fresh seasonal vegetables, and plenty of plump rolls.

Eleanor returned to their table, wondering if she would have room for dessert after eating everything on her plate. She had spotted key lime pie, as well as a few other scrumptious-looking dessert choices that had been placed on a separate serving table. Since this was their final day of vacation, Eleanor was determined to eat one last piece of key lime pie, which she had come to enjoy when they'd eaten out several times during the last two weeks. Eleanor patted her stomach. "I bet during this trip I've gained some weight."

Vic shook his head. "Naw, you look just as slender as you did before we left home." He gestured to their plates. "Guess we'd better close our eyes and pray."

With no thought of what others around them might think, Eleanor bowed her head and prayed. She thanked the Lord for the food they were about to eat and asked Him to give them and their driver a safe trip as they headed back to Pennsylvania in the morning.

When she'd finished praying and taken her first bite of food, Eleanor's eyes closed with pleasure. "Oh, this chicken is so flavorful and tender." She looked at Vic and noticed that he hadn't eaten anything yet. He sat staring out the window, a wide smile on his face.

"Look over there, Eleanor! Do you see those dolphins?"

She looked in the direction Vic had pointed. Sure enough, three or four dolphins were bobbing up and down in the water, not far from the boat.

About that time, the boat captain spoke through the loudspeaker. "If you look to the right side of the boat, you'll see some dolphins."

Everyone seated at tables on this deck were either commenting on the playful dolphins or taking pictures. Some had gone to the open-air outside deck for a better look. Since Eleanor had seen other dolphins at Lido and Siesta Beaches, she chose to stay inside and finish her delicious meal. Vic remained at their table as well.

As the boat continued to tour Sarasota Bay, the captain pointed out several attractions, such as the Ringling Bridge. When they approached the area he referred to as "Bird Key," the captain talked about some of the beautiful homes, many worth millions of dollars, that had gorgeous water views.

I think it would be quite difficult to stay humble if Vic and I possessed a fancy house and property like the ones we've seen along the water today. She pondered the thought awhile, trying to imagine what type of job it would take to own any of those expensive homes, not to mention what it would cost to maintain such a large estate year-round.

Eleanor gave a slow, disbelieving shake of her head. "It's hard to believe people have that kind of money." She found it especially surprising when the captain mentioned that some home owners were only part-time residents, using their houses for vacation purposes only.

"I agree." Vic pointed at one very large three-story home. In addition to having its own infinity pool, a dock had been built in front of the place and a pontoon party boat was secured at the dock. Some of the other homes with docks had bigger boats, but none were as large as the *Marina Jack II.* Even so, the day Eleanor and Vic had eaten lunch at Marina Jack's downstairs restaurant, she'd seen several large, expensive-looking yachts that had either been moored there or were for sale. Eleanor didn't know anyone who had enough money to buy a yacht or one of the expensive homes here in the Bird Key area. Although some of the houses in their part of Pennsylvania were larger than her and Vic's home, none were nearly as extravagant as what they were seeing now.

Vic cut up the last piece of chicken and ate it, then finished off the rest of his tea. "I hope you're not too captivated, seeing all these amazing homes and boats," he said, looking at Eleanor. "Even if I worked two jobs, I'd never earn the amount of money needed to own anything like what we've seen today."

Eleanor gave a quick shake of her head. "There's no need to worry about that, Husband. I have no desire to live like the wealthy." She smiled and placed one hand against her chest. "My heart is full, and I'm satisfied just being married to you."

A slow smile spread across Vic's face, and he reached across the table to touch her arm. "And you, sweet Eleanor, are all that I will ever need."

How good it felt to hear her husband's tender, loving words. At this moment, Eleanor was more convinced than ever that this getaway to Sarasota had been exactly what she and Vic needed. She felt confident that things really would be better once they returned home.

Chapter 26

Strasburg

Susie entered the kitchen to begin making supper preparations and glanced at the clock. According to the message they'd gotten from Victor that morning, he and Eleanor had left Sarasota and should arrive soon to pick up Victor's dog and hopefully share some details about their trip.

"I'm sure they'll be hungry and want to stay for supper," she told her oldest daughter, who had recently gotten home from her waitressing job at a local restaurant. "They will probably be tired from the long journey too, and I doubt that Eleanor will want to go home and cook a meal."

"You're probably right," Clara agreed. "And it will be a nice opportunity for us to sit and visit with them. I'd like to find out more details about their trip than just the few things Eleanor wrote about on the one postcard she sent." Clara filled the glass she'd taken from the cupboard with water and took a drink. "I know Eleanor wrote the card because I recognized her neat-as-a-pin handwriting."

"Your bruder is more into phoning than writing a letter, so it makes sense that Eleanor would be the one to drop us a line." Susie smiled. "She does have nice penmanship. Your brother did well choosing Eleanor as his fraa, and I don't mean because of her tidy writing or the way she describes things. Eleanor is a good cook and keeps their home and yard in excellent shape. She is also even tempered and kindhearted, and I am certain that she loves Victor with all of her heart."

Clara finished her drink and set the glass on the counter near the sink. "Living in Indiana for a while and meeting his future wife was one of the best things that ever happened to Vic. Eleanor was a big support to him when Eddie died too, and even since then, trying to help him deal with his depression and unwarranted guilt."

Susie moved across the room and placed her arm around Clara's waist. "You and Kate have been supportive to me and your daed since your brother died. Even Stephen, in his own way, has given encouragement by helping us with many things around here, and always without complaint." She teared up and sniffed to keep the tears from falling onto her cheeks. "I am sure the three of you miss Eddie too—the whole while offering your love and understanding to me and your daed. It's meant a whole lot, and we haven't told you thank you often enough."

Clara smiled. "No thanks is needed, Mom."

Just then, Kate came in the door, red-faced and panting.

"What's wrong?" Susie asked. "Why are you out of breath?"

Kate set her lunch satchel on the counter and removed her jacket and the black headscarf that had been holding her bonnet in place. "Things were super busy at the fabric store today, and my feet hurt from standing at the cash register for long hours, so I'm exhausted. On top of that, it's cold and windy out there, and when my driver dropped me off just now, that crazy hund of Vic's came charging right at me with muddy paws and his irritating yap. The next thing I knew, Eddie's dog came running out too." Her forehead creased. "I thought both dogs were supposed to be kept in the pen when no one was with them."

Susie looked out the kitchen window and grimaced when she saw Checkers and Freckles run past. There was no sign of Ethan or Stephan, so she was certain that those energetic dogs were on their own. "This is not good." Susie pointed out the window. "The last thing we need is for those animals to run off or—worse—go out on the road and get hit by a car. Victor would be very upset if he returned home to something like that. He doesn't need another tragedy to deal with, even if it happened to a dog and not a boy."

"I'll go see if I can chase them down." Kate reached for her jacket. "I tried once, but I'll give it another go."

"I'd better help too." Clara grabbed her jacket from the wall peg where she'd previously hung it.

"Let me know if you need my help," Susie called to her daughters' retreating forms as they headed out the back door. "I hope the girls manage to catch those mutts before Victor and Eleanor show up," she mumbled.

———— ≋ ————

From the back seat of their driver's van, Vic clutched Eleanor's warm hand and found it comforting. They would be at his folks' house soon, and he hoped the reminder that Eddie wouldn't be there would not cause him to feel stressed out. He and Eleanor had enjoyed themselves so much while in Florida, but now it was time to face reality again. As much as he may have wanted it, Vic knew they could not stay on a perpetual vacation. He had to get back to work to provide for their needs. He also had a dog waiting to be picked up and figured Checkers had probably missed him and Eleanor.

If I can keep from thinking about the loss of my little brother, I'll be okay, Vic told himself. *I just need to keep other things in my focus and knock any negative thoughts out.*

When their driver pulled into his parents' yard a few minutes later, Vic was surprised to see both of his sisters running and waving their hands as they chased after two dogs.

"What's going on?" Eleanor asked, leaning over Vic and peering out the window. "I wonder if your sisters are running after Checkers and Freckles because they are playing some kind of a game. Or maybe the dogs were trying to leave the yard for some reason, and the girls are trying to stop them."

Vic shook his head. "All I know is I'm gonna put a stop to it right now." He opened the door and stepped out. "I'll be back as soon as I capture my hund."

Vic moved toward his sisters, but he'd only taken a few steps before Checkers spotted him and began yipping and running around Vic in circles. Vic got down on one knee and called the dog to him. With no further encouragement, Checkers gave a mighty leap and slurped his wet tongue across Vic's face several times. Meanwhile, Freckles had stopped running and now stood close beside Clara with his tail wagging and tongue hanging out.

"Simmer down, boy. I know you missed me. I missed you too, but I don't need my face washed." Vic stroked his dog's head and ears.

Checkers tipped his head back and let out a weird-sounding noise that sounded more like a howl than a bark. There was no doubt about it—the dog had surely missed him. Vic couldn't help laughing at all the racket Checkers was making. With a greeting like this, who couldn't help feeling happy to be home?

Once the dog finally settled down, Vic rose to his feet and greeted his sisters with a hug.

"Welcome back. It's sure good to see you," Kate said.

"Same here." He gave her back a few pats. "Was my hund giving you and Clara a merry chase?"

"Jah," Clara said before Kate could respond. "He and Freckles escaped from the dog pen, and I'm guessing Checkers may have sensed that you were on your way home. So he probably got all worked up, which no doubt was the reason Freckles started carrying on too."

Vic tried to avoid looking at his little brother's dog. Seeing Freckles was always a painful reminder that Eddie was gone.

Vic's sisters gave Eleanor a hug after she'd exited the van. Then Clara stepped back and squinted as she stared at Vic and Eleanor. "Oh boy. . . I can sure tell that you two have seen a bit of sun. You both have such beautiful tans."

"It looks good on you," Kate chimed in. "Did you two have a good time in Sarasota?"

"Oh yes." Eleanor's lips curved into a broad smile. "Vic and I made the most of every single day, and the weather was nearly perfect the whole time we were there."

"How often did you go to the beach?" This question came from Kate.

"Every chance we got." Vic glanced toward the house. "Where are Mom, Dad, and Stephen? I'd like to say hello before we get back in the van and head for home."

"Dad and Stephen are still in the shop, and Mom's in the kitchen," Clara said. "She's hoping you and Eleanor will stay for supper."

He shook his head. "Sorry, not tonight. It's a tempting offer, but we can't hold our driver up for that long. He has family waiting for him and needs to get home." Vic slipped his arm around Eleanor's waist. "Besides, we're both tired and will probably go to bed early tonight."

"I understand," Clara said. "But you have to know that Mom will be disappointed."

"We'll come for a meal another time."

"You will go say hello to everyone, won't you?" Kate tugged the sleeve of Vic's jacket.

"Jah, of course." He turned to face Eleanor. "I'll help my sisters put the dogs back in the pen, and then we can go into the house to see my mamm for a few minutes. After that, we'll stop by the shop to say hi to my daed and bruder."

Eleanor nodded. "I'll let our driver know that we'll be back in the van shortly."

Paradise

When Vic entered the house behind Eleanor, a wave of exhaustion settled over him like a dark cloud about to dump rain. After two full weeks of doing whatever they wanted, it would be difficult to go back to work Monday morning. At least he had to do a few things around home tomorrow, and the next day would be their off-Sunday. Before leaving his folks' home, Vic had promised that he and Eleanor would attend church in Dad and Mom's district, then go to their home afterward to visit and stay for a light supper. Vic didn't plan to remain there too late, however, since he had to be up early for work on Monday.

After setting their suitcases on the floor in the entryway, Vic turned to Eleanor and wrapped his arms around her. "I love you so much, and I'm ever so glad you're my *fraa*." He bent his head and kissed her upturned mouth.

When the kiss ended, still leaning against him, she murmured, "I love you too, and I am glad that you're my *mansleit*."

Vic's stomach gave an unexpected noisy growl. "Sorry about that. A blaring belly rumble is not exactly romantic, is it?"

She giggled. "No, it's not, but it does let me know that you need to be fed. I'll head for the kitchen and see what I can fix for our supper."

Vic shook his head. "You're tired from traveling all day, and so am I. Think I should hitch Domino to the buggy and take us out to eat. How's that sound?"

Eleanor suppressed a yawn with the palm of her hand. "The thought of going out to a restaurant makes me feel even more tired than I am. If you'd be okay with a simple sandwich, or maybe some of the homemade chicken soup I have in the freezer that can be thawed in a kettle on the stove, I'd be happy to stay right here for our evening meal."

He nodded and gave her another meaningful kiss. Vic couldn't seem to get enough of those lately. "Staying here is fine with me. That way I'll have you all to myself."

———≈———

The following day after breakfast, Vic had gone out to the barn to clean the stalls and put Domino and Buttons out to pasture. It had been nice of their Amish neighbor, Omar Stoltzfus, to come over each day while they were away to tend to the horses, while his wife, Anna, got the mail and took care of feeding their cats. Vic would no doubt return the favor sometime when Omar and Anna went somewhere for more than a day.

Neighbors helping neighbors is the Christian way, Eleanor told herself as she returned from their neighbors' home with a sack full of mail. She placed everything on the kitchen table and began sorting through all the envelopes and magazines—one pile for the bills that had come in—another for advertisements and junk mail, and a third pile for letters and cards from friends and family in Indiana. Curious to find out who all had written to them while they were gone, Eleanor began with that stack of letters. The first one she picked up was from Doretta.

Eager to see what her friend had to say, Eleanor tore the envelope open and read the letter silently.

———— ≋ ————

Dear Eleanor,

I received the beautiful postcard you sent while you were in Sarasota. I loved looking at the gorgeous sunset on the front of the card. It reminded me of the time you and I went there with a few other friends during our rumschpringe days. Maybe William and I will take a trip there soon after we're married.

Yes, you read that right—it's not just my wishful thinking anymore. Last night when he brought me home from a young people's singing, William asked me to marry him. Of course I said yes. We haven't set a wedding date yet, but I will be sure to let you know as soon as we do. I would like you to be one of my witnesses at the wedding, just as I was at yours.

Oh, Eleanor, I can't tell you how happy I am today. As you well know, I was beginning to think maybe William didn't love me the way I did him and might never ask me to marry him.

William's twin brother still has no steady girl. William says Warren is too particular and will probably never find the right woman.

That's enough about me, now. I am sure you must be home

213

from Florida by now, and I'm eager to hear all the details of your trip that you couldn't squeeze into that little postcard you wrote.

Take care, and I hope to hear back from you soon.

Love,
Doretta

———≈———

Eleanor put her friend's letter back in the envelope. She would respond to it later today if there was time. Otherwise it would have to wait until early next week. Having been empty for two whole weeks, the house was dusty and needed a good cleaning. She also had to come up with something to fix for tonight's supper. It would be a busy day, and although vacations were nice, Eleanor had to admit that it was rather nice to be home again.

She stood and pushed in her chair at the table. It was time to fix something for her and Vic to eat, so she moved the mail to the opposite end of the table. Eleanor was sure that by the time Vic came back into the house, she would have their simple meal ready, and then they could sit down to eat and go through the rest of the mail together after they'd finished eating.

She smiled and released a contented sigh. *I think everything between me and Vic is going to be okay from now on. After our trip to Sarasota, he seems like a new man. I don't believe I have to worry about him drinking beer or getting drunk anymore.*

Eleanor closed her eyes and said a little prayer out loud. "Thank You, Lord, for everything that's been accomplished during the past two weeks."

Chapter 27

Eleanor stepped into the kitchen and took a carton of eggs from the refrigerator to begin making breakfast. She hoped Vic wouldn't want anything more than that this morning. It had been a little over three weeks since they had returned from Sarasota, and for the last several days she'd felt nauseous every morning. The pungent, fatty odor of bacon frying was especially repulsive, so hopefully he wouldn't ask her to fix any of that to go with his scrambled eggs. Eleanor hadn't said anything to Vic yet, but she suspected that she might be pregnant, because in addition to an upset stomach, Eleanor had also missed her monthly.

She set the eggs on the counter and glanced out the kitchen window at the dismal sky. They would be celebrating Christmas next week, and she wondered if they might have some snow by then.

"It would be *schee*," she murmured.

"What would be pretty?" Vic asked, stepping up to Eleanor and placing his arms around her waist.

"Snow, if we have any for *Grischtdaag*."

"It would be nice to have a white Christmas." Vic kissed the back of Eleanor's neck, causing goose bumps to erupt on her arms. "I hope you weren't planning a big breakfast for me this morning. I'm running late, and Tom should be here soon."

"No scrambled eggs then?"

"Nope, not today. I'll just fill my kaffi mug, grab a few kichlin, and be on my way as soon as I hear Tom honk his horn."

Eleanor turned to face him. Pressing both hands against her stomach, hoping to quell the queasiness, she forced a smile. "Sounds good. I'll put the *oier* away."

She reached for the carton of eggs, but Vic stopped her by placing his hand on her arm. "Are you feeling okay?"

"I'm all right. Why do you ask?"

"Because normally when I rush off without eating before leaving for work, you remind me that a healthy breakfast is the most important meal of the day, and you'd say that coffee and cookies were not substantial." He caressed her cheek with his thumb. "Besides, you look a little pale this morning. Maybe you're coming down with something or didn't get enough sleep last night."

"I'm fine, really. My suntan is probably fading, so that would explain the reason for pale skin." Eleanor didn't feel ready to tell Vic about her upset stomach. She wanted to be certain that she was pregnant before saying anything. When she felt well enough to hitch her horse to the buggy today, Eleanor planned to make a trip to the pharmacy in town and buy a pregnancy test.

———————≈———————

"How was your weekend?" Vic asked after he got into Tom's truck.

"Saturday was great. Sunday, not so much."

"Oh? How come?"

"Saturday, I went to a friend's keg party and had more than my share to drink. Sunday I woke up with a hangover and slept most of the day." Tom glanced over at Vic. "I thought about inviting you to join me on Saturday, but then I remembered you'd quit drinking again."

Vic bobbed his head. "Yeah, it wasn't doing me any good, and my marriage was being affected." He wondered if his coworker might comment or

216

LETTERS OF TRUST

say that drinking hadn't done his marriage any good either, but Tom kept quiet and headed down the road with a stoic expression. Apparently he was either unwilling to admit that drinking too much had affected his marriage, or he believed that it had nothing to do with his wife leaving him.

Vic was glad things were better between him and Eleanor now, and he hoped to keep it that way.

〰

Eleanor left the pharmacy with a paper sack. Inside was a pregnancy test and a few other items, including a package of mint-flavored gum, which she hoped might help to settle her stomach. She'd wait until she got to her buggy to try a piece.

Eleanor was almost to the hitching rail when she spotted Letty Zook coming down the sidewalk. Not wishing to appear rude, she paused and waited for the older woman to catch up to her.

When Letty approached, she smiled and gave Eleanor a sideways hug. With her black handbag in the way, it was probably the best hug the bishop's wife could offer. "It's good to see you. We haven't had a chance to converse since you and your husband got back from Florida." Letty shifted her purse straps to the other shoulder. "How was your trip, and how is Vic getting along? Has his depression lifted at all?"

Eleanor wasn't sure which question to respond to first, so she began by telling Letty a little about the trip. She ended by saying, "I think all we both needed was to get away for a while, where it was peaceful and warm, and we didn't have any distractions or things to remind Vic about the loss of his brother. To answer your other question, Vic is doing much better, with no sign of depression at all. "

"That's so good to hear. Michael and I have been praying for you and your husband, and it's nice to know that our prayers are being answered." Letty's lips parted slightly and then turned into a smile. "I will make sure to give my husband the good news." Her chin dipped down as she readjusted her handbag. "Of course, Michael might have already spoken to Vic, and he could be aware that things are going better now. Sometimes my mansleit forgets to share things with me. Although," she quickly added, "there are probably some things he doesn't share because they are confidential between him and the person he's spoken to."

Letty asked Eleanor what plans they had made for Christmas.

"Vic and I have been invited to join his parents at their home for a meal on Christmas Day," Eleanor replied. "We will spend Christmas Eve at home, just the two of us." She placed her free hand on Letty's arm. "What about you and the bishop? Will you be with your family for the holiday?"

"Oh jah, and since Michael and I live in the daadihaus next to them, we won't have far to go." Letty's face broke into a wide smile. "How about your family members from Indiana? Will any of them be coming to Pennsylvania to join you for Christmas?"

Eleanor shook her head. "Mom and Dad will spend the holiday with my siblings and their families, and I'm sure they'll have a pleasant time."

The cold wind shifted suddenly, blowing Eleanor's white head covering ties across her face and causing her to shiver.

"I should let you go," Letty said. "It's chilly today, and you appear to be kelt, as am I, so we'd both best be on our way."

"I am cold," Eleanor admitted. "I wouldn't be surprised if we didn't get some schnee pretty soon."

"Jah, snow can be quite lovely to look at, but it can also make a mess of the roads."

One more hug was exchanged between Eleanor and the bishop's wife, and then they said goodbye and went their separate ways. With her nausea increasing, and the chill from the wind seeping under the neckline of her jacket, Eleanor could hardly wait to get inside the buggy and head for the warmth and safety of her home. One of the first things she planned to do when she got there was to take the pregnancy test. If it was positive, she would happily share the good news with Vic as soon as he got home from work this evening. If Eleanor was expecting their first child, she felt certain that he would be as excited as she.

As Eleanor went about her chores for the rest of the day, a wonderful feeling of warmth and happiness infused her whole body. The results of her pregnancy test had been positive, and she found it impossible to keep a smile off her face. Based on when Eleanor had missed her last monthly, she figured that conception must have taken place while she and Vic were in Sarasota. That was logical, since they'd both been so relaxed and enjoyed each other's company to the full extent.

Eleanor entered the living room and lowered herself into the rocking chair to wait for Vic's arrival. She placed both hands on her belly and gave it a few pats. *I wonder if our baby will be a boy or a girl. Either one would be fine with me. I just want our child to be healthy.*

Eleanor had been thankful that the peppermint tea and saltine crackers she'd tried earlier had helped to settle her stomach. From what other women in a family way had said about nausea and sometimes vomiting, she knew it could hit anytime of the day, not just in the morning hours. Eleanor was also aware that for some women the sick-to-the-stomach feelings could continue for several months or even during all nine months of one's pregnancy. She hoped that would not be the case for her. Feeling nauseous would make it difficult to cook meals, not to mention doing housework, shopping, or attending church and social events.

I shall take one day at a time, she told herself, *and try not to worry, because that would not be good for me or the baby. I will also make sure to eat right and get plenty of rest.*

Eleanor leaned her head against the back of the chair and closed her eyes. *Thank You, Lord, for the new life growing within me. Please help me to feel strong and healthy during this special time in my life, and I ask that You would give Vic and me the wisdom and understanding to raise our child so that he or she will grow up to love and serve You.*

Eleanor's prayer ended, and she opened her eyes when she heard the front door open and Vic call, "I'm home!"

She rose from the chair and went to greet him with a welcoming hug. "After you take your hat and jacket off, let's go to the living room so we can talk. There is something important I want to share with you."

Vic's voice lowered as he gently touched her face. "You sound so serious. Should I be concerned?"

"No, not at all. Everything is fine. I will meet you in the living room to talk about it."

"Okay." Vic ambled down the hall to hang up his coat and hat, and he joined Eleanor a short time later.

"Come sit beside me." She sat in the middle of the couch and patted the cushion beside her.

Vic did as she asked and took hold of her hand. "Now what's that big smile on your face all about? Did you make my favorite chocolate chip pie today?"

Eleanor shook her head. "My news is much better than any dessert."

Vic tipped his head to one side. "I can't stand the suspense. What's going on, my dear wife? What is it that you have to tell me?"

Laughter bubbled up in Eleanor's throat as she moved his hand to rest on her belly. "I've been feeling sick to my stomach for the past several days, and I missed my last monthly."

He glanced around the room, as if looking for answers. "Wh–what are you saying?"

"I took a home pregnancy test today, Vic, and it was positive."

His eyes widened, and after letting go of Eleanor's hand, he leaned slightly away from her. "You're in a family way?"

"Jah. Isn't it exciting, Vic?"

"This can't be happening now!"

She blinked several times, surprised at his unexpected reaction. "What do you mean?"

"I am not ready to be a daed."

"Why would you say that?"

"Because I would not make a good dad, and you should know it, Eleanor."

She shook her head. "I don't know that at all. I think you would make a wonderful father. You're a kind, loving man, and—"

"Have you forgotten that I couldn't even look out for my little brother? How am I gonna be trusted to keep an eye on a baby?"

"You will, Vic. We'll both take good care of our child." Eleanor placed her hand on his arm. "And you've got to stop blaming yourself for Eddie's death."

"I can't believe this has happened."

She lifted her gaze toward the ceiling. "Seriously, Vic? We're married, and we share the same bed."

"Yeah, I know, but we've been married over a year and you've never gotten pregnant. Why now?" Vic shook his head vigorously and repeated, "I am not ready to be a daed." Before Eleanor had the chance to respond, he jumped up and raced out the front door.

Eleanor felt an unsettling heaviness in her chest as she clasped her hands tightly against her stomach. She had never expected that Vic would not share in her joy over the news that they were expectant parents. She thought he would be as happy about becoming a father as she was at the prospect of being a mother. Surely once Vic had the chance to think things through, he would change his mind and see her pregnancy as a blessing from God. Eleanor just needed to give him some time. She sat quietly for several minutes, until another thought crept into her mind, one that was quite unsettling. *I hope Vic doesn't go off the deep end over my news and start drinking again.*

Vic entered the barn and began to pace. He hadn't given any thought to the fact that Eleanor might get pregnant while they were on vacation. The simple truth was, after being married this long without her becoming pregnant, Vic had convinced himself that one or both of them was incapable of producing a child.

"And that would have been fine with me," he mumbled, kicking at a bale of straw outside of his horse's stall. When they'd first gotten married,

Vic had wanted Eleanor all to himself and hadn't relished the idea of them having children anytime soon. But after a time, he'd looked forward to the day that he and Eleanor would become parents. Then Eddie died, and from that time until their trip to Florida, Vic had not been intimate with his wife, partially for fear of her becoming pregnant and also because he'd turned to alcohol for comfort instead of finding solace in Eleanor's arms.

Vic looked up at the hayloft and grimaced as the urge to drown his sorrows gripped him like a vise. Vic wished he hadn't promised Eleanor that he would quit drinking. He put one hand on the ladder. *Maybe I have a few cans of beer still hidden up there somewhere.*

Vic climbed up and began searching. He looked under the scattered straw, behind bales of hay, and in every nook and cranny of the loft. Nothing. Not even one can of beer.

Vic had thought his craving for the stuff had disappeared, but after hearing the news that his wife was expecting a baby, he felt desperate to drink a beer or something else to help him relax and take his mind off the situation. Vic also felt betrayed by his own stupidity. He never should have allowed it to happen, and now he was stuck with the consequences of his unbridled passion.

Vic took a seat on a bale of straw and rested his head in the palms of his hands. "Dear Lord," he prayed out loud, "please help me figure out how to deal with this situation that I have no control over." Vic's ribs felt so tight he could hardly breathe, and he stood, raising his hands over his head. *Maybe it will help if I take a long walk and try to think things through.* One thing for sure, Vic could not go back into the house and face Eleanor right now. He needed some time by himself.

Chapter 28

Grabill

"What are you doing?" Doretta's mother called from the dining room.

"I'm reading the note Eleanor included in her Christmas card." Doretta left the kitchen to join her.

Mama looked up from her seat at the table and smiled. "Oh good. You're here. I thought we were going to play a few board games." She gestured to the game of Rook on the table. "Your daed went out for some wood for the fireplace, and as soon as he comes inside he'll join us. Your older brothers are at their girlfriends' homes this evening, but I think Karen and Jeremy would like to join us for a while before it's their bedtime."

"Oh, okay, but first I want to share Eleanor's good news." Doretta handed her mother the note she'd found inside her friend's Christmas card.

Mama's face broke into a wide smile as she read the note. "How nice it is that Eleanor and Vic are expecting their first baby. I'm sure they must be very excited."

"I know for sure that Eleanor is, because she's the one who wrote the note." Doretta wasn't about to tell her mother about the extra little sticky note Eleanor had included, asking for prayer. She'd stated in just a few words that Vic was not thrilled about the pregnancy and had said he would not make a good father.

Such a shame, Doretta thought. *This should be a happy time for both Vic and Eleanor. I'm sure Vic's attitude about Eleanor's pregnancy has to do with the grief and guilt he has struggled with since his little brother died. I need to write another letter to Eleanor soon and let her know that I'll be praying for both her and Vic.*

Paradise

"Would you like another open-faced sandwich?" Eleanor asked Vic as they sat quietly at the kitchen table.

He shook his head. He hadn't said more than a few words to her since they'd begun their Christmas Eve meal, and those only in answer to Eleanor's questions.

She took a bite of her sandwich and followed it with a drink of hot apple cider. Eleanor was relieved that the nausea she'd felt nearly every morning didn't last all day. At least she could enjoy two meals a day without stomach upset. Right now, however, Eleanor's belly felt like it was tied in knots. When Vic became moody or gave her the silent treatment, it stressed her out, which was not good for her or the precious baby growing inside of her womb.

Eleanor thought of the comforting words from John 14:27, a verse of scripture she'd read the other day during her morning devotions: *Jesus said, "Peace I leave with you, my peace I give unto you: not as the world giveth, give I unto you. Let not your heart be troubled, neither let it be afraid."*

Eleanor had to admit that she was fearful—afraid of Vic's sudden personality change since she'd revealed the results of her pregnancy test. Why couldn't he just be happy that they would become parents in about eight months? How was it possible for Vic to be convinced that because his brother had drowned while under their care, he would not be a good father?

Eleanor glanced at Vic as he sat staring at his empty plate. The way he sagged into his chair, with his shoulders curled forward, revealed the depression that had set in once again. If only there was some way to reach him. How could Vic have changed so much since their wonderful trip to

Sarasota? When they'd returned home, Eleanor had been certain that things would continue to be better for them. No more drinking, no more unhealthy silence, but instead of the joyful, loving spirit he'd had during their vacation, Vic had changed. His depression seemed to be spiraling downward, with more of his previous problems creeping back in.

Prior to coming home, Vic's attitude had been so pleasant that Eleanor had begun to dream of starting a family. The way things had been between Eleanor and Vic while they were in Florida had reminded her of the good times right after they married, when they'd talked about and looked forward to raising children someday. Vic's gloomy attitude was so bad now that Eleanor was afraid to talk about the upcoming birth of their baby. She wanted to choose names for a boy and a girl—something that she and Vic would agree upon. But no, the last time she'd brought up the topic of her pregnancy, Vic had said he didn't want to talk about it and abruptly left the room. Eleanor wondered if she might have to revisit the Zooks and tell them more of what was happening with Vic. She surely couldn't go through this alone. It wasn't a healthy situation for her, Vic, or their unborn child.

Eleanor had left a message on her parents' voice mail this morning, wishing them a Merry Christmas and revealing the news of her pregnancy. Of course, she hadn't said anything about her husband's reaction to the idea of becoming a father. It would be nice to unburden herself with what was so upsetting in her life right now. She longed to have her mother say she would be praying for them and if Eleanor needed anything to let her know. Unfortunately, if Eleanor told her mother what was going on with Vic, Mom would likely see it as an opportunity to put the blame on him. Why give her one more thing to criticize him about? It wasn't fair. Vic's sorrowful attitude had stolen some of Eleanor's enthusiasm about becoming a mother, and that was the last thing she'd ever wanted. Her pregnancy and the eventual birth of their baby should be joyous, and no matter how Vic acted, Eleanor did not want anything to put a damper on her happiness about becoming a mother.

Tomorrow, when they went to Vic's parents' house for Christmas dinner, they needed to tell his mom and dad that sometime around the middle of August, they would become grandparents for the first time. Eleanor felt certain that Susie, Ethan, and Vic's siblings would be happy to hear the good news. Shouldn't that be a normal response from anyone, especially from the father of the baby, who supposedly loved his wife dearly? The question was, would Vic be able to hide his disappointment about Eleanor's pregnancy from his family?

Grabill

"I have some *gut nei-ichkeede* to share with all of you," Lydia said after everyone took seats at the dinner table and their prayers had been said.

"I'm always up for some good news," her husband responded. "Please don't keep us in suspense. What's your good news?"

"I went out to the phone shed this afternoon and discovered a message from Eleanor."

"What'd my granddaughter have to say?" Lydia's elderly father questioned.

"Eleanor said that she and Vic will become parents sometime around the middle of August." Lydia couldn't keep the smile from her lips, because this exciting news meant that she and Al would become grandparents again. Although it was nice to have Gabe's, Sam's, and Larry's children all living nearby, Lydia felt bad because she wouldn't get to see her new grandbaby as often as she'd like. *But,* she told herself, *there's nothing I can do about the distance between us. With Vic's job in Pennsylvania, it's doubtful that he and Eleanor will ever move back to Indiana.*

Al reached over and touched Lydia's arm. "What's wrong? That smile you had on your face a few minutes ago has suddenly turned to a frown. Aren't you happy about having another grandchild to fuss over and buy things for?"

"Of course. I was just thinking about how nice it would be if Eleanor and Vic lived closer so we could see them and the baby as often as we like."

Gabe spoke up. "We would enjoy seeing them more frequently too. It will be harder for our kinner to get know their little cousin when they won't get to see him or her all the time."

"I'm sure Vic and Eleanor will bring their child here for visits," Larry said.

Sam nodded. "And we can all take turns going to Pennsylvania to see them too."

Lydia released a sigh. Since their daughter had gotten married and moved away, they'd only seen her on a few occasions. Between Vic's work schedule and the cost of hiring a driver, it wasn't likely she and Al would get to spend much time with their youngest grandchild. But Lydia was resigned to the fact that there was nothing she could do about it. Hopefully, Al would be able to take some time off from overseeing his bulk food store often enough to make trips to Pennsylvania. Otherwise, it would be a shame if Eleanor and Vic's baby grew up not knowing his or her maternal grandparents very well.

———— ≈ ————

Strasburg

While Susie sat at the dining room table with her family on Christmas Day, she kept eyeing Victor. He hadn't eaten much or said more than a few words since they'd all begun eating twenty minutes ago. *Could my son and his wife have had some sort of disagreement before coming over here today?* Susie wondered. *If so, I wish they had worked things out. Victor's melancholy mood does not set a good example for Stephen, Kate, or Clara. And no doubt his somber attitude is unsettling for Eleanor. Vic seemed so happy and upbeat when they returned from Florida. I wonder what occurred between then and now to bring about this negative side of him.*

"Did you and your fraa have a pleasant Christmas Eve?" Susie directed her question to Victor, making sure she looked right at him while speaking.

He gave a noncommittal shrug and mumbled, "It was okay."

"What'd you have for supper?" Kate questioned.

"Open-faced sandwiches, like the ones my mamm likes to fix on Christmas Eve," Eleanor responded when Vic ignored his sister's question.

"Those sound interesting. Maybe you could show me how to make them sometime," Katie said.

"I'd be happy to." Eleanor gave a sidelong glance at her husband. Susie was pretty good at reading people's body language, and she had a feeling that her daughter-in-law may have been trying to tell Victor something.

"This is another outstanding meal," Ethan interjected, reaching over and giving Susie's arm a pat.

She smiled and said, "Danki. There are plenty more mashed potatoes and ham in the kitchen, so if the bowls here on the table become empty, I'll bring more food out."

"Hey Vic, how come you're not eating much today?" The question came from Stephen.

"I'm getting enough. Just choosing not to make a *sau* out of myself." Victor pointed at Stephen's plate, piled high with ham, potatoes, creamed corn, pickles, olives, and one oversized roll.

Stephen frowned. "I'm not a pig, and you're a grouch. You have been ever since you sat down at this table."

Susie figured she'd better put a stop to this conversation before it got out of control with her sons trying to one-up each other. But before she had the chance to form a sentence, Ethan spoke.

"Let's not spoil the day by pointing fingers," he said, looking first at Stephen and then Victor. "I am sure we can all find something positive to talk about on this special day when we celebrate the birth of Christ."

"Vic and I have something positive to share," Eleanor said. "It's something that will affect each one of you in some way."

"That makes me real curious." Clara's eyes brightened as she nudged her brother's arm. "Please tell us about it."

Victor nodded with his head toward Eleanor. "Since she brought it up, I'll let her do the telling."

All heads turned in Eleanor's direction. A crimson flush quickly spread across her cheeks as she drew in a deep breath. "Well, uh. . .Vic and I have some happy news—we're expecting a baby."

Susie let out a squeal of delight, and everyone began talking and asking questions at the same time.

"That is great news. Congratulations!" Ethan looked at Susie and grinned. "Just think now, we're soon going to become grandparents, and it won't be long before the little one will be calling us *Grossdaadi* and *Grossmudder*."

"Or maybe, for short, our grandbaby will simply refer to us as *Daadi* and *Mammi*."

"Clara and I will both be *aendi*, and I can hardly wait to hold my niece or nephew." Kate pointed at Stephen. "And you, young bruder, will become an *onkel*."

Stephen's ears turned red as a ripe tomato. "I'm too young to be anybody's uncle, and I can't imagine being called Uncle Stephen."

"You'll get used to the idea," Susie said. "We all will, and it'll be so much fun having a little one around." Joyful tears sprang to her eyes. Although Victor and Eleanor's baby could not take the place of Eddie, it would be ever so nice to have a new member of the family to dote over and shower with love.

She glanced over at Victor, confused by his lack of enthusiasm over this wonderful news. Surely he must be happy about becoming a father. Or was he? Susie couldn't miss the wrinkles that had formed on her son's forehead, or the way Victor stared at his half-eaten plate of food with a look of disinterest. Was it possible that he did not share in his wife's excitement? Was that why he'd been acting so sullen today?

But why would Victor be unhappy about becoming a parent? Susie asked herself. She couldn't come right out and ask, but it was hard to watch her son acting like this. He didn't seem the least bit excited about becoming a father. There was trouble in paradise, and it appeared to be centered on Victor. Eleanor seemed pleased with the positive comments she'd received from his family over the wonderful news.

Susie looked at her sweet daughter-in-law and pursed her lips. *It isn't right or fair for Eleanor to have to deal with Victor behaving in this manner. If I could, I'd ask her to come and stay with us throughout the rest of her pregnancy, and let my son come begging for Eleanor to return home. He needs to wake up. That's all there is to it.* If her son was not pleased about the prospect of becoming a father, then he needed a good, strong lecture, which Susie would have given right now if the whole family hadn't been here. If Victor's attitude kept up, however, she wouldn't hesitate to talk to him, or maybe Eleanor, about it.

Chapter 29

Vic's stomach tightened as he watched Eleanor seated in the rocking chair, knitting a pair of baby booties. He should be happy about the prospect of becoming a parent—any normal man would be. But for Vic, things were not normal. No matter how hard he'd tried, he couldn't get past the idea that he was responsible for his brother's death, and he was still convinced that he could not be a good father, no matter how hard Eleanor tried to convince him otherwise.

Vic recalled the feelings he'd had in Sarasota. He'd felt calm and unencumbered in that homey little cottage not far from the beach. He missed the bike rides he and Eleanor had taken together. Going to the beach and doing anything they wanted without anyone's interference had been like healing balm. Why couldn't those feelings have lasted when he and Eleanor had come home? But those carefree days were over, and reality had set in. Even if they could take another trip to Sarasota, it would not change the fact that Eleanor was going to have a baby, and Vic's depression and his desperate need for alcohol had returned.

Vic was sure that if anyone in his family learned about his habit of lifting a bottle of beer to his lips to numb the pain, there would be problems and plenty of unsolicited comments. Vic's reason for hiding his need to drink was to avoid confrontation, because he was sure that if anyone found out about it, they'd be on his case. He had enough stress on his plate right now and needed to make sure the truth was kept hidden.

Vic also felt sure that Eleanor didn't know that he had started drinking regularly again about a month ago. If she did, she hadn't said anything about it. The day after New Year's he'd enlisted Tom's help and bought several cartons of beer. Since Eleanor had found his previous hiding place in the hayloft, Vic had had to unearth some other places to hide the beer: the back of the toolshed, inside an old crate he kept in the corncrib, and a few other places Eleanor was not likely to find. Vic had gotten good at covering his tracks and deceiving his wife. If he avoided her too often, she would become suspicious, so Vic had decided to do his best to act as normal as possible around her. However, he could not muster up the words to say that he was excited about them having a baby. But he didn't dare say anything that would be off-putting either.

Vic wished he could shake away the doubts and dislike of himself that loomed over his head like a dark, foreboding cloud. No matter what anyone had said about him being a good father or Eddie's death not being his fault, he couldn't accept their words or believe it himself. The one thing Vic had accepted was his need for booze, and he thought being dishonest with his wife was a necessity right now. He'd also been careful not to drink to the point of becoming intoxicated. He needed enough alcohol to help him relax, and it had quickly gotten to the point where he needed a few beers almost every day. Vic made sure to cover his breath after drinking with gum, mints, or mouthwash, and he only kissed Eleanor when he hadn't had a beer to drink.

Yesterday, in an effort to come to grips with his guilty feelings about Eddie's death, Vic had taken a walk and ended up at the pond where Eddie had drowned. He hadn't paid anyone to fill it in because of the cost and figured the best thing to do was either force himself to come here once in a while, or not come anywhere near the pond at all. Forcing himself hadn't helped—it had only made Vic feel worse—so he'd decided he would avoid the pond altogether. Maybe someday, when their finances were better, he'd see about getting the body of water filled in.

"Is there anything interesting in that newspaper you're holding?" Eleanor's question pushed Vic's thoughts aside.

He shook his head. "No, not really. Same old negative news, coupled with too many advertisements for things most people don't need." Vic forced a laugh to cover the hopelessness he felt.

"That's true." Eleanor held up her pale green yarn. "I'm almost finished with this project, and then I'll begin making a sweater. Since we don't know the sex of our child, I chose a neutral color."

"If the baby's coming in the heat of summer, why would he or she need a sweater or knitted booties?" he asked.

"I'm making them bigger than newborn size, so Paul or Rosetta can wear them during the cooler fall weather that will come in September or October and beyond."

Vic's brows furrowed. "Since when did you start calling our unborn baby by *naame*, and why those specific names?"

"Because those are the ones we chose. Don't you remember when we talked about it a few weeks ago?"

If he answered truthfully, Vic would have to admit that he had no memory of the discussion. It was probably one of those nights he'd had a few drinks with Tom after work before coming home and gargling with a strong, minty mouthwash. "Umm. . .yeah. . .I must've forgot. Guess either of those names would be okay."

Eleanor tipped her head and looked at him with squinted eyes. "You don't remember the discussion we had about baby names, do you?"

He scratched an itchy spot on the side of his nose. "Course I remember. It just slipped my mind. You know how forgetful I can be sometimes. Just ask my mamm—she'll tell you I've been like that since I was a boy." Vic tossed the newspaper aside and stood. "I'm gonna take Checkers outside to do his duty before it's time to get ready for bed."

"Okay." Eleanor yawned. "I'm really tired, so I'll put things away here and take a warm shower and crawl into bed."

Vic nodded, put his jacket on, and called for the dog. Checkers stretched lazily from the place where he'd been lying by the fireplace and trotted after Vic when he went to get his jacket.

Once outside, Vic paused in the yard and breathed in the cold night air. The first breath hurt his lungs, but after a few more inhalations, he felt energized. Shoving his cold hands deep into his pockets, Vic plodded through the snow as he made his way out to the toolshed. He would drink one quick beer and chew a couple of mints before heading back to the house. Maybe by then Eleanor would be in bed asleep.

<hr>

Eleanor crawled into bed and pulled the covers up to her chin. She hoped Vic wouldn't be too long. It was lonely going to bed without him, and without his body warmth, the sheets felt colder than usual.

Although Vic had been making an attempt to talk with her when she brought up the topic of the baby, Eleanor could tell by the way his gaze darted around the room that he had felt anxious tonight when she'd mentioned the possible names they'd chosen for their baby. She was still concerned about her husband's disinterest in this baby. Both of their families had reacted positively to their joyful news, yet Vic rarely talked with Eleanor about having their first child. This stifled her joy and left Eleanor in tears. She longed for peace and harmony in their home and wanted laughter, not tears.

She closed her eyes and tried to send her thoughts in another direction, but it was no use. Eleanor wanted desperately for Vic to share in her enthusiasm that she was carrying his baby. Why couldn't he put his faith and trust in God and ask Him for help in learning how to be a good father? Eleanor was smart enough to realize that the process of becoming a worthy parent took some time. It wouldn't happen overnight, and they would both make some mistakes along the way. Even so, it would be a joyous journey to raise their child and help him or her grow up to be an example to the people they met along the way and live the Christian life God intended for them.

Eleanor's eyelids grew heavy, and she was on the verge of drifting off when she heard the bedroom door open, followed by the shuffling of Vic's feet as he made his way across the room. Eleanor waited until he pulled back the covers and climbed into bed, and then she reached out and put her hand on his back. "I've been struggling to stay awake so I could kiss you good night," she said, scooching closer to him.

"My throat feels kind of scratchy," he mumbled, keeping his back to her. "So it's best if we don't kiss tonight."

"I'm not worried about you giving me a sore throat," she responded.

"Well, I am. It's bad enough that you're still dealing with morning sickness. You sure don't need to end up with a sore throat." Before Eleanor could comment, Vic said, "Good night, Eleanor. See you in the morning."

That was it. The next thing Eleanor heard was her husband's heavy breathing. He'd obviously fallen quickly into a deep sleep.

"Good night, Vic. I love you," Eleanor whispered, even though she wasn't sure he could hear her. She rolled in the opposite direction and closed her eyes. *Dear Lord, please show me what I can say or do to help bring my husband out of his depression before it gets so bad that he resorts to drinking again. Help me to be kind and patient with Vic and open his eyes to the truth that he can and will be a good father if he'll just allow You to work through him.*

When her prayer ended, Eleanor relaxed a bit, and soon she felt herself being lulled closer to sleep. She placed both hands against her stomach. *Good night, my sweet child. I love you already, and I'm sure that your daddy does too, even though he hasn't yet spoken the words.*

———— ≈ ————

The following morning it was all Vic could do to pull himself up off the couch. He'd gotten up during the night and snuck back outside for a couple more beers, and to keep Eleanor from knowing, he'd slept in the living room, with only the warmth of a blanket. Vic hadn't planned to get drunk, but after drinking his first can of beer, he'd wanted another, which had led to more. He liked the relaxed, untroubled way he felt after he'd downed enough beers. He wished he could remain in a perpetual state of intoxication, but it always wore off, and then he had to face reality again.

Vic's head pounded, and with closed eyes, he reached up to rub his temples. At the same time, he felt the slurp of his dog's tongue. Vic pulled his hand away and groaned. "Knock it off, Checkers! I'm not in the mood for your sloppy kisses."

"Nor mine, either, apparently."

Vic's eyes snapped open, and he jerked his head to the right. Eleanor stood looking down at him with her arms folded across her stomach and a scowl on her face. "Would you please explain why you got up sometime during the night and slept out here on the couch instead of remaining in our bed next to me?" The red in his wife's face let him know that she was quite upset.

Vic sat up straight and faced her. "I. . .uh. . .had a hard time sleeping and didn't want to keep you awake with all my tossing and turning. Besides, my throat kept bothering me, and I was afraid I might end up coughing all night." The words rolled off his tongue with ease. He'd gotten good at lying and only felt a twinge of guilt. Vic told himself that he had no choice. If he'd told Eleanor the truth about what he'd done when he got out of bed during the night, she would get upset. They'd probably have ended up in a heated discussion, which neither of them needed right now.

Eleanor leaned closer and sniffed. "Please don't lie to me, Vic. You have that rotten egg smell of beer on your breath, as well as your clothes. What'd you do—get up to drink some beer? Or did you take a bath in the horrible stuff?" Her lips pressed into a tight grimace. This was not a good way to start a new day.

Checkers nuzzled Vic's hand with his cold nose, and Vic pushed the dog away. "I don't want to discuss this with you right now, Eleanor. I need to get ready for work."

"When did you start drinking again? Was it right after I told you that I was pregnant?"

He shook his head. "No, but it doesn't mean I didn't want to."

"Do you want to right now?"

He gave a noncommittal shrug and stood. "I need to shower and change into some clean work clothes. Would you please let Checkers out? I'm sure he's more than ready by now."

She stood unmoving, arms still pressed against her slightly protruding stomach. "We need to talk about this, Vic. If you're drinking again, hoping it will help you cope, then you need to seek help for the problem. Maybe you could—"

"I don't need any help! I'm not an alcoholic, you know. I can quit anytime I want." Vic stormed out of the room before Eleanor could offer a retort. She didn't understand the guilt he still felt over his brother's death, or the fact that he wouldn't make a good father. He wished he could push a button and start his life over—or at least begin from that fateful day when Eddie had come here to stay with them. If it were possible, Vic would make sure to keep a close eye on his brother, and he would definitely teach the boy how to swim.

Eleanor let Checkers out the back door and collapsed into a chair at the kitchen table. Her eyelids quivered with the need to cry. So what she had suspected for the last several weeks was true: Vic had started drinking again. Eleanor felt like a fool for believing his lies, but she'd wanted to give her husband the benefit of the doubt.

If Vic kept this up, by the time the baby was born, his previous declaration would be true—he would not be a good father. No child could live a healthy, normal life if either of their parents had an addition to alcohol that went untreated. And with Vic unwilling to admit he had a problem and refusing to seek help, Eleanor didn't see how their marriage and family life could ever be happy or complete. It was upsetting to hear him deny that he needed help and say he wasn't an alcoholic. She could hardly believe that her husband had said he could quit drinking anytime he wanted. If what

Vic said had been true, then he never would have started drinking in the first place.

Frustration welled in Eleanor's soul. *I think my husband's lost his way. The taste for alcohol and the lies that spill from his lips seem to be Vic's only comfort these days.*

Eleanor's gaze went to the jar filled with shells she and Vic had picked up at Lido Beach during their stay in Sarasota. Her jaw ached from clenching her teeth as she struggled with the agony of the situation she and Vic now faced. It would take a lot more than a two-week vacation to make things right this time, but if he wouldn't seek professional help, Eleanor felt sure that more problems would develop between them.

Could Vic's drinking problem get worse after the baby was born? Might he ever become abusive to her or their child? So many unanswered questions rolled around in her head. The only thing Eleanor knew for certain was that she needed to tell someone about this, and it had to be a person she could trust not to tell anyone—especially not Vic. Eleanor could only imagine how angry he would become if his family or someone in their church district learned about his drinking problem and confronted him with it. No, she would have to reach out to somebody outside of the family, and Eleanor knew who it should be.

Chapter 30

Grabill

Doretta's heart constricted as she read her dear friend's recent letter. It was a shock to learn that Vic had begun drinking beer after his little brother died. Eleanor said that her husband had stopped drinking for a while but then started again after learning that he was going to become a father. Eleanor also stated that she couldn't take Vic at his word anymore because he'd been lying to her about his drinking habit and perhaps other things as well.

Clearly desperate to share her burden, Eleanor had reached out to Doretta, asking for prayer and pleading with her not to tell anyone about Vic's problem and how it had been affecting their marriage in such a negative way.

Poor, sweet Eleanor. You're my best friend and such a good person. It's hard to imagine that you are having to go through this and being forced to deal with such a stressful situation. Doretta's thoughts went in several directions as she tried to analyze things and seek some sort of resolution. Her mind skipped ahead to some of the possible consequences of Vic's behavior. Would things get so bad that Eleanor might consider leaving him—maybe not indefinitely, but until he sought help?

Using the tips of her fingers, Doretta made little circles across her forehead as she reflected further. *Has Eleanor tried to persuade Vic to get help? There was no mention of that in her letter. It is, however, something my friend*

*should consider. Would I be out of place to suggest to Eleanor that she should try
to get her husband some help? There are places like Alcoholics Anonymous and
many clinics that treat various addictions. There are also Christian counseling
services, and of course, talking with their church leaders could help.*

Doretta lowered her hands into her lap. *If only we lived closer and I could
be there for her. She needs a close friend for comfort now more than ever. I wish I
could talk to my mamm about this, but Eleanor asked me not to tell anyone, and
I won't break her trust.*

She got up from the foot of her bed, where she'd been sitting to read
Eleanor's letter, and took a seat in the chair in front of her desk. In addition
to praying earnestly for her friend's situation, the very least Doretta could
do was to write Eleanor a letter, offering some suggestions for where Vic
might find help for his addiction. Of course, he'd have to be willing to talk
about his problems, and since seeking professional help was something
he might not agree to, Doretta would let her friend know that she would
definitely be praying about the situation.

Paradise

Eleanor fought queasiness as she forced herself to get out the ingredients
for some baking. Lying around on the couch or in bed while feeling sorry
for herself didn't ease the nausea she felt or help her forget about the confrontation she'd had with Vic when he'd come home from work last night.
Vic had not only arrived two hours later than usual, but he'd been drinking
again. This was getting old, and her patience was about to wear out. Eleanor's
emotions were erratic and often ran high with the hormones of pregnancy.
Sometimes she would find herself crying easily over the least little thing.
But she had a right to her strong feelings regarding her husband's alcohol
addiction. He hadn't tried to hide it from her this time, the way he had
a few weeks ago when he'd slept on the couch. From what Eleanor could
tell, Vic didn't seem to care how much his actions hurt her. He'd made it
quite plain last night that she needed to stop nagging him about it. Eleanor

could still see her husband's flared nostrils and the tightness around his eyes. She replayed in her mind the way Vic had raised his voice at her, saying he could do whatever he wanted and she was not his boss. It seemed almost every day Vic said or did something to hurt Eleanor's feelings, and he never bothered to apologize.

"Such a contrast from the husband I spent two weeks with in Florida." Eleanor swallowed against the bile rising in her throat as she forced herself to take out a glass baking dish that she would use to make an applesauce cake. If Vic would only listen to reason and realize that he needed help now, before his drinking problem became worse.

Eleanor remembered an English man who'd lived in the community where she'd grown up. He had dealt with a serious alcohol dependency. Sadly, he had become known as the town drunk. The fellow had gotten so bad that he'd begun abusing his wife and children and finally ended up in jail when someone reported his actions.

Could things go that far with Vic? Eleanor asked herself. *I surely don't want anyone to think of my husband as the town drunk. Before Eddie died, Vic was always a gentle, kindhearted man, but I've witnessed how the influence of alcohol can change a person, and if he doesn't get control of his drinking habits soon, it will change him too.*

Eleanor's gaze came to rest on the stenciled lettering she'd put on one kitchen wall some time ago. It was a verse from the Bible that she'd read many times, Joshua 24:15: "BUT AS FOR ME AND MY HOUSE, WE WILL SERVE THE LORD." She had put it there before Vic had started drinking, believing that it would be a reminder for both of them to always put God first and seek to serve Him in all ways. Eleanor wondered if her husband noticed the stenciling anymore. If he did, he never commented on it, and worse, Vic was not doing anything that would indicate that he wanted to serve the Lord. Had he lost his faith in God altogether after the death of his brother?

Tears sprang to her eyes, and she whisked them away with the back of her hand. Crying would not solve the problem, and besides, she had already shed way too many tears.

Eleanor placed one hand against her abdomen and held it there for several seconds. *Feeling so stressed is not good for me or the precious infant growing within my belly. If Vic doesn't straighten out soon, I may have to go away for a while—at least until he wakes up to the fact that he has a problem and is willing to get some help.*

Eleanor leaned over the kitchen sink as a wave of nausea came so fast she felt sure that she would lose her breakfast. Despite the chill outside, she opened the window and took in a few deep breaths, hoping it would help calm her down and ease the nausea. Her thinking had become muddled due to all the stress she'd been under since learning she was pregnant, and something needed to change. Between the problems she faced with Vic and the hours she felt sick to her stomach every day, Eleanor was barely able to function. Yet she kept forcing herself to do things like cooking, baking, laundry, and other household chores. They all needed to be done, and she was the only person here to do them.

A blast of cold made a hasty entrance into the room, and she quickly shut the window. When Eleanor reached into the cupboard for a sack of flour, a knock sounded on the front door. Placing the sack on the counter and wiping away the tears beneath her eyes, she went to see who it was.

———— ≈ ————

Susie smiled when Eleanor opened the door, but seeing the grave expression on her daughter-in-law's face caused the woman's smile to fade.

"Are you feeling *grank* today?" she asked upon entering the house with a bag in her grasp, along with a plastic container.

Eleanor moved her head slowly up and down. "I felt quite ill a few moments ago, and nearly vomited in the kitchen sink."

"Oh my. I'm so sorry." Susie gave Eleanor a hug. "I've been worried about you, so I came by to find out how you're doing and see if there is anything I can do to help. Also, I've brought a couple of different teas. One is ginger and the other is peppermint. You can try them both, and hopefully at least one of them might curb your nausea." Susie set the container and bag down on the narrow wooden table inside the entryway. "There are a couple dozen ginger cookies in here that might be good later too." She tapped the top of the lid.

"I appreciate the cookies as well as the teas, and if you have the time and feel so inclined, I wouldn't mind your help with some baking."

"No problem. I'd be happy to help with whatever you need." Susie removed her outer garments and hung them on the coat tree in the hall, then picked up the items she'd brought and followed Eleanor to the kitchen. When they entered the room, she set the cookies and tea bags on the counter and asked what kind of baking Eleanor had in mind.

"Before you got here, I was getting ready to make an applesauce cake. It's one of the few things that actually appeals to me."

"I understand completely. When I was expecting Victor, I sometimes had to force myself to eat, because with the frequent bouts of nausea, my appetite often disappeared."

"That's how it is for me most days." Eleanor stood against the wall, her arms hanging loosely at her sides. "I don't have much energy either."

"Pregnancy does make a woman feel tired. That's why it's important for you to get as much rest as possible." Susie studied her daughter-in-law's face. The dark shadows beneath Eleanor's eyes were an indication that she either wasn't sleeping enough hours at night or the sleep she did get wasn't good quality. Susie remembered how during each of her pregnancies, she'd sometimes suffered with heartburn or simply couldn't find a comfortable position while trying to sleep. It had been a challenge to get enough rest in order to keep doing her chores every day. Thankfully, she'd had her mother's help during the first three pregnancies, and since her daughters had been older by the time she gave birth to Stephen and again when Eddie came along, Kate and Clara had chipped in and helped out.

Susie could tell that she'd made the right choice coming here today to check on her daughter-in-law. *I should make myself more accessible to Eleanor's needs. In addition to helping with chores, I can empathize more with how Eleanor feels physically and offer a mother's touch.*

"If you're tired and not feeling well, why don't you go lie down while I make the cake?" Susie offered.

"It would be kind of nice to lie down for a bit," Eleanor responded, "but I wouldn't feel right about doing that while you do my work in the kitchen."

Susie stepped closer to Eleanor and placed both hands on her slim shoulders. "I don't mind at all. In fact, I would count it a privilege to be able to do the baking for you."

Eleanor's eyes seemed to brighten a bit, and she smiled. "Danki for your kindness. I appreciate you coming by and offering to help, more than you know."

"I'm happy to do it. I'm also available to come back later this week if you need me."

"Are you sure that wouldn't be an imposition?"

"Not at all. Maybe you could figure out what you'd need to have done around here—like the laundry or some cleaning. Have you been up to going out shopping?"

"On some days, when I've felt up to it, I have been able to do a few errands, but other times the nausea has persisted, which has kept me close to home. And as far as getting chores done, that can be hit or miss, depending on how much energy I have."

"I can help you with your grocery shopping or other errands." Susie glanced at the door. "Have you gotten your mail today?"

Eleanor heaved a sigh. "No, I haven't been out to the box yet."

"Don't give it another thought. I'll go out right now and get it for you before I start the baking."

"Thank you. Guess I'll go lie down on the couch and rest awhile. If I fall asleep, please wake me."

Susie shook her head. "I'll do no such thing. If you doze off, I will not disturb you."

"Okay." When Eleanor brought a shaky hand up to her forehead, tears pooled in her eyes.

"Is everything all right? I mean, other than you being tired and nause-ated?" Susie couldn't help feeling concern.

A few seconds passed, and Eleanor said in a near whisper, "Things are a bit stressful for me and Vic right now. I'm hoping everything will be better soon." Before Susie could comment, Eleanor turned and shuffled out of the kitchen.

Susie pursed her lips. *I am almost sure now that there is some kind of a problem going on between my son and his fraa. I should have spoken to Victor about it like I'd planned to do, but I have yet to get that chance. Poor Eleanor. The last thing a woman in a family way needs is a struggle in her marriage. The next time I see Victor and no one's around, I am going to speak to him about this important matter.*

Lancaster

"How are things going with the old ball and chain?" Tom looked at Vic over the rim of his coffee mug as he lifted it to his lips.

Vic gave his left ear a tug. "What?"

"I said. . ."

Vic held up his hand. "I know what you said. What I don't know is what you meant by that."

"Ball and chain. You've heard the expression before, right?"

"I'm aware of what a ball and chain is, but I don't have one."

"Sure you do." Tom set the mug down and picked up his sandwich. "In this instance, ball and chain refers to your wife."

"Huh?"

"She ties you down, right?"

"I–I'm not sure what you're getting at." Vic blew out his cheeks and then released the air quickly. "Are you trying to make me feel stupid by asking questions you think I don't understand?"

"Not at all." Tom ate the piece of sandwich he'd put in his mouth and washed it down with more coffee. "When I picked you up this morning,

I mentioned going out for a few drinks after work and asked if you'd like to go with me."

Vic bobbed his head. "And I said, not this time. Eleanor and I had an argument last night, and I don't want to make things any worse by getting home late this evening with alcohol on my breath."

Tom lifted one hand with his palm up. "Ball and chain."

"Stop saying that. My wife is not a ball and chain. She's expecting our first baby and—"

"So now you've lost all your freedom. Next thing you know, she'll have you talked into going off to some stupid AA meetings." Spots of color erupted on Tom's cheeks. "That's what my wife tried to do with me."

"AA?"

"Yeah—you know—Alcoholics Anonymous, where everyone in attendance sits around in a circle and admits that they're an alcoholic." Tom scrunched up his nose as though some foul odor had permeated the booth where they sat inside the restaurant they'd gone to for lunch. "And then the ones in charge try to make you give up drinking," he added with a scowl.

Vic opened his mouth to say something, but, thinking better of it, he bit the inside of his cheek. He was sure that Eleanor would never expect him to attend an AA meeting. A place like that was for alcoholics, not someone like him who drank once in a while to relax and cope with the stresses of life. Vic figured all he needed to do to get back in Eleanor's good graces was promise to quit drinking and pay a little more attention to her. Starting tonight, that's exactly what he would do.

Chapter 31

"Are you sure you're feeling up to having supper at my folks' house this evening?" Vic reached across the buggy seat and touched Eleanor's arm.

Truth was, she'd been dealing with this terrible nausea for a good many weeks, and it hadn't really improved. Eleanor had been trying the peppermint and ginger teas, along with eating some ginger cookies—anything to curb the feeling of wanting to vomit. It was hard to know from hour to hour how she would feel throughout the day, but for the moment things were okay.

"Eleanor, did you hear what I said? Are you sure you're up to having supper at my folks' this evening? I can turn the horse and buggy around and head for home. You just have to say the word."

"I'm fine." Eleanor fought the urge to ask Vic if he really cared. He'd said he did a few nights ago when he'd come from work with a bouquet of red roses. Vic had also apologized for the things he'd said and done to upset her, and once again he'd promised that he would quit drinking, but she doubted his word. After all, he'd made that same promise before and then went right back to drinking as soon as she'd announced her pregnancy. Eleanor had no reason to believe her husband now. But the only right thing to do was give him the benefit of the doubt. Her other choice would be to say that she didn't believe him, which would undoubtedly make him angry, and then they'd most likely end up in another argument. For the sake of the baby, as well as Eleanor's health, she would accept Vic's apology and make every effort to be the kind of wife her husband needed. She also wanted to please God with her words and deeds, which would hopefully set a good example for Vic.

"Sure will be glad when spring comes and brings in some warmer weather. I'm kind of sick of the schnee."

For a brief moment, Eleanor would've liked to simply state that she was sick and tired of Vic's lies. But her honesty would have provoked an angry response, which neither of them needed. *If only I could trust Vic.* Eleanor gripped the handles of her black handbag. *Is he incapable of being honest with me?*

Eleanor eyed the glistening scenery out the buggy's window. "Snow is pretty, but I don't care much for it anymore. When I was a young girl, I thought it was fun to play in the snow, but not now. As an adult, I prefer warmer weather or to be inside during the cold winter months."

"Same here." Vic kept a tight hold on the reins as a big truck went past on the opposite side of the road, going much too fast. Dealing with crazy drivers, like the man behind the wheel of that truck, was enough to put Vic's nerves on edge. Of course, a lot of things made him tense up—including his obligation to spend an evening at his parents' house. Being in the home where he grew up was a reminder that one of their family members was gone.

Will the pain of losing Eddie ever go away? Vic asked himself. *Will I ever stop missing him or quit feeling responsible for his death? Can I ever walk past our pond without reliving that fateful day?* He'd asked himself these same questions so many times and always with no answers. Vic wished he hadn't promised Eleanor that he would quit drinking, because it was getting more difficult to keep his word. Whenever he'd had a hard day at work, he craved a drink. If Vic's boss got on him about something he hadn't done to his satisfaction, it filled him with the desire for a can of beer. Every day without drinking had become a big challenge.

Maybe if I only had a few drinks once in a while, when I'm not at home, Eleanor wouldn't know. Vic contemplated the idea. *Of course I'd have to come up with a better way to cover the evidence on my breath. I would also have to limit it to just one or two drinks and never come home drunk again.*

———————≈———————

Ever since that truck had sped by, aggravating Vic's horse, Vic had seemed to be concentrating on the road and controlling Domino. Eleanor had no problem with that. It was important that they arrive at their destination safely. She hoped the evening would go well, and that whatever meal her mother-in-law had fixed would not cause any stomach upset. It was bad enough when she got nauseous and vomited while at home, like she had when she'd fixed cabbage rolls two nights ago. Just the smell of the cabbage cooking had made Eleanor feel queasy, and the tangy tomato sauce covering the ground pork and beef that had been rolled up in the cabbage had given her a severe case of indigestion. Eleanor wouldn't want either of those reactions to happen at the Lapps' home. That would be most embarrassing. Well, it would do no good to worry about it now. Maybe whatever food had been prepared wouldn't bother her at all.

Eleanor glanced at Vic, noticing the firm set of his jaw. Was it from concentrating so hard on the road, or was there something else bothering her husband right now?

Eleanor thought about the letter she'd received from Doretta a week after she'd written to her about Vic's drinking problem. Would her friend's suggestion about the possibility of Vic attending AA meetings be helpful, even if he wasn't drinking right now? If he began attending the meetings perhaps it would help him if the urge to drink crept back in.

Of course, she reasoned, *I can't make Vic go. That's something he will have to decide for himself.* Eleanor pressed her lips together as she stared out the buggy window at the snow that had begun to fall in heavy, thick flakes. *I could definitely start attending Al-Anon meetings for spouses of alcoholics if Vic's drinking should start up again. At least there would be other people in attendance who have experienced the same kinds of things as I've had to deal with.*

———— ≋ ————

Strasburg

As Vic sat at the supper table in his parents' dining room, he forced himself not to look at the seat Eddie used to occupy. Of course it wasn't easy when he had to pass the food in that direction.

"How are things going in the construction business?" Vic's dad asked. "Has work slacked off due to the colder weather, or does your boss have plenty of jobs for you and his crew to do?"

"Everything's been inside work lately, so Ned's managed to keep us all fairly busy," Vic replied.

Dad nodded. "Good to hear."

"How are things in your shop here?" Vic asked as he helped himself to another piece of chicken breast.

"We don't have as much work as we do during the warmer months, of course, but there's still some work to be done." Dad looked across the table at Stephen. "I'm keeping you busy enough, right, son?"

"Jah, Dad. If not in the shop, then there are always other things to do around here and in the barn."

Vic thought about the days he'd still been in school and had worked for their father on Saturdays and even some late afternoons or evenings. For the most part, they'd gotten along okay, but sometimes Dad got on Vic's case, saying he wasn't working quickly enough or hadn't sanded a piece of wood as smooth as he would like. It all boiled down to one thing—his father was a perfectionist. Vic had always done the best job he could and still did. But he had learned early on that working for a boss he wasn't related to was a lot easier than working for a close relative who scrutinized everything he said or did. Vic figured if Stephen ever decided to go to work for someone other than their dad, he'd figure that out too.

"How are you feeling these days?" Clara asked, looking at Eleanor.

"Somewhat better. I get tired if I try to do too much, and I'm still dealing with stomach upset from time to time." Eleanor took a drink of water, and when she set the glass down, a sigh escaped her lips. "I'll be ever so glad when the baby comes."

Eleanor glanced over at Vic as though expecting him to agree with her, but all he could manage was a brief nod. With the way he still felt about becoming a father, it was hard to get excited about the big event. No matter what anyone said, Vic was still convinced that he would fail miserably as a parent.

———————≈———————

When the meal was over, Clara and Kate volunteered to clear the table and do the dishes. While they were doing that, Eleanor excused herself to use the bathroom. After Ethan and Stephen went out to the barn to check on the animals, Susie saw her chance to speak to Victor alone. "Let's go into the living room, Son." She gestured in that direction. "There's something I'd like to talk to you about."

Victor's eyes narrowed, as if in confusion. "What's up?"

She started down the hall and motioned for him to follow. When they entered the living room, Susie took a seat on the couch and asked Victor to sit beside her.

"What's going on, Mom?" he asked after seating himself.

She moved closer to him and spoke quietly. "I sense that there may be a problem between you and Eleanor and thought you might want to talk about it."

Victor looked down at the floor, avoiding eye contact with her. "What makes you believe that Eleanor and I have any kind of a problem?"

"Your lack of enthusiasm about her pregnancy is quite obvious."

He lifted his gaze and nodded. "It's not the right time, Mom. It's not even a quarter to the right time."

"Do you think there is ever a perfect time to have a child?"

Victor shrugged.

"That precious baby your wife carries in her womb is a gift from God. Surely you must realize that."

"A gift I'm not worthy of fathering," he muttered.

"That's *lecherich*."

"It's not ridiculous. It's the truth." Victor pointed to himself. "I do not have what it takes to father any child."

In her mind, Susie retorted, *If you didn't feel ready to have a child yet, then you should've been honest with your wife and not been trying to procreate.* She could see that her son showed selfishness and a certain lack of maturity. This didn't set well with her. The effects his actions were having on Eleanor were obvious.

Susie sat for several seconds, letting his remark settle into her brain so she could process it correctly and come up with the best response. "Do you think that your daed felt ready to raise a child when I got pregnant with you?"

"That was different." A muscle on the side of Victor's jaw quivered. "I bet Dad had done nothing to prove that he was irresponsible around kinner. Am I right?"

"Nobody is perfect, and accidents happen to a good many people. No one is immune to bad things while living in this world, either, but when they do happen, we need to allow God to work His power through us. Besides, this isn't about your daed, Victor. I suspect that this is about you piling the blame on yourself for your brother's accidental death. Is that correct?"

Victor stared straight ahead.

"It is. I can tell. And I'm also aware that things are not right between you and your fraa." She placed her hand on his knee. "You need to find a way to get past all this guilt and anger you're still harboring over losing Eddie. It's not doing you or your marriage any good."

Her son's facial features tightened. "I don't need a lecture, Mom. My wife and I are getting along just fine, and even if we weren't, it would be our own business."

Susie's jaw slackened as her mouth dropped open, but she held back from saying the words on the tip of her tongue because she heard footsteps coming down the hall. A few seconds later, Eleanor entered the room. Her face looked so pale, and she held both hands against her stomach. "I'm sorry," she said, looking at Susie, "but I think Vic and I need to go home. I'm not feeling well."

Susie's pulse quickened. "Do we need to call one of our drivers to take you to the hospital?"

Eleanor shook her head. "I'm sure it's nothing serious. I became nauseated soon after we ate, and unfortunately, I lost my dinner when I went to your bathroom."

Victor got up from the couch and went over to stand beside Eleanor. "You're right. We'd better go home. I'll get the horse hitched to the buggy while you put on your things."

"Danki." After Victor put on his jacket and went out the door, Eleanor turned to Susie and said, "Please don't worry about me. I'll be fine once I get home and go to bed."

Susie gave the young woman a gentle hug. "I hope you get a good night's sleep, and I'll be checking on you tomorrow to see how you're feeling."

Eleanor's eyes teared up. "I appreciate your concern."

"And I appreciate the fact that our son chose you to be his fraa. Ethan and I couldn't ask for a better daughter-in-law."

"I am grateful for both of you too."

Susie got Eleanor's jacket and outer bonnet for her. When she saw that her son had his horse and buggy ready, she stood in the doorway and watched as Eleanor walked carefully down the porch steps and across the snow-covered lawn to get into the carriage. Susie hoped the nausea would end soon and that Eleanor would be feeling much better. It didn't seem fair that the poor girl had to deal with that on top of Victor's ongoing self-guilt. To make matters worse was his negative reaction to the birth of their future child. *If I could,* she thought again, *I'd ask my daughter-in-law to stay with us right now. Then she'd get the proper care and support she needs.*

Susie reduced the opening of the door, trying to keep out some of the cold while she watched them get into their buggy and head out. *I hope I did the right thing by talking to Victor,* Susie told herself. *I only wish I could have gotten through to him. If he doesn't get rid of the guilt he feels about Eddie, things will never be right between him and Eleanor. and then he'll probably be right—my son Victor will not be a good father.*

Chapter 32

Eleanor entered the kitchen to check on the stew simmering on the stove-top, but before crossing the room to the stove, she glanced at the calendar hanging on the wall near the back door. Just three more months to go until the baby would be born, and she should have been filled with excitement. Instead, Eleanor looked upon the event with fear and trepidation because she wasn't sure what the future held for her, Vic, or their child. Vic had started drinking again, and this time it was worse than before. He'd hidden it well at first, and she hadn't caught on to the fact that he'd started up again until he'd begun making excuses about being late getting home from work. She had also smelled the sickening odor of beer on his breath several times. When Eleanor had confronted Vic about it, he said he'd only had one beer and that he wasn't drunk, so there was nothing for her to worry about.

"Nothing to worry about?" she muttered. "The signs are all there. I can see them as clear as glass, but I don't know what to do about it."

Checkers' ears perked up, and he gave a little bark before coming over to where Eleanor stood.

"Did you think I was talking to you?" Eleanor bent down and gave the dog's head a few pats.

Checkers stared up at her as he wagged his tail.

"Do you want to go out for a while?"

Woof! Woof! The dog ran out of the kitchen, raced down the hall, and stood at the front door.

Eleanor shook her head. "I don't know why you had to go out the front door when we were there in the kitchen by the back door." She let the dog out and stepped onto the porch, hoping to see Tom's truck coming up the road. No vehicles were in sight.

I may as well go ahead and eat without Vic, Eleanor told herself. If she didn't eat something soon, nausea could set in, like it still did on occasion when she'd gone without food for too long.

Eleanor waited until Checkers finished his business before she called the dog and they went in. Back in the kitchen, Eleanor dished herself a bowl of stew and took a seat at the table. She bowed her head, thanked God for the food, and asked Him to bring her husband home safely and soon.

As Eleanor ate her meal, she thought about the last letter she'd written to Doretta, giving her an update on things and asking for continued prayer. She'd begun the letter by posing a question for Doretta: *Did you ever talk to someone and think that everything they said was a lie? Well, that's how I feel now whenever Vic tells me anything.*

Eleanor's throat constricted as she glanced at the clock. It was eight o'clock, and she still had no sign of her husband. *Surely Vic would have called if he was going to be working this late. Maybe I should call his boss and ask. I need to know something because I'm starting to worry.*

Eleanor finished her stew, put the bowl in the sink, and went out the front door. Predictably, Checkers followed. Before she entered the phone shed, she threw a stick for the dog and stepped inside the small building as soon as Checkers chased after the piece of wood.

Eleanor took a seat and dialed the number for Vic's boss. She was glad when he answered the phone so she didn't have to leave a message. "Hello, Mr. Duncan. This is Eleanor Lapp, Vic's wife. My husband isn't home yet, and I was wondering if he had to work overtime this evening."

"No, everyone on my crew stopped working at five." The man paused a few seconds and cleared his throat. "I did hear Tom and Vic talking before they left the shop, though. One of them said something about going to a pub in Lancaster for a few beers."

"Oh, I see." Eleanor swallowed hard. "Thank you for the information, and I'm sorry to have bothered you."

"No problem. I hope your husband gets home soon. I'm sure you must be worried about him."

"Yes, I am," she admitted. *I worry about Vic all the time.* After Eleanor said goodbye, she checked for messages, but there were none. *Vic didn't even have the courtesy to call and say he was going to be late.* She sniffed deeply. *Doesn't he care about me at all? Does he not realize that I'm worried about him? Have I done something that would make Vic choose spending time with his drinking buddy instead of me?*

Eleanor felt so discouraged. She was tired of being on the verge of tears so much of the time. Her shoulders slumped as she left the phone shed and walked back to the house with her head down. Vic was off someplace drinking with Tom, and there wasn't a thing she could do about it.

Pray, a voice in her head seemed to say.

Eleanor closed her eyes and whispered a prayer for Vic and Tom. It was the only thing she could do since she had no idea where they were or when Tom would bring Vic home. The thought crossed Eleanor's mind that she could call one of their drivers to take her around in search of Vic. She quickly dismissed that silly notion, realizing that with all the taverns and pubs in Lancaster County, it would be difficult to find the one Tom and Vic had gone to. And even if by some chance Eleanor located her husband, she could only imagine how angry he would be if she walked into the establishment and asked him to come home with her. Vic would be embarrassed and so would she. No, the best thing she could do was to go back into the house and wait until Tom brought Vic home. Of course, he probably wouldn't be in the best shape to talk to about this problem tonight, but in the morning, when the alcohol had worn off, Eleanor was prepared to have a serious discussion with her husband.

~≋~

Eleanor felt a rush of adrenaline course through her body when she opened the blinds in the living room the next morning and saw Tom's truck parked in the front yard. She had fallen asleep, still wearing her clothes, while lying on the couch, as she'd waited up for Vic last night. Eleanor wondered what time they had arrived and where Vic and his buddy were. Surely she would have heard them if they'd come into the house during the night. *Could they be in Tom's truck? I need to go check.*

Eleanor got up and put her prayer covering on, then slipped on a sweater and opened the front door. Checkers made a beeline for the entrance before she had a chance to step out. Eleanor waited until he'd made it to the yard, and then she stepped off the porch and walked up to Tom's truck. Her heart pounded as she peered into the window on the passenger's side. There was no sign of Vic or his coworker. She squinted as she rubbed the bridge of her nose. *Where are those two men? Could they be out in the barn?*

Eleanor headed in that direction. At the same time, Checkers rounded the corner of the house and followed her. After opening the barn doors, she stepped in, allowing her eyes to adjust to the dim light inside.

Yip! Yip! Yip! The dog bounded in, bumping Eleanor's right knee. It threw her off balance, and she quickly grabbed one of the door handles to steady herself.

"Who's there?" a voice she didn't recognize called out.

"Eleanor, is that you?"

She recognized the second voice and took a few tentative steps forward. Then she saw them—Vic and Tom lying in a mound of straw on the floor. Checkers had seen them too and barked frantically as he crouched close to Tom.

"Knock it off, dog! Get away from me!"

"It's okay, boy. Come here, Checkers." Vic clapped his hands, and when the dog came to him, he looked over at Tom and said, "Don't worry. Checkers won't bite. He doesn't know you and is just being protective of me."

Eleanor's legs trembled as she moved closer to the men. "What are you two doing out here—sleeping off a drunk?"

Vic scrambled to his feet and reached a hand toward her. "We got here late and didn't want to disturb you."

"So you stumbled your way out here to the barn?" Her voice shook with raw emotion as she stared at her unkempt husband. "When you didn't come home at a reasonable hour, I called your boss."

"You did what?"

"I called your boss, and when I asked if you were working late, he said that he'd heard you and Tom talking about stopping someplace for a few beers."

Tom spoke up. "Yeah, it's true. When I brought your husband here, I was a little tipsy and didn't think it was a good idea to drive myself home."

"But you drove here, with my husband in your truck. Since you'd obviously been drinking, didn't you realize how dangerous it was to be driving your vehicle?"

"Yeah, that's why I bedded down in the barn with Vic."

As Vic moved closer to Eleanor, she focused on his bloodshot eyes, sallow skin, and disheveled hair. It made her feel sick to her stomach to see him that way.

With courage coming from somewhere deep inside, Eleanor planted both hands firmly against her hips. "You've been lying to me, Vic— promising to quit drinking, but like before, you couldn't keep your word." She gave her head a vigorous shake. "*Sis en sinn un en schand.*"

Tom crooked an eyebrow and looked at Vic. "What was the last thing your woman said to you? I couldn't understand the Pennsylvania Dutch."

"She said it's a sin and a shame," Vic replied.

Tom tipped his head back and let loose with a boisterous laugh. "She thinks a little lie is a sin and a shame?" He looked right at Eleanor and pointed at her. "Better get over that notion, lady. People stretch the truth and tell white lies all the time. It's just the way of things."

Vic said nothing in defense of Eleanor, and that fueled her anger even more. She shuddered, looking at these two men, both in such unsettling

WANDA & BRUNSTETTER

condition and apparently not the least bit sorry for their actions. Seeing Vic and his coworker like this was the last straw for her. In that moment, Eleanor knew that it was time to seek professional help of some kind for Vic, and perhaps she would need some counseling too. Eleanor couldn't wait for Tom to go home, because she and Vic had some serious talking to do, and she wouldn't take no for an answer this time.

Looking directly at her husband, Eleanor spoke in a steady, lower-than-normal voice. "I am going into the house to start breakfast now, and then we need to talk. Will you be coming in soon?"

He gave a slow nod and gestured to Tom. "What about him?"

"He should go home. I'm sure someone is there waiting for him."

"Not anymore." Tom clambered to his feet, brushing at the straw clinging to his shirt and pants. "But you're right, little lady. I do need to go home."

Yes, you do, because if you stay here much longer, I'm likely to give you a piece of my mind. Eleanor didn't voice her thoughts, because Vic's coworker was not her problem. He probably wouldn't have listened to anything she had to say anyhow. Without another word, she turned away from the men and hurried out of the barn.

———⋙———

"That went well, right?" Tom gave Vic's back a few thumps.

Vic cringed and muttered, "Yeah, real well."

"Guess you'll be sleeping in the doghouse with your mutt for a few nights." Tom gestured to Checkers, who stood near Vic.

Vic didn't appreciate Tom's comment and told him so. "For your information, I'm the man of this house, and my wife doesn't tell me what to do. Furthermore, during the night, Checkers has been sleeping in the house with us, here of late, not in his doghouse."

Tom flapped his hand. "Oh, don't look so serious. Can't you take a joke?"

"I could if it was funny." Vic flicked some straw off his shirt and headed out of the barn in a huff.

260

Tom followed. "Guess I'll head home and take some aspirin for my headache before I get cleaned up. See you Monday morning, Vic. Oh, and I hope your ball and chain doesn't give you too harsh of a tongue-lashing when you go in the house. Who knows—she might end up handing you your walking papers."

Vic clenched his teeth. It was all he could do to keep from punching Tom. It was bad enough that he had to face Eleanor right now. He sure didn't need to put up with Tom's snide remarks. Without another word, he walked off toward the house with his faithful dog at his heels. He'd messed things up with Eleanor again, and now it was time to face the music. Vic could only imagine what she would have to say to him during breakfast.

———≋———

Eleanor didn't say anything to Vic when he came into the house. She only nodded when he said he was going to take a shower and asked if she could hold breakfast until he was done. That had been thirty minutes ago, and still no sign of Vic. Eleanor wondered if he'd gone to bed after his shower. No doubt he was still suffering from a hangover, and he probably hadn't slept well on his mattress of straw in the barn.

She placed a box of cold cereal on the table, along with some blueberries she'd taken from the freezer. It wasn't an exciting breakfast, but Eleanor didn't feel at all like cooking. She just wanted to sit down with her husband and have a serious talk about his drinking problem and discuss some options for him to get the help he needed.

Another ten minutes went by, and Vic finally walked into the room. Like a shadow, the dog came in behind him and lay down on the throw rug when Vic took a seat at the table. He glanced at the box of cereal and frowned. "I'm not hungry; what I really need is a good strong cup of kaffi to clear the cobwebs outa my brain."

Eleanor poured him a cup of coffee and took a seat opposite him. "We need to talk, Vic."

"You're right, and I know I blew it last night. I promise to do better from now on, Eleanor."

"I've heard that before." She sat straight up and looked directly at him. "You have to get help for your addiction. You also need some counseling to resolve your guilt issues over Eddie's death, for which you were not to blame."

Vic breathed noisily through his flaring nostrils, and he glared at her with his bloodshot eyes. "I do not appreciate you telling me what I need. I told you I would quit, and I will!"

When Vic slammed his fist on the table, Eleanor flinched. She'd never seen so much anger pour out of her husband. It frightened her, but she couldn't back down. "Please, Vic." She spoke calmly and without raising her voice. "I'd be happy to go with you to an AA meeting, and we could talk to our bishop or one of the ministers about—"

"No!" Vic's face flamed a bright red, and he jumped up so quickly his chair toppled over, which caused the dog to jump up and scramble out of the room. "I do not want to hear another word about this, Eleanor. Is that clear?"

Her eyes burned, and she blinked away the moisture as she murmured, "Jah, Vic, I understand."

Vic grabbed his cup of coffee and headed out the door. Eleanor didn't bother to ask where he was going. This issue was not over, however, because if Vic wouldn't seek help for himself, then she would do whatever she needed to help herself.

Chapter 33

"How'd things go with your ball and. . . Sorry, I meant with your wife over the weekend?" Tom asked when Vic got into his truck Monday morning.

"Not well. Eleanor wants me to go to an AA meeting and get some counseling as well."

"You gonna do it?"

Vic gave a vigorous shake of his head. "No way! I'm not about to hang my dirty laundry out in front of people I don't even know. And if my wife thinks that talking to a counselor would help, she's wrong. No one and nothing is gonna convince me that I'm not the one responsible for my brother's death."

Tom's brows furrowed, but he didn't say anything. Vic figured his buddy either didn't understand his reason for drinking or had been dealing with issues of guilt himself. Maybe he felt responsible for the breakup of his marriage and drank heavily to deal with it. If that was the situation, Vic could certainly understand. Whatever the case, it didn't matter. He and Tom both had their own crosses to bear, and they each had their own reasons for turning to alcohol to help numb the pain. Vic didn't care for the dry mouth, twitchy muscles, and fatigue he often felt the day after he'd had too much to drink. He didn't enjoy the slurred speech and impaired coordination when he was drunk, but he liked the mellow, no-care feeling he got after downing a few beers. Even so, Vic knew that his marriage was in jeopardy, so he had to think of something to do that would get him back in Eleanor's good graces. He just hadn't figured out yet what it should be.

An hour after Vic left for work, Eleanor hitched Buttons to her buggy and headed down the road to see their bishop and his wife. It was time to let them know what was really going on with Vic and see if they had any suggestions or a contact number for Alcoholics Anonymous somewhere in Lancaster County. If Vic found out, he'd be angry, but Eleanor had to take that risk. Her biggest concern at the moment was not whether the bishop and his wife would keep what she said confidential, but whether Vic could be talked into going for help.

Eleanor's back became wet with perspiration as she drove the buggy. She wished it wasn't necessary to go behind her husband and defy his wishes, but she was desperate. Things hadn't changed with Vic, and his attitude toward her and their future child wasn't at all loving. After this trip, she would need to tell his folks about the situation, or else they might find out through the Amish grapevine. Either way, things were probably going to get worse before they got better at home. At least Eleanor hoped they would improve. As much as she hated to admit it, Vic might never get help for his addiction. If that happened, she didn't know what she would do.

Eleanor rolled her shoulders, trying to loosen the kinks and hoping she wouldn't be a sweaty mess upon arriving at the Zooks' place. At least it wasn't a long trip there, and Button's gait was a nice, easy trot. *Vic's and my future seems so up in the air right now,* she thought. *I can't help but worry how all this will play out. If only my husband could understand my reasons for trying to get him some help.*

She repositioned herself on the seat and tried to relax, but it was difficult. With everything that had been going on in her life, she felt stressed out most of the time. Her back and neck muscles often spasmed, her appetite had decreased, and the heartburn she'd often struggled with had increased.

In addition to those things, Eleanor had difficulty sleeping throughout the night and would often wake up feeling unrested and out of sorts. She prayed often and tried not to worry, but it had become increasingly difficult to cope.

Eleanor thought about her last appointment with the midwife, Mary Weaver, who would deliver her baby. If everything went well, the delivery would take place at Eleanor and Vic's home. Mary had mentioned that Eleanor's blood pressure was slightly elevated and suggested that Eleanor get a blood pressure monitor and check it a few times each day. The midwife had also reminded Eleanor to eat regular, healthy meals, stay hydrated, and get plenty of rest. Eleanor promised that she would do all those things, but she didn't mention the stress she'd been under due to Vic's drinking problem and the disagreements that had stirred things up.

Eleanor urged her horse to go a little faster. Soon she hoped to have some answers to all her questions.

Strasburg

Ethan had been in his shop a short time when his friend Lloyd Schmucker showed up. He hadn't seen Lloyd for a few weeks, since they were no longer in the same church district, and wondered if he'd come here to place an order for some item Ethan made in his shop.

After Lloyd entered the building, he approached Ethan with a hearty handshake.

"Good to see you, friend. It's been a while." Ethan smiled.

"It sure has," the other man agreed. "Since the number of families in our church increased and we divided into two separate districts, I miss the opportunity to see you regularly." Lloyd looked around the building, where multiple items sat ready to be sanded and stained. "Looks like you're keeping plenty busy here."

"Jah, I have enough work for both me and Stephen."

"So where is that young man?"

"He went up to the house to get us some water and snacks." Ethan chuckled and thumped his belly. "Gotta keep our energy up till it's time to eat lunch."

Lloyd grinned and fanned his face with the brim of his straw hat. "Feels like it's gonna be a hot one. If it's this warm during the month of May, I can only imagine what the summer months will bring." Lloyd moistened his lips and cleared his throat a few times.

"Is there something I can help you with today?" Ethan asked. "Are you looking to buy a piece of lawn furniture or maybe a new doghouse for Rufus?"

Lloyd set his hat down on a bench and reached up to rub the back of his neck. "No, I. . .uh. . .came by to tell you something."

Ethan tipped his head. "Oh, what's that?" *Poor fellow. He seems to be nervous about something.*

"Well the thing is. . ." Lloyd paused and cleared his throat again. "Maybe I shouldn't be saying anything, but if what I saw is true, then I thought you oughta know."

"What did you see?"

"Well, last Friday, when my driver took me and my wife to the Walmart in Lancaster, on our way out of town, I saw an Amish man who looked like Vic, and he was with an English fellow."

"Maybe it was Vic. He often does construction work in Lancaster, as well as many other towns in our county."

"He wasn't doing construction work when I saw him." Lloyd picked up his hat and began fanning his face again.

Ethan couldn't figure out why his friend seemed so jittery. It wasn't like him at all. "Where did you see Vic and the man that was probably one of his coworkers?"

"They were coming out of one of the pubs in Lancaster. From the way they both staggered, it appeared that the men were intoxicated."

Ethan lowered his gaze to the floor, focusing on a pile of sawdust near his feet. *Could it be true? Was my son one of the men Lloyd saw on Friday? If so, I need to speak with Vic about this as soon as possible.* He looked up at Lloyd and forced a smile. "It may have just been someone who resembled my son, but I'll look into the situation, so danki for letting me know."

"You're welcome. I'm sure you would do the same for me if you ever saw one of my boys coming out of a pub in a bad way."

"Jah, probably so."

"Guess I'd better head out. I have a few errands to run, and then I need to get back to my variety store. I left my wife and one of our daughters in charge, and if they've gotten real busy, they will need my help."

"I understand." Ethan put his hand on Lloyd's shoulder. "Before you go, I have a favor to ask."

"Sure thing. What do you need?"

"Please don't say anything to anyone else about seeing the Amish man who looked like Vic coming out of the pub. It may not have been him, and it wouldn't be good if a rumor got started."

Lloyd nodded. "I won't mention it to anyone, and I'm sure my wife, Elsie, hasn't said anything to anyone either."

"You told her?"

"Jah. There are no secrets between me and her."

"Could you please ask her to keep quiet about what you saw?"

"Of course." Lloyd slapped his hat back on his head, gave Ethan one final handshake, and went out the door.

Ethan drew in a couple of deep breaths in an effort to calm himself. With all of his heart, he hoped the inebriated Amish man Lloyd saw coming out of that pub was not Vic. But he would know soon enough, because this evening, after supper, he'd be making a special trip to Paradise to have a talk with his son.

---≋---

Paradise

Eleanor said a little prayer before she knocked on the Zooks' door. She hoped they were home and would have some good advice, because she was desperate.

When Letty Zook answered the door, Eleanor felt relieved.

The older woman smiled and gave Eleanor a hug. "It's nice you stopped by. I've been thinking about you and wondering how things are going with your pregnancy."

Eleanor placed both hands against her bulging belly. "I'm quite tired and will be glad when the baby gets here."

"I can imagine. And how are things with your husband these days?"

Eleanor swallowed hard. "Not good. That's what I came here to discuss with you and Bishop Michael. Is he here?"

Letty shook her head. "No, I'm sorry. He's not. My husband had some business to take care of today, and I don't expect him home until close to suppertime."

"Oh, I see." Eleanor's chin trembled. "Vic and I are. . . Well, we're having some serious problems, and I—I need to talk to the bishop."

"Please come into the living room and take a seat. If you'd like to talk to me about it, I'm more than willing to listen. Maybe there's something I can do to help."

"Thank you." Eleanor followed Letty into the next room and seated herself in an overstuffed chair. The muscles in her back had tightened again, and she hoped the comfort of the soft cushions might help her feel more relaxed.

Letty took a seat in the rocker and soon got the chair moving gently back and forth. "What's been happening with you and your husband that has brought you here for a talk?"

Eleanor began by telling the bishop's wife about Vic's drinking problem and how it had gotten worse since she'd become pregnant.

"I am sorry to hear that. When did it first begin?" Letty asked.

"After his little brother drowned in our pond. As you know, Vic took Eddie's death hard and blamed himself for not teaching his brother how to swim when he asked. He's also felt guilty for not keeping a closer eye on him when he was in our care. But then, I didn't watch Eddie close enough that day either, so Vic might blame me too, although he's never said so."

Eleanor paused, struggling to hold back the sob rising in her throat. "And now because of all that, Vic believes he will not make a good father."

Letty sat, as though mulling things over. Then she stopped rocking, leaned slightly forward, and said, "Your husband needs to do four things."

"What are they? I'm eager to know."

"First of all, he should acknowledge the fact that he needs help. Second, Vic should either come here to see Michael for counseling or talk with someone outside of our community who is a Christian and has been trained to help people who have been unable to deal with their guilt from past mistakes. He also needs to get help for his drinking problem, which could come from becoming involved with a program like Alcoholics Anonymous or a similar group."

"And what is the fourth thing Vic needs to do?"

"Get right with God. That's the most important. First by confessing his sins, and then by asking the Lord's forgiveness. Also, he needs to want to quit drinking."

"Vic doesn't read the Bible at home anymore, and he appears to be bored when we're at church." Eleanor paused to gather her thoughts. "I've suggested AA meetings and counseling, but Vic is against those things. He keeps saying he can quit on his own, but he's tried before and failed."

"That is because he has never gotten to the root of his problem, and acknowledging that he has a problem is the first step."

"How do I get him to do that?"

"You probably can't. Not on your own." Letty picked up the Bible lying on the small table beside her chair. "Let's see what God's Word says we should do when we can't solve a problem by ourselves." She opened the Bible and, after thumbing through several pages, read, " 'The eyes of the Lord are over the righteous, and his ears are open unto their prayers.' That's First Peter 3:12." She looked at Eleanor over the top of her reading glasses and smiled. "Prayer is the answer. Whenever we are faced with a problem, we are to take it to the Lord in prayer."

"I have been praying," Eleanor responded. "But so far, nothing has changed. Vic is still drinking, and it's affecting our marriage more every day."

"But you've come humbly here today, unburdening yourself and trusting me with the whole truth. That is a positive step in the right direction. Now our prayers will be direct, and my husband can focus on helping Vic get better." Letty put the Bible down, got up, and came to stand next to Eleanor's chair. "Continue to pray, and I shall tell Michael about your visit when he gets home. I'm sure he will make it a priority to schedule a meeting with Vic, and then we'll see where things go from there."

Tears streamed down Eleanor's face, and she nearly choked on a sob. "Danki for allowing me to share my burden with you." She stood up and gave Letty a hug. "And thank you for reminding me of what the Bible says about prayer."

"You're welcome. Now I'm going to the desk in my husband's study and get you the contact information we have about where the local AA and Al-Anon meetings are held."

Eleanor's eyes widened. "You have that?"

"Jah. In addition to a few older people struggling with alcohol addiction, we've dealt with drinking issues among several of our young people going through rumschpringe, and it helps to be prepared."

Letty left the room and returned shortly with a piece of paper that she handed to Eleanor. "Here you go." She gave Eleanor's arm a tender squeeze. "I'll be praying for you and your husband."

"I appreciate it. And now I need to pray that Vic will be open to whatever your husband suggests."

Chapter 34

Eleanor left the phone shed with a hopeful smile on her face. She'd made a call to the number Letty had given her and learned that there would be AA and Al-Anon meetings this Thursday evening in Lancaster. Eleanor was eager to go and hoped that after the bishop talked to Vic, he would be willing to go with her.

I'll go without him if I have to, though, Eleanor told herself as she approached the house. *I need the support of other people who are living with an alcoholic.* She had already called a driver about picking her up Thursday evening, so at least that much had been taken care of. It felt strange to go over Vic's head like this and make arrangements for something he might not agree to, but Eleanor was filled with determination. She had put serious hopes in their bishop getting through to her husband. She felt that if anyone could help Vic, it would be Michael. Eleanor wouldn't allow herself to carry any doubts over this matter. It was time for their situation to take a positive turn.

She stepped onto the porch and took a seat on the wooden bench near the front door. It felt nice to sit out here, enjoying the warmth of the sun, even though it was rather humid today.

Eleanor wrinkled her nose when Checkers brought a bone she'd given him this morning and dropped it on the boards beneath her feet. "I hope you don't expect me to pick that slimy thing up and throw it for you," she said, looking down at the dog.

Checkers flopped down on the porch, sandwiched the bone between his front paws, and started crunching.

Eleanor chuckled. It felt good to find something to laugh about. She tilted her head back and closed her eyes. The comforting sound of birds chirping nonstop as they flitted from treetop to treetop almost put her to sleep. She remained in that position for several minutes, until her stomach growled, which reminded her that it was time to fix lunch. After that, Eleanor planned to write Doretta another letter, giving her an update on things so she would know more specifically how to pray.

Eleanor pulled herself to a standing position, and then she reached around to rub the small of her back. The bigger the baby in her womb seemed to get, the more Eleanor's back muscles wanted to spasm. She opened the door and looked back at the dog. "You coming inside with me, Checkers, or do you prefer to stay out here with your *gnoche*?"

As though he had understood every word she'd said, Checkers picked up the bone with his mouth and followed Eleanor inside.

When Vic entered the house at five thirty, he found Eleanor in the kitchen, slicing a cucumber.

"I'm gonna go wash up," he said, kissing her on the cheek. "When I come back, I'll set the table."

She gave a brief nod. "Danki."

Vic hesitated a few seconds, wondering if he should say something more, but since he couldn't think of the right thing to say, he hurried from the room.

When Vic returned several minutes later, he noticed that the plates and silverware had been placed on the table. "What's for supper?" he asked while putting the plates in their proper places.

"I baked a ham earlier, and it's in the oven keeping warm." Eleanor picked up a tomato and cut it into small pieces. "And I'm making a tossed salad to go with it. Oh, and I have some frozen peas from last year's garden heating on the stove."

"Sounds good." Vic filled the glasses with water and ice and set them on the table. Finally, he got out their silverware, along with some napkins. "Is there anything else you'd like me to do?"

"You can take the ham out and slice it, if you don't mind."

"Don't mind a bit." Vic grabbed two large pot holders, opened the oven door, and removed the baking dish. "Yum. . . the odor of this hickory-smoked ham is appeditlich."

She glanced over her shoulder at him. "I hope it tastes as delicious as it smells."

Vic smiled. At least they were having polite conversation—no more arguing like they'd done Saturday morning.

Once the salad, peas, and ham were on the table, they both took their seats. As was expected, Vic bowed his head for prayer, but he couldn't think of anything to say to God. So he just sat there until he felt it was appropriate to open his eyes and waited for Eleanor to do the same.

"How did your day go?" Vic asked after he'd eaten some peas and a piece of ham.

"It went well." Eleanor kept her gaze on her plate and spoke in a slow, even tone. "I called and spoke with someone who heads up the AA and Al-Anon meetings in Lancaster today."

Vic's spine went rigid, but he kept eating and gave no response.

"Their next meeting is this Thursday evening, and I'd like to go." She looked up at him with pleading eyes. "Will you go with me?"

"No! I told you before that I can quit drinking on my own."

"I know you believe that, and you've said it before, but. . ."

"There are no buts about it, Eleanor. I said I'd quit, and I will."

"I don't think you can. You've already proven that by—"

He slammed his fist on the table, cutting her off again. "If you want to attend the stupid meeting, go right ahead, but I will not go with you!" Vic pushed his chair aside and stormed out of the room, refusing to acknowledge the tears streaming down his wife's flushed face.

"Wh–where are you going?" she called after him in a shaky voice.

"Anywhere but here. I need to be by myself!"

Vic hurried out the door and headed for the barn. He'd only been in the building a short time when he heard the rumble of buggy wheels and the whinny of a horse outside. He opened the barn doors and watched as his dad guided his horse and buggy up to the hitching rail. Vic thought it was strange to see his father show up at this time of day, so close to supper. He hoped Dad wasn't here to let him know that someone in the family had been hurt or fallen ill.

"Hey, Dad, what's going on?" Vic asked after he'd joined his father outside the buggy. "It's not like you to come by at this time of day by yourself. Is everyone all right?"

"We're fine. I came to speak to you about something."

"Oh, okay. Let's go in the barn to talk." Vic led the way, and once inside, they both took seats on bales of straw. "What did you want to talk to me about?" He turned to face his dad.

"One of my friends came by the shop today, and what he told me caused some concern."

Vic tipped his head to one side. "Oh, what was that?"

"He said that he saw an Amish man who looked like you coming out of a pub in Lancaster Friday evening." Dad's forehead wrinkled. "Was that man you?"

Vic's head jerked back slightly and his heartbeat began to race. He had to think quick and make sure he said the right thing. "Course not, Dad. Why would I be at a pub?"

"That's what I would like to know. Were you there drinking with one of your coworkers? My friend also mentioned seeing an English man coming out with the man who looked like you." The wrinkles in Dad's forehead deepened. "He said that the two men staggered and seemed to be making an effort to hold each other up. That would give an indication that they had not only been drinking but were both drunk."

Vic moistened his dry lips with the tip of his tongue as he struggled to maintain eye contact with his father. How was he going to wiggle his way out of this, other than to flat-out lie and say that the man Dad's friend had seen was definitely not him?

Using the back of his hand, Vic rubbed away the moisture that had formed on his forehead. *This rumor needs to be nipped in the bud right now,* he told himself. *Otherwise, it could not only travel through my dad's church district, but through ours here in Paradise as well.*

Vic closed his eyes, struggling to think things through. He could probably convince his father that it had just been a case of mistaken identity, but what if Dad went in the house and talked to Eleanor? He would not only be able to see Eleanor's tearstained face, but if he brought up the same topic to her as he'd asked Vic about, she might tell him about how she'd found Vic and Tom in the barn Saturday morning, sleeping off their drunkenness from the previous night. The best thing to do, Vic decided, was to stick to his original story, and if his father said anything about wanting to say hello to Eleanor, Vic would discourage it and say that she wasn't feeling well and wouldn't be up for having company.

Feeling a little more confident now that he'd made a decision, Vic leaned forward and placed his hand on Dad's arm. "As I said before, it was not me your friend saw, and I would appreciate it if you would let him know that, before any rumors get started."

Dad nodded slowly. "All right, then, Son, I'll accept your word and make sure that my friend knows the man he saw was not you." He started for the barn door but turned back around. "I'd better go into the house and say hello to your fraa. If your mamm found out I came by here and didn't check to see how Eleanor is doing, she'd probably send me to the doghouse to sleep with Freckles." He grinned and gave a wink.

Vic rubbed his sweaty hand down the side of his pant leg. "Umm. . .going into the house right now is not a good idea, Dad."

"Why not?"

"Eleanor isn't feeling the best, and she's probably lying down. I don't want to disturb her."

Dad's brows drew together as he pulled his fingers through the hair of his long beard. "I'm sorry to hear that. I'll give your mother that message, and we'll both be praying for Eleanor. Your mamm will most likely come by sometime tomorrow to check on your fraa."

Oh great. Vic's jaw clenched. *If Mom comes by, Eleanor might break down and tell her that I've been drinking.* He swallowed a couple of times. *Before we go to bed tonight, I'll need to make it clear to Eleanor that she is not to tell Mom, or anyone else, about our personal business. Anything that goes on between me and her is our business and no one else's.*

Vic felt relieved when, a few minutes later, his dad said goodbye and got into his carriage. At least he didn't have to worry about Eleanor saying anything inappropriate to Dad tonight.

Vic headed for his horse's stall. He would work his frustrations out by giving Domino a thorough brushing, whether he needed it or not. After that, he might groom Eleanor's horse before he went back in the house.

───── ≋ ─────

Vic's dad hadn't been gone more than ten minutes when Michael Zook showed up. Vic had heard the man's horse and buggy come in, and he'd hurried to leave Domino's stall and open up the barn doors, where he now stood waiting for the elderly man.

"*Guder owed.*" Michael held out his hand and greeted Vic with a hearty handshake.

"Good evening," Vic said. "What can I do for you, Bishop Zook?"

"I came by to have a little chat with you."

"Well, come on in and take a seat." Vic gestured to the bales of straw where he and his dad had sat.

Michael took a seat and turned to face Vic. "There's no point in me making small talk with you. I came here to say that I know about your drinking problem, and I'd like to help."

Taken aback, Vic blinked multiple times. "Who—who told you that?"

"Does it matter?"

"Jah, it does. I suspect some rumor may be going on about me."

The bishop folded his hands in a prayer-like gesture. "Your wife came by our house while I was gone today, and she and my fraa talked."

"Oh, I see." Vic flexed his fingers and gave each of his knuckles a good crack. "So let me get this straight. . .Eleanor told Letty that I have a drinking problem. Am I right?"

"Jah, and she is quite concerned about you."

Vic flapped his hand, hoping to make light of the situation, although he did not think it was funny. "I've only had a few beers now and then, and there's nothing in the Bible that says it's a sin for a person to drink. Right?"

"That is correct, but it does say, 'Be not drunk with wine.'"

Vic was tempted to remind Michael that he'd just said he had been drinking beer, not wine, but he figured that comment wouldn't go over too well. So instead, he said, "I am not an alcoholic. I can quit drinking anytime I want."

"Are you sure about that?" Michael leaned forward, one hand on his knee, as he seemed to look into Vic's soul.

"Of course. I quit before, and I can do it again."

The bishop's bushy gray brows drew close as his face tightened. "And you're sure about that?"

"Absolutely."

"All right, then, I won't hound you about it, but if something happens, and you are not able to control the desire to drink on your own, I hope you will take my advice and seek some help." Michael clasped Vic's hand and gave it a shake. "Please remember that I'm available to listen anytime you want to talk, about anything at all."

"I appreciate that." Vic walked the elderly man to the barn door and told him goodbye. He felt relieved when the bishop's horse and buggy left the yard and were out of sight. It seemed like everyone was on his case today—first Eleanor, then his dad, and now their bishop. Hearing everything they'd all said to him was enough to make Vic long even more for a few drinks.

One thing's for sure, Vic told himself, *I am not going to any AA meetings or seek counseling. I am a grown man, and I can beat this on my own, without anyone's help. All I need is a little self-control, and then I'll have the problem licked.*

Chapter 35

Eleanor sat at the picnic table under the cooling shade of a maple tree in their yard, reading a letter she had just received from Doretta. Things seemed to be going along well for her friend. After saying that she felt concern for Eleanor and Vic and would continue to pray for them, Doretta mentioned that she'd been working on the dress she would wear the second Tuesday in November, when she and William became husband and wife. Eleanor was glad for her friend, but she couldn't help feeling a bit envious. She and Vic had been so happy when they'd first gotten married, and now their marriage was in shambles. She felt thankful, at least, that her dear friend had been praying for her and had not condemned Vic.

Things hadn't changed like Eleanor had hoped. The bishop had talked to Vic a while back, but if anything, Michael's talk with Vic had made things worse. Vic was angry with Eleanor for having told the bishop's wife about his drinking problem, and he had continued to drink. Eleanor had remained silent, not wanting to stir up anything more with her husband. It seemed that rather than things improving between them, their relationship had become even more strained. Vic was more distant than ever and didn't engage Eleanor in much conversation unless they were quarreling about something. At least when Eleanor's mother-in-law came by she could have quality conversation with her. Eleanor missed the old Vic, the fun-loving man she once knew, before the alcohol had taken him hostage.

Eleanor's nausea had been bothering her less, which made the days a bit easier. Her pregnancy was otherwise going well, and Eleanor's weight was right where it needed to be. When she ate her meals, she tried to avoid as much sugar as possible and use less salt in her diet. It wasn't easy cutting back on those two items, since she had been used to eating them before she'd become pregnant, but if it meant keeping her and the baby healthier, it was worth the sacrifice.

Attending Al-Anon meetings for the past two months had helped Eleanor see things more clearly, and she'd learned a lot concerning what to say or not say to her husband, with the hope that he would quit drinking. During Eleanor's first meeting, she'd been told that alcoholism was an illness, and that some of the things she'd been saying and doing may have hindered her husband's recovery. She'd been surprised to learn that when the spouse of an alcoholic says or does certain things, it can enable the one with the drinking problem, which only makes things worse. She was reminded that her husband was not a bad boy who deserved to be punished; he was a sick, confused, guilt-ridden human being.

Eleanor fanned her flushed face with the envelope Doretta's letter came in as she reflected on one of the meetings she'd attended when someone in the group mentioned the topic of covering up for the alcoholic so his family and friends wouldn't find out about his drinking problem.

I did that before, but not anymore, Eleanor told herself, flapping the front of her skirt to cool the lower half of her body. Up to this point, she had only told Bishop Michael; his wife, Letty; and Doretta about Vic's addition. She'd been ashamed and afraid to admit it to Vic's parents or hers, believing they might think less of him, or even her for putting up with it and trying to hide the truth.

Trying to shield the alcoholic from an inevitable collapse as his disease progressed was an impossible task. Eleanor had learned that it would be far worse if she tried to protect Vic than to allow him to face up to his mistakes, free from her interference. So toward the end of last week, she had written a letter to her parents, telling them what had been going on, asking for their prayers, and explaining about the Al-Anon meetings she'd been attending weekly. Eleanor had not heard anything back from them yet and wondered if they'd received her letter. Last Wednesday, when Vic's mother came to help Eleanor clean the house and do laundry, Eleanor had opened up and told her about Vic's addiction to alcohol. Surprisingly, Susie hadn't seemed that taken aback by the news. In fact, Vic's mother had stated that both she and Ethan had sensed something serious was going on with their son, and they thought it might involve alcohol. Her suspicions were in part due to the way Vic had acted around them lately—nervous and like he had done something wrong. Susie had also shared with Eleanor that a friend of Ethan's thought he'd seen Vic and an English man coming out of a pub in Lancaster. When Vic's dad had confronted Vic with what he'd heard, Vic had said he wasn't the person the man saw. Ethan, however, did not believe him, telling Susie that Vic had the look of guilt written all over his face.

During Susie's visit, Eleanor had told her about the Al-Anon meetings she'd attended, and Susie agreed that it was a good idea and should be helpful for Eleanor. She did show some concern, though, that Vic wasn't interested in attending AA meetings. Her parting words to Eleanor that day were: "Ethan and I will definitely be praying for both you and Victor, and especially that he will see his need to get help and do it soon. As you know, others in our family have also struggled with grief over Eddie's death, but none of us have turned to alcohol to squelch the pain."

Eleanor had agreed with her mother-in-law's final statement, but since Vic had already acquired a taste for beer during his youth and knew that drinking seemed to help him relax and forget about his troubles, he was a prime candidate for becoming an alcoholic. She'd learned that at one of her meetings. And although it didn't excuse her husband's behavior, it did shed a better light on things.

Well, at least now the truth was finally out in the open, and Eleanor felt relief because she no longer had to hide Vic's drinking or make excuses for him. Her biggest concern, as it had been when she'd first married Vic, was that now her parents really would think he'd been a poor choice for a husband. It was quite possible that her mom and dad might never again have anything nice to say about their son-in-law.

"Well," Eleanor murmured, blotting her damp face with a tissue she'd taken from the band of her apron, "that's just the chance I will have to take. Maybe after they've read my letter about some of the things I've learned so far at Al-Anon, they'll have a better understanding and not be so quick to condemn."

Grabill

Lydia looked away from the harsh glare of the sun and turned her face toward the faint breeze coming from the eastern side of her garden. It was another hot and humid day, but she wouldn't quit weeding until the chore was done. Nothing grew well when it was crowded with weeds, and she was determined to get every single one. Working in the garden had always been a good stress reliever, and this morning Lydia's stress was at an all-time high. She'd received a letter from Eleanor today with some shocking news. Vic was addicted to alcohol, and Eleanor had been attending Al-Anon meetings.

"Why am I not surprised?" she muttered. "I knew even before they were married that Vic would not be a good husband." He had always seemed too sure of himself to suit Lydia, and she hadn't liked the rumors she'd heard about some of the things he'd done before joining the church.

She gritted her teeth and gave another handful of weeds a good yank. It would be wrong to suggest that Eleanor should divorce her husband, but Lydia worried what it would be like for her daughter once the baby came. She wanted to shield Eleanor from the agony of dealing with a man who had a drinking problem. Lydia had to wonder just how long this had been going on and why Eleanor hadn't said something before now. She also wondered what Al would say when he got home from work this evening and she shared Eleanor's letter with him. Would he suggest, like she hoped, that they invite Eleanor to move back home to have her baby and remain there with them until Vic straightened out his life? The muscles in her arms tightened as she pulled another handful of weeds. *If he ever quits drinking, that is.*

Paradise

As the weeks passed and the summer months had grown hotter, Vic's drinking had gotten worse. He'd said he could quit, and he had made a feeble attempt, but the closer Eleanor's due date came, the more frightened he became about becoming a father. He'd tried on his own not to think about Eddie's death and the responsibility he still felt for it, but self-talk wasn't working for him, and he wasn't about to see a counselor or attend AA meetings where he'd be expected to sit around with a bunch of people he didn't know, talking about why, when, or how often he drank. If Eleanor wanted to keep going to the Al-Anon meetings she'd been attending on Thursday evenings, that was up to her, but Vic didn't want anything to do with it.

"Before you go home, I need to talk to you, Mr. Lapp," Vic's boss called as Vic started to gather up his lunch pail and thermos.

Vic stepped into Ned's office. "Oh sure, no problem. Did you want to tell me something about the work you have lined out for tomorrow's job before Tom and I head for home?"

"It's not about the house we've been remodeling. This concerns you, and the way you've been showing up for work here of late."

Vic rubbed the bridge of his nose. "Tom and I are on time most days. In fact, we're rarely ever late."

Ned nodded his balding head. "I'm not talking about getting here late. It's the condition you've been arriving in that has me concerned."

"What do you mean?"

"On several occasions, you've had all the indications of having a hangover." Ned stood in front of his desk and shifted his weight. "On top of that, some of the guys have complained to me about you sleeping on the job."

Vic put both hands firmly against his hips. "That's not true. I've never slept while working on any jobsite." His cheeks warmed as hot as if he'd been sunburned. "Well, maybe I've dozed off during lunch break a couple of times, but then who hasn't?"

"What about the headaches you've complained of?"

Vic's only reply was a brief shrug.

Ned looked closely at him and frowned. "Your eyes are dull and blood-shot, and there are times when you've had an unfocused gaze. I can't have a man working for me who isn't fully focused on his work."

Vic's features tightened. "What about Tom and all the other guys who work for you? I've seen a few of them doze off during break times. Have you gotten on their cases, or are you just picking on me?" Vic's voice had taken on a challenging tone, but he couldn't seem to stop himself.

"I am not picking on you." Vic's boss lowered his voice, looking at Vic through squinted eyes. "But if you don't get your act together and improve that attitude of yours, I'll have no choice but to let you go."

"What?" Vic's gaze flitted around Ned's office, never settling on one place very long.

"You heard what I said. I won't tolerate any worker who doesn't pull his own weight, and I don't appreciate your tone of voice, either." Ned pointed at Vic. "I could fire you right now for that alone."

A vein on the side of Vic's neck pulsated, and his face became warmer. "Well, if that's how you feel about it, then go right ahead. I'm sure I could get a job working for one of the other contractors in the area. Or for that matter, I could even start my own business."

"There you go with that attitude again." Ned lifted his hands, holding them palms up as he shook his head. "You know, I had previously thought that hiring an Amish man was a good idea, because it's been my under-standing that most of them are honest, hard workers, with good principles and proper manners." He pointed at Vic one more time. "You're forcing my hand, so therefore—"

Vic knew he had pushed his boss too far, but he wasn't about to back down now. He pulled his shoulders straight back, and looking Ned right in the face, he said, "You don't have to worry about firing me because I quit!"

"Fine, then, you can pick up your personal tools and go. Oh, and you can come by for your check from this week on Friday. Or, better yet, why don't you ask your buddy, Tom, to get it for you?"

"Great! I'll just do that!" Vic whirled around and stomped out of the man's office. He couldn't remember when he'd been this angry at someone.

After Vic gathered up his lunch items and all his personal tools, he stepped outside and spotted Tom in the parking lot, waiting by his truck.

"What was up between you and the boss?" Tom asked. "I saw him talking to you through the open door of his office and heard your raised voices."

Vic's facial muscles quivered as he ground his teeth together. "He was on the verge of firing me, but I quit before he got the words out. I'd like you to pick up my check on Friday."

Tom's eyes widened. "You're kidding, right?"

"No, I'm not. I didn't like the things he accused me of." Heat spread throughout Vic's body. "And who needs this job anyway? I can do better on my own."

"You think so?"

Vic held his hands up and took a defensive stance. "Yeah, I sure do. I am not bragging here, but I've been told many times that I'm an excellent carpenter."

"Never said you weren't. There must be some reason, though, that Ned was on the verge of letting you go."

"Yeah, he stated that there's been some indication of me coming to work with a hangover on several occasions. He also said that some of the guys have complained to him about me sleeping on the job." Vic grimaced and shook his head. "It's not true. I told the boss that I've never fallen asleep while working on any jobsite."

"What did Ned say about that?"

"Not much. He just mentioned the headaches I've complained of. Can you believe that? I mean, who hasn't come to work with a headache sometimes?"

Tom nodded. "That's true."

"Oh, and the boss also said that my eyes looked dull and bloodshot, and that there were times when I've had an unfocused gaze." Vic scuffed the heel of his boot across the pavement. "That's when he said he couldn't have a man working for him who wasn't fully focused on his work."

"Is that all?"

"No. He threatened to let me go if I didn't improve my attitude. So I told him I quit, and after he said I should pick up my tools and either come by for my check on Friday or ask you to get it, I walked right out of his office."

Tom expelled a breath so hard that it raised the hair on his forehead. "Whew! You really blew it, buddy."

Vic offered no response, just stared at the ground and breathed deeply.

"What are you gonna do now?"

"If you don't mind stopping at one of the taverns on the way home, I'd like to have a few beers to help me relax and think things through. Then tomorrow morning, I'll either look for another job or figure out some way to start my own business."

"You'd need money to start your own business." Tom put his hand on Vic's shoulder. "I don't mean any disrespect, but do you have the knowledge of what it takes to open and run a contracting business, hire enough employees, advertise, and—"

"It doesn't have to be a full-fledged contracting business. I can do some woodworking jobs on my own, and I'm sure I'd get along fine." He shrugged Tom's hand off his shoulder. "Are you gonna stop somewhere so I can have a few beers or not?"

Tom, slowly, almost unwillingly, gave a brief nod. "Okay. Throw your tools and lunch box in the back seat of my truck, and let's go."

Chapter 36

It was almost time to start supper, but there were still a few items on the clothesline, so Eleanor left the house, carrying the wicker basket to get them. She'd just gotten to the line and set the basket on the ground when she heard the phone ringing from the shed. Thinking it might be Vic calling to say he was going to be late, she hurried into the building, picked up the phone, and said, "Hello."

"Oh, Eleanor, I'm so glad it's you. Your letter came today, and I just had to call."

Eleanor's shoulders curled forward. She wished time would speed up and she could end this call right now. Eleanor could only imagine what Mom would say concerning the thing she'd written about in the letter she had sent to her and Dad. They were probably shocked to learn about Vic's drinking issue and the problems it had caused with Eleanor and Vic's marriage.

"I...um...figured you would have probably received my letter by now." Eleanor spoke quietly, as she fought to keep her composure.

"The things you said were quite shocking. How long has this all been going on with Vic drinking beer and becoming intoxicated?"

"It started after his brother drowned, but then it got better for a while." Eleanor bent down and picked up the stick Checkers had brought into the shed when he'd found his way in through the open door. She tossed it outside and waited until the dog ran after it before resuming her conversation. "After Vic found out I was expecting a baby, things got worse. As you know, he's blamed himself for Eddie's death, and he is convinced that he won't make a good father."

"Why didn't you let us know sooner about what's been going on?"

Eleanor sighed deeply. She'd figured this question was coming. She moistened her dry lips and drew in a quick breath. "I kept hoping the problem would be resolved."

"I don't think it's a good idea for you to stay in that house. I'd like you to pack your suitcase and come here to live with us."

"Are you suggesting that I should divorce my husband?"

"Certainly not. I just don't think it would be good for you to stay there when your husband's been drinking. People do strange things when they're under the influence of alcohol."

"Mom, like I mentioned in the letter I wrote, I've been going to regular Al-Anon meetings, which is helping me to cope."

"Is Vic going to AA meetings or getting some other kind of professional help for his problem?"

"No, not yet, but I'm sure he will see the need to go soon."

Silence. Then Mom spoke again. "Please give some thought to my invitation. It isn't good for you to be living with the stress of Vic's problem. And how are you feeling, by the way?"

"I'm tired, but not so nauseous these days. And as I said, Al-Anon is helping me cope, and it's reduced my stress." Eleanor hoped the positive tone she had used would ease her mother's mind.

"What about when the baby comes? How's it going to be for your child, living under the same roof with an alcoholic father?"

"Hopefully, by then, Vic will be doing better."

"And if he's not?"

"Then I'll figure out what to do when the time comes." Eleanor glanced at the battery-operated clock sitting on the wooden bench next to the phone.

"I need to hang up now, Mom. Vic will be home from work soon, and I need to get my laundry off the line and start supper."

"All right, but please think about what I said. If things get to be more than you can handle, please don't hesitate to come here. We only want what is best for you and the baby."

"I know, Mom. Danki."

"Before we hang up, though, I have one more quick question."

"What is it?"

"Does your friend Doretta know about the situation with Vic?"

Eleanor shifted on the unyielding wooden stool she sat upon. She wouldn't lie to her mother, but at the same time, Eleanor saw no reason to tell Mom that Doretta had known for some time and had offered advice regarding Vic's addiction.

"Jah, Mom," she replied. "I've let Doretta know as well."

"That's good. Maybe she will also suggest that you come back to Grabill."

"We'll see, Mom. Now I really do need to go."

"Okay, I understand, and I'll be in touch with you again soon. Take care, Daughter, and please know that your daed and I, as well as others in our family, will be praying for you."

"You'll pray for my husband too, right?"

"Jah, of course."

Eleanor said goodbye to her mother and hung up the phone. It was good to have that conversation over with. She couldn't help feeling sad that the relationship with her mother felt strained because of what Mom thought of Vic. Although her parents had been disappointed when Eleanor married Vic and moved away, at least they had accepted Eleanor's decision to marry a man from Pennsylvania—a man she truly loved. Now, however, if Vic didn't get help for his drinking, Eleanor figured her folks would not want anything to do with him. And the idea of Eleanor moving back home to live with them would no doubt come up again. Eleanor would have to deal with that issue when the time came.

Strasburg

When Ethan and Stephen came in from his shop that evening, Susie followed Ethan down the hall to the bathroom where he'd gone to clean up. "As soon as you're done, could you meet me in our bedroom? There's something I need to talk to you about, and I don't want any of our kinner to hear what I have to say."

Ethan nodded. "Is there something seriously wrong?"

Her voice lowered to a whisper. "It's about Victor and Eleanor."

"Oh, okay. I'll meet you there shortly."

Ethan stepped into the bathroom, and Susie went straight to their room. After closing the door, she took a seat on the bed. In less than five minutes, Ethan showed up with a clean face and hands and his hair combed neatly. "If this is about Vic's drinking problem, we've already discussed it, and I thought we'd decided that we are going to do what Eleanor is doing and not try to force him to get help. If and when he reaches rock bottom, his eyes will hopefully be opened to the truth that he needs to seek professional help." He sat down beside Susie and took hold of her hand. "We're also going to continue praying for Vic and Eleanor, right?"

"Definitely, but I believe we can do more."

"Such as?"

"I've been thinking about this for a while, and I would like to invite Eleanor to come here to stay with us. She's due to have the baby in a month, and she does not need the ongoing stress of never knowing when Victor will come home drunk or what his response to her will be."

"That's not a good idea, Susie."

"How come?"

Ethan let go of her hand and reached up to massage his damp forehead. "Our son wouldn't be happy if you asked his wife to move in with us. It could cause even more problems between him and Eleanor. It might also be another excuse for Vic to keep drinking."

She tipped her head. "You think so?"

"Jah. Vic's pretty unstable right now, and his emotions are up and down like a yo-yo. I don't want us to be the cause of setting him off."

Susie pulled her bottom lip inward. "I suppose you're right, but I can't help being worried about our daughter-in-law and the precious baby she'll be giving birth to soon."

Ethan rested his hand on her arm and gave it a few gentle pats. "Try not to worry. Just pray. I feel confident that God will work things out in His time and His way."

Susie gave a deep, weighted sigh. She wished she could be so sure. Perhaps her faith wasn't as strong as Ethan's, but she would pray and try to leave the situation in God's hands. She would also continue to check on Eleanor often by dropping by and leaving phone messages.

———— ≈ ————

Lancaster

"Are you sure you want to do this?" Tom asked when he pulled his vehicle into the parking lot of the tavern on Prince Street.

Vic bobbed his head. "Sure am. I'm not going home till I've had a chance to calm down and come up with something to tell Eleanor when I get there."

"How about telling her the truth—that you walked away from a perfectly good job because you didn't like what the boss said."

Vic winced, feeling as though he'd been slapped in the face. "All right, I did, but I couldn't stand there and let Ned say all those things to me and make a threat to fire me on the spot."

Tom looked straight at Vic. "Yeah, you could have. If you hadn't mouthed off, you'd still have a job. What you should have done is promised our boss that you would do better from now on and asked him for another chance to prove yourself."

291

Vic's gaze flicked upward. "Yeah, right. I'm sure that's what you would have done."

"That's correct. Ned's gotten on my case a few times since I began working for him, and I've never argued with him or smarted off." Tom shook his head. "I can't believe you, Vic. You don't act like any Amish man I've ever known."

"What's that supposed to mean? How's an Amish man supposed to behave?"

Tom scratched his head. "I'll admit, I don't know many Amish men, but the ones I have met were hard workers and polite."

Vic couldn't think of a good enough response, so he opened the truck door and stepped out. "You coming or what?"

"All right, I'll come in for a couple of beers, but then we need to go. Today's my mom's birthday, and I told my stepdad that I would stop by their place for cake and ice cream. I bought a plant to give her too, which is at my house. So after I drop you off at your place, I'll need to stop at my house to change and get the gift."

"Okay," Vic agreed. "We'll have a few quick drinks and be on our way."

———— ≈ ————

Paradise

Eleanor went to the front door, opened it, and peered out. It was almost eight o'clock, and there was still no sign of Tom's truck. She'd gone out to the phone shed again, half an hour ago, but there'd been no message from Vic or anyone else. Eleanor hoped Vic and Tom hadn't stopped off for a few drinks somewhere. She knew all too well that a couple of beers could easily lead to more, and the end result would be her husband coming home drunk. Even after so many times of him pulling this same stunt, she couldn't get used to it. All Eleanor could see was that her husband wasn't strong enough to handle adult life. At this point, she was trying to trust in the Lord, but it was hard not to fret, and she had to remind herself to think about her own needs right now.

She'd thought about fixing herself a healthy snack. There were some cut-up veggies in a plastic container inside the refrigerator that she could enjoy with some flavorful dip. She was hungry and needed to eat before nausea set in. She'd been better in that regard for the most part, but whenever Eleanor went too long without eating, her stomach still felt a bit queasy.

With a heavy sigh and the dog at her heels, Eleanor entered the kitchen and got out the veggies. She would heat up some leftover potato soup to eat after her fresh vegetable snack. And if Vic came home late or didn't come home at all, she would find the strength from deep within to deal with it.

———— ≈ ————

Lancaster

"We've gotta go, Vic. I need to be at my parents' house in one hour, and you've had one too many beers."

Holding tight to the glass of beer in his hand, Vic shook his head. "You go ahead. I'll find a way home on my own."

"Don't be ridiculous. I can't just leave you here. It's too far for you to walk to your house. Besides, you're in no shape to be going anywhere by yourself." Tom nudged Vic's arm.

Vic shrugged it away and narrowed his eyes. "Just let me be. I'm not ready to go home and face my wife yet."

"You'll have to face her sometime and admit what happened at work today. There's no point in putting it off."

Vic picked up his glass and took another swig. A few seconds later, he moved away from Tom and plunked down on a different barstool.

"Come on, man. You can't stay here by yourself."

"I'm not alone." Vic made a sweeping gesture of the room. "Look, there's a whole room full of drinking buddies. I'm sure one of them might live out my way, and I can catch a ride home with that person whenever I'm ready to go." Vic hunched over the bar. "I mean it, Tom. Just leave me alone."

"Be reasonable, Vic. You don't know any of these guys well enough to trust them—especially in the condition you're in right now."

Vic didn't respond to his buddy's comment. He just looked away and took another sip of his beer.

"You're just being stubborn is all, and I can't wait around here any longer, my friend." Tom looked at his watch. "Okay, have it your way. You can stay here till the place closes if you want, but I think you'll be sorry in the morning." Tom walked away, paid his tab. and left the building.

What does he know about how I'm feeling? I just want to be free from all my troubles, and this beer is making that happen for me. Vic ordered another beer and ended up spilling part of it on his chicken strips. He didn't care. He had no appetite for food, anyhow. All Vic wanted to do was numb the pain gnawing at the core of his being, and he hoped a few more beers might do the trick.

———≈———

Vic had no idea what time it was. He weaved back and forth on rubbery legs, barely able to walk when he stepped outside, leaning on some guy he didn't know, who'd said he would drive Vic home. He blinked rapidly, trying to focus on something familiar, but everything seemed kind of blurry. His body felt tingly, and he had a weird fuzzy feeling in his head. The fellow with him didn't say anything as he led Vic along. Suddenly, with no warning whatsoever, Vic felt a blunt object hit the back of his head. Then everything started spinning and Vic blacked out.

Chapter 37

Paradise

At midnight Eleanor let the dog out to do his business one final time until morning, and then she locked the front door and went down the hall to her and Vic's room. He was obviously not coming home—at least no time soon. She could almost picture her husband sitting in a noisy, dim bar somewhere with his buddy Tom. They were both probably quite drunk by now and might have decided to sleep it off somewhere before coming here.

Maybe tomorrow morning I'll find them in the barn again. Eleanor's lips pinched together as she removed her head covering and placed it on the dresser. *Sleeping in the barn would be better than Vic coming into the house in a drunken stupor.* Eleanor opened the closet door and removed her lightweight summer nightgown. If he should enter the house in an intoxicated state, she would not engage in any negative confrontation. Eleanor had learned from Al-Anon meetings that the worst time to attempt communication with her husband was when he was drunk. All that would accomplish was to trigger a blowup, which neither of them needed, and it would solve nothing. She also reminded herself that shielding Vic from the consequences of his drinking would only prolong the course.

Eleanor pulled the pins from the bun at the back of her head and picked up her hairbrush. She sat on the end of the bed, brushing her hair with one hand and gently massaging her stomach with the other hand.

"Dear Lord, what should I do?" Eleanor prayed out loud. "Should I go back to my parents' house to have this baby, like Mom suggested? Or would it be better to stay here so that Vic can be a part of the event if he wants to?" She set the brush down and squeezed her eyes tightly shut in an effort to keep tears from spilling over. "Please, Lord, open my husband's eyes so that he sees the need to get help for his drinking. Help Vic come to the place where he will forgive himself and be absolved of the guilt he feels for Eddie's death. And most of all, Lord, please restore his faith in You so that he can become the spiritual leader of this home, as You intend."

Lancaster

"It's good to see that you're awake, sir. Can you tell us your name?"

Vic blinked at the invading light and the two faces looking down at him: one male, one female, both wearing white hospital-type garb.

"My name's Vic—Victor Lapp. Who are you, and where am I?"

"I'm Dr. Warner, and this is your nurse, Mrs. Daniels. You're in the hospital. You were brought here in an ambulance last night."

"Ambulance?" Vic repeated. He had no recollection of that. He barely remembered leaving the tavern with some man who had promised to give him a ride home.

"Yes," the doctor replied. "You were badly beaten, and whoever found you in the parking lot of a tavern here in town called for help."

Vic grimaced as he turned his head to the right. "How bad am I hurt?"

"You have a nasty cut on the back of your head and some facial contusions. You also received several broken ribs from whoever beat you up." Dr. Warner shook his head. "It could have been much worse, though. You might have been killed."

"Where are my clothes?" Vic asked without responding to the doctor's last statement. He was embarrassed by his actions and didn't need to be told that he'd messed up.

The nurse spoke up. "They were dirty and had bloodstains on them. They also smelled heavy with alcohol. We put them in the closet for you. I'm sure when you're discharged you'll want to take them home for a good washing."

"Oh, I see." Vic's mouth seemed terribly dry and felt like it had been stuffed with a wad of cotton when he spoke. He was overwhelmed and powerless, lying in the hospital room in his condition. It was the first time in Vic's life that he'd been beaten up by anyone. He couldn't help feeling sorry for himself, not to mention ashamed, because the truth was, he'd brought this on himself by getting drunk and not letting Tom take him home when he'd asked.

"From the looks of your clothes and your bobbed haircut, I'm guessing you must be Amish. Am I right?" Nurse Daniels asked.

"Yeah," Vic mumbled. He felt embarrassed to admit it—not because he was ashamed of his heritage, but because getting drunk was not a good testimony to others, who most likely thought Amish people were religious and wouldn't do something like that.

People should realize that we're all human, and sometimes we do things we shouldn't, Vic thought. *Just because we get baptized, join the church, and go to worship services regularly doesn't mean we're perfect, by any stretch of the imagination. Of course,* he had to admit, *I'm among the minority, not the majority. Most Amish men I know do not have a serious drinking problem that ends up landing them in the hospital, beaten, ashamed, and hurting all over.*

"Where's my wallet?" Vic questioned.

The nurse shook her head. "There was no wallet in your pockets when you were admitted, and no other form of identification. Is there a family member we can call to let them know you are here and what happened to you?"

Vic knew he could never make it home on his own. He was in too much pain. He also figured since he hadn't come home last night that Eleanor must be worried sick about him. Vic felt like a heel. He wanted to go home—real bad, in fact—but he didn't want Eleanor to see him like this or know what had happened to him last night when he'd walked out of that bar.

Vic remembered back to when he'd thought his buddy Tom should have gotten counseling to save his marriage. Now Vic's own marriage was in trouble, and he'd foolishly believed he could solve their problems with no outside help. Vic had made promises he hadn't kept. He'd lied to his wife and others multiple times. He had said unkind things to Eleanor, often without so much as a weak apology. The guilt Vic felt was overwhelming. He didn't think he deserved his wife's forgiveness, although that was what he wanted so badly. He had messed things up and he owed God an apology too. Oh, how Vic wished he could wipe the slate clean and start over.

"Sir, is there someone we can call? You'll be discharged later today and will need a ride to your home."

The doctor's question drove Vic's thoughts aside. "Uh, yeah. I'll give you my phone number, but you'll have to leave a message. We don't have a phone in our house. It's inside a little shed near the end of our property, so my wife would not be likely to hear it ring."

The nurse placed her hand gently upon his. "If you'll provide me with the number, I'll give her a call and leave a message."

Vic swallowed hard. He really had no other choice. He sure couldn't give the nurse his folks' number. Vic could only imagine what they would have to say when they heard about the condition he was in right now.

———— ≈ ————

Paradise

A woodpecker's incessant tapping on a tree outside Eleanor's bedroom window pulled her out of a deep sleep. She forced her eyes open and looked at the clock on the nightstand by her bed. It was well past 8:00 a.m., which was later than she normally got up, but she'd needed the extra sleep, considering how late she'd gotten to bed last night.

Eager to see if Vic had made it home and might be sleeping on the couch or even in the barn, Eleanor got up and hurriedly dressed. When she left her bedroom, she was disappointed to see that there was no sign of her husband in the living room. However, she found Checkers at the front door, waiting not so patiently to be let out as he whined and pawed at the door.

Eleanor turned the knob, and as soon as the door swung open, the dog darted out and raced into the yard. There was no sign of Tom's truck outside, so if he had brought Vic home and stayed the night, he'd obviously gone home already. Back and forth, up and down, it seemed that Eleanor's life had become like riding a roller coaster, never knowing from one moment to the next what to expect where Vic was concerned.

Guess I'd better go out to the barn and see if Vic might be there, she told herself.

A few seconds after Eleanor went out and stepped off the porch, it began to rain in fat, skin-soaking drops. Oddly enough, the birds in the yard sang cheerfully, in spite of the rain pelting the ground. Eleanor figured maybe they appreciated the reprieve from the hot weather. She was glad for it too, but she needed an umbrella for her walk to the barn so she wouldn't get soaked to the bone.

Eleanor went back inside and came out shortly with a black umbrella, which she opened and held over her head. Carefully stepping around puddles that had already formed, she made her way out to the barn. Upon entering, the only sounds that greeted her were the huffing breaths and thumping hooves coming from the horses' stalls, along with the creaking boards beneath her feet. She checked each area of the building while calling Vic's name, but there was no sign of him anywhere.

I'd better go out to the phone shed. Hopefully he called and has left me a message. Eleanor's heart thumped in her chest. *What if Vic's been hurt and is unable to call or come home? He could even be—*

Forcing the disconcerting thoughts to the back of her mind, she made her way down the driveway and entered the shed. The light on the answering machine blinked rapidly, so she sat down and pushed the button.

Beads of sweat erupted on Eleanor's forehead as she listened to the one and only message. It was from a woman who said she was a nurse at the hospital in Lancaster. Eleanor's breaths burst in and out when she heard that Vic had been admitted to the hospital during the night with several injuries and the nurse explained the details of what had happened to him. Fortunately, the woman said that none of Vic's wounds were life threatening.

"I need to call a driver right away so we can go get him." Eleanor reached for the phone, but then she paused and closed her eyes. "Thank You, God, that my husband is still alive. Please calm my nerves and give me the right words to say when I see Vic face-to-face."

Lancaster

When Vic saw his sweet wife enter the hospital room, tears gushed from his eyes, and he sobbed like a baby. Pressing both hands against his hot cheeks, Vic continued to weep and didn't look at Eleanor again until he heard her say, "I brought you some clean clothes, Vic. Are you ready to go home?"

He nodded slowly, feeling such relief. "I'm sorry, Eleanor—not just for putting myself in danger last night by getting drunk and ending up with my wallet stolen, but for all the stupid, hurtful things I've said and done since my little brother died. Can you ever forgive me?"

She took a seat in the chair beside his bed, then reached out and took hold of his hand. Her skin felt soft, warm, and reassuring to the touch. "Jah, Vic, I forgive you, but you need to forgive yourself and come to the realization that you are not responsible for Eddie's death."

"I know you're right, but I can't stop thinking about it. My emotions are a tangled mess of guilt, anger, sadness, and confusion, and I can't seem to control any of those feelings." He paused and sniffed deeply as more tears dripped onto his cheeks. "I've been using my brother's death as an excuse to drink. All the pain I kept bottled up inside me is what led me to even start drinking. I knew it was wrong, but I couldn't help myself. And now I'm struggling with an addiction I can't control, no matter how much I want to or how hard I try."

"Jah, Vic, I know. That's why you need to seek help."

"Lying here in pain while hoping you would show up to get me, I had already come to that conclusion."

Tears glistened in Eleanor's eyes as her lips parted and a smile spread across her face. "I am so thankful you are ready to take the necessary steps for your recovery, Vic. Are you willing to attend AA meetings while I go to Al-Anon?"

"Yes, or maybe I'll go to a clinic my nurse told me about. The organization treats people who are alcoholics, like me, and they deal with other types of addiction too. It is a faith-based, Christian establishment, and they offer group therapy one evening a week, as well as individual counseling sessions that would give me the support I need to deal with the guilt I've struggled with over Eddie's drowning. I would also be taught stress management, the importance of meditation and prayer, and many other things to prevent relapses." He paused to take a few painful breaths. "They have clinics, like the nurse mentioned, here in Lancaster, as well as in a few other towns in Pennsylvania, including one in Quarryville. I could go there as an outpatient, and I'm willing to attend AA meetings on a different night each week too."

"That sounds wonderful, Vic. You will have my full support."

"There's something else I need to tell you, though." Vic winced as he rolled over and tried to sit up. "I did a really stupid thing at the end of the workday on Friday."

"You mean by getting drunk?"

"Yeah, that too, but it was before Tom and I went to get drinks at a bar that I made a huge mistake." A knot formed in Vic's stomach. "I quit my job."

Her eyes widened. "Seriously?"

"Jah."

"Why would you do that, Vic?"

He explained everything that had been said and ended it by saying, "I don't know if my boss will take me back now, after all the rude things I said to him, but I'm going to apologize, tell Ned that I plan to get help for my drinking problem, and see if he'd be willing to give me another chance."

Eleanor leaned closer and spoke softly. "Once you're feeling up to going to see your boss, I'd be willing to go with you."

Vic shook his head. "I appreciate your offer, but pleading for my job back is something I need to do on my own. Even if Ned agrees to hire me back, I won't be able to start working again until my injuries heal. In the meantime, we can contact the clinic and begin my journey back to sobriety." He stroked Eleanor's face with the back of his hand and touched her stomach. "I never want to hurt you again. I want to become the kind of loving father our precious baby will need and deserves."

She nodded and tears seeped from her eyes. "I want that too, Vic, because our little one needs two loving parents. From this moment on, we shall move forward, with God leading the way, as we face the unknown future. As we are well aware, there will be good days and bad, but whatever life brings, we'll face it together, always looking to Jesus, the author and perfecter of our faith." She paused, gently stroking Vic's forehead. "We just need to remember, and cling to the words found in Psalm 46:1: 'God is our refuge and strength, a very present help in trouble.' "

Epilogue

Paradise
Two months later

Eleanor entered the living room and smiled when she saw Vic sitting in the rocking chair, holding their precious baby girl. They'd named the child Rosetta Sue, in honor of three people: Eleanor's mother, whose middle name was Rose; Vic's mother, Susie; and Eleanor's special friend Doretta. Their baby girl had been born a month ago, here in this house with the aid of Eleanor's capable midwife. There had been no complications, and Rosetta was healthy, growing, and contented.

Although Vic was still early into his treatment for alcohol addiction, he'd been sober since the day he'd come out of the hospital. His sessions at the clinic in Quarryville were going well, and he'd found more help by attending AA meetings and counseling with the bishop and other ministers of their church as well. Vic had also recommitted his life to Christ and had been doing his best to be the spiritual leader in their home. Eleanor continued to practice the things she'd learned at Al-Anon and encouraged Vic regularly with her positivity. Both Vic's family and Eleanor's had become encouragers too.

"I'm going out to check the mail," Eleanor whispered as she approached her husband and sleeping baby. "Should I put Rosetta in her crib before I go?"

Vic shook his head. "I'm content to sit with her awhile longer. I enjoy being a daadi and want to spend as much time with our daughter as possible on my days off from work."

Eleanor nodded and smiled. It had been an answer to prayer when Vic's boss gave Vic a second chance and hired him back. Ned had said that he supported Vic in his decision to get help and would keep him working as long as Vic didn't mess up. Fortunately, things had been good in that regard as well.

Eleanor kissed the baby's soft cheek, and she gave Vic a kiss too. With their trusty dog following on her heels, she went out the front door. She'd no more than stepped off the porch when Checkers looked up at her and gave a *Woof! Woof!*

"Okay, I know what you want, boy. Some things just never change." Eleanor picked up the dog's favorite stick and flung it into the yard. When Checkers took off after it, barking all the way, Eleanor chuckled and began her trek to their mailbox. In addition to several other pieces of mail, she found an envelope from her dearest friend.

Eager to see what Doretta had written, Eleanor brought the mail up to the picnic table and took a seat. When Eleanor tore open the envelope, she was pleased to discover an invitation to Doretta and William's wedding, which would take place the second Tuesday of November. Eleanor looked forward to going to the event and also showing everyone her precious daughter. She was eager to see her good friend get married and hoped that Doretta and William would have many happy years together. *Perhaps our childhood friend Irma will be at the wedding too. How nice it would be to see her again and reestablish a relationship.*

Eleanor put the invitation aside, closed her eyes, and thanked God for reminding her daily of the vow she had made on her wedding day, to love and honor her husband, through the good times and the bad. Although her and Vic's life was not perfect, it was much better than it had been a year ago. She thanked the Lord too for the friendship she had with Doretta and for all the letters of trust she'd received from her dear friend. Good friends were important, and so were families. Eleanor felt blessed because she and Vic had both. She would continue to write letters to her friend in Grabill and hoped that something she might write in the days ahead would be as beneficial to Doretta as her friend's letters had been to her.

Recipe

Eleanor's Chocolate Chip Pie

Ingredients:

1 stick margarine or butter

2 eggs

1 cup white sugar

1 teaspoon vanilla

1 cup chocolate chips

1 cup nuts, chopped

1 (9 inch) unbaked pastry shell

Prehcat oven to 325 degrees. Melt margarine or butter in small saucepan and set aside. Beat eggs, sugar, and vanilla in bowl. Add chocolate chips and nuts. Add margarine and beat well. Put in unbaked pastry shell. Bake for 50 minutes or until done. One pie will serve 6 to 8 people.

Dear Reader,

You may be wondering why I chose to write a novel that included the topic of alcoholism. It's a sensitive subject, for sure. Having grown up in a home with an alcoholic father, I am well acquainted with the shame and stress that was put upon not only my mother, sister, and me, but also my dad. During the early years of my life, I was instructed not to tell anyone about his drinking problem. Keeping it bottled up inside was almost as difficult as dealing with the fear I felt every day of not knowing when, or if, he might start drinking again.

When Dad was sober, our lives seemed somewhat normal, but during his bouts of drinking and sometimes being gone for several days, I lived in fear of what could happen to him and us. I worried that my father might leave and never come back. My mother attended several Al-Anon meetings, but she struggled with her own emotional problems and didn't always follow through with the suggestions she'd been given. Sometimes, when she knew Dad was not coming home because he'd gone off somewhere to drink, she loaded my sister and me up in the car and went searching for him.

With Mom's continued persuasion, my father did finally go to some AA meetings, and for a while he did better, but then something would set him off and his alcoholic binges would start up again. Dad knew he had a serious addiction, and he tried many other things to squelch his desire for alcohol. One day, in his later years, he checked himself into a rehab center in a town not far from ours. The methods they used there were more drastic than some, but my father came home from the treatment clean, and he stayed that way until his death at the age of sixty-two.

When asked by several Amish and English people to write a novel dealing with the topic of alcoholism, I felt a bit of concern. What if my English readers thought that all Amish people struggled with an alcohol addiction? Also, I wondered if my Amish or English readers might find the topic to be offensive. But after praying about it and seeking God's will, I came to the realization that people from all walks of life can be affected by various addictions. People who are addicted to alcohol, as well as those who have been affected by someone who has the disease, need encouragement and information about where they can go to get help.

If someone close to you is struggling with an alcohol addiction and you need help to cope with the situation, you may contact the Al-Anon Family Group Headquarters, Inc., at the following address: 1600 Corporate Landing Parkway; Virginia Beach, VA 23454-5617. Phone number: 757-563-1600; email: wso@al-anon.org; website: al-anon.org/members.

If you or someone you know is struggling with an addiction to alcohol and would like to seek help through Alcoholics Anonymous, you can reach out for help at the following website: www.alcoholicsanonymous.com. Their hotline phone number to call for immediate help for a problem related to alcoholism is 1-800-839-1686.

There are also many churches and faith-based ministries that offer help to people with addictions, using programs like Celebrate Recovery, and other facilities are available, like the one I mention in *Letters of Trust*. It is my hope that if you or anyone you know is struggling with alcohol or some other addiction, you will seek help and walk the right path that will end in recovery.

Love & blessings,
Wanda Brunstetter

Discussion Questions

1. Eleanor's parents had some reservations about her marrying Vic. They'd heard rumors about some of the things he'd been involved with before he joined the church and worried that his old habits might resurface. Do you think their concerns were founded? Is there ever a time when a parent should speak up or intervene when their grown child wants to marry someone of whom they disapprove?

2. It was difficult for Eleanor to move from her home in Grabill, Indiana, to Vic's home state of Pennsylvania. However, she was able to keep in contact with her family and close friend Doretta, to whom she wrote letters. Have you ever had a good friend who lived some distance away? How did you keep in touch with them? Did your friendship grow stronger or begin to fade away?

3. Things were going well in Vic and Eleanor's marriage until his young brother died. Do you think Vic was justified in blaming himself for his brother's death? Why do you think some people have a tendency to blame themselves when a loved one dies?

4. Vic's guilt and depression eventually led him to drink alcoholic beverages in excess. This, in turn, caused more problems within his marriage. What do you think Vic should have done when feelings of depression and guilt overtook him?

5. When things became difficult in Eleanor and Vic's marriage, why did Eleanor feel that she could tell Doretta about them in the letters she wrote and not worry about Doretta telling someone else?

6. Do you know anyone who has struggled with an addiction to alcohol or some other substance? If the person is related to you, how has it affected your family?

7. Eleanor kept her husband's problem with alcohol a secret from her and Vic's families for several months. Why do you believe she chose not to tell them for such a long time? Do you think it may have had something to do with her embarrassment of him, or did her reasons go deeper than that?

8. What are some ways we can help someone who is struggling with an addiction? How can we help a friend or family member whose loved one is an alcoholic?

9. Is there ever a time when a spouse should consider leaving their mate who is struggling with an addiction? Why did Eleanor choose to stay with her husband? Do you think she would have left Vic if his drinking and negative behavior had worsened?

10. Quite often an alcoholic blames their problem on someone else. Why do some people going through a difficult time or doing something they know is wrong blame others instead of themselves?

11. Should Vic's parents have stepped in and tried to get help for their son? Or did they do the right thing by simply praying and offering their support when needed?

12. Eleanor's first attempt at trying to help Vic was when she went to see their bishop and received counseling from him and his wife. This step gave her the courage to go to Al-Anon meetings, where she learned some things she'd been doing that may have aggravated the situation with Vic. She also learned better ways of communicating with him when he was sober. What are some ways a married couple can communicate their feelings without arguing or hurting someone's feelings?

13. Who was your favorite character in this book and why? What was the one thing you found to be most special about them?

14. What did you learn about alcoholism while reading this novel? Did it give you a better understanding of how and why the addiction can begin? Have you or a family member ever dealt with the problem of alcoholism? If so, did you (or they) find the help needed through counseling or an organization like Alcoholics Anonymous or Al-Anon?

About the Author

New York Times bestselling and award-winning author Wanda E. Brunstetter is one of the founders of the Amish fiction genre. She has written more than one hundred books translated in four languages. With over twelve million copies sold, Wanda's stories consistently earn spots on the nation's most prestigious bestseller lists and have received numerous awards.

Wanda's ancestors were part of the Anabaptist faith, and her novels are based on personal research intended to accurately portray the Amish way of life. Her books are read and trusted by many Amish people, who credit her for giving readers a deeper understanding of the people and their customs.

When Wanda visits her Amish friends, she finds herself drawn to their peaceful lifestyle, sincerity, and close family ties. Wanda enjoys photography, ventriloquism, gardening, bird-watching, beachcombing, and spending time with her family. She and her husband, Richard, are blessed with two grown children, six grandchildren, and two great-grandchildren.

To learn more about Wanda,
visit her website at www.wandabrunstetter.com.

The Friendship Letters Series

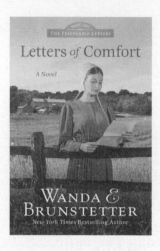

LETTERS OF COMFORT (COMING AUGUST 2023)
Book 2

Doretta Schwartz used to be so happy and passed her positive attitude along to friends in several letters she wrote each month. But that all changed the day she learned of her fiancé's death and a heavy weight of depression fell upon her. Feeling empty, she puts away her letter writing and won't even respond to calls from friends. William's twin brother, Warren, is also grieving his loss, while at the same time trying to be supportive to his parents and Doretta. Doretta responds to Warren's friendship, but is he just becoming a replacement for the once-in-a-lifetime love she lost?

Paperback / 978-1-63609-487-8

More from Wanda!

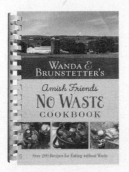

WANDA E. BRUNSTETTER'S AMISH FRIENDS
NO WASTE COOKBOOK

More Than 270 Recipes Help Stretch a Food Budget

When times are hard, the family budget gets tighter. Brand-new from *New York Times* bestselling author of Amish fiction Wanda E. Brunstetter is a useful cookbook from Amish and Mennonite cooks who offer recipes and advice for saving money, stretching a meal, and eliminating waste in the kitchen. Over 270 recipes are divided into traditional categories from main dishes and sides to desserts and snacks. Encased in a lay-flat binding and presented in full color, home cooks of all ages will find this cookbook to be a valuable addition to their collections.

Comb Bound / 978-1-63609-385-7

THE PRAYER JAR DEVOTIONAL: HOPE

Inspired by Wanda E. Brunstetter's The Prayer Jars series, this encouraging devotional will help transform your prayer life. With each turn of the page, you will discover unchanging truths of God's Word alongside meaningful prompts that guide you to write out your personal prayers or favorite hope-filled Bible verses and then add to your very own prayer jar.

Hardback / 978-1-63609-374-1

Other Fiction Works by
Wanda E. Brunstetter

Amish Cooking Class
The Seekers (Book 1)
The Blessing (Book 2)
The Celebration (Book 3)
Amish Cooking Class Cookbook
The Amish Cooking Class Trilogy (All 3 books in 1)

Amish Greenhouse Mystery
The Crow's Call (Book 1)
The Mockingbird's Song (Book 2)
The Robin's Greeting (Book 3)
The Amish Greenhouse Mysteries (All 3 books in 1)

Amish Hawaiian Series
The Hawaiian Discovery (Book 1)
The Hawaiian Quilt (Book 2)
Amish Hawaiian Adventures (Book 1 & 2)
The Blended Quilt (Book 3)

Amish Millionaire
The English Son (Book 1)
The Stubborn Father (Book 2)
The Betrayed Fiancee (Book 3)
The Missing Will (Book 4)
The Divided Family (Book 5)
The Selfless Act (Book 6)
Amish Millionaire (All 6 in 1)

Brides of Lancaster County
A Merry Heart (Book 1)
Looking for a Miracle (Book 2)
Plain and Fancy (Book 3)
The Hope Chest (Book 4)
Brides of Lancaster County Collection (All 4 books in 1)

Brides of Webster County
Going Home (Book 1)
On Her Own (Book 2)
Dear to Me (Book 3)
Allison's Journey (Book 4)
Brides of Webster County Collection (All 4 books in 1)

Creektown Discoveries
The Walnut Creek Wish (Book 1)
The Sugarcreek Surprise (Book 2)
The Apple Creek Announcement (Book 3)

Daughters of Lancaster County
The Storekeeper's Daughter (Book 1)
The Quilter's Daughter (Book 2)
The Bishop's Daughter (Book 3)
The Daughters of Lancaster County (All 3 books in 1)

The Discovery – A Lancaster County Saga
Goodbye to Yesterday (Book 1)
Silence of Winter (Book 2)
The Hope of Spring (Book 3)
The Pieces of Summer (Book 4)
A Revelation in Autumn (Book 5)
A Vow for Always (Book 6)
The Discovery Saga Collection (All 6 books in 1)

The Half-Stitched Amish Quilting Club Series
The Half-Stitched Amish Quilting Club (Book 1)
The Tattered Quilt (Book 2)
The Healing Quilt (Book 3)
The Half-Stitched Amish Quilting Club Trilogy (All 3 in 1)

The Hochstetler Twins
The Lopsided Christmas Cake (Book 1)
The Farmers' Market Mishap (Book 2)
Twice as Nice Amish Romance Collection (Books 1 & 2)

Indiana Cousins
A Cousin's Promise (Book 1)
A Cousin's Prayer (Book 2)
A Cousin's Challenge (Book 3) ·
Indiana Cousins (All 3 books in 1)

Kentucky Brothers
The Journey (Book 1)
The Healing (Book 2)
The Struggle (Book 3)
Kentucky Brothers (All 3 books in 1)

Prairie State Friends
The Decision (Book 1)
The Gift (Book 2)
The Restoration (Book 3)
The Prairie State Friends Trilogy (All 3 books in 1)

The Prayer Jars
The Hope Jar (Book 1)
The Forgiving Jar (Book 2)
The Healing Jar (Book 3)
The Prayer Jars Trilogy (All 3 books in 1)
The Prayer Jar Devotional: Hope

Sisters of Holmes County
A Sister's Secret (Book 1)
A Sister's Test (Book 2)
A Sister's Hope (Book 3)
Sisters of Holmes County (All 3 books in 1)

Historical Series -- Brides of Lehigh Canal
Kelly's Chance (Book 1)
Betsy's Return (Book 2)
Sarah's Choice (Book 3)
Brides of Lehigh Canal Trilogy (All 3 books in 1)

Stand Alone Novels
Lydia's Charm
White Christmas Pie
Woman of Courage

Novellas and Collections
Amish Front Porch Stories
The Beloved Christmas Quilt
The Brides of the Big Valley
The Christmas Prayer
The Christmas Secret
A Heartwarming Romance Collection
Love Finds a Home
Love Finds a Way
A Time to Laugh
Twice Loved
Return to the Big Valley